COURAGEOUS BOOKS

THE EYES OF BEL NISHANI
Book two of the Planet Walkers Series

A.V. Shackleton

Published by Courageous Books
1081 Wallaces Gap Rd
Ballalaba
NSW
Australia 2622

ISBN 978-0-9925814-5-9

Thank you to my family for your tireless support, and to my Father – may you rest sweetly in the Breath. Thanks also to my intrepid fellow Planet Walkers, I'd be lost without you.

GLOSSARY

(Go to www.avshackleton.com for more detail)

NAMES
Andel of Trianog, diviner for Uri'madu
Brätan Gok, Clan leader of Gok
Daric Enna, assassin working for Mirashael of Cantori
Duvät Gok, former member of the Uri'madu
Huldar of Leth, leader of Uri'madu
Inshogi of Trianog, Andel's father
Leahät Gok, Duvät Gok's wife
Lucaät of Faytha, mining magnate
Mirashael of Cantori, café/restaurant proprietor
Ninjay of Trianog, Andel's mother
Pieru of Leth, lord of the Explorers' Guild
The Agent, Lucaät's chief operator in the field

GENERAL GLOSSARY
Annangi: a dimorphic race consisting of angels and archangels
Chapter-House: Naghari house of healing. All major cities have at least one Chapter-House
Djan'rū: the point at which one planet can be joined to another by a navigator's song
El: Deity. Annangi believe that the Breath of El blows through all. Asheru is El's consort

Great House: There are ten Great Houses, each with a home planet and a leader accepted by El

Haze: easily visible aspects of an individual's aura

Kommer-sta: a large insect with a lethal bite, native to Giahn

Mark:

- The soul mark granted by El to those who become proficient in a particular psychic gift. The Mark appears as a symbol shining through the skin.
- Or the symbol of a Leader's Great House, granted when the potential heir sits upon the Throne of El. This Mark shines through the skin of a House Leader's back.

Qalān:

> **Personal Qalān** is a sub-dimensional space that surrounds every individual. Annangi access this space for storage of personal items.
>
> **Planetary Qalān** surrounds every planetary body in a web of interconnected wormholes. Skilled Annangi can create portals in this Qalān for instantaneous travel between locations on a given planet.
>
> **Galactic Qalān** connects the stars and planets of the galaxy. It merges with **planetary Qalān** at specific points known as Djan'rū. **Navigators** travel between Djan'rū.

Sajhar: both Mark and title of one who has mastered all powers entailed with the working of metal.

Screen: internally, a psychic construction that hides private information; or externally, a shield that hides one's presence.

Shamkar: the Mark of one who is a master of the power of voice, also the name of that power.

Shamkarun: the title of one who bears the Shamkar.

Tiamät: the Imperial House; the God-Emperor and Empress are of House Tiamät.

The three clans of Tiamät – Gok, Enna, and Ashik.

Tsemkar: the Mark of a master of mind power, also the name of that power.

Tsemkarun: the title of one who bears the Tsemkar.

Veil: a psychic construction that hides thoughts and feelings from the perception of others.

Ziquarra: the Mark of one who can leave their body at will and send their soul to far distant locations. Ziquarra is also the name of this gift.

Ziquarran: an unmarked practitioner of Ziquarra.

Ziquarudjan: the title of one who bears the Mark of the Ziquarra.

IMPERIAL CITY, CRAFTERS AND BEYOND
NORTHEAST

KARESK
CASCO
GOLDEN WHEEL
OLDTOWN
CLAN GOK
DUVAT GOK'S HOUSE
RED WEYFAL
FORGES
WAREHOUSES
MIRASHAEL'S CAFE
NAGHARI CHAPTER HOUSE
CRAFTERS
CLAN ASHIK
IMPERIAL CITY, CRAFTERS AND BEYOND
SOUTHWEST

THE GOOD WIFE

In the still mid-morning, the time between the rush hours for those who worked in the Imperial City and those who merely wished to go there to shop, a single non-descript female figure made her way through the streets of Amensay. She walked with purpose between the rows of plain terraced housing, brown brick walls and wooden doors, then turned toward a better-class area with clean pale stonework and carved lintels … gardens with flowers, patterned fencing, and gateways charmed to admit only select individuals.

A group of parasol-waving chatterers dawdled in the same direction. She glimpsed a glittering array of headdresses such as the Empress Ishiquel had made fashionable, but thankfully saw no one she knew.

As she neared the portal that led to the Imperial City, her pulse raced. Was it excitement she felt, or dread? The appointment she had made was of the utmost secrecy – afterward she would have to forget the outcome as if it had never occurred. The last thing she wanted was to meet anyone who knew her, or worse still, wanted to talk, so when she heard a familiar voice call her name, it was all she could do not to run.

"Leahät Gok?" *Leahät! Wait!*

She sighed and slowed her pace. The dainty trip, trip, trip of stylishly clad feet drew closer.

"So, is it true?" Rina Gok clasped her hands together in excitement, and Leahät couldn't help noticing the sparkle of painted fingernails.

"Is what true?" Leahät glanced downward. Her own shoes were plain and worn, her fingernails clean but ragged. There was no sparkle there.

"They'll be back next week?" Rina asked brightly.

"I suppose so," she answered.

"Aren't you excited?"

"Excited?" Leahät made a pained expression, but the petite blonde seemed hardly to notice. Leahät shook her head and walked on. She had an appointment to keep.

"Maybe he's turned over a new leaf," Rina said.

"He told me he had a surprise for me," Leahät admitted. "Breath knows what he meant by that. At least when he gets here I'll be able to pay some bills, so long as can I get to his wages before the Faythans do. But with my luck they'll be waiting right there in the Imperial Bays as the navigator chimes in."

Rina paused. Leahät thought she was probably in shock. But the dainty feet soon hurried to catch up, as bubbly as if the comment about their financial situation had never been made.

"I just couldn't bear it if Garshät was away for such a long time," she said. "I'd be lonely."

"Well, I'm not." Leahät scowled.

"How can you say that?" Rina said. "He's your husband! Don't you love him at all?"

"No ... although he wasn't so bad when we were first married ... and I thought, perhaps, he cared for me. Huh!" She snorted. "That soon changed."

They walked on in silence. Leahät remembered Duvät Gok as he had been: an archangel of modest power, plain and a little pedantic, but her first look into his heart had revealed the dreamer inside. Now, the dreamer had become a schemer and the gambling bug had claimed him for its own. Slowly, with each new defeat he'd become more bad tempered, vindictive and petty, and ever more obsessed with coin. Even her own inheritance had been traded to buy him out of trouble and keep his disgrace from the Guild so that at least his job would remain secure; and she had continued to hold her head up as if all was well.

"My coin ran out," Leahät said. "Since then I've meant nothing to him."

"Surely not."

"If I find work, I'm 'shaming' him," Leahät said caustically, "but I'm just a 'liability' when he's got no coin. I thought I was getting a husband with prospects, a life of adventure, an explorer with the Guild. How naïve I was! But not any more, Rina. Not any more."

They halted before a portal paved with yellow tiles and covered with a sturdy stone roof. The ring of pillars was carved with characters rendered in the Tiamäti style; a series of hints in case the portal keeper wasn't there to assist.

"Look how the years have blurred the words," Leahät said sadly. "That's how I feel sometimes, as if I'm faded beyond recognition and no longer know myself."

Rina looked at her and Leahät wondered what she saw.

"Please don't be sad," Rina said. "I'm sure Duvät Gok will be pleased to see you, and maybe his surprise will be something wonderful, something to brighten your day … a sign that El will bless you at last."

Leahät blinked back unexpected tears. El's Blessing? She had given up hope, and if today's meeting achieved its goal …

"Well, maybe so," she conceded, but the words sounded thin as the veneer they were. She tried for a more uplifting tone. "And I'm off to the city today to organize my own surprise for him."

"That's the spirit!" Rina smiled. "What part of the city are you going to? Maybe I could join you?"

The portal keeper waved. "I'll step you through if you wish, Ladies Gok."

Leahät nodded, then said to Rina, "I have some business to attend to first, but perhaps you and Garshät Gok would like to come for a meal some time soon? No doubt Duvät will have many entertaining stories to tell."

"Thank you! That would be lovely," Rina said.

Leahät smiled, hoping her expression looked genuine enough to mask the darkness in her heart. Part of her wanted to grasp Rina's head and show her exactly what she'd had to endure over the past few years – the horrible things her husband had done, first to helpless creatures and then to his team-mate, Lind. He'd known she'd see them too, be forced to share the experience through their marriage bond. It had taken all her strength and the help of a Shamkarun to narrow their connection to the shallowest possible, and her dearest wish now was to sever it for good. No surprise present from Duvät Gok could ever be enough to clean the away the stain, but if things went well today, her gift to him would mean freedom at last.

There was warmth in the crowded streets of the Imperial City, and Leahät quickly removed her cloak.

"Be careful if you're heading for the charm-singers," Rina said. "Half-breeds rioted there just last week, hadn't you heard?"

Leahät hadn't heard, but she nodded as if she had. She watched her friend vanish among a tide of colorful parasols, then struck off for Crafters, the industrial quarter, charm-singer stalls and all. At least there her shabby clothing would be unlikely to stand out.

Down an alley of woodworkers and artisans she found a café with grubby wooden tables and just enough space between chairs for someone to squeeze through – just as her contact had described.

Sitting in a shadowy corner was a lean male, possibly Enna. He was busy with something in his hands; Leahät started when she noticed it was a knife. Sure this was the person she had come to see, she began to make her way through the clutter, but every time a chair squealed against the floor or banged against its neighbors, her cheeks flamed.

The knife-wielder did not look up.

"Wait, my lady, wait!" A floridly dressed Cantori appeared from the back room. "Please, sit down. Perhaps I can help you?"

"I …" She glanced in desperation at the Enna. "I'm here to see someone."

"Yes, yes!" the Cantori said enthusiastically. "Of course! Why else would such a fine lady come to my miserable establishment?" He danced expertly between the chairs and was quickly at her side.

"Mirashael of Cantori at your service," he said, then continued in quieter tones. "And you must be the esteemed lady, Leahät Gok?"

Leahät glanced again at the Enna still polishing his knife.

"A regular patron," Mirashael said. "No one you need worry about, I'm sure. Would you like to sit?"

"Here?"

"Yes of course," her host assured her. "Plain sight is often best when one wishes to go unnoticed." The Cantori smiled engagingly. "Sometimes a memory can be disguised by its very ordinariness. Please?" He waved toward the back of the closest chair. "Or perhaps one would prefer to rest on a divan?"

She followed his gesture and noticed a cluster of grubby divans in one corner, strewn with motley cushions. "I think I'll sit here," she replied.

"Very good, very good. I will fetch refreshments and a range of our finest wooden handicrafts for you to peruse while we talk of life – and other things."

Leahät nodded, realizing this was another wise ploy. It would be easy to shape her memories of their encounter around the purchase of something … a new set of wooden bowls, perhaps, or of carved hanta for guests to eat with – it didn't matter what.

Mirashael returned with a tray of drinks balanced on one upraised palm, and a plate of bite-sized seafood parcels on the other. "The Realm's finest omosa," he said. "You'll get none better!"

He set the food and drinks before her with great aplomb, then withdrew a clunking bag of wooden objects from Qalān and arranged the contents on the table. There was a set of finely turned wooden bowls, enameled around the lip with a pattern of bright, blood-red flowers; a larger stand-alone piece with grain that seemed to wave like a heavy green ocean; a set decorated with the rune of Tiamät around the borders; and another set that she actually liked – red-ochre rims with the inner bowl enameled in simple pale green. The shape felt comfortable in her hand. She looked up and met Mirashael's gaze.

"Simple is best," he said. "No fuss, no … difficult explanations. And this glaze, it seems almost … accidental, would one say?"

"Yes," she answered. "Accidental is a style I like."

He looked at her knowingly. "And would the lady like these hanta to match? So smooth and sharp – one could shred one's food, piece by piece until it is no more. This is an extra charge, of course, but if one needs to truly relish …?"

She held up her hand to stop him. The thought of Duvät being tortured to death was not unpleasant, but would she want to share his pain?

"Tempting," she said, "but I prefer to eat neatly." She picked up an omosa, popped it into her mouth, chewed once and swallowed. "No mess and the food is just gone, never to be seen again."

"Ah. A lady of discernment! Then it is done," Mirashael said. "The accidental bowls, and for a bargain price, let's say, one thousand gold imperials?"

Leahät nearly choked. "One thousand?" Leaden disappointment filled her stomach.

Mirashael frowned. "Surely you did not think such excellence would come cheaply? This accidental glaze, so smooth, the work almost undetectable …"

"Almost?" She shook her head. "I would think that for such a price the work should be entirely invisible!"

"Not too invisible." Mirashael winked. "After all, we do want some effect." He studied her. "Then, as a special favor, I will sell these bowls for half price, just for today, just for you, since I can see you are a lady of honor – and who knows, perhaps you or one of your friends might come back and buy from me again."

Leahät picked up one of the bowls. They were a set of four. The work really was quite fine. "Perhaps if I took two of the bowls now, just to see what my husband thinks of them? If the reaction is to my satisfaction, I will collect the remaining bowls as soon as may be."

"Ah! Half now and half when the task is complete. A gamble … but then, that is what your husband likes, is it not?"

"Sadly, yes it is."

"Then I will take these bowls and wrap them for you, Lady Gok. The other two I will keep until you return." He paused. His gaze hardened. "It would be a shame to … break the set."

"I hope it won't be broken, but that depends on my husband, now."

Leahät's heart hammered as she handed Mirashael of Cantori a purse. When he seemed about to take it with him into the back room she stopped him. "If you don't mind," she said, "I'd like you to count it where I can see."

"You don't trust me?" Mirashael smiled shrewdly. Coin clinked onto the table.

When the count was done, the Cantori left to wrap the bowls, leaving Leahät to look around. Several new guests had arrived, but the knife-wielding Enna had gone. It worried her that she had not sensed his departure.

"Your bowls, Leahät Gok." Mirashael returned and presented her with a neatly wrapped parcel. He bowed. "Until we meet again?"

As she reached for her purchase, thoughts of Lind's suffering and her husband's betrayal steadied her hands. The lead in her stomach became steel in her spine. She tucked the package into Qalān and nodded coldly as she turned to leave. "Until we meet again."

HOME TO GIAHN

Duvät Gok sighed and looked around as their envelope dissolved.

"Padmil," Gento said. "Food's good here."

The translation bays rang with the sound of navigators coming and going. Chords chimed, customers chattered, spinners and lading crew called instructions and sang goods from place to place.

Kandät Enna had taken on extra cargo at their last stop, and while Arko, Bush and Topper helped unload it, Duvät Gok positioned himself at the back of the group, trying for invisibility. He needed to speak with the Faythans, but at every rest stop the same thing happened; the Uri'madu wouldn't let him out of their sight. In a scant few hours they would head to Doch, then to Mecca before the final jump to Giahn itself, and by then it would be too late to take advantage of his foreknowledge of the nacrite. Or, worse still, Lucaät of Faytha might think he was being avoided.

A Hermes started toward him. Anxiety gripped his chest. What would a Hermes want with him? He tried to blend between the Rukh.

"Watch it, Gok," Gento snarled.

Before he could reply, a soft voice at his elbow said, "Lord Duvät Gok?"

How had the Hermes gotten so close so quickly? She must have been waiting for them. The message must be from someone who knew their itinerary. The Explorers' Guild? The Navigators' Guild …? No, they had no reason to contact him …

She bowed. "I bear a message from Lord Lucaät of Faytha. It is a verbal message. Shall we engage here, or shall we adjourn somewhere more private?"

Duvät's heart fell further.

As the Faythan's name was mentioned, he felt Huldar of Leth's cold glance. Gento jostled him again, and this time he was sure it was deliberate. Seconds earlier he had been trying to find a way to make this meeting happen, but now the initiative was lost, he dreaded it. It was Huldar's fault. Everything was Huldar's fault.

"The refectory?" the Hermes suggested.

Duvät Gok cleared his throat. "Yes, an alcove perhaps?"

The Hermes bowed and led the way. For a fleeting moment, Duvät considered escape. The amount of coin he owed Lucaät of Faytha was enormous. He could run from there, hide until he could bribe someone to take him to … anywhere really, but Gento and Cobar followed not too far behind and his hopes faded. If only he could have made plans – but there was no one to help, no one on his side. He sighed in resignation. One day, the scores would be evened, but today was not that day.

With a burst of noise and the smell of hot food, the refectory doors opened. He followed meekly as the Hermes led him through a line of navigators and spinners impatient for their turn at the counter. He bumped someone and the predatory green eyes of a Maatu glared coldly down into his.

"My apologies, Lord Maatu," he stammered. The Shamkarun's Mark on the navigator's cheek seemed intimidatingly extensive. "The crowd ..." he continued, but the navigator moved on.

Breathless Maatu, Duvät thought to himself, *the way they look at you!*

A gaggle of spinners laughed and joked nearby. A group of brightly clad Nhadu took their places at a long bench. Patrons carried trays of steaming dishes, or made their way through the crowd with drinks in hand. Except for the cold gaze his Rukhish babysitters had welded to his back, no one paid him any further attention.

The Hermes indicated a semi-circular nook at the back of the room, somewhat isolated from the main press of diners. "In here, Lord Duvät Gok?"

Duvät nodded agreement. What choice did he have?

The Hermes seated herself opposite. "Shall we begin?" she asked. "The message is direct. Lord Lucaät of Faytha awaits your reply."

"What, he's here?" Duvät imagined the squinty-eyed face of the moneylender.

The Hermes nodded. "Yes. He is standing by."

"Very well. Go on," Duvät said.

A tight screen closed around them and he swallowed nervously. This was definitely to be a private transaction. The Faythan had spent a good deal of coin to ensure it.

The Hermes's face went blank. Her voice became a little deeper and took on a nasal Faythan accent.

"Ah, Duvät," Lucaät said. "You neglected to tell me you were on your way home. How long have you been travelling now?"

"I … ah …"

"No matter. I have followed your movements as best I can. Your arrival on Giahn is a moment I anticipate with great relish! I shall be there to greet you, of course."

"Of course." Duvät closed his eyes and gathered his wits. The Faythan would no doubt want the promise of some actual coin before their negotiations could even begin. At least with Lind dead he would not have to pay her compensation. Perhaps he could use that amount as a starting offer? But his hopes were soon dashed.

"And before you start wasting our time with convoluted terms," Lucaät said, "I have made a friend of the Explorers' Guild's paymaster. He will see that your entire wage is handed directly to me."

"My what? My … entire wage?" Duvät spluttered. "But –"

"Ha! No buts, Gok. This amount merely covers the interest you owe. Be thankful you've got home in three years, not ten."

"The interest? You never charged so much interest before!"

"Times have changed, it's true."

"But that's not fair! What will I live on?"

"As if I care," Lucaät said. "Sell your wife. Sell your house. You should try and pay before the interest rebuilds. That's why they call it interest," he chuckled. "Makes things more interesting for me."

Duvät leaned toward the Hermes and whispered urgently, "But I have other things, much more valuable than coin. I know things. I –"

"Like what?"

He looked over his shoulder. The Rukh were standing not too far away. Their faces were stony. Because of the Hermes's expert screen, they could not hear what was being said, but still, their proximity made him nervous. "Not here! I tried to tell you sooner," he said. "I wanted to, but there was no chance! They wouldn't leave me alone!"

"What, has your team become so fond of you?" Lucaät sniggered. "Have you and Shamkarun Huldar become lovers?"

"Listen! Please! This is no joking matter. What if I told you about the riches on the planet we just surveyed? Rare goods ... very rare. What would that be worth?"

"Well, since the planet – Went I think they're calling it: ridiculous name. Where Duvät Gok *went* broke!" Lucaät laughed. "Or where he *went* to hide ... Ah, I'm too funny."

The Hermes's laugh was shrill, not at all like Lucaät's. Duvät waited. Suddenly the laughter stopped. "The planet Went has been claimed for the Imperium, Gok," Lucaät said. "What use are its riches to me?"

"Get in now with a mining offer," Duvät suggested earnestly. "I would – if I could. You have friends within the Imperium. You have friends everywhere."

"And just what will we be mining? And why the urgency? It will be a hundred years or more before your people sign off on the place."

Duvät steeled himself. "What's it worth for you to know?" he suggested levelly.

In the short silence that followed, he could almost feel Lucaät's mind ticking over. The moneylender wouldn't be able to resist the offer of insider knowledge. The promise of easy profits … This was what Duvät was betting on.

"All right, I'll only take half your wage," the Faythan said at last. "Make it good!"

"It's worth more."

"We're getting nowhere," Lucaät snapped.

"Fine." Duvät said. "Take my coin. I'll go to Brätan Gok, the head of our clan."

"I know who Brätan Gok is!"

"It won't matter if you take my wages," Duvät continued smoothly. "I'll be able to pay you twice over … at least!" *At least,* he emphasized to himself, careful, of course, that his mind was tightly sealed. If Lucaät could see him through the Hermes's eyes, he'd also see his confidence.

Lucaät was quiet for a moment then asked, "Why are the Rukh tailing you?"

"They are concerned for my safety," Duvät said. "The knowledge I have," he paused. "If it got into the wrong hands …"

"Wrong hands!" Lucaät laughed. "What wrong hands? Mine?"

Duvät gave a derisive grunt. "Well, if you are not willing to negotiate sensibly, I'm sure Brätan Gok will be." He shrugged. "I've tried to be reasonable, but it's your loss. Do as you must. I'll see you when we arrive on Giahn."

"Now wait," Lucaät said, and Duvät relaxed a little on the inside. The Breath was still with him. Even the presence of Cobar and Gento had been played to his advantage – and all this without a whisper yet of the Eyes of Bel Nishani. He spread his hands as if open to offers.

"You can keep your wages …"

"Go on," said Duvät Gok.

"… and I'll reduce your debt by half."

Duvät shook his head. "I think you should be the one to pay me!" he said, and deep inside, he was already crowing his victory. "You have no idea what secrets I have," he continued. "The coin I owe you? Just a note in the Chime. Think again, Lucaät. Perhaps we'll speak again on Doch?"

"I'll get to the truth one way or another, Gok," Lucaät said nastily. "Deceive me and you'll find me most unreasonable!"

"I have already found you most unreasonable, Lucaät of Faytha. Enjoy the rest of your day." Duvät pushed back in his seat. "Thank you, Hermes. I trust –"

"Breathless Gok!" Lucaät snarled.

In the ensuing pause, Duvät strove to maintain an air of indifference. His haze might show some excitement, but that was not unreasonable given the magnitude of the knowledge he was about to impart.

"Yes?" he said at last. "I haven't got all day. I'm hungry and tired."

"Don't push it!" Lucaät snapped. "This better not be mere gold. This better be far more than gold."

"Oh, there's gold there," Duvät said, "and easily mined. Surface deposits of copper and silver as well."

Lucaät seemed taken aback by this easy admission, and Duvät allowed himself a moment of pride for another piece well played. The Hermes's face went blank for a moment, presumably as Lucaät broke contact for discussion with a third party. When it reanimated, Duvät almost smiled. He could tell from the Hermes's posture that Lord Lucaät of Faytha was about to capitulate. Eventually, perhaps, the Faythan would find out that the Rukh were not an actual bodyguard, but by then, what would it matter? The information about the nacrite alone would be enough to make his creditor very happy indeed, and perhaps give him time to consider his options regarding the eyes.

Ah, yes, he thought. *My fortunes are definitely improving.*

When the negotiations were over, Duvät dismissed the Hermes with the traditional phrase, "I trust I need not ask for your discretion?"

The Hermes bowed. "It is my honor to serve."

Duvät watched her depart. *What a strange people they are*, he thought. Each so alike they could hardly be told apart. And they never betrayed the messages they conveyed – utterly trustworthy.

"Come on, Gok," Gento growled. "Fun's over. I'm hungry."

"Do they gossip when they get home – to their home planet – do you think?" Duvät looked up at the stone-faced Rukh. "Do they smile and joke about us then?"

"Get moving!" Cobar rumbled.

"Very well," Duvät waved his hand forward. "Lead the way."

Gento shook his head. "Maybe his wife's forgiven him?" he said to Cobar.

"Would you?" Cobar rumbled dourly.

Gento shook his head again. Across the refectory the Uri'madu spilled through the doors. Huldar had his arm across Andel's shoulders. Nachiel and Ronnin chuckled together. Even the healers seemed more light hearted than usual.

One day they'll regret the way they've treated me. Duvät thought, *and I'll wipe those smiles from their faces!*

RECEPTION

Huldar looked up at the vaulted ceilings of the Imperial Navigation Bays on Giahn, seeing their splendor as if for the first time. The pearly ribs of the building, the skeletons of giant creatures who had walked this planet eons in the distant past, branched between fans of vitrified sandstone. Colors ranged from pale rose-pink to deepest red, orange to bright sunshine yellow, and some panes were so clear as to be invisible.

Andel stood beside him, her body language cool, as if they hardly knew each other – exactly as it should be now they were back in the Imperial City and in public view.

He looked up again. "I've been here hundreds of times," he said, "but I don't think I've actually seen it before."

"It's magnificent," she said. "The colors, so vivid and fresh. Completely remarkable."

"Physical heat and specialized charms, Zaīkhanun and Sajhar working together. What did you think, the first time you saw it?"

"The first time I was here was to meet you – too worried to give it a second glance, and the second was when we were preparing to leave."

He closed his eyes and recalled the scene of their first introduction. "You didn't seem too nervous." Even then, she had made his heart race – so much so that he'd forgotten to introduce himself. "But you were excited. I remember being annoyed because you showed so much of yourself, then sad because you hid it again."

"Contrary one!" She grinned, then her expression became thoughtful. "I was afraid I'd never fit in."

"But you did."

She gave him a wistful smile. "It takes effort to withdraw, doesn't it?" she said. "I've become so used to mind-speech and familiarity, it's hard to be distant again."

"I know. Takes a little while. Funny how it doesn't seem restrictive till it's gone." He felt Casco's mental prompt and nodded. "We'd best get back to work."

While Casco supervised the unloading of their goods, Huldar bowed to the navigator. "Thank you, Shamkarun Kandät Enna for your excellent services. A difficult journey expertly achieved."

"My honor!" Kandät bowed slightly in return. He glanced toward Casco. "And thank you for having your half-breed's papers in order. You've no idea how much trouble it causes if they're not."

A polite smile was the best Huldar could muster. Things had changed in the three years they'd been away. This was a stark reminder of how difficult his friend's readjustment to the strictures of the Imperium would be.

Kandät seemed not to have noticed. "So, maybe I'll see you on your next rotation to Went," he said. "It's a strange name you've chosen! By all accounts a fascinating place, if a little too cold and wild for my liking."

Huldar nodded, but Kandät hadn't seen the planet at its best during the long summer. For him, the beauty and mystery of Went was intrinsically bound up with his feelings for Andel, and seven years seemed a long time to wait for their return. How did those mysterious creatures, the went, survive the planet's long freeze? He hoped to discover that and more when the iceball world thawed once more and it was time for them to return.

He looked toward Casco, still directing the ground crew, checking lists and making sure everything was accounted for. It seemed ridiculous that he should need special certification to be part of their team.

Andel stood apart and comforted Sari, and again Huldar was reminded of Lind's absence. He could almost hear her sharp and sassy tongue ordering everyone around, chiding mistakes with droll exasperation.

He turned to the sound of marching boots and saw a thin-faced Faythan leading an entourage of four stony Ashik warriors toward him. The Ashik stopped at an unspoken signal and the Faythan advanced the last few paces alone.

"Is there something I can do for you?" Huldar asked politely.

The Faythan seemed about to answer, but Huldar was distracted by another arrival: a Guild official approaching from the opposite direction. Casco shrugged a tacit query. Huldar shook his head and prepared to greet Marick of Cantori, the Guild-Lord's personal assistant.

"Ah, Shamkarun Huldar of Leth," Marick bowed. "On behalf of Guild-Lord Shamkarun Pieru of Leth and the Imperial Explorers' Guild, I congratulate the Uri'madu on your safe return." He glanced quickly toward Duvät Gok. "However, may I express condolences for the loss of your team member, Lind, under the most tragic of circumstances?"

He handed Huldar a sealed scroll. "There are matters of urgency to discuss. Our Lord, Shamkarun Pieru of Leth, requires your attendance at your earliest convenience, along with certain members of your team. The scroll should make things clear."

Huldar bowed. "It's good to see you too, Marick of Cantori, and good to be back in Giahn. Of course, I and my team will be happy to attend Lord Pieru. It will be a great honor."

"The details are in the scroll," Marick said. "We have made arrangements for Duvät Gok to be held here, for the time being. Perhaps these worthy Rukh could be detailed as an escort?" He indicated Cobar and Gento.

Of course." Huldar bowed slightly.

Marick turned to the Faythan, who waited to one side. "And Lord Lucaät of Faytha? To what do we owe the pleasure?" He took a moment to study Lucaät's entourage. "I see you have brought some companions along. Have the Imperial Bays become so dangerous?"

Lucaät stretched his lips in a smile. "I have come to meet my friend, Duvät Gok." He eyed the two Rukh who had sandwiched Duvät Gok between them. "My … associates … are here to ensure the Overlord's safety."

"Ex-Overlord," Marick corrected. "Very well, you, and your associates may assist these good Rukh to escort Duvät Gok to the secure accommodation we have prepared."

"Why must he stay with the Guild?" Lucaät asked. "Surely my own rooms will be secure enough to ensure his protection?"

Huldar felt his brows begin to knit. Lucaät of Faytha had never called Duvät Gok a friend before, far from it! And why did he think he needed protection?

Marick smiled. "I assure you, Lucaät of Faytha, the Explorers' Guild will not allow him to come to harm before he stands trial."

Lucaät's haze shivered slightly. "Trial?"

"Duvät Gok must answer for his crimes."

After a brief hesitation, Lucaät nodded patronizingly. "Oh! I understand," he said. "Crimes, is it? Of course! I know what's going on here. The Guild is always loathe to share information with honest entrepreneurs."

Behind him, Huldar heard Casco's soft snort. *Unbelievable!*

Marick gave Lucaät a pitying frown. "You may be unaware of the severity of the charges against Duvät Gok. If you wish to speak on his behalf, please register your intention with the Guild, however, since his crimes took place while the Uri'madu were on assignment, and beyond communication with the Realm, I doubt you will have anything of relevance to add."

The Faythan first eyed Huldar, then Duvät.

Duvät Gok studied the ground.

Cobar and Gento stared stonily ahead.

"Nothing could surprise me now," Casco muttered.

Careful! Huldar warned.

"A talking half-breed." Lucaät's nose wrinkled slightly. "How novel." He half-turned his head toward the Ashik at his back and said, "We are far from satisfied with your explanations, Marick of Cantori, or that the Guild's detention of Imperial Overlord Duvät Gok is justified. What are you hiding? I must be allowed to speak with him."

"Ex-Overlord," Marick corrected patiently, "and by all means, take your concerns to Guild-Lord Shamkarun Pieru of Leth, or to whomever you think might be interested to hear." He returned to Huldar. "Once again, Shamkarun Huldar, congratulations on your return. Now, if you will excuse us?"

"Certainly," Huldar said. He signaled Cobar and Gento, but as he did so, Lucaät's Ashik also stepped forward. For a tense moment, Duvät Gok's presence seemed almost inconsequential as Rukh and Ashik stood chest to chest.

"Lucaät of Faytha, stand down!" Marick barked.

Cobar's and Gento's eyes warmed in the slightest of smiles to see the Ashik back off.

Marick glared at Lucaät and his retainers. "Under Imperial and Guild law, section thirty-eight," he recited, "Imperial provision number three point seven, as decreed by the God-Emperor Tsemkarun Harshät'aht'el Ashik, thirteenth God-Emperor of the Realm, it is for the Guild to decide in the first instance whether or not Duvät Gok, former Overlord to the Uri'madu and Imperial representative, must answer to the Imperium for his crimes." He paused. "Lucaät of Faytha, do you have grounds to contest this?"

Lucaät bowed and stepped back. "My apologies, Marick of Cantori. I am merely concerned for my friend's welfare."

With his gaze still firmly on the Faythan, Marick gestured to Gento and Cobar to bring Duvät Gok forward.

"Don't worry, Lucaät," he said. "When the trial is over, he's all yours."

Marick departed alongside Gento and Cobar who kept Duvät Gok firmly between them. Lucaät and his Ashik followed close behind. The Uri'madu gathered in their wake, minds abuzz with speculation. Warm sunshine spread over bobbing heads as folk came and went through the elaborate doorway to the outside world. Duvät glanced back for an instant before the crowd swallowed him.

"I could have sworn the Gok was smiling," Huldar murmured.

Casco sniggered. "Probably just wind."

"Wasn't that a performance?" said Nachiel. "And the Ashik? Very appealing in those dark uniforms – in an austere sort of way, of course."

Bush elbowed his brother. "Wonder what t'new Overlord'll be like then, eh Topper?"

"Can't be worse," said Tam.

Casco sniggered. "Don't bet on it."

"What time is your appointment with Lord Pieru?" Andel asked Huldar.

He unrolled the scroll given to him by Marick. "Ah …Tenth hour tomorrow." He unrolled a little more. "He wants the healers … and Tsemkarun Andel … and Casco."

"Me?" Casco seemed apprehensive.

"Yes," Huldar replied. "I'm sure it's nothing to worry about. Your permit's up to date, isn't it? They'll just want evidence for the trial." He resumed reading. "And … the rest of you are to stand by." He looked up and grinned. "So, for the moment, here we are, home safe. Let's get ourselves a meal and make ourselves comfortable, and all at the Guild's expense! Says here they've assigned us full accommodation at the Guild-Hall and free meals at the refectory."

"Ooh!" said Nachiel. "That sound's wonderful, eh Ronnin?"

"For how long?" Andel asked.

"Yes," said Sari. "For how long? My sister is waiting for me – the Sword Ceremony, the party and all? She'll need to know."

"It says here we're to remain at hand until the trial is over," said Huldar. He sighed, understanding Sari's frustration. For himself, although the rooms would doubtless be opulent, all he really wanted was time alone with Andel. "If it looks like dragging on," he said, "I'll see if you can be released early."

"Well, let's hope they're good rooms then," said Casco.

"They will be," said Huldar. "I've stayed there before."

"And free food? The refectory here is Realm-renowned!" said Tam.

"So long as you like talemgal," Casco said.

"Navigators," said Bush, his gaze followed as one walked by, head and shoulders above the work-a-day crowd. "All those great tall Maatu peerin down at you, like."

Topper nodded sagely. "And them Maatus, they love their talemgal."

"Like mother's milk," Bush agreed.

"I mean no offence, Tam," Andel said, "but even talemgal has to be a vast improvement on little attar … at least for now."

"Point taken, Lady Andel," Tam grinned. "And fair enough too."

Huldar smiled wearily and tipped his head toward the exit. "Come on, people, let's get ourselves a well-earned feast, talemgal or no, then we'll get these rooms sorted."

But as they made their way toward the refectory doors, Duvät's crafty smile played on his mind.

THE TRIAL

Andel gazed blearily at a series of incomprehensible shapes … rounded red blobs, gilded yellow lines, mottled patterns … and slowly their meaning registered. Not flowers on grass and weathered red boulders, but a broad soft rug on the floor and a red divan with yellow tasseled cushions against a pale blue-green wall. She was warm, swathed in soft creamy sheets that smelled so clean … and she was smiling. Then the lean body beside her nestled closer and she remembered why.

When it came time to register for their accommodation, Casco had seen them hesitating.

"For Breath's sake!" he said. "You two haven't had a moment's privacy since we left Went. Take the double room and be done with it!"

How her cheeks had flamed!

Sari had made a point of sitting her next to Huldar at the refectory. Bush and Topper's food 'accidentally' formed into ribald shapes. There'd been lots of elbow-bumping and jokes in broadly rhyming Lethian dialect that she'd found quite impossible to unravel and which Huldar had refused to translate.

Then, when they returned to the Guild-Hall, Huldar whisked her from her feet and carried her up the stairs.

"You're full of surprises!" she said.

He shut the door with a backward kick. *You have no idea!*

She grinned as she remembered landing on the bed, her head submerged between mounds of plump cushions.

"Ah! That's the answer," she patted them. "More than two pillows!"

She'd attacked him with one in each hand, and in the ensuing wrestle she was sure she'd never laughed so much – her sides actually hurt – but it had ended in the wildest, most care-free sex she had ever experienced. She smiled again, remembering. The joy of it had surprised them both.

He stirred, and she felt him waking. His hand moved slowly over her bare shoulders. Fingers roughened from outdoor work vibrated against the smooth skin of her bicep. Desire tingled against her haze.

Don't turn over, he murmured. *Not yet …*

She let his voice play her. Soft at first, it rippled over her senses like molten honey, then as she became more aroused it flicked pleasure like a whip, goading her toward ecstasy. She arched her rear toward him, and in one smooth motion felt herself impaled. There was no structure to their love-making, no explanation or thought to the rules of touch. Only instinct and answer, hunger and desire.

Afterward, they dozed again, reveling in the warmth and softness after so many months of sleeping rough on a planet that was rapidly freezing over.

He brushed loose strands of hair from her face. "W-a-a-n-t some food?" he said.

She rolled her eyes. *Isn't that joke a little tired?*

Huldar grinned. *I know I am! And hungry.*

As they finished their meal, Andel looked with dismay at the growing crowd in the refectory. After years of isolation, the pressure of many hazes bore down on her, and ether thickened with psychic exchange seemed oppressive.

She raised her voice to be heard over the noise. "Is there a way out that doesn't go through the bays?"

Huldar nodded toward an alcove across the room. "The long way round."

"How long?"

His eyes twinkled. " … Is a spinner's song?"

"As long as it has to be!" She laughed.

"Well," he said, "we're used to walking, so about fifteen minutes."

She pushed her empty bowl aside. "Better get going then."

But I haven't finished my drink!

"Don't want to be late, do we?" she retorted.

Huldar took a last mouthful and hurried after her, weaving through the crowds as he made his way toward the refectory's back door.

As they spilled out onto the street, she turned her face to the sun and breathed deeply of the balmy morning air.

"It can affect you like that," Huldar said. He tipped his head to the right. "The Guild is this way. I thought you didn't want to be late?"

"I don't, but there's no rush just yet, is there? This architecture, such massive buildings! That one across the park there, the one with the plaited columns, what is it?"

"You're pointing like a tourist," he chided. "Never seen the sights of Giahn, the wondrous Imperial City?"

"Exciting, isn't it?"

"So, lords and ladies," he said. She laughed as he postured like a tour-guide. "Here we are in Sadir, the ancient and magnificent district of the Guilds. If you look there," he indicated a tall pink building with frond-like minarets, "you'll notice the spires of the Weavers' Guild, and there," he directed her attention to an open-sided structure with swathes of greenery spilling down from a dozen gardened tiers, "the bureau of the Gardeners' Collective. They share most of the office space out," he commented, "but it's surprising how many gardeners there are, and someone has to represent them. And in the heart of the building is a massive conservatory with a fantastic collection of rare plants."

Andel turned on the spot. "It's so beautiful," she said, "and grand, but there's something forbidding about it too, don't you think?"

Huldar hesitated then started walking. "Too many Tiamäti, for one thing." He shrugged. "And too many Faythans. But there are some beautiful places, and the palaces are remarkable. I'll take you to the Palace of Winds if you like. It's on Ilanath, the western continent – the most amazing building I've ever seen."

He shared an image of a multi-tiered edifice clinging to the side of a vast precipice in a series of pavilions so delicate they seemed to have grown, like flowers, from the rock itself. The colors of the strata, pale pink and white, were continued in the bands of stonework.

Andel sighed. "Ephemeral … like lace. How did they shape the stone so finely? I can't wait to see it. Isn't that where the iskilatu gates are?"

"*The* iskilatu gates? Yes. The Imperial Palace has a pair too, but I don't know anyone who's ever seen those. They say they lead to the inner sanctum, where the God-Emperor holds his most important meetings and such."

"But we can see the gates at the Palace of Winds?"

"Yes, but you can't touch them of course. You can even go up to the turret where the God-Empress and Ziquarudjan Ulisharu used to meet – where the greatest of scryers once ranged the skies."

"Oh! Is that the turret you showed us in Casco's story of the Terric?"

Huldar frowned. "Not so loud," he whispered. *Remember, the Terric have been expelled.*

He pointed across the street to a broad portico supported by translucent yellow pillars. "Ah! There it is."

Gento moved from the shadows and waved them over.

Casco ushered them up the steps. "Took the long way round?"

Topper and Bush peered up at the sky. "Day's a heatin'!"

Andel stroked one of the columns. "This stone is only found here on Giahn. Spectacular, aren't they? And what stories they could tell!"

Nachiel put his ear to the stone. Refracted light lit up his face. "Nothing to say just yet." He winked at Ronnin. "Can you hear anything?"

"Only that them beds be mighty comfy if Lord Huldar here be late." Bush laughed.

Sari frowned at him. "Pay no attention to their teasing, Lady Andel."

Huldar gestured to the imposing doorway. "Shall we?"

Inside, the noise of the street faded. Across a floor of polished yellow stone was a round-edged desk that looked to have been fashioned from a single giant seed-pod.

An officious receptionist looked them up and down. "Shamkarun Huldar of Leth?" He pointed to the passage on the right. "Third door on the left. Wait for the usher, please."

As the Uri'madu followed their escort down the cavernous hall, their feet echoed conspicuously on the polished stone. Crystal globes cast a web of muted shadows.

"You'd think there'd be a rug," whispered Nachiel.

The third door opened into an alcove lit by a window in the ceiling high above. They were met by a tall archangel in the flowing robes of a court official. Silently, she indicated for Huldar to follow and led him through to the chamber.

As the doors parted, Andel bobbed forward to glimpse an older archangel, plainly dressed, flanked by two taller officials also wearing Imperial colors.

She turned to Casco. "Is that the Guild Lord?

Casco leaned closer. "Arien Leth's uncle," he murmured.

"I've heard Arien Leth is a real firebrand," Andel remarked, "or at least that's the word everyone seems to use."

"Aye, well, his mother was Ashik," Casco said.

"Ashik?"

Casco nodded, smiling at her surprise. "Ekarät Ashik became Ekarät Leth. Not what anyone would expect, yet the match was well made by all accounts."

"Is she still alive?"

"Alive? No, she died long ago," said Sari. "I was barely come of age."

They settled on cushioned benches to wait, but before long the door opened again.

"Tsemkarun Andel of Trianog," the usher said firmly, "come forward please."

"You'll be all right," Sari said. "We'll be waiting right here when you've finished."

Andel took a deep breath and followed into the next room. To calm her nerves, she focused on Huldar. His bright blue eyes sent a message of reassurance. His fair hair was uncharacteristically tidy, a fourth-level braid in a distinctively Lethian style, close and practical with a bun at the back. Lit by an oblique shaft from the skylight above, it shone in stark contrast to the deep brown of the wood-paneled walls.

She echoed the usher's formal bow to the Guild-Lord. Huldar nodded faintly as she was escorted to her place beside him.

"Greetings, Tsemkarun Andel." The master's voice was warm and fluid. "It is good to meet you," he continued. "By all accounts your work on the planet Went was outstanding."

She bowed politely. "It is my honor, Lord Shamkarun Pieru of Leth."

When she looked up, he searched her face as if seeking confirmation of something, then came to stand in front of her.

"Please, if you will permit a level of sharing?" he asked calmly. His gnarled hand opened.

Andel nodded automatically, though this was not what she'd expected.

"I sense your misgivings," he said, "but this will be the best way for me to see exactly what you saw." He smiled gently. "If you don't wish to connect, I'll certainly understand. Perhaps Huldar can vouch for me?"

Huldar smiled at her. "I'm sure it will be all right."

Again, Lord Pieru held out his hand.

Andel had a moment to feel the rugged texture of his skin, then his mind swept into hers with the coolness of a wave to the shore. She was surprised to sense he was not more powerful than she, but vastly more skilled, and very competent with this kind of link.

I have had to become so, he said. *As Master of the Explorers' Guild I deal with many individuals of varying strength and intention.*

Intention?

You'd be astounded, Lady Andel, and Lucaät of Faytha is not least among them. Now, show me Lind. Take your time. Do not be ashamed to reveal your emotions. I will filter them as best I can, but they are important too. We will pause if the memories become too much to bear.

Andel was amazed by the small details that came to light under Pieru's scrutiny: Lind's expressions, the tone of her haze, subliminal messages revealed while her veil was still imperfect, then details of its strengthening and repair. But when she revisited the sight of her counting her toes, the pain became overwhelming.

It was the only way she could be sure she was still alive. Andel's breath caught in her throat, and tears slid down her cheeks. *She couldn't tell any more what was dream and what was real – even after we found her. No one has ever been so alone.*

She felt Huldar's arm around her. *We should pause,* he said.

Pieru gave her hand a gentle squeeze. *You are not to blame for Lind's death,* he said. *You interpreted her earlier distress as the result of her interaction with Huldar – and afterward? You did the best you could. The difficulties of interpersonal relationships can cloud even the most acute of minds, and Duvät Gok hid his tracks remarkably well.* He paused. *We will stop now. I have seen enough.*

Andel shook her head. *I am strong enough to go on.*

I have no doubt of it, Lady Andel, but truly, I have seen enough. Thank you for your trust.

He disengaged smoothly and turned to Huldar.

"In this matter, Shamkarun Huldar, my initial impression is that your judgment was sound – although I have yet to speak to the Naghari. I am also keen to speak with Casco. As a half-breed, he may have been underestimated and seen or heard things while Duvät Gok was incautious."

Huldar frowned. "Casco is invaluable to the Uri'madu. He is highly skilled and talented."

"I meant no disrespect," Pieru assured him. "The same Breath blows though us all."

"His heritage has no bearing on his importance to the team," Huldar insisted, "or as my friend."

"Understood."

Pieru looked into their faces as if he saw through them to Went itself. "Poor Lind … and her death-cry, *'Duvät Gok has eyes'* – he must have followed her every move – his gaze haunted her. And if that were not enough, she faced the absolute terror of being trapped in Qalān." He shook his head sadly. "No wonder we lost her. May she rest sweetly in the Breath," he said reverently.

Huldar lowered his head. "And now I have lost two team members in as many rotations."

"There is no shame on you for this, Huldar," Pieru insisted. "No dishonor, I assure you. On the contrary, no one could have done more. Ours is a dangerous occupation. And benefit has come from tragedy in the amazing ability you have found – to hold open the gates of Qalān – and another even more extraordinary gift! But we will talk later."

He nodded at the usher. "I will speak with the Naghari now."

As the marshal came forward to lead them out, Pieru opened his hand toward the door and said, "Please, wait outside until we are ready to pass judgment. I understand your entire team is here? Such support warms my heart, Shamkarun Huldar of Leth, and speaks loudly of your qualities as a leader."

In due course, Ubaid and Alis of Naghar emerged from the chamber and it was Casco's turn.

"You'll be fine," Andel said breezily. "Lord Pieru is …" she looked to Huldar for inspiration.

"He wants to understand what happened," Huldar said. "How an Imperial Overlord could do such things and think he could get away with it. He suspects you may have something to add."

Casco nodded. It hurt Andel to see him so anxious. Was this how life was for a half-breed on Giahn? Permits and humiliation? On Frith, her own homeworld, people married as they chose. Intermarriage was uncommon, but perhaps that was due to differences in life expectancy – archangels lived much longer. But as her father said, length of life should not be the focus, rather what you did with the time allotted, and there was no segregation for mixed marriages, only admiration for a couple who chose love over the inevitable pain of loss. As for travel permits, on Frith, she had never heard it mentioned.

The Uri'madu nibbled half-heartedly on the remains of a plate of small biscuits and a selection of cheeses. When the doors opened, Casco waved them in with at least some of his usual confidence, and Andel smiled with relief.

"He wants us all present when judgment is passed," he said solemnly.

Bush and Topper shared a nervous glance.

Nachiel blinked. "All of us? Well!" He stood and brushed the crumbs from his clothes. "Glad now I wore my nice new vest."

Andel walked beside Huldar as they led the way into the Guild-Lord's chamber.

"Welcome, Uri'madu," Lord Pieru said. "Your loyalty as a team is something others should aspire to. Now, if you would please remain silent as the respondent makes his entry?"

Pieru gestured and Duvät Gok was brought in, flanked by two stern officials. He seemed clean and rested and had the temerity to be dressed in Imperial colors, but his haze was far from steady and apprehension stained his usually impeccable veil.

The usher approached Pieru with a shimmering white shawl. The Guild-Lord bowed, first to the garment itself, then again to the Keeper as he accepted it. When it was draped over his shoulders, he crossed his hands over his heart and bowed to them all.

"Bey Maat'aht ej El a'sien." The sound of the ancient words invoked a deep solemnity.

"Breath blow truth," they intoned in response.

"I call Duvät Gok of Tiamät to trial on the basis of information presented by those who bore witness to his misdeeds," Pieru began. "During the course of this day, information pertaining to the case has been shared with me by way of direct imagery which cannot be manipulated or false."

The Uri'madu responded, "Breath blow truth."

"Shamkarun Huldar of Leth," Pieru said. "Will you stand for your fallen team member, Lind, and make the accusations?"

Huldar stepped forward. "Yes, I will."

His strong voice rolled over them, reminding Andel of that final, bitter night on Went. She saw again the dazzle of sparks held by his charm, heard the hiss of snow and the crackle of flame – it had been the last time Lind would hear his voice. Could they have stopped her if they had known?

He turned to face Duvät Gok. "This I say – that over the course of many months while the Uri'madu were isolated from the Realm during the progress of their explorations of the planet Went, Duvät Gok, our then Overlord and Imperial Representative, did rape and terrorize our team member Lind. This I say, as the Breath blows."

"Breath blow truth," Andel whispered, but she remembered Lind's eyes, huge and terrified, and her breathing tightened with the burn of unshed tears.

Pieru nodded. "Duvät Gok, before the Guild and these parties who bear witness, do you admit to these allegations?" He gestured toward a steely-veiled Enna standing among the officials and said, "If you do not, an Imperial interrogator is standing by to ascertain the facts."

Duvät Gok's expression wavered.

"Feel free to tell the truth," Pieru said. "If you are innocent of these charges, this highly skilled interrogator will quickly and painlessly determine the veracity of your counter claim."

Duvät glanced at the Enna and cleared his throat, a habit Andel had come to detest. "I … do admit," he said.

Pieru bowed. "So it is told!" he said. "Is this your final word?"

"It is," Duvät mumbled, then he repeated more clearly, "Yes, it is my final word."

Shamkarun Pieru fingered the shawl for a moment as if composing his thoughts, then lifted his head. His voice rang out as he proclaimed, "Therefore I, Shamkarun Pieru of Leth, Master of the Explorers' Guild, say that Duvät Gok is no longer fit to be associated with our Guild in any way. His entire wage for the Went expedition is forfeit, and since Lind has no direct relatives, it shall be divided equally among the remaining Uri'madu. Lind's wage shall also be divided equally among you as compensation for the emotional damages inflicted.

"Further to this, as Duvät Gok has been a representative of the Imperium, it is my duty to decide whether he should face the God-Emperor to answer for his crimes."

Duvät Gok's eyes widened. Andel glanced Huldar's way. Would their Overlord be made accountable to the God-Emperor in person? Huldar shook his head minutely to show he had not anticipated this either.

At last, Pieru came to a decision. "Since Duvät Gok did not directly or deliberately end Lind's life, he shall not face audience with the God-Emperor, Tsemkarun Ishät Ashik; however, the Imperium shall be notified of this trial and its result. The shame of Duvät Gok shall be known."

Ceremoniously, he turned to Huldar. "Shamkarun Huldar of Leth, on behalf of Lind, is honor satisfied?"

Huldar bowed and said, "Breath has blown."

Andel closed her eyes as a wave of grief swept over them all. It was finished, but nothing could bring Lind back.

The Guild-Lord sighed. "Duvät Gok, please await your escort."

As the rest of the Uri'madu turned and filed toward the door, Huldar touched Andel's mind with a gentle caress. *Shamkarun Pieru wants to talk to me. You go on with the others. I'll catch up when we're done.*

"Red Weyfal?" Casco suggested.

"Sounds good to me," said Topper.

"Huldar will catch up later," Andel said. "So, where is this place I've heard so much about?"

"The bartender's as big as a house!" Nachiel said.

"Sounds interesting."

Slowly, they made their way onto the street. It was late afternoon and many well-dressed officials were on their way home.

"Crafters first," said Sari, "then we're off to the outer reaches of the enclave."

"The enclave?" Andel said. "What's that?"

"Karesk," Casco corrected her.

"Where the half-breeds live," Gento explained.

"We call ourselves Kareski," Casco said. "But we won't be going all the way into Karesk, Lady Andel. The Red Weyfal's on the pure side, so you needn't worry."

"Worry?" she said. "I'm not worried, but I'm certainly curious. Why is there such a place? There's nothing like that on Frith."

"You can tell she's not from around here." Nachiel laughed. "Come on, let's show her the sights!"

On the edge of a forested area they stepped through a portal to Crafters, then after negotiating a twisted warren of streets and portals, they came to the district of weavers. In the distance she could see a vast swamp and high alps beyond it. There was no sign of the huge buildings of the Imperial City, but the portal connections they'd crossed were so smooth and direct it seemed that these areas really were just one street over.

On a cobbled lane they passed a family carrying bundles of stout reeds on their backs while the adults ferried an even bigger load on the ether before them. In a nearby workshop she saw a mother teaching her son how to sing a special pattern into the basket he made. Then, just as they reached an open square lined with vendors' stalls, she stopped, surprised by a familiar hail.

"What is it?" asked Sari.

"Sorry, everyone," she said. "I'll have to share the joys of Crafters and the Red Weyfal with you another time. My parents have just arrived."

There you are! Her father sent her an image of the translation bays and her mother's glacially calm expression as she ordered the spinners to be careful with their luggage.

"There's a quicker way back to the Bays," Casco said. He held out his hand. "Do you mind?"

"Of course not," Andel replied.

Through their contact, Casco passed a set of instructions and images. "Had to make a quick getaway from time to time," he said, "so I know all the ways – or most of them. If you get lost, just give me a shout."

With a cheery smile, she waved good-bye to her friends and started back.

This is a lovely surprise, she said to her father. *We didn't expect you till late tomorrow.*

Yes, the navigator was one of the best and here we are, a day early! Her father smiled broadly. *Your mother is quite ready for a soothing drink or two – you know how she is after traveling. Is there somewhere close by where we can meet?*

I'm already on my way, she replied.

Her parents, Ninjay and Inshogi of Trianog, waited just inside the Imperial Bays beside the huge double doors. Her mother, small and slight as herself, was already quite ruddy from the unaccustomed heat, a shade that contrasted with her coolly correct outer veil. On the other hand, her more robust father seemed quite excited, his gaze darting between architectural marvels and the press of the city's populace with equal enthusiasm.

"One of those spinners was a half-breed," her mother said irritably. "I'm sure of it!"

"Ninjay!" her father scolded.

Andel blinked in surprise. She'd hoped for a warmer greeting.

"An archangel was killed by one of them," her mother rounded on him. "Right here in the Imperial City. Just a few days ago!"

"Exclusion is not our way!" he muttered. "We don't know what happened or why."

At last, Ninjay reached out and drew Andel in for a perfunctory hug and she was inundated by vast relief for her safe return. Enveloped by her mother's familiar scent, she was momentarily transported to her beloved home on Frith in much the same way as a navigator's envelope would take her there for real.

Then the elegant arms pushed her back outward, a warm but critical gaze looked her up and down, and she was pleased she had dressed well. Her mother seemed in no mood for the more casual style she had adopted with the team.

"And you, my dear?" Ninjay said. "Have you been affected by these dreadful riots? Perhaps you can tell us what happened."

"Riots?" Andel shook her head. "We only just got here ourselves."

A party of angels giggled as they walked by. Ninjay looked at them coldly. "Is there somewhere suitable where we can eat?"

Andel glanced toward the refectory.

"Never mind," her mother declared. "I have a brochure that shows all the best places."

With the pamphlet in hand, Ninjay set off for Al Bayut, the district closest to the Imperial Palace. Andel and her father smiled resignedly and followed.

MEET THE PARENTS

Huldar strolled down the front steps of the Guild-Hall and took time to gather his thoughts. How quickly the afternoon had passed! Already, chains of crystal globes along the streets had begun to glow as the light-singers started their rounds. A cool breeze sifted some of the day's heat from between the buildings, and the psychic buzz grew steadily as the disciplines of a day at work eased.

He felt calm but exhilarated after his meeting with Shamkarun Pieru. It had felt good to share his experiences on Went with someone who truly understood. He'd thought that the song he'd devised to hold open the gates of planetary Qalān would be foremost on the agenda, but Pieru had been far more excited to find another who was, as he put it, sacred to Leth.

Sacred to Leth? Huldar looked up at the sky, feeling the Breath in his heart. Was he truly so … exalted? His Mark now reached down his cheek all the way to his neck, and he'd noticed that the space beneath his eye was also covered with intricate patterns. There were even tendrils of light shining through the fine skin by the bridge of his nose … and the planet Went *had* spoken to him.

No doubt Pieru would report his findings to Arien Leth, his House Leader, at the first opportunity. Maybe he was already doing just that.

He imagined Arien's craggy face, avid and proud. Would the Leth ask to see him again? Present him with another jacket? With broader epaulettes, and even wider lapels? The thought almost made him chuckle aloud. Reflexively, he tried to share the joke with Casco, but although he could sense his friend's presence, their normal camaraderie was closed.

"You have a lady now," Casco had said. "You need to spend time with her … private time. And I have some catching up of my own to do."

Huldar sighed as he remembered agreeing to this. Apart from missing his friend, their separation worried him. In the company of an archangel, Casco's presence would not be questioned and he could move freely around the planet. But recently, riots had been sparked by the imposition of a new half-breed travel levy, or so he'd heard. Navigators would have to pay every time they transported a half-breed, and anyone who employed one would be charged an additional cost in taxes. Extra Imperial peacekeepers, the so-called ashessé, had been signed on to enforce these and other new laws … but Casco was no stranger to the Imperial City, Huldar reminded himself, and well able to look after himself.

There was so much to think about, and just to complicate things further, Lord Pieru had offered him a position within the Guild. But even as he thought about the prestigious appointment, his mind shied away. Acceptance would mean the end of the Uri'madu. He took a steadying breath. Pieru had warned him that now his true status had been revealed, his path might not be easy. Huldar nodded to himself. Best to keep news of the Guild's proposal quiet until he and Andel had time to share fully.

He pictured her, already at the Red Weyfal no doubt, sipping tea with Sari while the others drank stronger stuff. He imagined her animated eyes creased in laughter as someone told a joke – she was one of the team now, just as she had longed to be. But when he located the Uri'madu in a downtown tavern, Andel was not there. He cast about more widely. Surely it was too early for her to have retired to their rooms at the Guild?

Ah! There you are, she greeted him warmly. *Emerged from Lord Pieru's clutches at last?*

I found the others, he said, *but where are you?*

Al Bayut. It's called the Winds of Hesh, a Nhadu place – well you'd have guessed that from the name, wouldn't you? She visualized the restaurant's colorful façade. *Can't quite remember how we got here, but it's near a boutique that sells jewelry, and there're gardens with a fountain on the other side of the street …*

… And distant glimpses of the Imperial Palace? He knew the place. Very stylish.

Andel heard the question in his mind and chuckled. *The others went to the Red Weyfal and from there they were planning quite a night.*

The Red Weyfal, he laughed. *I thought so. Casco's favorite watering hole.*

Yes, I had to leave them to it. My parents arrived soon after we left the Guild-Hall. They wanted to eat somewhere nice.

Your parents?

Huldar felt his spirits slump. After the rigors of the trial then Pieru's proposal, he'd looked forward to an easy night with the team. To be on show for Andel's parents was not what he had hoped for. He turned toward the wealthier region of the Imperial City, following his sense of Andel's location.

She broke his silence with a wordless enquiry and he grimaced.

I told you they were coming, she said. *They're eager to meet you.* She pictured her parents as they watched her talk with him.

Yes, but I thought we had days yet, he replied, *at least one; and I was looking forward to a drink with everyone before we say goodbye.*

So was I. That's why they've agreed to get together again for a second farewell feast tomorrow. Don't worry, my parents will love you!

He could feel her enthusiasm, and even some welcome reassurance, but his mood continued to plummet.

Did you tell them I've asked you to be dabaku? He said.

There was a momentary pause, then, *No, not yet. We'll tell them when we're ready, together.*

Perhaps we shouldn't tell them at all, he suggested ruefully. *Perhaps we should just do it.*

Huldar! That would be so rude!

It's dabaku, he shot back. *Not marriage.*

He felt her recoil and his mood hit rock bottom.

Better get cleaned up before you meet them, she said at last.

Cleaned up? He looked down at his soft ketta-fiber shirt, pale blue-green, his favorite color. *What's wrong with the way I look? I've been to a meeting with the Guild-Lord, not climbing cliffs or working up a sweat.*

What about your dress coat? The one with the lapels?

He sent her a sensation of residual summer heat. *No problem, if we were still half frozen on Went!* he snapped. *I think I'm fine just how I am.*

Well, it's up to you, of course.

Yes, it is, he said. Why should he change? Ketta was a prized hard-wearing material that breathed in the heat. The clothes he had on were perfectly suitable for an important meeting – good enough for Guild-Lord Pieru. Surely it was best to be himself, and comfortable … not dressed up like some glittering Faythan merchant ready to cheat them out of … their daughter? No, he was as well dressed as he would ever be, and that would have to do.

A passer-by gave his haze a pointed look. Embarrassed, he clutched for the residue of his former buoyancy.

As he entered the restaurant Andel waved, a small, self-conscious gesture. She was sitting toward the back, and he hardly noticed the spectacular view from the huge window behind her. Her parents' attention prickled over his skin. He smiled as he made his way between the tables.

Andel's father got to his feet with a convivial grin. "Inshogi of Trianog," he said heartily, "and my wife, Ninjay of Trianog."

Huldar introduced himself with a short bow. Ninjay nodded but made no attempt to rise.

Inshogi bustled around the table to pull out a chair. "Come, come!" he said. "Welcome, Huldar, welcome! Please, sit down. Our Andel has shared so much about you, but I must admit, you're taller than I imagined. Almost as tall as a navigator, eh?"

"Not all navigators are tall," Huldar said, "but I am told there is Maatu in my distant heritage."

"Good, good. Ah, yes," Inshogi said. "Navigators. What a romantic life they lead." He held up a fluted glass. "Here's to the endless song between hearth and stars. Wine? Or perhaps you'd prefer some of that Lethian Besh?" He murmured the words again, "Lethian Besh," and gave a broad wink. "I've heard it's what you explorers like best, eh?"

Huldar felt Andel's inner cringe and smiled.

"There's a fine wine here on the table –" he started, but Inshogi was already signaling the waiter.

"Yes, one of those Lethian Beshes please," he called out, "for our good explorer here!"

"Besh it is then," Huldar nodded. "Thank you, sir."

Inshogi beamed, but Andel's mother sat without moving. Her haze was tightly bound and her veil icily perfect. She glanced briefly at her husband; there was a rapid exchange and his exuberance was quickly contained.

"How was your meeting with the Guild-Lord?" Andel asked Huldar.

Inshogi nodded. "Guild-Lord, eh? Sounds important, Ninjay, doesn't it? An important young fellow this, and on the up and up, eh?"

"The meeting went well, thank you," he said.

"No doubt discussing the death of your colleague, Lind," Ninjay remarked.

Andel's father shook his head. "Terrible business. Terrible."

"Exploration is a dangerous occupation," Ninjay said brusquely. "Death must be expected."

"Expected?" Huldar's anger rose to the accusation in her tone. It had been a long day.

In her heart-shaped face he could see the resemblance to her daughter, but her eyes were like shutters braced for a storm. "You must realize by now that Andel is completely unsuited to such conditions," she said.

"On the contrary –" Huldar started.

"And the sooner she comes to her senses about that the better." Ninjay glanced coldly at her husband as if he was somehow to blame. "I hope she wasn't too great a liability for you?"

"A liability?" Huldar clamped his veil down tightly and wondered how best to respond. Through the window, the distant turrets of the Imperial Palace gleamed in the late afternoon light.

Andel rested her forehead against one hand as if blocking out the scene. Her other index finger made small circles on the tablecloth. He almost expected the fabric to swirl.

"Ah! Here's your drink," Inshogi said brightly.

Huldar took the glass with relief.

"Don't mind my wife," Andel's father continued. "The rigors of travel, eh my love?"

Ninjay glared. Andel continued to draw figures on the cloth.

"Let's order, shall we?" Inshogi's jollity was edged with a touch of desperation. "Lucky your meeting finished when it did, young Huldar, or we'd have started without you."

"Thank you for waiting," Huldar said.

"I'm sure he wouldn't have minded," said Ninjay. "He must understand what hunger is, given his profession."

Inshogi gave his wife a forced grin, then turned back to Huldar. "Yes, yes. Breath has blown you to us just in time, eh? Our Andel tells us that you are quite famous among the explorers at the Guild?"

"Does she?" Huldar knew he should say more, use this opportunity to break the ice, but he couldn't think. He imagined Casco would have known how to find safe conversation. He took a deep draught of Besh and was met again by Ninjay's disapproving glare.

"Ah, here comes the waiter!" Inshogi announced.

He took another drink, and Ninjay's gaze narrowed as if war had been declared.

"By the Breath," Inshogi said warmly, "that meeting must have been thirsty work."

"Yes, it was," Huldar replied. The glass felt cool in his hand. He longed to hold it against his forehead.

Once their selections were made, Inshogi turned to him again.

"Tell us about your parents, Shamkarun Huldar. What do they do?"

Huldar hesitated. "My parents rejoined the Breath – many years ago."

Ninjay's frozen demeanor softened just a touch. "May they rest sweetly," she said reverently. "You are young to be alone."

"I am not alone," Huldar said. "I have my team, my friends, the Uri'madu."

"But no true family?"

"I have a brother on Lentath, First of our family, married and blessed with a beautiful daughter. He grows vines."

"Easanberry, eh?" Inshogi was visibly relieved to have found a safe subject. "We've seen the vines, haven't we, Ninjay? And the perfume in the morning, yes, marvelous! Well, this brother of yours, he'll be chuffed when he sees you home again safe, no doubt."

"No doubt," Huldar said flatly. Then, to fill the ensuing pause he continued, "It's not that we don't get along, but he disapproves of my career choice."

"As would any responsible First!" Ninjay snapped.

"Mother, please!" Andel said, but Ninjay's control had already slipped.

"Exploring new planets?" Her chin jutted forward. "The dangers you ask your team to face! How can you answer to Lind's parents?"

"Lind was an orphan, mother," Andel said. "She had no family, only the Uri'madu." Although she hid her feelings well, Huldar could hear the strain in her voice and knew she was close to tears.

"Nevertheless, she is gone!" Ninjay retorted. "How would you have answered to us if Andel had not come home!"

"How would I answer?" Huldar breathed deep and tried to level his emotions. "Andel *has* come home and you should be tremendously proud of her. I say to you now that she is a powerful Tsemkarun and a fine and resourceful archangel with great inner strength and resilience. She is capable and thinks on her feet. I know of no one more suited to the career she has, of her own accord, chosen. Within the first few days of our assignment on the planet Went, many of the Uri'madu already owed her their lives to her courage. And you should also know that I love her."

Ninjay turned to her daughter.

"It's true, mother," Andel said. "Huldar and I are in love."

"In love?" Ninjay gave her daughter a look of desperation. "So, you would doom yourself to a life of uncertainty? Of fear? The both of you never sure that the other will survive?"

"Yes, Mother." Andel lifted her chin defiantly. Her tawny gaze found Huldar's and he nodded. *As good a time as any.*

They stood up together and turned to her parents. "We have decided to become dabaku."

Ninjay slumped. Her veil returned to its frozen neutrality. Inshogi, on the other hand, opened his arms and beamed his happiness to them both.

"My darling daughter! Such news. Congratulations, young Huldar. Breath blows love to us where it will, hearts captured by Asheru's gift ... Wonderful! When is the ceremony to be performed?"

"Inshogi!" Ninjay hissed.

Around them, diners busied themselves with food and drink, but their attention on the Trianogi table was plain.

"What?" Inshogi frowned. The quick flush of red on his haze was masterfully contained. "Our beautiful daughter has found love, and a career that matches her talents and stretches her to do great deeds. She can follow her heart with joy. How can we not be happy with this news?" With a gentle sigh he opened his hand to Ninjay and spoke to her, mind to mind.

Huldar took Andel's fingers, determined they would not stay another minute unless there was some evidence of change in her mother's attitude.

Wait! Please … Andel returned his grip. *Father would be devastated.*

An emotional bombardment flooded through their contact, but there was little he could do to soothe it. *Perhaps Ninjay's fear for you has some justification,* he conceded. *Some of what she says is true, if exaggerated.* Her near-death experience in Qalān weighed on his mind.

She lost her son. My brother was swept away in a caving accident – remember? It haunts her.

Another burst of communication sizzled between Andel's parents.

At first, the softening of Ninjay's demeanor was barely perceptible, perhaps just a change in the tone of her haze, then she rose and bowed with her husband.

"My apologies, Shamkarun Huldar of Leth," she said. "I want only what is best for my daughter."

"Of course. I understand," he said, "and I hope that in time you will accept that is also my desire."

"Please, may we start again?" Inshogi said. "Our meal is ready, and the cook has gone to a lot of trouble."

Please? Andel looked up into his face.

He nodded and with a reluctant smile they returned to their seats.

"Let us tell you about our home on Frith," Inshogi said. He glanced pointedly at his wife.

"Yes," she said. "I hope you will come back with us to Aventhe and stay a while?"

"Of course," Huldar said valiantly. "Andel has shown me the beauty of Aventhe many times. The perfume of the rayno blooms is among her fondest memories. I look forward to observing these wonders for myself."

"I think I'll try some of that Besh," Inshogi said, and he signaled the waiter.

Andel squeezed his hand. Her sympathetic inner smile softened his heart. To lose a child must be a dreadful thing, he thought. Perhaps her mother's hostility would ease with time.

LET THE GAMES BEGIN

As he was escorted from the Guild's chambers, Duvät Gok tried to look contrite, but the welling gratification of a move well played was hard to repress. However, satisfaction dimmed when he saw Lucaät of Faytha's tame troop of Ashik awaiting him in the foyer. They were clad in the black leather of Imperial ashessé, but Duvät had no doubt who they were really working for.

He looked into the hard-eyed gaze of the troop leader. "I don't think we've been introduced."

The Ashik replied calmly but firmly, "This way, if you please."

"To Lord Lucaät of Faytha?" Duvät asked.

He was answered with a grunt.

As Duvät hurried along beside the hard-muscled soldier, he hoped he looked more like an important archangel with an escort than a prisoner. He saw someone in the crowd who reminded him of his wife, and wondered why she hadn't yet greeted him. Perhaps she was angry, but that wouldn't last when she found out how clever he'd been – how wealthy they would become.

The Ashik marched at pace. Sweat trickled down his back.

"Isn't there a portal we could use?" he asked.

The guards sniggered.

"Lord Lucaät will hear of this!" he said.

"Up to you, of course," the leader muttered.

The hairs on the back of his neck lifted as if he was being watched. He looked around, but saw no one. They trudged on in the sweltering heat. The distant song of builders at work grew louder. As they neared a construction site they were asked to wait as several Zaïkhanun wrapped a huge stone in song, ready to lift it into position. Duvät craned his head to watch the majestic rise of the mighty block, weightless on waves of sound, but then something glittered on the ground and he stepped forward to see if it was a coin. The shadow of the stone fell around him, dark as a pit. The telltale prickle of surveillance returned, and in that moment the Zaïkhanun lost control.

Someone swore. There was a blazing burst of sound as they tried to stop the plummeting stone.

He knew he should move, but his feet seemed frozen in place.

Then the wind was knocked from his lungs as someone hurled him aside. Dust billowed as the stone crashed onto the space where he had been standing. The ether shuddered with a vast roar of pain, and Duvät realized that the Ashik who had saved him was now trapped. Blood seeped from beneath the rock, its metallic aroma beguiling to his senses.

"Call the healer!" someone yelled. *Get the healer!*

Workers scurried as if the expenditure of energy would somehow make things better. The Zaïkhanun stood at the four corners of their stone, waiting anxiously for the healer's advice before they lifted it from the victim's torso.

"What went wrong?" one whispered.

"I don't know," the other replied. "It was as if someone was inside my head. I lost concentration and all went awry."

Light fingers touched Duvät's shoulder. *You were lucky, my friend!* their owner said.

He turned to see sardonic eyes shining from beneath the shadows of a wide-brimmed hat, then the brim dipped and vanished into the growing crowd of onlookers.

The healer gave a nod. The song of the Zaīkhanun swelled. As the stone began to lift, the smell of gore sent him back to the long beach on Went, and the stench of the dying sea-creatures. The victim's agony flooded his soul with the remembrance of power. His knife hand clenched and unclenched as he relived the joy of the kill.

"Keep moving," the Ashik lieutenant barked. He gave Duvät a rough shove. "Let's go!"

Reluctantly, he stumbled forward.

After an age of steady marching, a winding forest path and a river spanned by an ornate if flimsy bridge, they reached Al Bayut, and there, within actual sight of the Imperial turrets, the lavish gate of a manorial home slid open. Metalwork tingled with expensive ward-charms. Once more, Duvät felt the prickle of observance and he smiled cheerily. It must have been Lucaät who'd been watching him.

"I hope you have a cool drink waiting," he said for his creditor's benefit, "and a healer to tend my over-used feet."

Behind him there was a derisive snort, but the Ashik's attitude was unimportant. The Breath was with him. He had vital information for Lucaät of Faytha – and the eyes of Bel Nishani? That secret was buried as profoundly and completely as he knew how.

Inside Lucaät's foyer, coolness bathed the overheated skin of his face.

"Wait here," the Ashik ordered. One remained on guard while the rest tramped off down a side passage.

The polished stone walls were invitingly chill. A water fountain tinkled nearby. Then he heard brisk footsteps, and with an oily smile, Lucaät of Faytha appeared and beckoned him toward the end of the atrium.

"Sit, sit!" Lucaät waggled his finger at a wooden divan. "Did you enjoy your little walk?"

"Desai Forest? The river Khal'a'din? I'm exhausted, and your guard were quite rude."

"My apologies," Lucaät said. "I thought that one newly returned from the wilds of the Guild might value such a chance for self-reflection."

A slim angel carrying a tray of icy drinks entered the room. She studied the tray as if it was the most fascinating thing she'd ever seen. Terror coated her every move. A fine silvery chain glinted at her neck.

"Never seen one before?" asked Lucaät.

Duvät had heard of slave-chains, of course, and seen one or two in the distance. He'd even fantasized about owning one. In his mind's eye, he superimposed Lind's features over the slave girl's, but the reality was even more delicious than he'd imagined.

"Touch her if you desire." Lucaät shrugged as if he'd offered up a bowl of nuts. "She'll even believe she wants you to – if that's what you want … or not."

The girl stood in front of him. Four hundred summers, no more. Her skimpy garment hid little.

"You control them with your mind," Lucaät drawled. "They can't stop you … can't resist. Some call it an atrocity, against the tennets of El; at least, I've heard that's what they say in quiet corners – but I'm a bit bored with it, really."

The girl continued to stare at the tray. Memories of past abuse fluttered from her defenseless mind. Duvät found her attempts to stop them quite fetching.

"Lethian?"

Lucaät nodded.

"Where did you get her?"

"I have my ways."

Lucaät's finger flicked. The girl tensed to leave.

"My drink!" Duvät cried.

She turned back. The tray vibrated with the shaking of her hands. Lust stirred in Duvät's loins. He closed his fingers around the glass.

The girl quickly turned and fled.

The Faythan sniggered. "Time for that later, if your information lives up to its claims. If not …" He shook his head. "… I doubt you'll be pleasuring yourself with anyone."

Duvät took a long mouthful of chilled juice and tried to focus.

The Faythan leaned forward. "You noticed Pieru didn't report you to the Imperium?"

Duvät nodded. "Your work?"

"Things are so bad in the palace now – it didn't take much."

"Bad? How so?"

Lucaät smirked. "You've heard, of course, about the God-Emperor's notorious temper? There's talk that El no longer favors him and that's the reason he has only one child."

"Who would dare?"

"It's all around the palace," Lucaät continued. "And now his son's latest Bride Choice fiasco? Said none of the candidates were suitable and walked out. Our Exalted One is certainly not known for his diplomacy – it'll take years to smooth the ruffled feathers there – on both sides! I think the recent half-breed riots were engineered in an attempt to give people something else to gossip about." Lucaät gave a dry laugh. "Hasn't helped with his irritability, but it's certainly helped me."

Duvät shook his head. Besides being the embodiment of El, the God-Emperor was a powerful Tsemkarun. He could kill someone just by looking at them: everyone knew it. How could such internal conflict help Lucaät – or anybody?

"You Gok; so naïve!" Lucaät waved his hand as if the answer was obvious. "Nobody wants to be the one to tell him anything, of course – and the less he knows, the less he wants to know and that, my friend, means that the Realm is run by the bureaucracy, and they can be owned – by greed – by the promise of power and the desire for self-preservation. Perfect, don't you think?"

"But the Ashik?" Duvät argued. "They won't stand for it. They guard him day and night."

Lucaät tilted his chin toward his personal garrison. One side of his mouth tightened in a smile. "They guard him from anyone who might annoy him with the unpleasant truth. It's amazing what you can get for coin these days, yes, and for information cleverly applied." His gaze sharpened. "And that's where you come in. Information." He leaned back against the soft padding of the divan. "I'm sure you won't mind if I use an interrogator to verify whatever it is you have to give?"

"Such intrusion is ill-mannered and completely unnecessary." Duvät swallowed his fear. "What do I have to gain from hiding anything?"

Lucaät looked at him doubtfully.

"I'll show you myself," he said. "Then you can make up your own mind."

Duvät held out his hand. It was a gamble, but working with Huldar and the Uri'madu had honed his native Gokish ability to conceal, and above all he was certain Lucaät would be far easier to deceive than a trained interrogator.

Manicured fingers closed over his own and the invasion began. Their polished blue nails helped him focus on trying to hide the blue calcite deposits. It would seem suspicious if he didn't try to keep something back. The fire-opal beds formed the next layer of encryption. If Lucaät found the nacrite too easily he would be suspicious, but once he had discovered it, Duvät was certain his ordeal would be over – so long as it was believable that there was nothing else.

Images flickered. There was a stab of pain as Ulisharu's map was found, then hints of gold and copper, ice and snow as Lucaät pushed deeper, chasing the trails he had set. He gasped as a wisp of glittering opal was thrust aside, lured by a glimpse of Lady Andel speaking to the Uri'madu, making her report. Its significance loomed large despite his best efforts. He'd only watched from a distance but every nuance was uncovered in an agonizing rummage – the written, the spoken, the subverbal, the moaning of the breeze outside the tent, the stillness of the group as nacrite was mentioned, then the buzz of subliminal excitement.

Nacrite?

Lucaät's surprise came as a jolt. As their contact wavered, Duvät focused all his efforts on hiding the fire-opal. Pain ripped through his head as Lucaät took the bait. It wasn't that it stopped him delving for every shred of information about the nacrite, but the fire opal was also rare and exceedingly valuable, and the idea that Duvät had tried to keep it from him would be logical enough to stop the Faythan searching beyond it.

Fire opal? Blue calcite? Oh … does it feel it's earned a small reward for itself? Why did you even try? Lucaät sneered. *Another bet that didn't pay off.*

As Lucaät withdrew, Duvät mopped his brow. The Faythan's sense of superiority had saved him. The Eyes of Bel Nishani were safe. An interrogator might not have been fooled, but the Breath was still with him – he could feel it.

Lucaät of Faytha sat back, taking time for self-control. To have information about the nacrite before the Guild went public was a real gift. Duvät Gok had put up more of a fight than he'd expected, but capitulated easily at the end … was it possible he'd missed something? More likely he'd grasped at the opportunity to avoid unnecessary pain once his little ruse was discovered.

Duvät Gok sank lower into the divan, his gaze locked on his crushed fingers. As he massaged the life back into them, beads of sweat leaked slowly from his face. His veil seemed tight and anxious, his haze all spikes, as if expecting the worst.

"My apologies, Lord Lucaät," Duvät mumbled. "Alas I am no match for you."

Lucaät considered his position. Duvät should be punished, but ultimately, he had delivered the prize as agreed. If he'd succeeded in hiding the fire opal, with clever planning the returns would have been enough for him to live in comfort for the rest of his days, if he didn't gamble it all away – but this was a mere drop in the ocean to the wealth the nacrite represented.

"Duvät, I should let you sweat a little longer," he said at last, "but in truth, I can't be bothered. You have made me a very, very wealthy person today, and wealth is sacred to my House." He snapped his fingers for food and drink. "Instead, on behalf of Faytha itself, we shall celebrate!"

A wave of relief crossed the Gok's veil, his haze shimmering into rosy smoothness, and Lucaät almost chuckled aloud, though still something seemed out of kilter. Was there too much contrition … too much relief? The Gok definitely smelled of victory, and not just a victory over the Explorers' Guild … had he managed to keep something from him? The Duvät he remembered was nowhere near skilled or powerful enough to achieve such a thing, but something significant had happened to him on the Imperial Planet Went, and whatever it was, it had changed him.

He decided on a test.

Duvät stilled as the slave came in and placed a tray of colorful fruits before them, then Lucaät reached into Qalān with a dramatic flourish and announced, "The girl or the purse? Duvät Gok, my friend, I offer you a reward for your … honesty. You must make a choice!"

As the Gok wavered between the prizes on offer, Lucaät searched him intently.

"I thought we had agreed on a price?" Duvät said.

"Of course we did!" Lucaät smiled airily. "Do you doubt my word? This is a little extra – an expression of appreciation. I thought it might please you."

"Oh, it does!" Duvät reached out to stroke the girl's fine skin. "But such a dilemma."

While the Gok's repellant fingers reached beneath the girl's shift to explore, Lucaät studied his haze. Psychic emissions were much harder to control than a veil and took skill to interpret, but this ability was the secret art of House Faytha, and Lucaät's gift was the key to his great success.

Duvät was almost drooling with lust, but there was something obscene about the intensity of his regard and Lucaät fought the urge to look away. With one hand still on the slave, Duvät lifted the purse and jiggled its weight. Through slightly narrowed eyes Lucaät saw avarice gust through the Gok's aura, and there – oozing beneath it – the deep, muddy blue of hubris.

"The slave is tempting," Duvät said with a crafty smile, "but with this much gold, maybe I can buy one of my own."

"Very well, the choice is made." Lucaät smiled inside, knowing his intuition had been correct. Duvät was hiding something, but the information he had already divulged was explosive enough. Nacrite! He could still hardly believe it. The most precious of metals, so treasured by swordsmiths. Riots in the Imperial City were already driving trade in the armorer's shops. Only news of an impending battle could make his day brighter. No, the rest of Duvät's offering would come in its own good time.

He waved lazily toward the door. "Karmät Ashik will show you out."

Despite his haughty escort, Duvät Gok's haze was irritatingly smug.

Summon the Agent and set a tail on him, Lucaät said to Karmät, but he had to ask himself, what could be more precious than nacrite?

He watched as Duvät Gok was escorted through the gates, then cleared his mind. He must act before anyone else got wind. His factor within the palace was very well placed, and although the planet was claimed for the Imperium, mining was always left to the Faythans. Ashik were too proud, Enna too lofty and Gok too lazy. He must secure an exclusive contract over the Planet Went without delay and negotiate commissions as soon as possible.

DUVÄT GOK FINDS MIRASHAEL

Duvät glanced nervously over his shoulder. Since leaving Lucaät of Faytha, his neck had prickled constantly. The same feeling had plagued him during the incident at the building site – faint but detectable.

'You were lucky, my friend,' the stranger had said, but far from putting him at ease, the glint of those eyes stayed with him like a dire foretelling.

Was someone spying on him? Did they know about his purse from Lucaät? Well, if they did, it was safe in Qalān and he would never give it up!

He ducked down a sidestreet, flattened himself against the wall and waited. His heart beat fast. A lone bird clack-clack-clacked in the heat. After several moments pressed against the cool stone, no one had followed. Cautiously, he extended his senses. Nothing seemed out of the ordinary, but someone could well be tailing him, content to merely observe. He recalled a hint of shrewdness in Lucaät's parting glance.

The side street emptied onto an alley where a little-used portal led to the Basket-weaver's Collective. From there he thought to make his way to the Crafters district, a riddled maze where he'd be able to lose any tail.

As he stepped through the portal, the glimmer of the surrounding swamps and dank smell of reeds told him he was in the right place. He flitted through the outskirts and set out on a narrow trail that led across the wetlands to the rain-forests that rimmed them, but a short way down the track his hackles prickled. He turned to look. Was that a shadow? His instinct said not.

Shrill creatures called rhythmically from reed-beds taller than himself. Humidity sent clammy sweat trickling down his back. Ahead was a portal – he could just make out its glow, but it was small and he would have to get his feet wet to use it.

Steps crunched behind him, coming closer. Ahead, a hulking figure rounded a corner and started toward him. With a burst of speed Duvät splashed into the portal's field and with great presence of mind, sang himself through with a twist that sent him to the Glassworkers' Co-op.

Cold slapped him in the face. The Glassworkers lived in an alpine precinct close to the snow-line. Wet trousers clung to his rapidly cooling legs. Ahead was a large stone dome that radiated heat and he squelched eagerly toward it.

Inside among the furnaces and kilns, steam rose from his pants and shoes. Heat burned the inside of his nose. He stopped to watch an archangel moulding molten glass. The noise of singers was loud, some managing fires while others cajoled the bubbles at the end of their blow-pipe.

Then a hulking figure passed between work-stations. It seemed to be searching.

Duvät toughened his screens to the best he knew how and hurried for the exit. Outside, he sidled down a chilly alley to where he knew another portal waited, and instead of a direct route to Crafters, sang a detour to an area where charmsingers and substrate merchants plied their trade.

The familiar warmth of the City proper was a great relief. He paused by the portal to see if the hulk had followed. Several minutes went by before a group of Faythans came through, then a short time later, a Cantori with what looked to be a bag of pumice. Neither party saw him, but just to be sure, he decided to use the same portal to access the forges district, then, with the clang of metal ringing in his ears, he made a quick dash to another little-used portal and stepped into Crafters at last.

The scent of timber and sawdust was everywhere. He set off immediately and merged with the evening stream of dusty artisans intent on finding food. There was no more sense of being followed and he congratulated himself on his cunning. Years of dodging debt-collectors had paid off. Then the blurred outline of a heavily screened person made his heart skip a beat and he turned left into a workshop-thoroughfare. In the next alley a shadow made him jump. He cursed his over-active imagination, but veered hard right just the same and found himself in a dingy back street lined with bars and cafeterias.

Sounds of laughter carried with the gusting scents of exotic spices. Some teashops were so small he wondered how they could make a living. There were no more phantoms. His nerves began to settle. At length he came to a quieter café where he pushed between grubby bits of wooden furniture to get to an empty divan at the back.

A florid Cantori leaned from the kitchen at the rear.

Duvät studied a menu scrawled on a battered board, and a bright young angel came to take his order.

"Soup," Duvät said. "There's little you can do to ruin soup. And some roshan … oh, wait. Does it have little attar in it?"

"Yes, my lord," the waitress said. "Of course."

"As if that's a good thing," he grumbled. "I'll have the kavesh instead. No attar in that, is there?"

"No, my lord."

"Should be banned. And a long glass of guerdi – a long one, mind. Don't think you can bring me a half cut and call it long. And make sure the glass is clean!"

"Certainly, my lord." The waitress bowed and scurried away.

He looked around. There were few patrons and none gave him the slightest attention.

At first, the tattered cushions on the divan had seemed soft and welcoming, but as he sank lower their musty smell made him sneeze. He dragged himself more upright as footsteps started toward him but it was only the colorfully dressed person he'd seen as he entered.

"Mirashael of Cantori at your service," the archangel said, "proprietor of this humble establishment. My lord will forgive me, and I apologize profusely, but the kavesh is no longer available. It has been quite popular this evening and we have no more left."

Duvät felt the stresses of the day bearing down on him – the trial, the stone, the interrogation, the spy, and now this? All he wanted was some nice kavesh to go with his soup. He looked up just in time to see a steaming serve of the savory loaf being delivered to another table.

"Tsemkarun," the proprietor said apologetically. "They took the last of it. Perhaps I can interest my lord Gok in a plate of omosa? The house specialty? ... Garnished with cilfra?"

Duvät scowled.

Mirashael smiled ingratiatingly. "At a special reduced rate to reflect the anguish I have caused by preparing insufficient kavesh to meet your needs?"

The lucky diner nearby lifted the last wedge of kavesh to his mouth and bit into it with great relish.

Duvät's frown deepened. "Very well," he snapped. "Half price."

"Half price it is!" The proprietor's smile never slipped. "Your gamble will pay well, lord Gok. My omosa are the finest in the Realm. All the great lords eat at my table."

Duvät looked around. The claim seemed unlikely.

A hearty bowl of soup was duly delivered in person by the proprietor, accompanied by a plate of juicy brown omosa. "Crisp on the outside, scrumptious within!" the Cantori announced.

"They'd better be," he grumbled.

Although the cilfra garnish was a little less than fresh, his first mouthful of soup was encouraging. The Cantori watched from the kitchen doorway. For an instant, his expression smacked of a bento eyeing prey, but seeing Duvät take another mouthful he smiled and turned his attention elsewhere.

As his stomach filled, Duvät's tension eased. The omosa had an unusual sweetness about them, and were delicious, as promised. The glass of guerdi was indeed long and clean. All in all the meal turned out to be quite satisfactory, and cost far less than similar fare at a restaurant in the fancier end of the city. A pleasant lethargy crept through his bones, and as he walked down the street after leaving the café he was surprised to catch his face smiling. The thought that his face could make its own decisions made him giggle.

A pretty angel looked his way and his loins tingled. She whispered to her friends and they laughed, a sound reminiscent of water tinkling over shiny pebbles. The tingle became a throb. What he needed now was sex! And if he went to a Naghari Chapter-House, he wouldn't have to pay much for it – in fact it would be free if he didn't leave a donation. Fortunately the nearest one was only three streets away.

The night was balmy, the lights so pretty … Duvät whirled on the spot, entranced by the lilting streamers they made as he turned. Happy voices filled the air. The prickle on his neck was merely a cool breeze wafting by. As he neared his destination his legs became harder to move, but sex, yes! Sex was what he needed. A vision of Lind's face flashed through his mind, at first brazen and street-wise, then fearful and defiant, seeing him for the great lord he was.

All the great lords ate at Mirashael's – he could see now that it was true.

His legs labored on. Only one street to go. The night was so hot. He unbuttoned his shirt. The crowds seemed thicker, but his destination was in sight. When a wiry archangel bumped his shoulder, he barely noticed, but a sharp pain stabbed more aggressively at his side: the prick of an insect bite.

"Breathless zilla!" He cursed and swatted at the scurry of tiny legs beneath his shirt, then chuckled – zilla belonged to Mathas, a scantly populated Lethian planet.

"There's no zilla here!" he laughed. "How funny is that?"

"Steady there, my friend!" the stranger said.

Duvät peered into his face. Was he familiar? "Out of my way!" he cried, and was shocked to hear himself chuckle. "Yes!" He laughed. "Out of my way, or join me with the Naghari!"

"You don't want to go there, my lord," the stranger murmured. Duvät heard the cultured accent of Enna. "No, why go there when I have something far more attractive to offer?"

Duvät shoved the Enna away. Whatever he had to offer, it was sure to involve more coin than he intended to part with. He lurched on. He could see the Chapter-House steps. The serpent of Naghar branded on the door seemed to writhe invitingly.

He brushed at his side again as something leggy scuttled beneath his shirt, then lifted his elbow as pain flared from his ribs. His head reeled. Strong arms caught him as he collapsed. The serpent door opened. Laughter faded. Bare feet ran toward him, but not his wife's … her feet were far more dainty.

"Stand back!" someone said. "Get him inside, quickly!"

"Yes," he laughed. "Take me! Take me now!"

Sometime much later, he awoke to the sound of running water. Soft fabric rustled. Heat spread through him as a gentle hand touched his side.

You were lucky. The deep, calm Naghari lilt swam through his head.

Kommer-sta, the healer said, and pictured a beetle with a shiny black carapace shaped like a sword. *A big one. Rarely see them in the city. Highly venomous. If you hadn't been right at our steps, Breath would have claimed you.*

Duvät still felt as if death might come at any moment. *I feel sick.*

I'm not surprised. The healer stood up. *There's a bucket by the bed. I'll leave you to it.*

ANDEL AND HULDAR

In the back room of the Red Weyfal, two burly angels cleared a long wooden trestle littered with empty trays and tureens, used bowls and platters, and not a grain of little attar to be seen. They barely looked up as Topper darted in.

"Sorry, mates!" he said cheerfully. "Forgettin' me beverage here. How could that 'appen, eh?"

By a window in the front, the Uri'madu had gathered around a group of tables pulled together for the occasion. Another bowl of greasy omosa was plonked down in front of them and the Planet Walkers tucked in with gusto.

"And there she was," Casco raised his hands theatrically. "Eyes of a startled maffit! The great hairy beast reared up before her, trying to sniff her face." He waved his arms and cried, "Get away, get away!" in a high-pitched, girly voice. The group roared with laughter.

"I didn't sound like that," Andel spluttered. She turned to Huldar. "Did I?"

He shrugged. "Casco's telling the story …"

"Beast!" She laughed and slapped his chest.

"Wae-e-nt some help with that?" Tam called out.

Huldar's arms wrapped warm around her. "I think I'll be right thanks, Tam." He grinned.

"Thanks, Tam, yes," Sari said. "Now, let Casco finish his story."

"Thanks, Tam, thanks, Tam!" the group echoed. "Casco, finish your story!"

"Finish my story? Yes, Sari!" Casco teased. "Right away!"

As he launched back into "The Tale Of The Diviner And The Went", Sari leaned toward Andel and said, "You didn't sound like that at all. And it was mean of them to play such a trick."

A little later, Casco came over to Huldar and tilted his head toward the door. "Got a minute?"

"Of course." Huldar smiled down at Andel, *Won't be long*, and followed him out onto the street.

Andel's back was cold where she had been leaning against him.

"He seems … a little quiet," Sari said.

"It's the noise, I think. The ether is alive – all the people everywhere. I think I prefer the peace and quiet too, now that I've experienced it."

"Yesss!" said Tam. "She's definitely one of us!"

"No escape now, Lady Andel." Nachiel crowed. "Seven years will be gone before you know it then we'll all be back together …"

"And off to sunnier climes!" Topper laughed.

"To Went!" they toasted.

Behind the bar, the rugged barkeep shook his head.

"To Went," Sari repeated thoughtfully. "And life in the Imperial City? Your parents?" she prompted. "That must have been a nice surprise."

"Yes, it was," Andel said. "But … I don't think Mother likes him very much."

"Your mother? Ah." Sari's smile was knowing. "I daresay Huldar has little to do with it, Lady Andel. She hardly knows him. More likely she fears losing you."

"Losing me?"

"Is there an echo in the room? Now you sound like me!" Sari laughed. "Well, I've got to go, I'm sorry to say. Navigator's booked. I'm off home to Lentath for my sister's party and all."

"We'll go with you, Sari, and see you off in style," said Andel. She looked up as Huldar returned.

"To the bays? Good idea," he said. "If Sari doesn't mind?"

"Uri'madu!" the company roared. "To the Imperial Bays!"

Sari shrieked as Gento lifted her off her feet and carried her over his shoulder.

After her departure, the Uri'madu said good night. Giahn's huge moon sailed through the sky with a trail of minor moons behind it. Through silvered streets, Andel and Huldar laughed and talked as they returned to the Guild-Hall lodgings. At the front desk, the concierge yawned to attention.

"Lord Shamkarun Huldar," he stammered. "We were not expecting you."

"Not expecting us?" Huldar's focus sharpened.

"My lord," the attendant floundered, "the Lady Andel's mother ..."

"My mother?" She and Huldar shared a puzzled glance.

"She insisted that you were staying with them," the attendant stammered, "at the Jewel of the Imperium. I'm sorry. I'm so terribly sorry. I just assumed – she is your mother, my lady, and she sent someone to transfer your belongings."

Your mother has cancelled our room? Huldar said. *Why would she do this?*

Andel held up her hand. "One moment." It was considered rude to use mid-speech overtly in public, but under the circumstances … *I'll ask.*

She found her mother still awake with a drink in her hand and a bowl of toasted nuts by her side.

What's going on? she snapped. Her attempt at calm was not hugely successful. *Why have you cancelled our room?*

Daughter, please! Ninjay rubbed her temples delicately. *Your anger is most unseemly. Years in the wilderness have done nothing for your self-control. I merely assumed you would want to stay here with us, and not in some musty old Guild-Hall.*

Musty? Have you seen it? Andel choked back her anger. *You have no right! We are so embarrassed!*

She heard Huldar ask the attendant, using his most reasonable voice, "Is there another room available?"

Well, if you don't want to spend time with us … Her mother's tone was indignant.

That's not the point! Andel shot back at her.

Huldar put his hand on her shoulder. "We're here at the Guild-Hall now," he said. "It's late. There is a room available. Tell your mother we'll come over tomorrow and sort things out."

After a restless night spent agonizing over how her mother would react to her outburst, Andel could barely face breakfast. While Huldar finished hers as well as his own, she tried to decide what to wear. Eventually, she slipped on a blue over-shirt and asked him to show her what she looked like. In his mind's eye, the color made her skin look pale. She seemed dainty, yet somehow fierce.

Not to be trifled with! Huldar assured her.

Lucky we're used to keeping a wardrobe in Qalān. Everything we left in the closet is gone! After a short pause she held another blouse against her torso. *This green one?* It had rayno flowers picked out in pink-silver thread, reminding her of home. *Perhaps Mother will like it better.*

Maybe … he said.

You're no help! she snapped.

He glanced toward the turrets of the Jewel of the Imperium, several blocks away. *Whatever your mother is playing at, I doubt your outfit will make a difference.*

Don't you care how I look?

Of course! he said. *But I see inside as well, and I'd still love you if you were wearing a coal sack.*

He sent an image of a stained, coarse-woven bag with holes for her neck and arms, and she had to laugh.

I'll wear the blue.

Good choice, he said. *And no, I am not going to wear my formal jacket with the lapels.*

On any other day, Andel might have enjoyed the walk through the vibrant city, but as they neared the Jewel its façade seemed to loom down at them – gilded balconies like jutting eyebrows, bowed doorway a frowning mouth. Huldar radiated reassurance, but her heart was coiled with the pent energy of years of her mother's disapproval, and her only hope was that she would not lose her composure. Ninjay would see that as another victory.

The door of her parents' suite opened as they grew near.

"Are you coming in?" her mother called.

Andel and Huldar shared a brief touch of hands, then went inside.

Ninjay stood to greet them. "Good morning, Shamkarun Huldar." She nodded the briefest of bows. "I trust you slept well?"

Huldar bowed. "Very well, thank you, Ninjay of Trianog."

"Please, just Ninjay, and I shall call you Huldar. No time for formalities now." She waved graciously toward a low table surrounded by plump cushions. "I've ordered tea."

A male attendant stepped forward with a tray of cups and steaming pots.

Ninjay turned to Huldar. "Urmahji?" When Huldar nodded, she glanced Andel's way. "And galano of course."

"Thank you, Mother," Andel said tightly.

"Always so difficult," Ninjay murmured to herself. "Your father will be along shortly. You took so long to get here … Well, he's just stepped out for a breath of air."

They sat quietly as the attendant poured. Andel breathed over her cup to cool the contents. She could hear her heart beating in her ears. Were they supposed to pretend nothing had happened?

"Your rooms are adjoining," her mother said. She pointed to a pair of mottled cream-colored doors and said grandly, "Carved from a single garsha carapace, I believe."

"Garsha?" Huldar seemed genuinely interested. "Intrinsic to Giahn's eastern ocean. Quite a majestic beast."

Ninjay almost smiled. "This sitting room and dining area are shared," she continued. "Lovely aspect, don't you think? And the furnishings, genuine Harrik of Nhadu, not cheap Cantori imitations."

Huldar's eyebrows lifted.

"The Guild's furnishings too are the very finest, Mother," Andel said. "Rare materials drawn from the furthest reaches of the Known. Hardly musty, and certainly not imitation!"

"Yes, well, perhaps it seems so. The Explorers' Guild are your employers, after all."

Andel's cup clattered firmly onto the table. "You didn't even tell us. We arrived back – such a lovely night. I was so embarrassed."

"And when were you going to tell us about your dabaku?" Ninjay retorted. "Dabaku leads to marriage." The pitch of her voice climbed higher. "How could you do this to me?"

"We're not dabaku yet!" Andel cried. "And it's my decision, not yours!"

When Andel's father opened the door, she felt like running to him as she would have when she was young. If anyone could talk sense into her mother, he could.

Huldar got to his feet. His mind was so tightly veiled she could not be sure what he was thinking.

He bowed respectfully. "Inshogi of Trianog …"

Andel's father flattened his hand. "Just plain Inshogi, please." His head tilted slowly as he absorbed the situation.

He looked at Huldar's Shamkar. "If custom were to be followed to the letter, it is I who should bow and call you lord." His gaze traveled between them. "The decision to become dabaku is yours and no one else's." He turned to Ninjay. "And of course Andel couldn't tell us beforehand, my dear. The planet Went is beyond contact for the most part, and when they came home, I'm sure these two wanted to tell us of their plans together, as is right."

"And we will be happy to stay here with you, of course," Huldar said smoothly. "But I must say, the change of room did come as a surprise."

"More a shock," Andel added sullenly.

"You were out, having fun," Ninjay said. Her tone was slightly injured. "And yes, I thought I would surprise you. A gift …"

"You were spying on me? A gift?" Andel shook her head. "You always do this! Do something rude, or controlling, then act as if I'm in the wrong!"

"Controlling?" Ninjay glanced at Huldar and gave a tiny, dismissive shake of her head. She looked Andel up and down. "And speaking of gifts, my daughter, where did you get that outfit? Dressed in Cantori hand-me-downs?

"You took the clothes from my closet!"

"Yes, and found nothing more inspiring there. It's time we went shopping, and here we are in the center of all things, the heart of our Realm. I'm sure your fine Shamkarun here will be happy to show us the sights, and, if you are to be dabaku, perhaps even stretch to buying you something suitable to wear?"

Huldar nodded agreeably and Andel almost laughed. Even with the concealment she could see the monumental effort he was putting into remaining calm. He could face any geographical disaster with ease and had no trouble managing a bunch of unruly explorers stranded on a lonely planet – but apparently her mother was a cut above.

Inshogi stepped forward. "Come, Huldar. Have you seen the view from the balcony yet? Quite splendid really. You can see right into the Imperial Palace grounds – if you look sharply enough."

Andel and her mother sat with their cooling tea.

"It's just that I worry about you, dear," Ninjay said at last. "All alone in such an inhospitable environment … it was bad enough when you chose to become a diviner. Of all the ways you could have used your talents!"

"What do you mean?"

"You could have worked with the healers and learned to influence thought-processes –"

"Invading people's minds?" Andel looked at her mother aghast. "Do you really see me enjoying that?"

"Well, what about bones? You could be helping them set bones. Bones are not unlike stone."

"Mother!"

"Or why not a meseq if you must work with stone … you'd be designing for the Zaīkhanun – helping create new cities, move water, circulate air, nurture gardens, all safe, respectable and socially responsible occupations …"

Andel got to her feet. "I think I'd like to see the view now too," she said, leaving Ninjay to finish her tea alone.

DUVÄT GOK COMES HOME

Duvät Gok looked up into the Naghari's care-worn face. He still felt terrible. His shirt was stained, but he lacked the energy to sing it clean.

"You're well enough to go home," the healer said.

He shook his head.

"Come on, up you get!" the healer insisted. "You may feel nauseated for a day or so, but the Breath has blown you a narrow escape. You should treasure the life that remains."

"Someone tried to kill me. I know it! I was poisoned!"

"Yes, bitten by a kommer-sta. Nasty. Few survive one. There's a tale for your grandchildren."

Duvät Gok sighed irritably. "I don't have any." There was more to this story, he was sure of it. His memory of the meal, the walk to the Chapter-House – all so vague and dream-like.

"Someone bumped into me, I felt a stab, a prick …" He touched his side. The bites were still raw and itchy despite the healer's best efforts. His face puckered as he chased dim recollections. "There must have been a reason I wanted to come here." When a nubile young healer sauntered past, the answer dawned on him … a far cry from his interests now.

"I wanted sex," he said morosely. "I was happy, so happy."

"Well, it may be a few days before you're ready to explore the rules of touch again," the Naghari smiled, "but when you are, by all means return. You are welcome to learn, and in doing so, we will learn from you. The beauty of sexual transaction mirrors the desire of El for Asheru. Through constant learning we strive to share the perfect joy of the Seventh Word."

"The Seventh Word? A little lofty for me." Duvät sniggered. "I still think I was deliberately poisoned." The image of an Enna's crafty eyes flashed through his mind.

Duvät swung his legs to the ground.

The Naghari smiled gently. "Here, drink this, and take some with you." He handed Duvät Gok a glass with a small amount of murky fluid and a sachet of powdered herbs. The medicine tasted vile, but the effects were rapid. Energy flowed back into his veins.

"Have you seen anyone suspicious?" he asked. "Maybe loitering around the door?"

"Why would anyone wish to harm you?" The healer looked around. "Come, I'll walk with you if it helps."

Duvät followed the healer through several ward-rooms where the sick and injured lay recovering from treatment. Then they passed a room where group of injured half-breeds waited for attention. A small child clung to her mother. The Mark on the healer's hand flared as she gently set the little one's broken arm.

"Riots," his companion said. "They're getting worse. Soon no Kareski will feel safe in the Imperial City, but where will they go? And who will replace them?"

"Half-breeds?" Duvät grunted. "What are they good for?"

The healer looked gently toward the forlorn group awaiting treatment and shook his head. "People say they're unpredictable, neither one species nor the other, but not too many injured pures among this lot are there?"

Duvät Gok shrugged. Half-breeds *were* unpredictable. Everyone knew it. "Disgusting that they would involve a child in their petty disputes."

"Involve a child?" The healer rounded on him. "Do you know why these poor people are here? No, of course you don't, and nor would you care, I daresay."

Despite his studied lack of interest, Duvät knew he was going to hear anyway.

"The child, Kisha, the one with the broken arm, was playing with her friends and accidentally crossed the enclave borders. A gang of larger children from the neighboring area set on them, resulting in this little one's fractured arm. When their parents came to their aid, the parents of the 'pure bloods' called on some nearby ashessé and this is the result."

Duvät made no comment and hoped that would be enough to shut the healer up. As they neared the exit, he hung back and tried to see who was outside before he stepped from shelter. As the doors opened, a haughty Ashik waiting on the steps turned toward them.

"Is there a back way?" he asked, ducking behind the door before the guard saw him.

The healer considered for a moment, then inclined his head. "Very well. Follow me, please."

Eventually they came to the laundries and he was shown onto a dingy alley. The door closed behind him with a decisive snick.

Suddenly, he felt very alone.

With a nervous glance up and down the street he headed for home, anxious to get away before the Ashik noticed his absence.

He stepped from the portal nearest his home and brushed past the keeper. Soon, he was walking up a street defined by a barrier of walls. Flat-roofed houses, each much the same as the last, were replicated in monotonous lines. Then came a row with front gardens and gates and a path.

He paused outside his own and let his senses range. There was no sign of anyone following.

Leahät!

It was like yelling into stone. His wife had reconfigured their bond so he could barely even sense her location. The changes hurt, but he was confident she'd open up again when she saw how wealthy he'd become.

The door swung open to his song and shut quickly behind him. He called again, *Leahät!*

She was not at home. The Breath was still with him! He hurried down the hall and into the bathroom. From Qalān he fetched the charm-stone he'd used to screen his activities on Went. It was not powerful, and would provide just enough cover to hide what he was doing without arousing suspicion.

Beneath a polished flagstone he'd hidden a small hole. Even Leahät had no idea of its existence. The smooth slate made barely a sound as he lifted it aside, and the smell of damp soil drowned the perfume of cheap toiletries. He stashed all but one bag of the Eyes of Bel Nishani in the hole, then raced to the hallway and placed a last bag inside the strongbox beneath the hall-stand. If it was found, a thief might assume this was the only one and not even try to find more.

He kept the lesser eyes with him in Qalān as a first line of defense. Even if he was forced to relinquish those, he might still be able to hide the others, and if they weren't physically with him, he couldn't be forced to give them up.

The box closed with a soft clack. He turned as Leahät pushed open the door.

"Wife?" He opened his arms hopefully. "I've been waiting for you. You must have known I was home?"

Her haze radiated disgust. She pushed past with barely a glance.

Annoyed, he followed to the kitchen and set Lucaät's purse heavily on the bench.

"What's that?" she asked. There was little curiosity in her tone.

"Take a look," he suggested. "Open it." There was nothing like gold imperials to sweeten a wife's heart. But she eyed the heavy fabric as if it were poisonous.

"If you've so much as touched it, I want no part of it."

"But I have suffered to bring this to you," Duvät cried. "I nearly died – twice!" He pushed the bag closer. "It's not winnings. It's fair payment!"

"Fair payment? Payment for what!" Leahät cried. "I have been informed by the Guild that they have terminated your employment. Your wage has been divided among the team, and Lind – yes, Lind! –is no longer with us."

"I didn't kill her!"

"Just get out!" she yelled.

Duvät could hardly believe what he was hearing. "Jealousy was always your downfall!" he hissed.

"Jealousy?" She shook her head – seemed genuinely puzzled.

"If you'd reopen our bond," he pleaded, "you'd understand."

"Open our bond?" Rage swelled through her haze – her veil fairly rippled with it. "I would rather die than defile myself in that way ever again!"

Her teeth were bared. Her eyes flashed. He had never seen her so angry. "Get out!" she stormed. "And never come back!"

"But I have nowhere else to go." Panic rose in his chest. Why wouldn't she listen? "I've worked so hard," he said, "and I've paid Lucaät off – it was he who paid me this time. I did it for us, so you could have the house you want, the status. I did it for us, for our future."

She folded her arms and wouldn't look at him.

"Why won't you open your bond!" He hammered his fist on the table. "Open to me!"

But the more he pushed, the harder her walls became. He tried to explain, but his words and even his thoughts bounced off her frozen veil. At last he stood mute, seething with frustration.

After a time, she took two bowls from the shelf, wooden bowls with green enamel lining. He couldn't understand why she held them so fondly.

"With the coin I have," he suggested as sweetly as he could, "you could get new bowls, much nicer than those."

She ran her finger round the rim, first one, then the other, as if she was considering his words, but just when she seemed on the verge of relenting, she returned them decisively to the shelf.

His anger flared. "If you'd open to me, you'd know how hungry I am!"

She looked him up and down then turned away as if bored.

Duvät leaned forward until they were almost nose to nose. "You'll thank me one day!" he snarled.

She made a show of wiping droplets of spittle from her face. Hatred permeated his soul. If she knew his true power, his strength, she'd never look at him like that! An image flashed to mind of Andel of Trianog gazing up at Huldar, her haze all rosy and warm. Once, Leahät had looked at him that way.

Without taking his eyes from her, he jerked the purse open. Predictably, her gaze followed the shiny coins as they spilled onto the counter. With the side of his hand he scraped a small portion back into the bag.

"The rest is yours," he snapped. "Do with it as you will!"

As he stalked from the house and slammed the door, he wondered if the gold would still be on the counter when he returned, or if her apparent abhorrence would evaporate as soon as he'd gone.

He marched along the pavement with no clear destination in mind, but soon slowed as an audacious plan took form. If he delivered the second-rate eyes directly to his Clan Chief, Brätan Gok, at least some of the honor he'd lost by being expelled from the Explorers' Guild might be regained. Then, as the eyes were sold, the clan coffers would bulge and his own prestige would bulge accordingly! But in the meantime, as Clan Chief, Brätan would be obliged to find him somewhere to stay.

As for the true Eyes of Bel Nishani, the best course was still unclear – but with Brätan's support he would be in a position to wait and take whatever opportunity benefited him most.

He smiled as speculation took wing … With such wealth as the Eyes would bring, who knew, maybe he would one day replace Brätan Gok – but for that to happen, he must ensure that the clan saw his value. Then Leahät would view him differently. She'd understand how clever he'd been. His foresight would bear due reward … and if she came sniveling back, would he even want her?

His daydream ended with the thought of the pain that would be caused if their bond was actually severed. Such wounds could take many years to heal and occasionally even caused permanent damage – the last thing he needed if he was to become Clan Chief.

Maybe I should buy her a gift, he thought. *A piece of jewelry might do the trick …*

He remembered a deep purple stone she used to wear as a hairpiece, and a brooch to match. It was a long time since he'd seen them. Yes, a sparkly new trinket was just what she needed, a symbol of his brilliance as a forward-thinking entrepreneur.

The rhythm of his steps became lighter as he congratulated himself on yet another problem solved.

MEETING WITH THE CLAN CHIEF

The sign on the wall read *Imperial Office of the Fifth Sector Urban Drainage and Waste Disposal*. Even after being made Clan Chief, Brätan Gok had retained his sector office, and if one wished to make an appointment, this was how it was done.

After checking yet again that no one was following, Duvät presented himself to the front desk.

An elderly archangel peered up at him. "Yes?"

He cleared his throat. "I want to see Brätan Gok."

"Oh, yes …" The clerk's long fingers wrapped like vines around his stylus. He stared at the page before him.

"Brätan Gok, the Clan Chief?" Duvät prompted.

"Brätan Gok, you say?"

The archangel paused for a moment longer then began to scratch neat characters in orderly lines. None were related to the Clan Chief in any way that Duvät could see.

"I have urgent business with him!"

The clerk nodded his head. "Urgent business, you say?" He kept writing.

Duvät glared down at his thinning braid, tempted to set it on fire.

At last he looked up. His old, grey eyes were steely. "Duvät Gok, late of the Explorer's Guild?" The way he emphasized 'late' was most insolent. "State your business."

"I have an offer for Brätan Gok that will benefit the entire clan," Duvät said.

"Come back tomorrow at three after midday."

"Tomorrow? This is an emergency. A most important matter!"

"Is there anything else?" The clerk asked.

Duvät cleared his throat again. "In that case, I need somewhere to stay … just for the short term."

"I expect you do." The old clerk rummaged in his desk drawer for a moment then slid a rounded pebble toward him. "Take this. The address is imprinted. The charm will let you in. It must be returned tomorrow. Don't lose it."

Duvät Gok leaned forward to take the pebble and planted his fists on the desk. "We'll see how you speak to me after Brätan has accepted my offer," he hissed. "Oh yes, then we'll see!"

The clerk twiddled his stylus briefly then returned to his writing.

The next morning Duvät woke to the clang of metalwork pounding up through the floor. He felt sick and sore all over – no doubt the residue of the near-fatal bite. Slowly it came to him that he was in a small apartment above a shop in the metalworkers' district.

He stumbled to the water jug and tried to retrieve the powder the Naghari had given him. It took several attempts, but at last he had it mixed and ready to drink. As the bitter fluid went down his neck, the clanging from below continued. He was surprised the clan even owned such squalid premises. Last night, he'd congratulated himself on getting free accommodation, but Breath be stilled, if Brätan couldn't do any better he'd use his own funds to find himself a decent room tonight.

"Why am I even bothering with them?" he grumbled. "I should just walk away." But he was in danger of being outcast. He knew it in his heart. Even if he became the wealthiest person in the Realm, to live without clan … one might as well be a half-breed. Such a situation was unthinkable. Already things were difficult. Look at the way the clerk had treated him. Then his favorite gaming den had refused him entry even though he'd shown them a gold piece. In the end he'd been forced to patronize the far less salubrious Breath's Bounty. His skin still itched.

Bang, bang, bang … the rhythmic din travelled up through his feet into his tender, sleep-deprived brain.

He dressed quickly and withdrew his somewhat slimmer purse, but the sight of the remaining imperials only increased his frustration. He'd been left with nothing of the wage he'd worked so hard for – let go from the Guild without so much as a thank you for three years of life spent under the most appalling of conditions. Pretentious Lethians! How could they even begin to imagine they were above the Tiamäti, El's chosen people? He was not outcast yet – and what's more, he had a hunch Brätan would look after him much, much better once he'd seen what he had to offer.

The rickety stairway swayed as he trotted down, anxious to leave the clamor of blacksmithery behind. As he passed the forge doorway, a deep voice began to sing charms into the metal. Steam hissed, and through the cloud he saw the glow of the smith's Shamkar.

You were lucky, my friend. Unbidden, the words flowed through his mind. Had someone said that to him? He wasn't sure, but they felt right.

He mouthed them again and answered, *Yes, I am! The Breath was with me yesterday, and it's with me now.* Today he would regain his honor, and tomorrow? … Brätan could not live forever.

An image of Leahät came to him and he wondered if the gift he had in mind would help dissipate her jealousy.

A clan chief had to be married, but as things stood, he doubted Leahät would be singing his praises. Didn't she realize Lind was just something he'd used to stave off the boredom of exile? A common angel could never be anything but a toy to an archangel such as him. Leahät would have felt that through their bond … wouldn't she? And besides, Lind was dead – no longer a problem.

The incessant din vanished as he set out for the jewelers' precinct. Even the shortest way involved several steps, but the route would take him past a lovely Nhadu bakehouse where he could eat his first meal of the day in peace.

LUCAÄT OF FAYTHA

In a room jammed with stylish furniture and exotic ornaments, two heads bent over a game of ashut. Lucaät's concentration faltered as he felt a query nudge his mind – his agent checking in with the latest report on Duvät Gok's movements.

He looked up at his opponent. "We'll continue later."

The Ashik archangel wove a quick stasis charm over the boards, then bowed and left the room.

News of Duvät's visit to Brätan Gok came as no surprise. It was understandable hat he would go to the head of his clan for support since his wife had kicked him out.

Cheapskate, he sniggered. With the coin he'd been given there would have been many other ways he could have found accommodation.

It's a ploy to regain face, the Agent suggested.

Lucaät nodded. Duvät would be hoping for sympathy now word had spread about the fiasco with the Explorers' Guild, but it was unlikely anyone would want to be seen in his company at all, let alone employ him. If Brätan made him outcast as well, his life would become unpleasant indeed.

Keep watching, he said. *He's up to something.*

They briefly lost contact as the Agent stepped through another portal.

Where's he off to? Lucaät asked as their connection snapped back into place.

Heading for the jewelers' district.

Ah. The wife!

No doubt … The Agent paused.

What is it?

There's someone else following him.

Who?

I'm not sure. He's very good …

Duvät Gok has never been so popular! Annoyance gave Lucaät's sneer a nasty edge. *Get closer. See who it is.*

Lucaät closed his eyes and stayed in his agent's mind. He had a sense of people on the street, sights and smells of mid-morning pavement. The Agent's gaze lingered on a poster proclaiming the importance of half-breed permit requirements, then was taken by a street vendor with a tray of teserid fruit. Their distinctive aroma filtered through. The only place they grew on Giahn was inside the Imperial Palace. Was someone stealing Imperial produce?

They passed a shop where bright headdresses adorned ceramic mannequins, and another where expensive shoes were displayed on cushions. There was a burst of shrill chatter as a group of shoppers went by, then the movement slowed. The Agent seemed to hold his breath, then release it.

Well, well! Our rival is Daric Enna. One of Mirashael's. The Agent snorted. *The finest omosa in the Realm, and the finest assassin.*

Someone wants our subject dead, Lucaät remarked.

It's whispered that even the God-Emperor himself has tried the Cantori's omosa – the aphrodisiac version …

Oh yes! Lucaät assured him. *I have it on good authority. Perhaps the Imperial couple imagine it will help El to bless them if they give Him every opportunity.*

If that worked, the Agent sniggered, *we'd be overrun with Naghari before we knew it. And on Hesh!*

Lucaät paused to think. Mirashael of Cantori was a powerful player with an extensive web of thugs at his beck and call. Angering him would be like stepping on a thuja nest. Was it worth continuing his surveillance? Duvät's life meant nothing to him really, but the growing puzzle intrigued him. Why was this sorry Gok's life under threat? Did someone know more than he did?

The stakes just got higher, he decided. *Let's not interfere with the Cantori if we can help it, but don't let Duvät Gok get killed before we know what he's up to.*

Right you are, the Agent said. *And about my pay … What about it?*

This mission just became more sensitive.

Lucaät paused again, but the adrenalin of challenge was already running and this agent was the best he could buy. *Very well, I'll see that you are compensated. Don't let me down.*

I never do, the Agent replied. *The extra is just to help me focus.*

Lucaät caught a brief sense of movement, then left him to it. This operative was as Cantori as Mirashael, and making things happen was what Cantori were all about. They were also highly adaptable and capable of extreme focus – and totally loyal to whoever paid them. In a sense, Lucaät had just secured insurance, and to pit these top assassins against each other could be as diverting as a round of ashut.

BRÄTAN GOK

The ancient desk clerk waved his finger toward the back of the foyer. Duvät moved off obediently. Time passed. He tried not to fidget. Eventually, the tack, tack, tack of footsteps announced a sallow usher in dark robes come to lead him into the bowels of the Fifth Sector Urban Drainage and Waste Disposal building. He followed silently through corridors lined with anonymous doors. Behind each one, he assumed, was a diligent Gok organizing whatever there was to organize about sewage and rubbish.

At the end of the passage was a slightly larger entrance.

"Wait here," the attendant said shortly.

With a tight swish of fabric, she turned and left him.

As her footfalls receded, Duvät studied the wood grain on the paneled door. Should he wait for it to open, or try to push it himself? If it had a special song, he would seem an impatient fool, but if he waited too long, how would that make him look? He damned the nervous perspiration that formed on his face – as if he were an amateur in a gambling den. He looked down the corridor at the departing attendant. There was an annoying swagger to her walk. At least she could have announced his presence.

Without fanfare, Brätan Gok's office entrance swung ajar.

Duvät's heart raced. The space was modest but for the huge silver and white banner of Tiamät draping the full length of the wall behind the Clan Chief's desk.

He swept a respectful bow. "Greetings, Lord Brätan Gok."

Brätan's attention remained on the papers before him.

The silence stretched on.

The Clan Chief's hostility was palpable.

Duvät kept his thoughts to himself.

At last Brätan scrawled his signature on the bottom of the page and looked up. "Out with it," he said tiredly.

"I-I-I …" Duvät stammered back to silence. How to start? After a heavy pause he whispered to Qalān and withdrew a bag of eyes. Brätan watched as he undid the drawstring and pale rainbow light scattered about the room. His astounded frown was intensely gratifying. Duvät almost laughed. If Brätan was so taken with the 'dead' eyes, how would he have reacted to the unspeakable brilliance of the live ones?

For a time, the Clan Chief seemed lost in wonder.

"Gems I discovered on Went," Duvät informed him. "I, myself, recovered them at great personal danger."

Brätan winced. "You? Danger?" His gaze became clear and direct. "And what do you intend to do with them? How many do you have?"

Duvät stepped closer to the desk. "I have several small bags such as this." He raised his brows. "I thought I could, that is, I brought them here because I thought the Clan would benefit from their sale."

Brätan snorted. "Things are bad then, Duvät."

"No, not really." It took effort to keep his psychic emissions steady and his veil firm and unrippled. As Brätan reached for a jewel, he had to stop himself from snatching it back.

The Clan Chief held the orb to the light and searched it deeply. Soft colors bathed his face, shining in his eyes. It was a moment of beauty, yet Duvät's wariness increased as he sensed indecision.

The gem clacked softly against its brethren as it was returned.

"The planet Went has been claimed for the Imperium," Brätan said. "By rights, these belong to the God-Emperor."

Duvät Gok's heart plummeted. He looked up at the huge silver rune of Tiamät. Of course Brätan would see it that way. He was directly answerable.

Stupid, stupid, stupid! he berated himself. "But I found them before it was claimed. Surely that means they are mine?"

"Is there a record of this? A report perhaps?"

"Well … no."

Brätan shook his head. "I might have known! There's something underhand, something you're not telling me. You come looking to reclaim your honor, but honor can't be bought, and especially not with gems stolen from the Imperium!"

Duvät raised his shoulders. "You could take them to the God-Emperor, say I kept them apart because I wanted such rarities to go directly to him … couldn't you?"

"Put them away."

Hesitantly, Duvät tied the drawstring. If the Imperium knew these as the ultimate gem, how could he make the most from the live ones? And once they knew he had hidden his discovery, he'd be branded a thief forever in his people's minds. All he wanted was a little respect. Why was it so hard to find? He pushed the bag toward Brätan Gok.

Brätan raised his hands. "I don't want them!" He took a long look at Duvät and grimaced. "What am I to do with you now – with the situation I have before me?"

"You could say they came from a secret source?"

Brätan's sneer was pitying. He continued as if he hadn't heard, counting off options on his fingers. "If I do nothing, and the Imperium finds out that you came to me? That would be bad. Bad for me, bad for the Clan."

"You could say I made a mistake," Duvät pleaded. "Say I found them before the planet was claimed and kept them secret so the God-Emperor himself could see them first!"

"Please stop," Brätan barked. "You expect me to implicate myself in your wrongdoing? There are no lies the God-Emperor cannot see through!" He raised another finger. "If I present the eyes and tell him exactly what has happened …"

"You can't do that!"

Brätan rocked his hand. "… things could go either way. But if I present you and the eyes together? There will be no blame or loss of honor for Gok, or for me – no hint of collusion. You, on the other hand, must take your chances."

"Me? Take me to the God-Emperor?" Duvät Gok felt his gut churn.

"Yes, you. You might need a change of underwear." Brätan stood up from his desk and started for the door. "Come on."

"Now?" Duvät barely registered the squeak of terror in his voice. "The God-Emperor can kill with a single glance!

"Yes he can." Brätan gave him a measuring look. "I've seen him do it."

"Don't you need an appointment?"

"Certainly one does! But in the meantime let's find somewhere to keep you. Somewhere secure. Think of it as a holiday rather than house arrest, if that makes you feel better."

LUCAÄT

Lucaät waved his secretary aside as the Agent made contact.

I can see him now, he said. *He's coming out of the building … oh.*

Oh?

He's surrounded by ashessé.

Lucaät sighed. Why was nothing ever simple where Duvät Gok was concerned? Brätan was no fool. They had not been quick enough, and unless he moved decisively now, the game would overtake him. His agent shared an image of Duvät marching between his black-clad escort. People darted out of their way as if mere proximity was dangerous.

Follow them, Lucaät said. *Keep clear of Daric Enna, but don't let him kill Duvät before we can get hold of him. We have to know what that Breathless wretch is hiding!*

Four ashessé, the Agent pointed out. *Only one of me.*

Take your chance when it comes. I have every faith.

The Agent moved forward, trying to keep within eyeshot of their quarry. A kaleidoscope of images flowed second-hand through Lucaät's vision. It was frustrating to have to be so careful, but too dangerous for his operative to follow the ashessé with the mind's eye. The God-Emperor's forces were trained to detect such scrutiny. Their response would be quick and, at best, debilitating. Yet, as they shadowed the troop and remained unobserved, Lucaät sensed the Agent's enjoyment.

The ashessé paused. The Agent crept closer.

If they get in my way? he asked.

Lucaät knew him to be adept at the quick kill, but this time? *Better to stun.*

The Agent grunted. *Easier said than done.*

Send even one to the Breath, it's like kicking a thuja nest. They'll swarm all over the city. Bad for business!

Bad for business, the Agent echoed dryly.

Don't forget who pays you, Lucaät warned.

The ashessé stopped outside a non-descript two-story villa and Duvät Gok was shoved through the door. Two guards remained at the front and the other two moved off toward the back.

Lucaät studied the dwelling through the Agent's eyes. It had few windows and those seemed small. *How will you get in?*

Leave me alone and I'll work something out, the Agent snapped.

Touchy!

My life here, not yours.

You're the best, Lucaät assured him. *Keep me informed … Daric?*

Still no sign, the Agent said, *but he'll be here somewhere, you can bet on it.*

Betting's for fools, Lucaät sniggered.

Fools like Duvät Gok, the Agent retorted. He watched the ashessé for a moment. *Looks like they're settling in for the duration. I'd best try and get comfy.*

Lucaät withdrew and summoned his secretary again. There was still just time enough to prepare for a meeting that afternoon with the commissioner of mines in the Imperial court.

MEETING AT COURT

Five times as tall as an angel and carved from a single massive calipas shell, the gates of the Imperial Palace Compound were certainly a sight to behold, but Lucaät had passed through them many a time and barely gave them a second look. The guards nodded respectfully as he passed. He glanced longingly at the portal by the gates, but it was strictly off limits to all but the most trusted of courtiers. Instead, he was obliged to choose the long, covered footpath that wound through the gardens toward the Imperial Offices.

Among the greenery, gardeners in large straw hats shaped hedges with staccato bursts of energy, and sang flowers to abundant life. Insects chimed in the lazy afternoon heat. Lucaät's step crunch-crunched on the gravel while he fanned his face and wished for winter.

Once inside, he shed his walking shoes for ornate court slippers and the sound of silken soles and softly chinking jewels was far more satisfying than the brutal tramp outdoors.

As he strode through the winding galleries of the palace, gilded wall-patterns flowed as if they were moving, not him. Anshät of Faytha minced past and gave him a decorous nod. As he returned her gesture, he noted the spectacular belt flashing at her waist – surely the work of Mina of Nhadu – and made a mental note to order one for himself. A sensual perfume wafted in her wake and he made another mental note: find out what Anshät was up to.

By one of the many fountains, a colorful knot of courtiers loitered with their heads bent close. Perhaps they thought the tinkling water would disguise their words, but it took little effort for Lucaät to listen in.

"Every other God-Emperor has had at least three children," one muttered. She looked nervously over her shoulder. "Yet ours, only one?"

"Not since the Empress Manük Enna ..."

"And she died horribly, or so it's said!"

"That's just myth ... isn't it?"

"Well, I heard ..."

The murmurs faded. Lucaät's lips compressed. The God-Empress Manük Enna ... who was she? He wracked his brain for clues. Then it came to him, a long-ago lecture from a boring old Enna – a cautionary tale for the young – the only one of El's Chosen ever to be deposed.

Whether it had really happened was doubtful, but sedition must be rife for a group of non-entities to risk airing such tales within the palace itself. Even with the distraction of half-breed riots and the inevitable disruption that caused, or perhaps because of it, it was clear unrest with the God-Emperor was growing.

Sword-makers will be busier than ever, he thought, *and my nacrite worth more than the Breath itself.*

Buoyed by such musings, it seemed to take less time than usual to come to the Offices of Mining Options and Commissions; flanked by garish panels shimmering with polished crystals, his destination was hard to miss. Very slightly, his lip curled. The Tiamäti had wealth, mostly thanks to House Faytha, but style? He shook his head.

"Lord Lucaät," the receptionist started, but he continued past him, confident the door would open. Sure enough it swung wide just before he reached it. He marched in and made the smallest bow he politely could.

"Dendar Gok," he said solemnly. "I trust you are still enjoying nature's bounty?"

The folds around Dendar's eyes puckered in a nervous squint. "Sshh! Not here!" she rasped.

A smirk danced beneath Lucaät's lips. Ever since he'd supplied the Chief Commissioner with a pair of bissara, rare snake-like creatures that could be latched onto certain organs for an exotic sexual thrill – highly frowned upon, of course – Dendar had been very eager to please.

"My apologies," Lucaät said.

"But one can never be too careful," she said quietly. "Especially here! Slaves – are everywhere. I am certain that everything they hear is pass on to … certain others. They tell me I'm paranoid, but who would dare take the risk?"

Lucaät took a seat and shrugged. "Oh, I don't know. I find mine rather useful."

At the same time as Dendar Gok's veil shivered with disgust, her haze shrank with fear and Lucaät smiled. This one would refuse him nothing.

"Commissions and options with regard to the new Imperial Planet Went," Lucaät said briskly. "I'm sure you can do better than the usual rates. After all, it's quite well known that my operations run more smoothly than any of my competitors'." He nodded. "The most for the least, that's my motto."

Dendar laughed, a short, derisive bark. "The least what?"

"The least cost, the least effort on the Imperium's part …" Lucaät slowed as the commissioner imaged a particular mining camp.

"The Padmil operation?" he blustered. "A triumph of profitability."

The Commissioner's palms lifted wide. "Too many shortcuts. Angered the Lethians no end. Irreparable environmental damage, they said." She waved her hands theatrically. "Ecosystems disrupted! Arien Leth himself paid us a personal visit and you could hear him shouting right through these chambers."

"I heard nothing," Lucaät said innocently.

Dendar rolled her eyes. "I was told to give you a warning."

"Told?" Lucaät sat straighter. "I thought you were in charge."

"Told," Dendar assured him. "A most unpleasant experience which I have no wish to repeat." She leaned closer and used her index finger as punctuation. "Pay more attention to detail. Follow the protocols. Make sure paperwork and reports are completely up to date for each and every part of every process."

Lucaät groaned. "Time wasted! Increased costs!"

"And that's not all," Dendar continued. Lucaät was sure she was enjoying herself. "Henceforth you must include a full Explorers' Guild party – and if we are talking about a new planet, the original survey team if possible – to monitor, advise and report on each and every mining operation performed."

"What!"

Dendar's expression grew pained. "Rest assured it's not just you who's screaming. The same edict applies to everyone."

"I see." Lucaät breathed deeply. A team of Lethians monitoring his every move? Questioning his every innovation? He rubbed his forehead, already thinking of ways such a team could be kept occupied while he got on with the real business of increasing his personal wealth. And the original team from Planet Went was now without an Overlord … his head wavered from side to side … perhaps there was an opening there?

"A full team?" he said. "I'll definitely need my terms adjusted."

"I'll take that into consideration," the Commissioner replied.

"But you will grant me full mining rights over Planet Went's assets?"

Dendar nodded slowly. "On the proviso that you agree to follow the Lethian Edict … as they're calling it."

"That depends on my margins."

"No Leth, no rights." Dendar folded her arms.

"Come now, Chief Commissioner, we are all friends here!" Lucaät said. "Are you serious? This edict will be enforced? Madness!"

"The God-Emperor demands it and I dare not – will not – be the one to anger him. His temper is very uncertain of late, especially since the latest bride-choice fiasco. Everyone is on edge. I want to retain my office … and my life."

"That bad?"

Dendar beckoned Lucaät closer. He could smell the faint scent of her body. "Every time Aqumät spurns his father's selections, the God-Emperor becomes unapproachable, sometimes for weeks, sometimes months. And that's not all. In quiet corners it's whispered …" she looked over her shoulder "… that Aqumät follows the Breath in this. The God-Emperor … how can El condone his actions? Levies and taxes. Slaves! Children ripped from their mother's arms … little wonder there is only one heir. The succession is vulnerable," she rasped. "El has not blessed!"

"Quiet corners indeed." Lucaät resisted the urge to scan for listeners. "I will try and forget that such scandalous gossip ever crossed your lips."

The Chief Commissioner drew back and was still.

Lucaät smiled inside. Oh yes! Dendar was sorry she'd spoken.

"And my commission?"

"Certainly. I'll do what I can," Dendar said.

"Of course you will." Lucaät eyebrows flickered. "One would hate to become the subject of idle chatter, eh? Especially one so close to nature as yourself."

"My reputation would be destroyed!"

Lucaät looked her in the eye. "That's why I'm so successful."

Blue fingernails flashed as Dendar wiped imaginary dust from her desk. "As I've said, I will do my best."

"And I thank you for your assurances." Lucaät gestured expansively. "But the action is many years off yet. Plenty of time to get organized."

Dendar beckoned him close again. "Don't be surprised if the Imperium moves more quickly on this," she said quietly.

"Oh? How quickly?"

"Whispers of rare substances. I will keep you informed, of course."

Lucaät's gaze tracked Dendar Gok as she stood to end their meeting, but he didn't follow suit.

"There is something else you can do for me," he said.

Dendar glanced toward the door. "Yes?"

"I hear Brätan Gok has made an appointment." He tipped his head toward the Palace proper. "I need to know when."

"You spy on my Clan Chief?"

"It's my nature."

Dendar's haze showed fear and intense irritation in almost equal portions, but nonetheless she closed her eyes. When she returned, she seemed puzzled.

"Farun Gok, the Imperial secretary, informs me that Clan Chief Brätan Gok has an appointment with the God-Emperor Tsemkarun Ishät Ashik for ten in the morning, two days from now. This was arranged only moments ago. How did you know?

"The voice of the Breath." Lucaät raised his hand to his heart. "A person of your standing should stay more in touch!"

"Voice of the Breath?" She grunted derisively. "If we are done now?"

"Yes, of course." Lucaät stood up. He answered her bow with one that was little more than an inclination of his head. "Our meeting has been most profitable."

"Brätan is a fool to speak with God-Emperor directly," the Commissioner murmured as she walked him to the door. "Just last week Ishät got so angry with Ashemar Rukh … I saw his tentacles."

Lucaät paused as a chill of foreboding washed over him. "Tiamät showed itself?"

Dendar's glance was fearful. "We all saw it. I wouldn't go near him at the moment. It's this business about brides – and heirs. They're shipping in new and novel aphrodisiacs by the box-load, anything they think might … but El Blesses as El will," she rasped. "The quality of the Imperial sex-life – I can't see how that can help, do you?"

"No, indeed." Lucaät made a mental note to go through his inventory of sexual enhancements and make sure they were made known to the Imperial suppliers, then retreated quickly through the maze of the complex, anxious to escape. Once he'd reached the safety of his own home, he would contact his agent in the field with news of Duvät Gok's appointment with power – still two days off, so there was time to plan.

ABDUCTION

Except for the ashessé's occasional change of posture, nothing moved on the empty street. There were few trees to attract wildlife, no gardens. Each house was much the same – flat topped, two story, butted up against its neighbor on one side and with a narrow alley on the other. Some roof-spaces were shared and sported colorful awnings, but the house Lucaät's agent watched had no such enrichment. The front door opened directly onto the cobbles, and two black-clad ashessé stood like ebony pillars guarding either side.

The Agent pursed his lips as he digested Lucaät's new information. Duvät's audience with the God-Emperor would be in two days' time. The directive was to watch and wait, but it was not Lucaät of Faytha out there doing all the hard work. The weather was hot and humid. His covering song required constant maintenance lest the ashessé see him loitering and become suspicious. There was no tavern or café within eyeshot, and with every house on the street privately owned and occupied, where was he supposed to sleep? There in the alley across the road? There'd been no mention of sending another to take over 'watch and wait' duties while he took a much-needed break. If he'd been working for Mirashael things would be different, but Lucaät paid more.

He studied the house again, designed by the Gok, no doubt in compliance with edict number whatever and amendment number blah blah from Fifth Sector Urban Drainage and Waste Disposal. The alley between the villas was just wide enough for two people abreast. There were three small windows on that side of the safe house. Carefully, he bent his mind to view the back of the building. The second pair of ashessé stood by a featureless back door that opened onto a narrow paved yard. Nowhere to hide; little room to maneuver.

Perhaps the best way to get in might be by breaking into the adjoining villa, the home of a respectable angel family. From the top floor, the outermost windows were very close. The jump would be risky but achievable with care.

He gave a crafty smile and hunkered down to wait. The guards would be alert for Duvät's attempt to escape – not a daring break-in through a top-floor window.

At last, when the first almost imperceptible light of the new day began to silhouette the villas against the eastern sky, the Agent limbered up, ready for action. Slowly he made his way across the street toward the outer wall of the next-door villa. After so long in stillness, it felt good to move.

A kitchen window opened into the alley. It was sealed, as one would expect, but the charm was a cheap one any half-note thief could nullify. The overall house screens were also low cost and easily negotiated, and he could sense no alarm.

The sill felt gritty against his palms. He hoisted himself lightly through the opening and landed silently between the utensils on the bench. The smell of herbs and baking bread made the corners of his mouth twitch with an involuntary smile. From the aroma, the loaf would need tending soon.

The stairs creaked faintly as he crept upward. Every sense throbbed with life. He was a shadow, no more. He could kill these people while they slept. He sniggered at a toy bird left abandoned in the upstairs corridor. This young Gokish family may never wake up, and never know why.

A boy of forty summers occupied the back room, no doubt the owner of the errant bird. A mobile, also featuring birds, dangled above the child's bed. The Agent paused to study his sleeping face, so innocent. He sensed another child in a cot beside his parents' bed. To be blessed in succession so quickly … this must be a happy family indeed. An unexpected pang welled from his subconscious and was quickly stifled.

He touched the window's surface and breathed the nullifying sequence. As it dissipated, a slight breeze tinkled the mobile. The Agent froze, a stun-charm ready on his lips – but the child never stirred.

The next trick was to negate the window next door without alerting the guards below. From a pocket in his shirt, he retrieved a slim wooden box. Inside was a small sliver of pure iron, his secret window-opening weapon. When he held the exposed metal in his hand it would nullify the screens he'd set to hide his presence, but when it passed through a window-charm, that barrier would dissolve also.

With his back to the wall, the Agent set his mind free to manipulate the impressive stack of protections on Duvät Gok's prison. After a careful time spent unraveling screens and alarms, he opened his eyes to the pure but puzzled blue of the little boy's gaze.

He held his finger up to his lips and whispered, *Sshh…* His mind held a charm poised.

Are you really here? the boy asked sleepily.

Not for long. Go back to sleep.

The Agent smiled. Behind his back, he already clenched the hilt of his knife.

Surprisingly, the young one did as he was told, but as the small eyelids closed the Agent released the stun-song anyway, just to be sure.

Back at the window he took aim and threw the iron sliver, then, after a moment to refurbish his personal screens, threw himself across the gap. There was a light thud as his boots impacted, then a soft scrape as drew himself over the brink.

After a quick scan, he flitted down the stairs toward Duvät, asleep on a couch on the lower floor.

He gave the reprobate a psychic nudge. His eyes blinked open.

Who are you? he said. *What do you want? I feel sick.*

The Agent tilted his head and sent an image.

Lucaät? Duvät said warily. *What does he want?* With fumbling hands he emptied a sachet of powder into a glass of water on a nearby table.

I hear you have an audience with the God-Emperor. The Agent smiled.

Duvät drank thirstily then slumped back on his makeshift bed. *My life is over; I know it!*

Not yet, the Agent said. *I'm here to help you avoid that unfortunate circumstance. I just need you to do one thing.*

What thing?

Help me get past the ashessé at the door.

Duvät sat up. His eyes narrowed. *How? What do you want me to do?*

The Agent handed him a small globular fungus. Duvät shook it.

"Careful with that!" the Agent whispered. "Seshura. Puff it into the guard's face and you'll knock him out, but I only have two – one each."

"Seshura?" Duvät muttered. He shook the ball of fungus again, but more carefully this time. "It's rare, and very costly." He squinted into the Agent's face. "How do I know you're telling the truth?"

"Take a guess, Gok," the Agent snapped. "Why would I lie?" *Our Lucaät has wide resources*, the Agent assured him. "There's a portal up the road, two hundred paces, no more. Get dressed. Something unremarkable. I'll have to hide us both," he said evenly. "Keep that in mind."

As Duvät Gok emerged from beneath his covers, the Agent was surprised by his physique. True, his outline was softened by a layer of blubber, but life as an explorer had made demands even on this puffed-up waste of space.

At least he can probably run. "Ready?" he said aloud.

"Not quite."

The Agent shuffled impatiently. "You waiting for fresh guards to arrive?"

"I'll look like a common angel!" he complained.

The Agent ignored him. A subtle probe revealed the two guards slumped on either side of the wall.

"Two at the front and two at the back," he said, "drowsy and at the end of their resources. Once the two at the front are down, we'll have to run before the others process the incident. Hold the seshura like this," he whispered. "Be ready to puff it into the guard's face when I open the door – and be quick or he'll sing a counter-charm."

"I'm sure I can manage," Duvät said stiffly.

"Let's hope so," he muttered. He tipped his head to indicate the guard on the left.

Duvät nodded to the right and adjusted the seshura in his palm.

The Agent held up his hand and signaled, one … two … with the third count he pushed the door open and swung to the left as planned. His mark blinked in surprise and went down as planned but there was a scuffle as Duvät missed his moment with the other and struggled to raise his arm to his opponent's face.

The Agent looked over his shoulder. It was only a matter of time before the ashessé at the back of the house were alerted. He grabbed at Duvät's loaded hand. "Give it to me!" he hissed, but the Gok wrenched away and almost puffed himself.

Then there was a flash of metal and the guard collapsed. Duvät Gok stood above his body, breathing heavily. Blood dripped from the knife in his hand.

"I've killed him," he said blankly.

There was a shout from the back of the house and footsteps hammered toward them. It was too late to run. The Agent slipped into the house next door, dragging Duvät in his wake.

Put that knife away! the Agent snapped.

What about the screens? Duvät asked. *How did you know the song?*

Shut up and let me think! Why did you kill him?!

With eyes half closed, Duvät Gok opened his mind, inviting the Agent to share as if they were peers, and the Agent recoiled from the red morass of Duvät's bloodlust. The smell of baking bread wrapped his nose in incongruous pleasure. He thought of the little one sleeping upstairs. The noise outside would wake someone soon. They had to be gone before that happened.

Thankfully, Duvät had his mind veiled once more, but the Agent strained to reconcile the inner Gok with the outer. He thought back to the interview with Lucaät. It seemed the Gok was far better at hiding himself than they had anticipated. At the same time, a plan began to form. If the ashessé assumed Duvät had enacted his escape alone – and there was nothing to indicate otherwise – maybe they wouldn't look too closely at a couple. If he and Duvät touched, their psychic signature would blur just a little, maybe enough. But as he reached out to take Duvät Gok's hand, the thought of such intimacy made him waver. Would he see the monster again?

In an act of will he completed the gesture. *Even Lucaät of Faytha couldn't pay me enough for this*, he thought to himself, then he pushed his mind forward. *This is what we're going to do …*

The Gok relaxed. *Lovers? How titillating!*

Don't get your hopes up, the Agent snapped. Together they slipped out the kitchen window and sidled down the alley toward the back.

The ether hummed with messages. At last Duvät he seemed to recognize the danger. When his mind began to probe, the Agent warned, *Use mundane senses only. Ashessé may sense you.*

With screens as tight as he dared, he boosted his captive over the wall. They darted across one backyard to the next, then it was a short scramble over the wall and into the adjacent laneway.

Duvät grinned a little when the Agent pulled him close and prepared to enact their disguise. Their hazes crackled, then smoothed. To complete the picture, he touched Duvät's pleasure with the eighth rule and the fool almost turned to water.

You can do that again, Duvät gasped. His eyes laughed, but behind them was a discomfiting darkness.

The Agent hugged Duvät's shoulders in a shameful display of affection, *Just wait till I get you home!* and they lurched out onto the street, close as lovers. In his mind's eye the Agent saw the ashessé glance their way then quickly return to their own problems, but while his attention was thus occupied, something bumped his shoulder and the shimmer of a well-wrought screen crossed his path.

Never would have picked it!

The sardonic voice spoke directly into his mind, and even as the Agent's heart fell, he almost laughed aloud. Daric Enna! How long had he been watching?

Who's there? Duvät asked nervously.

No one, the agent replied. If Daric had wished them harm, they'd have known it by now. He nodded ahead. *The portal's not far now.*

Duvät squeezed him lightly. *I'm disappointed.*

The Agent tried to project a promise of lust returned – anything to give their disguise veracity, but all the while he could feel Duvät Gok's inner monster living and re-living the moment of the ashessé's death. The crunching slide of the knife as it entered the ashessé's chest, the jolt of pain that leaped through the contact, relished as if it were a rare perfume. The evil was not so close to the surface as it had been, but he'd seen its raw hunger. How could they have so thoroughly underestimated this one, the pathetic gambler, always whining, always losing?

Another probe skipped over them, paused for one chilling moment then moved on. He turned to smile, as if they really were lovers.

Duvät seemed to stumble and the Agent held him tighter to stop his fall, but then a clammy hand grasped at his penis and he understood the ruse.

Are you completely mad? He slapped the hand with mock playfulness and dodged aside.

Such a pretty dance, Duvät whispered.

The Agent's skin longed to crawl. He could feel Duvät's eyes, anticipating – glanced across to see his slack mouth leering. Although he was not averse to male sexual partners, to touch Duvät Gok was akin to bathing in a sewer.

As they reached their goal, he risked another backward glance. Brätan's safe-house was a hive of activity but no one looked their way. A hundred paces to the right was a nicely paved city portal with a tiled dome above it. For a moment, he was tempted to go that bit further and lose the two of them in the Imperial maze, but then he glimpsed the shadowy blur of well-screened guards and another probe raised the hairs on his neck.

Duvät looked at the shabby space before them. *Ah, Qalān*, he said. *All those little holes, thrusting through barriers, getting us where we want to go …*

The Agent tried not to shudder. He closed his eyes and listened for the portal's song then stepped them through to the outskirts of a tiny alpine hamlet. Muted mid-morning sun seeped through dank mist. Droplets quickly settled on their hair and clothing. On steep mountainsides, herds of wooly kreth yodeled quietly to each other and the few shops in the settlement seemed sleepy despite their brightly striped awnings.

The Agent tore his mind from Duvät's and pushed him away. For a fleeting second, his prisoner seemed disappointed, then the flinty gaze returned. "Where are we?" he said.

"Ganos," the Agent replied. "Southern continent."

"Well," said Duvät Gok. He peered down the single cobbled street. "I see another portal at the far end there, so I'll be on my way. Give my thanks to Lucaät."

"Wait," the Agent said.

Duvät slowed.

"You killed an Imperial ashessé!" the Agent called quietly. "They'll find our ruse and be here any minute." He walked closer and softened his haze. "There's a place I can take us to. Somewhere no one will find us."

"Privacy?" The corners of Duvät's lips quirked. "Why didn't you say so?"

As Duvät opened his mind to say something more intimate, the Agent took the final step into his personal space and sent a vicious burst of power arrowing through his defenses. The seductive gaze lingered on a face too stunned to react. With a derisive grunt he started for the portal at the other end of town and Duvät followed, step for step, barely capable of resistance.

The next portal delivered them to Traps, a small mining town in the North. From there, with a small twist of song he took them to the bustling hub of Clouds, the city at the foot of the Palace of Gates, the palace of the scryers.

"What have you done?" Duvät mumbled. "The Ziquarudjan will see through any hidey-hole you have here!"

The Agent winced as he realized Duvät still half-believed this was some sort of love play.

"I don't think they will," he said, or at least they hadn't so far. Lucaät had kept a safe-house there for eons: sometimes it was best to hide in full view. He led Duvät through winding cobbled streets to an unpretentious shanty with a brown stone door.

Is this it? Duvät shivered with excitement.

The Agent almost laughed aloud. Of all the ways to trap someone, this must be the least dignified.

As the stone slid open, a cold draft brushed by. Duvät made a sudden attempt to escape but the Agent was well prepared. The door closed silently. The noise of the outer world shut off and there was a prickle as the house screens intensified. A single globe gradually illuminated Lucaät of Faytha's predatory smile.

"Glad you two sweethearts could make it," he said mockingly. Another loomed behind him in the shadows.

The Agent let his mind slip free, interested to see how the Gok would respond.

"What's happening?" Duvät rubbed his head. "Lucaät of Faytha?"

He lunged for the door but the Agent stepped in his way.

Duvät whimpered.

"They brought you here for me," the stranger said. He had a soft, nasal voice. "In fact, I'm rather looking forward to getting to know you better."

Duvät slowly turned. Lucaät's smile broadened. "Meet my inquisitor," he said. "I'm sure you'll get along."

The whites of the inquisitor's eyes glinted in the low light.

Duvät backed away. "You can't do this," he moaned. "I won't let you!" but the inquisitor grasped his arm with preternatural speed. The spider-like grip barely tightened, but Duvät's eyes almost popped out of his head. His next moan was a strange hybrid, somewhere between a squeak and a sob.

The Agent tried not to smile.

"I thought you had a soft spot for him," Lucaät chuckled, "but it seems you're enjoying this."

"You have no idea," the Agent replied.

"We will take our time, Duvät Gok, my friend," the inquisitor said lovingly, "just as you hoped ..."

Duvät shrieked. His free hand flew down and clutched his genitals.

"As long as you need," said Lucaät. "We'll be in the back, taking refreshments. It seems my ever resourceful Agent has had a harder time of things than expected." He turned from the spectacle of Duvät and opened his arm toward a shadowy door. "This must be worth an extra bonus!"

ANDEL AND HULDAR

It was a typical summer evening in the Imperial City. While the setting sun blazed its last, cool air descended from the western mountains and whispered through the maze of streets and districts like a lover's sweetest promise. In the Jewel of the Imperium, muted windows admitted sensory sketches of the streets below.

From the relative privacy of their room, Huldar let his senses range until he found a place where insects and birds chirped by a fountain nestled in an overgrown garden. The sounds were almost Wentish, if he let his imagination work at it.

Andel stroked his face thoughtfully. He caught her hand and kissed it.

Is everything all right? she asked.

He sighed and relaxed his veil to share the sounds he listened to.

I know there's something, she said softly. *Ever since your meeting with Shamkarun Pieru.*

The tinkle of birdsong was relinquished. Huldar hung his head, unsure how to broach the subject of Pieru's offer. He had seen the damage wrought by secrets, they both had, and she had every right to know, but while they were sharing her parents' suite … He felt awkward.

Can we make time to be alone? he asked her.

Is it serious?

He nodded, then sensing anxiety he hurried to add, *Nothing to worry about!*

Her honey-brown eyes found his, then lowered. She fingered the lace on the end of her sleeves. *You and Mother – I know it's difficult.*

Gently, he turned her chin toward him. *I would walk on higa shells for you. I opened Qalān itself to find you! I'm not going to give up because your mother hates explorers.*

She doesn't hate you, Andel said earnestly. *Not really.*

A number of difficult moments flashed through his mind, accompanied by vivid recollections of Ninjay's many grades of frosty stare.

I'm sorry, Andel said.

Not your fault. A slow smile spread over his face. *How about dinner tonight, just the two of us?*

Andel hesitated. *She's bound to have something organized – I heard her mention the Palace of Winds …* but her haze began to brighten.

I'll tell her, Huldar said. A soft laugh blew through his nose. *It can't get worse …*

His mind reached beyond the door and quickly scanned the sitting room. If Ninjay of Trianog lurked in wait it was best to be prepared – but instead he found Andel's father, Inshogi, sitting alone by the window, perhaps enjoying the breeze as he had been a few moments earlier.

They opened the door.

"Ah! There you are!" Inshogi said. "My lovely Ninjay is just getting ready. We thought we'd treat you to a meal at a place that was recommended by the concierge, somewhere over on the Western Continent, I think, in the city below the Palace of Winds. It's by the beach. Morning over there – fresh breezes, islands, seafood, very nice!"

Andel gave Huldar's hand a small squeeze. *Told you so!*

Inshogi sensed the exchange and looked at them expectantly.

"I'm sorry, sir, it's just that I wish you had told us earlier," Huldar explained. "We've already made plans."

"Oh?" Andel's father's eyes narrowed kindly. "Well, I can see you two want some time to yourselves, eh?" He tipped his head toward the door. "Best if you go now, then! Go on!" he said to Andel. "I'll deal with your mother."

Huldar gave Inshogi a heartfelt bow, and Andel ran to give her father a quick kiss.

Inshogi blinked. "Is it that bad?"

Andel nodded ruefully and turned for the exit. Huldar hastened in her wake.

Out on the street, the last rays of sunset beat against the tops of turrets and spires leaving doorways cool and dark with shadow. Andel took his arm and shared her enjoyment. Trust flowed through their contact like a tacit accusation, and he was glad he'd decided to share his dilemma – as soon as they were settled to dine and the time was right.

Father likes you, she smiled.

Perhaps it was our trip to the Guild library. Huldar envisioned Inshogi's wondrous expression as they entered the great hall full of books and scrolls devoted entirely to the exploration of planets most people never knew existed.

He hasn't stopped talking about it, she said. *It's probably why Mother is so cranky.*

Cranky? he replied innocently. *How can you tell?*

Beast! she said, and gave him a playful shove. As she took his hand, their connection ebbed and flowed with comfortable ease until a passing Tsemkarun looked them up and down. Her censure was cut short when she noticed their extensive Marks.

"My lord, my lady …" She gave a light bow. Huldar shared Andel's giggle, but they yielded to decorum and walked without touching.

I wish we were still on Went, she said. *I miss the freedom.*

Their subvocal exchanged garnered another look.

"Everybody does it!" Andel complained. "Why do these people make faces?"

"'Everybody' does it less noticeably," Huldar replied. He gave her a cheeky grin. "Too long in the wilds, and this is the result."

Up ahead, a canopy of silver-pink blooms arched over the pavement.

"Rayno?" She beamed up at him. "I didn't know it grew anywhere but Frith!"

"This is the only other place … right here in this restaurant."

Beneath the bower, porcelain petals tinkled musically. Dusky fragrance bathed their faces while a series of angled window charms protected them from the constant misting the delicate plants required. Above them, fine droplets vanished into a shielding charm, and as he breathed in the soft perfume, shared happiness coursed through his heart.

"Shall we sit here?" he said. "I thought the Trianogi menu might be welcome."

"That's right," she grinned, "you've never been to Frith, have you?"

Huldar smiled ruefully. "All that exploration, you'd think I'd have been to Trianog Frith."

He sat back to survey the parklands surrounding the Imperial Palace, a citadel of stone fading in the last light of day. With a little sharpening of vision, Huldar would have been able to see the delicate outer carvings the Palace proper was famous for, if it hadn't been for the shimmering net of screens and protections that surrounded it.

Andel's attention came back to him. He resisted the urge to clear his throat. Had he acquired the habit from Duvät Gok? It annoyed him to think so.

"Shamkarun Pieru," he blurted at last. "The Guild, that is … I've been offered a job, a position at Guild headquarters."

"A job? Permanent, here on Giahn?"

He nodded. "Pieru feels my experience on Went makes me – holy to Leth." He grimaced, struggling with the notion of his own sanctity. "He wants me to take a position, an advisory position. Imperial Advisor."

Andel blinked as if she too wrestled with the concept. "Imperial advisor?" she said at last.

He reached for her hand, but she moved it away.

"Give me a minute to process this," she said.

He contemplated the manicured fields of the Imperial domain, not sure what to say, wishing he'd been able to tell her sooner. Now the words were spoken, he could feel the power they held. The voice of the planet came back to him, *The sacrifice begins* … For a moment he relived the pain, the terrible fear he might have overextended himself – that he might fail and Andel would be lost to him forever. The immensity of the song he'd wielded over Qalān … the joyous terror he'd felt as it gusted through him and the door was held open. The exhilaration when he'd found Andel and drawn her back to safety. From that moment on, whatever path they chose, their future had been shaped by Went. This choice about the position, although it seemed momentous, was merely an extension of that single, overarching instant when everything had changed and he'd defeated Qalān.

When at last Andel spoke, he only half heard.

"Huldar?" she repeated. "What does it mean?"

He blinked his reverie away. "What does what mean?"

"Imperial advisor – isn't that Shamkarun Pieru's job?"

"I would be his understudy – adding my voice. And he wants me to try and teach others to manipulate Qalān." He paused to gather his thoughts. "Who knows where that might lead, or if it's possible to teach it at all? I'm not sure … and not sure that I want to try. The planet herself showed me the key, but that's the thing, isn't it? If communing with a planet is a sacred experience, do I have the right to share what she said? To impart her knowledge without her permission?"

"You shared with me," Andel said.

"Yes, but that was part of it. *Only as one*, she said – that meant we had to join forces."

"Can you remember the song?"

"Of course. But it feels too big … as if that's what's sacred, not me."

She pulled a few pebbles from Qalān and toyed with them in her palm. He recognized a striped one from Went.

"I'm sorry I waited so long," he said, "but the time never seemed right."

"Now where have I heard those words before?" She grinned and took his hand at last. *Whatever you choose, I will be right beside you.*

Suddenly, he felt very small. *Do I deserve such riches?*

Yes, you do, she whispered, and through their touch he felt it to be true.

Their food began to arrive, every bit as colorful and fragrant as promised.

"So," Andel said brightly. "When do we tell the others?"

Huldar's heart fell. The Uri'madu had scattered and under normal circumstances would not reconvene until the next rotation, which in this case would be in seven standard years when Went finally began its thaw. "Let's leave it for a while," he said. "I don't have to make up my mind immediately. Shamkarun Pieru said to take all the time I needed."

"What about Casco? Have you told him?"

"Not yet, although he guessed something was up. Remember the farewell party?"

Andel nodded. "Is that why he called you outside?"

"Partly." Huldar picked at a plate of varicolored vegetables. It had been hard enough to tell Andel the news – how could he begin to tell Casco their partnership might be over?

"Let's keep it between ourselves for the time being," he said. "We'll be leaving for Frith in a few days, and I'm still coming to terms with the idea. I need to think this through, Andel. It's an important choice. Maybe the most important one I'll have to make ... besides marrying you, of course."

"Marriage!" She laughed. "What would mother say? We aren't even dabaku yet."

People looked around. Huldar blushed.

Andel laughed softly again. Her haze glowed with joy. "I do love surprises," she said.

DUVÄT GOK MEETS INQUISITOR

The ashut players looked up as the door creaked open. Low light bled over the inquisitor's thin features.

"What is it?" Lucaät snapped. "We're trying to enjoy a game, here."

The Agent looked up from the boards. This would be his third victory in a row. Perhaps he should let his boss win the next one, just to be on the safe side.

"He's passed out again," the inquisitor said.

"You haven't killed him?"

"Not yet, my lord, no."

"Probably wishes you had," the Agent said cheerfully.

"What have you found?" Lucaät asked. "What's he been hiding from me?"

"Eyes." The inquisitor shrugged. "He found some creatures on that last planet – Went, they're calling it – and he took their eyes."

"What?" Lucaät's face twisted in disgust. "Distasteful, but there must be more."

"No, it's the eyes – The Eyes of Bel Nishani. Even if his recollection is exaggerated … my lord, they are of priceless magnificence."

"Really?"

The inquisitor nodded.

"Eyes?"

The inquisitor nodded again.

"Well where are they? Does he have them with him?"

"I had to rip his mind to bits just to get this far. His hold on secrets is remarkably strong even for a Gok. Now he's unconscious."

"Wake him up!"

"Do you want him to live?"

Lucaät pursed his lips as if unsure.

"Don't be too hasty," the Agent said reluctantly. "He might be the only one who knows how to get these things. If you remember the edict – you have to take the original explorers …?"

"Only if possible," Lucaät countered.

The Agent shrugged. "On a completely wild planet, local knowledge might make the difference."

Lucaät studied the ashut boards. "Maybe …"

The inquisitor held up one spidery finger. "There is more information there to take, my lord. Locations, gates …"

"The more he fights, the greater the pain," the Agent said.

Lucaät gave him a puzzled look. "You really don't like him, do you?"

The Agent flickered his eyebrows and returned his attention to the game boards. Lucaät's subtle invitation to share was ignored. Duvät Gok relished the agony of others in a way even he couldn't fathom. He didn't want to relive his experience.

His boss turned back to the inquisitor. "My opponent here thinks we ought to keep the wretch alive, and he's besting me at ashut, so perhaps I should listen." He seemed to consider for a moment, then said, "Give him time to rally then hit him again. Get as much as you can. If he dies … well … just do your best. Report to me immediately after the next session."

"Very well, Lord Lucaät."

"Are they really so beautiful?"

"I could show you what I have seen," the inquisitor offered.

Lucaät hesitated, wisely wary of the inquisitor's capabilities. The Agent waited to see whether Faythan greed would win over native caution, then smiled to himself as Lucaät put out his hand. He watched with interest as hints of expression moved across the Faythan's face, then the hand-grip was released.

"Astonishing," said Lucaät.

The Agent waited for more, but Lucaät merely closed his eyes and breathed deeply as if reexamining the information he'd received.

Without a word, the inquisitor bowed himself back into the gloom. The door closed, and still Lucaät remained silent. The Agent twiddled with some of the ashut pieces he'd won – an ivory ranger inlaid with silver and a fish of green cosa-wood so polished with age that much of the fine detail was now mere hints and traces.

When Lucaät finally opened his eyes, they were bright with excitement.

"I have a plan," he said. "I have no idea what that plan is as yet, but it's there. This is the find of a lifetime, my friend. The find of a lifetime."

The Agent looked at him askance. "'My friend' is it, now? These rocks must be something marvelous."

"Rocks? These are not rocks, not mere gems!"

"What are they, then?"

"The Eyes of Bel Nishani … and I will have them!"

"For the honor of Faytha?" the Agent quipped.

Lucaät's gaze sharpened. "You may snigger, but yes, this is something I must do for my House. Only Faytha can truly understand the value of such splendor. "

"The Planet Went belongs to the God-Emperor. The eyes will be Tiamät's."

"Some, maybe. But who shall obtain them in the first place?" He nodded with great satisfaction. "Now I've secured exclusive rights."

"Dangerous …"

"We shall see. I've word that operations on Went may begin far sooner than would normally be allowed." He returned to his consideration of the Ashut boards. "Let's continue our game, shall we? I think I've seen a way to win."

The Agent gave a soft laugh as Lucaät's Great Mother sailed across hevahni, the third tier. In a convoluted move that even he hadn't anticipated, the Palace was claimed. The game was lost. Maybe the boss was onto something after all.

"Again?" he suggested.

"Why not?" Lucaät replied. His expression seemed bemused, as if even he was surprised by his win.

The pieces rattled into position.

"You first," the Agent said.

Midway through their next game, Lucaät lifted his head.

The Agent waited, aware his boss was in communication with someone he considered important. A nobody would have been dismissed with barely a sign.

"You wouldn't believe it," Lucaät said at last. His attention snapped back to the here-and-now. "Ashessé at the manor!"

The Agent's eyebrows flickered upward. "Didn't take them long."

They looked to the door as the inquisitor entered.

"That didn't take long either," the Agent remarked.

"Lord Lucaät prefers him to live," the inquisitor said dourly. He bowed. "My lord, good news and bad. Duvät Gok …"

"Formerly Gok," Lucaät interrupted. "I've just had word Brätan Gok has severed him from the clan. Go on?"

The inquisitor took a breath, no doubt as shocked as the Agent to hear that Duvät's House affiliation had been revoked. Such measures were only taken under the most dire of circumstances.

"So, what do we call him now?" the inquisitor asked.

Lucaät shrugged.

The inquisitor continued. "Duvät … has divulged this sack from Qalān. I have it here." He held a soft leather satchel by its drawstring. "But Brätan Gok has already seen the contents. He refused to take them, pointing out that they were the property of the Imperium. Brätan made an appointment with the God-Emperor – the actual God-Emperor – for himself and Duvät to take the gems to him in person."

Lucaät held out his hand for the bag. With a murmur, he loosened the string. The contents seemed to glow with their own faint but glorious light. With finger and thumb, Lucaät pulled out a crystal and held it up for examination.

"What is that?" The Agent leaned forward, not quite sure of what he was seeing.

Rainbow emanations transformed Lucaät's pale visage. "The Eye of Bel Nishani," he answered.

The inquisitor shook his head. "He almost had me fooled," he said. "He is far stronger than we ever could have suspected. I feel he has practiced this one skill, the art of concealment, most diligently."

Lucaät squinted at the gem in his hand. "What is it then? It is certainly exceptional."

"Yes, these are the eyes he showed Brätan, but he has others – he thinks of them as the True Eyes, the ones taken 'live'. My lord, I think these are indeed eyes, taken by force from living creatures, not mined from the ground as we might have assumed. We must tread with great caution. There is grave misdoing here …"

"And now Ishät Ashik, our mighty God-Emperor, is involved," Lucaät murmured, "or at least his personal secretary is."

Lucaät and the inquisitor paused again as if transfixed, and even though he'd been told these gems were in some way inferior to the True Eyes, the Agent also had trouble wrenching his gaze away. His skin crawled with premonition. With such a prize at its heart, this tangle could not end well.

"Give Duvät back to the Gok," he said. "The God-Emperor will kill him and that will be that."

But his boss seemed not to have heard. Blue nail varnish glinted softly as he stroked his chin with one hand. "And Brätan is knocking at our door …" He closed his eyes, but they reopened as if by the subtle call of the gem.

The Agent waited for his employer to speak, but in the pit of his stomach he knew that there was no way Lucaät of Faytha would, or could, relinquish the challenge. It was as if Faytha itself looked through his eyes and coveted what it saw.

"Brätan Gok is not greedy," Lucaät said sharply, "and Ishät has not yet seen them …" The Faythan's gaze locked onto his. "Think! What do we have that Brätan wants? There must be a deal, here, a … a way to win."

The Agent almost groaned as a viable plan came to mind. He tried to drive it out, but he was Cantori, and Lucaät of Faytha had paid.

"If we give Brätan what he wants," he said grudgingly, "let him take Duvät, formerly Gok, to the God-Emperor and show him the eyes he thinks are the real ones. Meantime, if we can recover the true eyes … Brätan has no interest in delving beyond what he already knows. When you show the God-Emperor the real ones – which must be even more beautiful than these – and tell him you have already discovered how to get more, you will make Brätan look like a fool who has wasted Imperial time without full knowledge of the issue, and yourself as the only possible candidate to mine them."

"But what of the Eyes themselves?" the inquisitor said. "They are not mined, but taken. This is not ethical. Somehow Duvät has managed to keep this from the Leth, and they must not find out or else the operation will be cancelled before it starts and we – as in you, my lord – will take the blame. There must be utmost secrecy. How can this situation be managed?"

Lucaät held the eye forward. "We must find out all we can about the creatures these came from." Slowly, as if with great reluctance, he placed it back inside the bag. The drawstring eased shut. "It is obvious, as you say, that the Lethians don't know," he reasoned, "If they did, they would certainly have stopped him. The charges against him would have been more severe. He would have been obliged to face the Imperium."

He stroked his chin again. "Secret knowledge … a great opportunity! We must speak to the God-Emperor in private."

"The God-Emperor! Why?"

"We must convince him that the creatures are plentiful and not particularly important to the ecology of the planet, and that the eyes can be taken … painlessly? Yes! It could even be true!" He turned back to the inquisitor. "Milk that wretch for everything he has. We must locate the true gems quickly, then give him back to his Clan Chief. It would be better if he's still breathing – but the worse condition his mind is in, the less chance he'll contradict me later on."

The inquisitor bowed and backed through the door.

"Can you actually speak to him?"

"Ishät Ashik?" Lucaät studied his fingernails for a moment. "Maybe not ... But I do have a cousin who can get me an appointment with the Empress Ishiquel, and from there ..."

Lucaät turned to him. "Go to Brätan Gok, tell him Duvät is recovering and we'll return him as soon as possible." His eyes burned with the energy of this new scheme.

"But he killed an ashessé," the Agent pointed out.

"Yes, an unfortunate accident. Insinuate that he may also have been harmed in the fray."

"But he wasn't."

"Don't be obtuse!" Lucaät growled. "Buy me some time."

"Let's talk recompense," the Agent said. If the God-Emperor was involved, the stakes could be no higher.

Lucaät shook his head. "Perhaps your spirit was Faythan before it joined House Cantori."

"You say I'm the best," the Agent insisted. "This will be a highly sensitive and difficult project with many disparate aspects to consider."

"Disparate aspects?" Lucaät considered him shrewdly. "Have you been studying again? Very well, for the duration of this assignment, I'll double whatever it is I pay you."

The Agent blinked in surprise and got to his feet, ready to make a start for Brätan Gok before Lucaät could change his mind, but the Faythan gestured him back to the ashut boards.

"Your enthusiasm is noted," Lucaät drawled, "but we haven't finished our game. Don't worry, this is part of the new mission too ... and this one I'm winning for certain."

"Brätan is no fool," the Agent retorted. "He'll find us if he turns his mind to it. Won't it be better if we reach him before he comes knocking?"

"Relax!" said Lucaät. "No one has found us yet. Intrigue and secrets, reading the field, that's the game I'm best at."

The Agent stifled his reservations and settled to the boards as he was bid, but he wasn't about to let his boss win this one.

LEAHÄT

Leahät Gok slumped in her seat and lowered her head to her arms. At last, Duvät's pain had subsided. Perhaps he was unconscious again. The silence in her home was complete.

She had not wanted him to suffer. After the horror of Lind and the other poor creatures he'd tortured, she'd just wanted him dead – but now, the torment he endured was so terrible it could not be blocked out. Surely such agony could be no worse than what she would have experienced if their marriage had been excised. If only they would let him die!

Weary to the core, her fingers traced familiar textures on the battered kitchen table, thankful for its solid presence. When he was at home, her husband insisted it be covered with a cloth, but now it was bare and she soaked up the precious memories it retained. Happy sounds – her mother's laugh, the smell of cooking and treasured moments of her father's warmth as he taught her how to read. That scattered streak there … she touched it with her finger … that was where she had spilled a ladle of ackway soup and scalded her leg. With all the fuss of calling the healer, the rich purple of the ackway had been allowed to seep into the wood. Her parents had left the stain as a reminder to be more careful.

She surveyed her sparse shelves, then with a little concentration widened her awareness to include the other rooms of the house, all bare now but for a few last things. The brightly colored blanket on her bed seemed incongruously cheerful.

Visible over the lip of one of Mirashael's bowls, the top of Duvät's purse leered down at her. She could not bear to store anything he had touched in Qalān. The ether around her would be tainted by its presence. She had struggled for so long, but the thought of using his gift was abhorrent. Where had it come from? Inevitably someone would come knocking and demand its return.

Her attention lingered on the trunk in the hallway, with its shiny straps and complex lock. It was there she had hidden what she needed to pay for her other two bowls … when the job was done. She hadn't dared open it, lest she be tempted to spend the small hoard on other needs. To jilt an assassin of his pay would not improve her situation.

Only moments later, she looked toward the front path. A group of ashessé approached. Their stony haze chilled her.

A heavy fist hammered at the door.

Fear made her heart beat loud. The back door beckoned, but where would she go?

What do you want? she asked fearfully. The coins seemed to laugh at her. *I have done nothing wrong!*

She hurried down the hallway, hoping to get to the door before it splintered.

"Who are you?" she cried. "Why are you here?"

The door swung open. Black leather creaked as the ashessé barged in.

One stayed to loom over her while the other three dispersed and began to search the house.

"What do you want," she cried. "My husband is not here!"

"Where is he?"

She cowered as the guard flexed his knuckles.

"I don't know," she said. "Please! I have done nothing wrong."

The guard's head tilted menacingly. Leahät stiffened as an ashessé came up behind her.

"You are his wife, yes?"

Nervously, she bobbed her head.

The first guard nodded to his partner. "Take her," he said flatly. "Follow the bond."

The one behind her slipped off his gloves and flexed his fingers.

She snatched her arm away. "No! You can't do this!" But his iron grip was quick and cruel. The chill as a foreign awareness ploughed through her screens made her choke.

The assault hesitated as a shadow crossed the doorway.

She dared not look up.

"Now, now! What have we here?" someone said cheerfully. The voice seemed familiar, male, but she could not place it. Tears stung her eyes.

"Senlät Gok, Derrel Gok?" the stranger continued. "Surely this is too fine a day to be harassing innocent ladies?"

"We are here on orders from Brätan Gok," the ashessé leader rasped coldly.

"Brätan himself? Ahh yes, very good, very good."

Cautiously, Leahät lifted her head. Surely it was not Mirashael of Cantori who stood just inside the door?

"Yes. Brätan," Mirashael continued. "Quite a regular client of mine. I'm sure he'd be interested to hear all about how you spend your time, Senlät … only when you're not too busy with your duties as an ashessé, of course! And Derrel? We both know how diligent you are …"

Derrel released her arm and stepped back. Free to turn, she saw Mirashael standing on the step, his colorful clothing and affable expression quite at odds with the grim, dark ashessé.

"Good!" Mirashael congratulated them. He gave her a quick wink. "Much better! Now, if you ask the lady nicely, I'm sure she will tell you what she can."

"Her husband killed one of us," Senlät grated. "Cheated Brätan Gok. Disgraced our clan!"

"Hmm." Mirashael nodded thoughtfully. "Well, I've not seen the less-than-esteemed Duvät of late, but I may have heard somewhere that he's hiding out at a location near the Palace of Gates."

The ashessé looked at each other. A spark of cognition seemed to fly between them.

"The Palace of Gates?"

"Just a rumor, of course," Mirashael nodded, "but on quite good authority. Clouds is a big place, I know, yes, but you're the sort that likes a challenge. If I were you – and this is just a suggestion – I'd leave this fine lady alone and spend your efforts elsewhere."

After a moment's hesitation, the ashessé leader nodded. "We have already heard something along those lines."

"There you are then!" Mirashael beamed. "Way ahead of me, and I daresay of this poor lady as well."

The ashessé called to his cohort to stand down. As his underlings gathered behind him he gave Leahät a shallow bow. "Please accept my apologies, Lady Gok. I did not know you were a friend of Mirashael of Cantori."

He gave a much deeper bow to Mirashael, then motioned his head toward the street.

Completely bewildered, Leahät watched them go.

"Come, come, Lady Gok …" Gently Mirashael pushed the door closed behind him. "Some tea might help?" He smiled reassuringly. "If you would lead the way?"

"Tea?" She choked back fresh tears and started for the kitchen, where Mirashael's gaze came to rest on a particular pair of bowls.

"I … I can't even make a fire." Leahät tried to keep her emotions under control, but her voice caught in her throat and the effort seemed impossible.

"Don't fret, dear lady, no! It is no problem. I make tea all day long." His expression radiated concern. "Just sit here, yes? I'll have a nice pot for you before you know it!"

"I just wanted the bowls," she cried, "the accidental bowls! You asked me if I wanted the hanta, but I didn't. Just the bowls. But now Duvät is in such agony, and I … I can hardly think!"

"Oh my lady, such terrible things you have suffered, and now the ashessé here, so rude! So rough!"

"Just end it please!"

"I would. I have tried," he assured her. "But matters have been taken from my hands, and your husband, Duvät, formerly of Gok …"

"Formerly?" Leahät felt as if her head was gripped in a closing vice.

Chagrin welled in Mirashael's otherwise smooth and perfect veil. Evidently, he'd assumed she had been informed.

"How can I show myself in public again?" she gasped. This ultimate shame … was she the last to know? Her mind darted between contingencies. The vice drew tighter.

Mirashael busied himself with preparations, and within a few minutes had a steaming cup before her.

"The shame is not yours, Lady Gok …" he said, but she hardly heard him.

"I must leave here!" Her gaze darted toward the trunk in the hall then into his rugged Cantori face. "You have been so kind, but I have no coin of my own, just what I owe for the bowls."

Abruptly, he turned away. His roving gaze lingered on empty cupboards.

She hugged her arms defensively, embarrassed by how thin they had become.

"Come to my place," he said at last. "A lovely hot meal? Omosa? The finest in the Realm?"

"But –"

"There is no need for payment," he said kindly. "You have suffered enough, and it's the least I can do … but if you feel inclined, there is something you can do for me."

"There is?"

"Yes: my bookwork. I came here to offer you employment. I find myself in need of someone to keep my accounts in order."

She was almost sure he was lying. "But Cantori are well known for their bookkeeping skills," she said.

"Not this one I'm afraid." He shrugged his lips ruefully. "It's mainly the café. I have so many other concerns. It would be of great help to me if I had someone there I could trust."

"Well, I ..."

"I would expect a certain discretion, of course. I have many high-profile patrons."

She nodded as if she understood, but in reality, she struggled. Mirashael of Cantori, someone with whom she was barely acquainted, someone she knew to have underworld dealings, had come all the way to her home to personally offer her employment? It seemed unlikely to say the least, but why else was he there? Should she be flattered, insulted, concerned or all three?

"If you like, I can help you get started," he said brightly. "Just until you are familiar with my techniques. And there are rooms above the shop if you need them." He smiled encouragingly. "I sense you have great strength, Lady Gok, but it has been underutilized. Perhaps this catastrophe is, instead, an opportunity for you."

"An opportunity?" Her mind wrestled with this reversal of fortunes. Perhaps she would not need to consider her husband's gift after all.

"Yes, yes!" Mirashael said. "A chance for you to become yourself." He looked her up and down. "And what a magnificent self that might be!"

Leahät's heart plummeted. Suddenly it seemed she understood.

"You're laughing at me!" she cried. "Well you can take your bookkeeping and your café and your lies and, and … I don't need your charity! I will pay you for the bowls when and if you deliver!"

"But no! No!" Mirashael lifted his hands. "It was no jest, no disrespect. A genuine offer!"

She pointed to the door. "Leave!" she cried. "Just leave!"

"My lady, I would never hurt you!"

She pushed her tea aside and turned away. There was an intake of breath as the Cantori started to say something more, then nothing until his feet receded, treading soft and rapid on the bare stone floor. He paused briefly by the trunk in the hall, then continued with greater conviction. The door creaked shut behind him.

Good, she thought. *Maybe he'll work harder to fulfill the bargain, and I can have peace again.*

Her mind went to the pantry where a small bag of little attar and a few greens sat dejectedly on the shelf, but then, wherever he was, her husband awoke. Fresh waves of pain welled through what remained of their marriage bond and she began to cry in earnest.

BRÄTAN GOK

Outside the shanty-style safe-house in Clouds, morning light flitted through gaps in the mist that gave the city its name. Deep within, the ashut tournament was long over, the eventual outcome indecisive. Lucaät's eyes flew open as the Agent sat bolt upright and looked toward the door. Seconds later, an alarm was triggered.

"Ashessé," the Agent said. "Four of them. Brätan Gok's, I'd imagine."

"So, I should have listened to you," Lucaät sighed. "But the game was good, was it not?" He looked around. "This has been a good place. Should bring a decent price to the right people."

"Clan Gok, maybe?" the Agent quipped.

The inquisitor came into the room. "The seals are sound, my lord. If you meet them in the front room?"

Lucaät nodded. "Have we finished with Duvät?"

"Not quite."

There was a loud rap on the door.

"Disappointing," Lucaät remarked. "Get him ready to travel."

The knock came again, this time louder and more insistent.

He turned to the Agent. "Stay out of sight and be ready to leave by the back."

The Agent shook his head and muttered, "Just hand him over."

"Don't forget who pays you!" Lucaät growled.

The door swung open and the pale light of dawn revealed four muscular silhouettes. The Agent hovered in the background, screened from view. The ashessé oozed brutality, but unless it came to actual blows he was certain his boss would be more than a match.

Their inward barge stopped as Lucaät held up his hand.

"I am Lucaät of Faytha," he declared, "nephew to Fayenätu Faytha himself. Manners, please!"

The leader glared down at him, then sketched a bow. "We come in the name of Brätan of Tiamät, Chief of Clan Gok."

Lucaät bowed slightly in return. "I am honored," he said smoothly. "What is it you seek?"

"The criminal, Duvät."

"Duvät?" Lucaät said carefully. "Yes, I heard of his … de-clanment – if that's what it's called. Terrible business."

"We know he's here!" the ashessé snarled. "Lord Brätan Gok demands he be surrendered."

"I am happy to comply with Brätan's wishes, of course!" Lucaät countered. "But Duvät's current health is quite uncertain. It seems he was injured in some sort of affray. Would it be possible for you to return? Perhaps tomorrow?"

"No," the ashessé said flatly. "We have been ordered to deliver him to Lord Brätan Gok as soon as possible. He must honor his obligations."

"Unfortunate," said Lucaät, "but very well, so long as you have a healer to attend him?"

The ashessé squinted uncertainly. "We were not advised of the need for a healer."

"Well, without one," Lucaät said firmly, "I doubt Duvät will live long enough to face your lord."

"For Breath's sake!" the leader said. His face went blank as he conferred with a higher authority, presumably Brätan himself. "Very well," he said at last. "We will wait here until the healer comes."

"How long will that be?"

"Several minutes."

Lucaät nodded as if he was concerned for Duvät's health, which the Agent supposed he was, in a way.

"Please excuse me then," Lucaät said, "as I prepare our guest for the healer's attentions. I can only hope he survives so long."

"If his health is so dire," the ashessé sniggered, "where's your own healer, Lucaät of Faytha? Can't afford one?"

Lucaät pretended not to have heard. He closed the door, signaled the inquisitor to activate their strongest screens, then the Agent followed him to the dingy back room where Duvät sat slumped in a chair. Strings of saliva hung from the prisoner's mouth. His eyes fluttered open and fixed blearily on the Agent's face.

"My lover, come to save me …" he mumbled.

Lucaät waved his fingers at the Agent. "Pick him up. Follow me."

There were several alternative escape routes, each at the end of a branching tunnel. He hurried after Lucaät as best he could with Duvät half dragged beside him. If their physical contact had been repellent before, it was stomach-turning now. The Gok's inner monster roiled. Painful moments of interrogation bled through ravaged screens and filled the Agent's body with echoes.

As they reached the outside, chill, damp air sucked the oxygen from the Agent's lungs. Lucaät hurried them along narrow cobbled streets until they reached a row of cheap shops and an alehouse. Peeling orange paint flaked from the architrave around the door. Above it a grubby sign proclaimed, *The Sunset Soiree – No Tea Served Here.*

"Why this place?" the Agent grunted.

"There's a portal behind it," Lucaät said quietly.

"And I thought I knew every one."

"Leads to the Imperial City," Lucaät told him. "With luck you'll make it back to the manor and our friend the inquisitor will extract the last bit of information from our guest before I'm forced to hand him over." He gave a sharp nod. "Good luck! I'll leave you to it."

"Why am I always the one?" the Agent said sourly. He hoisted Duvät into a more balanced position. "You better make good with the pay. And his absence when the ashessé return?"

"I'll alert them when I get back – before they come knocking. I'll tell them he's escaped." He turned and hurried away. *You've less than two minutes to be gone.*

The Agent shouldered through the alehouse door, and Duvät's feet scraped across the mucky floor. The few patrons seemed like dregs left over from the previous night's session. Most barely looked up from their slops, and those who did returned to them as if nothing had happened.

The inquisitor waved him on. *Through here ...*

They shuffled quickly past several stinking toilets then back into the fresh air. The Agent struggled to think clearly. Duvät's tattered defenses were destroying his.

There's a gap in the back wall ... The inquisitor indicated a narrow opening where the stone had decayed, then slipped between the worn blocks and continued into the scrub beyond.

The Agent tried to maneuver Duvät's dead weight through the breach.

Hurry! the inquisitor called. Twigs cracked amongst the trees. *It's right here.*

With another great heave from the Agent, Duvät's semi-conscious body squeezed through the hole, but as he went to follow, a sudden force crashed through his screens and stunned him. Duvät's limp form seemed to disappear before his eyes. He tried to sound an alarm, but his head spun from the impact. Helpless, he watched the inquisitor fall, then the portal hummed faintly and all went dark.

It felt like only moments later that Lucaät's voice shook him awake.

"You there! Are you all right?"

Lucaät's tone was impersonal. The vague outline of several ashessé surrounded him.

"What happened?" the Agent mumbled. His head felt like it had been crushed by a shuna.

"Healer, tend this person," Lucaät ordered.

The Agent felt a firm, feminine touch on his head, then a brief white explosion rearranged his brain. His mind cleared. He peered through the gap in the wall. There was no sign of Duvät, or the inquisitor.

"Better?" The healer's soft Naghari lilt was a comfort in itself.

"So, Duvät has outwitted you," one of the ashessé said almost proudly. "That's a Gok for you – slippery when cornered."

"What happened?" the Agent said. "I came out for a piss … and then …"

"Through here!" a voice called. "Portal! Recently used."

The ashessé almost trampled him in their haste to get through the wall. Lucaät gave him a look as he passed.

The healer touched his arm. "Are you sure you're all right?" she said. Her peat-brown eyes examined his aura. "Whoever did this, they've left a stain. I've cleansed your soul as best I can, but you may have periods of nausea until the influence is completely cleared."

"Thank you, I feel much better," he said stoutly. "A good sleep will do the trick."

"I daresay it will help."

He saw a hint of amusement in her smile, and wondered how much she'd really seen.

The wall crumbled beneath his fingers as he hauled himself to his feet.

"I'd best be going then," he said.

"I think you'll find your friends have left without you," the healer replied softly. As she ducked through the gap to follow the others, she gave him a wry smile. "Take care, now. Be sure to have that sleep!"

DUVÄT

Sunny skies warmed him from above, dainty wavelets lapped at his toes and all was at peace. He raised his hand to shield his eyes from the glare and looked down the long arc of the inner sea to the drama of the volcano, still belching smoke and flame. His skin began to crawl. The mountains were watching him: he could feel it. He backed away from the waves as seething monsters began to crawl blindly toward him. They sang in eerie screams, their tortured voices calling his name – "Duvät! Duvät Gok!"

He tried to run, but even with no eyes the creatures followed. Sand clung to his feet. Nameless refuse gripped his legs. He was sinking. He couldn't run fast enough.

"Duvät!" the voices howled. *Duvät Gok …*

He woke with a gasp. The wailing receded. His eyes slowly focused on the wiry Enna above him. At least it wasn't Lucaät's inquisitor.

"Who are you?" he said. His voice rasped in his throat. "What's happening?"

"Never you mind," his new captor said. "Luckily I have a little healing ability. You were in bad shape, my friend."

"Friend?" Duvät felt his mind begin to clear. "I have no friends."

"Ahh!" The Enna cocked his head. "I can see why that might be the case. Can you walk?"

He struggled to rise but fell back against his pallet. Fragments of dream still adhered. How much information had Lucaät stolen? He could barely remember what had happened – only the fight to save the most important bits for himself. If he'd told them where he'd hidden the eyes, they would have had no more use for him.

The creatures from his nightmare reached out to him with fading voices. *Duvät Gok*, they whispered, *we are coming for you …*

He peered at the shadows around the shabby room. "Why are you helping me?"

"Helping?" The Enna's expression was speculative. "Let's just say I'm acting on behalf of someone other than Lucaät of Faytha or Brätan Gok."

"Why?" Duvät demanded.

His captor cocked his head. "Would you rather I delivered you back to them?"

The creatures cried out again. Duvät looked up at the stained ceiling and shuddered, his fingers twitching against rough bedding. Light sifted through a dilapidated curtain nailed above the doorway. Sounds and smells of a low-class ale-house filtered through, but although he listened, speech patterns were hard to catch. "Where are we?"

"Karesk, or the borders of it."

"The half-breed enclave?" He groaned. *Why would anyone deliberately come here?*

The Enna gave a derisive chuckle. "No one looks closely at pariahs." He slipped into the local patois, speaking slowly as if Duvät might understand. "Pick a nary speak, ja?" He winked. "Be learnin de local lingo an be fittin fairly, sho la."

Duvät's mind flailed for comprehension. 'Fit right in?' He, a full Tiamäti archangel, fit in with half-breeds? The very notion drove the last of the voices from his head. Then Casco came to mind. Perhaps he lived somewhere near here. Casco would lead him to Huldar – and Huldar would pay for the pain he'd caused.

Huldar of Leth, I'm coming for you …

"Now, you should eat something, regain your strength." The Enna winked. "It could have been much worse."

"Worse!" Duvät rubbed his forehead. He would make things so much worse for that smug, self-righteous Leth …

"Be gebbin sometin ota the cookouse ere an chippy me later, ja?" the Enna said. As he pushed the curtain aside he looked back and said, *You were lucky, my friend* … but the glint in his eyes said something quite different.

Duvät's thoughts of revenge came to an abrupt standstill. … *You were lucky my friend* … The Enna's words echoed in his psyche. Alarm zipped through weakened muscles. That glint, he'd seen it before, and he'd heard that voice – first with the falling block of stone that nearly killed him, then when he was bitten by the kommer-sta. Both times he'd nearly died. A horrible comprehension dawned. This 'savior' was not what he seemed!

With a heavy thump, he threw himself to the floor and crawled to the doorway. It took effort to pull himself upright, but the terror of a fresh inquisition spurred him on. He peered through the tattered curtain – the Enna was nowhere to be seen – and tottered toward the exit, thankful for his stained clothing. The Enna was right. At this superficial level at least, he did fit right in.

Out on the street, light stabbed at his eyes. With one hand against the wall he made his way up the cobbles, moving faster as power returned to his limbs. Down alley after alleyway he ducked and wove until he came to a borderland of open fields and a portal he hoped would return him to the city.

He activated the gate, but the street he stepped onto was so similar to the one he'd left it was as if he'd gone nowhere. Delicious smells poured through an open doorway and his stomach rumbled. The sign above it proclaimed an eatery of some sort. He lurched toward a table near the back and signaled the waiter. He had to eat. He had to think! But as he reached into Qalān for his purse, anger gutted what little equilibrium he'd regained. He'd been forced to give up his bag of eyes.

He imagined Huldar writhing as he had, forced to relinquish the things he loved … the ones he loved …

A patron looked at him, radiating concern.

Screens, Duvät said to himself. He had to reestablish some screens! His mind was so addled that all he could accomplish was the most basic of inner ward, but then he remembered the charmstone – thankfully still his. With a perimeter set around his table he could relax a little.

Hot soup arrived. He tore at a knob of bread, and when the broth had barely cooled upended the bowl and drank, scarcely pausing to chew the chunky bits. With his free hand he signaled for more.

After another round of the same, still no one had come for him. He could feel his strength returning but a mental scan remained beyond him. He looked around, trying to seem casual. The serving boy had fine hair and skin like his own, yet the rounded pupils of an angel. He tried not to stare.

Although he knew not to think of them directly, he was comforted in the knowledge that he had somehow retained the location of the true Eyes of Bel Nishani. They were his and his alone. And now he had escaped. A new opportunity. It was as if the Breath had blown him to the right place again.

He signaled for more food. It seemed an age since he'd eaten. *Hungry as a weyfal!* he thought to himself … *The Red Weyfal* – Casco had often mentioned it. He was still in or near the enclave, so maybe it was nearby.

Fresh platters arrived and Duvät savored every mouthful. He was still alive, he still held the secret of the eyes, and now the bones of a new a plan! But first he had to rest.

"I need a room for the night," he said.

The boy tipped his head toward the back. Duvät looked at him in silence.

"Or mebee tryin de Golden Wheel," the boy continued hurriedly. "Sa bit furder down de street – one a right then tird a left – travelin til you be crossin de creek. Oer de bridge, sho la. Ye'll no be missin it."

Duvät's coin shone bright against the grubby tabletop. Every ache reawakened as he stood up, but despite the complaints of his body he poked the charmstone back into his pocket and headed for the Golden Wheel. Casco and the Red Weyfal could wait, just for a while.

Out on the street, there was still no sign of his savior/assassin but every gloomy corner held the prospect of disaster. The thought of the Enna's bright eyes peeping from the shadows, or worse still, Lucaät of Faytha's oily smile, kept his heart at the gallop.

Deeper into Karesk, the cobbled streets wound in a complex tangle between houses that seemed jumbled on top of each other, as if the whole settlement had emerged by chance from the landscape. Like fungus, he thought angrily, or a cluster of tickery burrs. Colorful awnings billowed over shabby chairs and divans left out on the street. All around, people prattled in their incomprehensible singsong dialect. Even when they spoke plain annangi it was with their own accent – as if Karesk was another planet, not just a small and insignificant part of the Imperial City.

By the time he arrived at the Golden Wheel, he was exhausted. The lady behind the counter smiled pleasantly. At least her physiology matched her round pupils. She looked almost pure, but for a particular fineness to her skin.

"Name a ples?" she asked.

"Can't you people speak properly?" he snapped.

Unruffled, she waited.

Obviously, he couldn't give her his actual name. As he searched for inspiration in his surroundings. a dark flicker in the common room caught his eye. His heart thundered, sure it was Daric Enna.

How could he have found me already? Duvät asked himself. But this was the nearest guest house – his movements had been too predictable. Had he been seen? There was no sense he'd been noticed.

"Where is the Red Weyfal?" he asked quietly.

Desk lady looked him up and down. "You be needin da heala, ja? No lookin so good."

"Keep your voice down!" he muttered, then bent forward to give her the name again.

She leaned back and wrinkled her nose. "No smellin so good eider."

Duvät looked over his shoulder, then down at his badly stained shirt, once an elegantly understated garment from a well-known maker. His trousers were sullied with the aftermath of unmentionable torture. Even his shoes bore witness.

Desk Lady's veil showed a whiff of remorse. She took a deep breath of fresher air and leaned closer. "Be takin de step down de street den a turn to de left," she murmured. "Anoder step dere should take you direct to it."

He nodded in thanks, appalled to think a half-breed could see him as an object of pity – another thing for which Huldar would pay. He tried to blend with a couple on their way toward the exit. They looked back and picked up their pace.

When he reached the portal, a last glance toward the Golden Wheel eased his mind. There was still no sense he'd been recognized. He activated the song and stepped through to an area just as bewildering as the one he'd left.

Lights glowed softly. Mixed groups of young and old gathered around collective cookfires where strips of food sizzled on metal plates and filled the air with the smell of spices. Outside one place, people lined up with bowls in hand, ready to be served from a huge communal cauldron. Many wore ill-fitting hand-me-downs, some were barefoot, yet they laughed and joked among themselves as if nothing troubled them, perhaps so ignorant that they were unaware of their shame.

"Ready for de big game!" one called up the line. He pointed to his shirt, inexpertly daubed with orange and black stripes.

A yellow-haired female waved a vivid red and blue hat. "Rangers be trumpin, sho la!" she yelled in reply.

"Sho la," Yellow and Black replied, "iffin dat limp-legged scuse for a fledder be mindin how to run, ja!"

Duvät hurried on. Clearly Karesk held more than its fair share of the insane. Little wonder, he thought, given the disgraceful parentage of its denizens. That an angel might aspire to marry above their station should be no surprise, but that an archangel, born to lead, should go along with it? Disgusting! And sometimes, Breath forbid, it went the other way round.

As he continued down the winding cobblestones in search of the next portal, a lilting voice caught his attention. Inside a doorway a young halfbreed sang over a carved amulet. She saw him pause and invited him to look. Hesitantly, Duvät stepped through the door. In her hand was a black onyx carved into the shape of a kommer-sta. He shuddered and backed away.

The next step, as they called it there, hummed so faintly he almost missed it. Clearly it was rarely used. From the dimly lit alcove he closed his eyes and opened them onto a normal city backstreet. Just two doors down, he saw a red sign with a weyfal painted on it.

The half-breed behind the bar had a face like a sandstone cliff.

"I'm looking for someone," Duvät said.

Cliff Face grunted, but his attention was on two patrons at the other end of the room. One knocked the ale from other's hands. The victim stood up and pushed his attacker's chest.

Cliff cocked his head and two meaty Rukh appeared from the shadows. They made their way toward the escalation. There was a slight scuffle and peace resumed.

"I'm looking for someone," Duvät repeated. "Casco? Tallish? Half-breed like you?"

Sandstone hardened into granite. "Kareski," Cliff-Face said flatly. "Who wants to know?"

The two Rukh came up on either side of Duvät.

"A friend," Duvät stammered. "Just a friend. We work together."

"His friends were here the other day." The cliff peered into his face. Vertical pupils constricted to slits. "You weren't with them." He cocked his head toward the door. Duvät felt huge hands grasp the back of his collar.

"No, wait!" he squeaked. "I was detained! I should have been here … missed them – sho la! But I'm back now and I have news he'll want to hear, sho la – great news. Good news, yes?"

Bar Attendant looked past Duvät as if his feet weren't dangling above the ground.

"You know 'im?" he asked.

"Put him out," came the reply.

Duvät squirmed in the Rukh's grasp. "Casco?" he said. "Is that you? Tell this monster to put me down!"

He landed face-first in the gutter. Grit stuck to his mouth, refusing to be parted from his tongue. Slowly he got to his feet and dusted himself off. When he turned, a powerful blow rocked his jaw and sent him reeling back into the gutter.

"Sho la?" Casco spat. "I've been itching to do that for years. Piece of filth!"

"No, wait!" Duvät said. "Please! I need your help."

Casco snorted disdainfully. "That's too bad." He turned away.

Duvät crawled after him. "Please! I'll pay you! You'll never see me again!"

Casco continued to walk as if he hadn't heard him, and Duvät's bravado crumpled. Slumped in the gutter, he began to sob. Hot tears stung fresh grazes on his cheek. Why was everyone so hateful? Why wouldn't anyone help him?

Steps came toward him, and he cowered, certain of another beating.

"I despise you," Casco said evenly.

Duvät shook his head. Tears greased his palms.

"Are you listening? I despise you!" said Casco. "Look at me!"

Duvät caught his breath and peered upward, flinching as the tirade went on.

"You are a hateful, stinking piece of shit – no, wait – at least shit fertilizes the ground. You poison the very air you breathe!"

Casco studied his face for a moment and smiled at the bruising there. His gaze moved down to his shirt, then lingered on his trousers as if reading the stains. "Seems someone's already gone halfway to giving you what you deserve," he said, "but I notice you're still breathing."

"I have coin, enough to set you up for life," Duvät mumbled.

"I am set up for life."

Despair turned to rage. "You're a half-breed," Duvät yelled. "A *half-breed*! Huldar's left you all alone, has he? Gone off to play with his pretty little diviner?"

"Shut-up!" Casco's haze flushed red.

"Where are they then?" Duvät looked up and down the street with all the theatricality he could muster. "Dabaku with Andel? Why not you after all these years? I thought you were so close, like brothers almost – like lovers, yes?" He looked Casco up and down "… Kareski? Is that what they're calling it?"

Another blow sent him reeling. He pushed himself up on one elbow and wiped blood from his nose.

"I don't need or want your coin." Casco snarled. "Unlike you, I got paid. You sicken me."

Casco turned to leave again and Duvät redoubled his efforts. "But I can help you," he hissed. "Hide me, and you'll have my gold! All of it!"

Casco hesitated. His veil seemed to waver. In desperation, Duvät pulled out the brooch he'd bought for his wife. "And this, it's real orusite, inlaid with silver, see? It's flowers." He twisted it back and forth to catch what light there was.

"What gold, and why would I help you?" Casco said. "I'd have Faythan debt-collectors breathing down my back before you could say El's Breath."

"If you don't," Duvät grated, "I'll make sure you have the Faythans after you anyway, and no fancy Shamkarun Huldar to stave them off!"

Casco narrowed his gaze. "What are you up to, Gok?"

Duvät decided on honesty, of sorts. "You're my last hope! I have to get away. I have to find a navigator. Please?"

Casco paused. Duvät relaxed. A bit of poison, a bit of promise, the old recipe had worked again. He would have smiled but his lip was already too swollen. "Do this for me and I'll never bother you again," he said earnestly. "I swear it."

Casco looked him with loathing. "You? Swear? You have no honor to swear by. Nothing could possibly hold your word." But then he paused. Duvät's hopes soared.

"Give me the coin now, and the brooch," Casco snapped. "You better hope there's enough to pay for your trip. If not, I'll hand you back to the tender mercies of Lucaät of Faytha's pet Ashik. Perhaps there's even a reward in it … perhaps I'll do that anyway."

Duvät tried not to shudder, but some of his fear leaked through.

Casco examined the brooch and weighed the purse in his hand. "Get up," he said. "Follow me."

Across the way a well-used portal hummed. At the instant they stepped through, Duvät looked back and gasped in fear. Something glittered in the shadows beyond the Red Weyfal – surely it wasn't the Enna, watching them depart? But in the pit of his stomach he knew it was.

LIFE IN KARESK

The house was bigger than some in Karesk, but certainly not palatial. A paucity of resonance spoke of absence. Casco wondered if that would change now that Huldar and he would no longer be spending their off time together.

He sank wearily onto his favorite divan, too tired to contemplate cooking as yet, and gazed at furnishings reflective of a life of travel and adventure – a cupboard he'd picked up on a trip to DuMah, low table made of variegated shara shell, bright fabrics from Hesh and a creamy white light stand made of fossilized wood he'd collected in the wilds of Manziat.

There were other mementos … a twisted twig, a sparkling blue stone, a spiky seedpod filled with wispy purple feathers, and shelves lined with crystals and books he had yet to read. Few Kareski had had his opportunities, but while trying for a position as a spinner he'd met Huldar and his life had changed. A few hundred years later, the Uri'madu had formed and he'd been dumped into logistics, a position that at first seemed beyond him. But despite his heritage he'd found that most suppliers were interested only in coin, and the math and instinct necessary to anticipate the company's needs had come easily to him, as Huldar had predicted.

In the far back room, Duvät's psychic presence had been screened to less than a whisper, but his thunderous snores were plainly audible. Casco leaned back on the cushions, gangly legs akimbo, and rubbed his knuckles. Well worth the graze. He owed Duvät Gok nothing, knew no one who liked him, and after what had happened to Lind … how good it had felt to finally knock him down and see him sprawling in the gutter. So why had he offered him shelter? Residual loyalty? An opportunity for control? He shook his head. It had happened, and this was the result – so far.

Eyes closed, he searched the neighborhood for any anomaly that could spell danger. After a millennia of planet walking, he was confident there was not much that could get past him. He was also fairly accomplished with portals, and, considering the sort of people that Duvät might be on the run from, he'd used every trick in his arsenal to lay a convoluted trail.

The scan revealed nothing untoward, but whoever had been watching them outside the Red Weyfal had been exceptionally skilled.

He rechecked the house screens, made sure the alarm would wake him if anyone tried to intrude, then let himself drift into a shallow sleep.

A buzz in his brain woke him with a start.

Casco! Trouble at Old Town. Looken a scrap, yeah.

He recognized his friend, Shen – not one to dramatize.

Wa de go? he asked.

Permies look a takin yon Tessa's bless. Shen sent an image of a troop of four ashessé with badges on their arms – permit inspectors – banging on Tess's door. Her family had been caught in the street-ball riot a few days back and ended up in the Naghari Chapter-House, battered and bruised.

Deys sayin she sa no fit moder on account of de youngun's busted arm. Kana's away, ja? Sho la, you gotta be comen quick!

Kana was Tess's husband, a mountain of half-bred Rukh who'd given quite an account of himself in the street-ball fracas. The ashessé had probably waited until he was off-world before making their move. Casco knew his help was needed, but he hated to leave Duvät unsupervised in his house.

Canna be doin, ja? he said. *Pic a nary … wha be Gruk? Gruk? You slippin de pram?*

Be minded … Yea giddy trap, sho la. He shook his head. Perhaps he was a bit unbalanced. There was no other way to explain the strange position he'd put himself in – but now he was home in Karesk he had a duty to his people, and Shen was right, Gruk would be more likely to stir trouble than diffuse it. He sighed heavily. *Minutes, I be dere.*

Although it was illegal for half-breeds to own a sword, he had one hidden in Qalān and had done a little training while on assignment. He recalled Cobar's deep rumble … 'To raise a weapon is to accept responsibility for the death of another. There should be no hiding from that choice, once made.' He hoped it wouldn't come to that.

Duvät was still snoring. With luck, he would have this new mess sorted out before his houseguest even realized he was gone. As he closed the door he whispered a particular charm. If he did wake before he returned, he wanted his goods unpilfered.

After three short steps through Qalān he could hear the sounds of an uproar and broke into a run.

Shen beckoned from the sidelines. *Rattle dem bones! Sa gettin over-wild, ja!*

Casco pushed toward four ashessé who loomed over a mother and child in the doorway of their weatherboard shack. A crowd of Kareski jeered and heckled.

Little Kisha cowered as the ashessé reached for her and, quick as a startled maffit, span back into the house. In his mind's eye Casco saw her dart through a neighbor's cottage. Panic clouded her thinking. Her headlong dash held no goal – just away. He flashed the image to Shen and his friend melted away from the back of the crowd to give chase.

"Don't come any closer!" Tess said.

The tallest of the raiders, every inch an Ashik warrior, tried to barge through, but the doughty householder stood her ground.

"Get back!" She cried. "My husband will …"

Without fuss, the Ashik tapped her on the forehead. Mid-sentence, she slumped on the doorstep.

A roar went up from the onlookers.

"Gruk, no!" Casco called, but the incensed Kareski threw himself at the nearest ashessé and was immediately knocked to the ground. Casco surged forward.

The Ashik pointed through the doorway. "Get her!"

"Wait!" Casco yelled. "Stop, all of you! What is happening here?"

The tall one paused.

Kareski jostled closer. "Look what deys done to Tessa!" someone called out. "Deys got no right!"

The ashessé looked him up and down. "Do you speak for this rabble?"

"Sometimes," he answered.

All four focused on him with disconcerting stillness.

"Bring the child to me," the leader said.

"Why would I do that?"

"It's the law."

"A law that deliberately separates mothers from children?" Casco fought to keep his anger contained. "There is no bond more sacred."

"The child must be protected," the ashessé sneered, "and the mother cured of her unnatural tendencies. She is pure, but her husband and child are not. She cannot care for the child while this illness is upon her."

"Illness? What illness? Is it an illness to love?"

"The child must be taken while she is still young." The leader's gaze flicked to a point further up the street. "She must be educated about the condition her parents have inflicted upon her. So our God-Emperor has decreed."

His gaze flickered again. Fear welled in Casco's chest. The potential for violence surrounded them like a living force.

"I'm sorry," Casco stalled. "Please excuse me if I ask for confirmation of your orders?"

Another of the ashessé sneered. "Mighty uppity for a Kareski, eh mates?"

Casco schooled his voice to utter calm. "We want no trouble."

"Then bring us the child."

"No!" someone in the crowd called.

"No right!"

"Leave us be!"

Casco was certain these four had not come without back-up, but the Kareski were so focused on the outrage at hand he doubted sensed the danger.

"One of us is searching for her now," he said, "but you know these wee ones – no one can find them if they're panicked – not till they calm down." He caught Gruk's eye and continued, "There are others up the street ..."

Up de street? Gruk echoed. *Breat!*

As he'd hoped, the volatile Kareski broadcast a warning to those closest. *Be minded! Deres a whole ganga bidin up dere, and deys armed!*

While the message passed from mind to mind Casco continued as if speaking only to the Ashik. "Yes, up the street, keeping a look-out. We'll let you know when we've found her. Let's hope the poor bless is safe – it's what we both want, isn't it?"

"You refuse?" He tossed his head and the nearest ashessé picked up Tess and hoisted her over his shoulder. "Then we'll take the mother as security."

The Kareski pressed forward, shouting their protest.

"No, please!" Casco cried. "This isn't right!"

The leader's lips moved. As he drew his sword from Qalān, the mob went silent.

"Casco, is it?" He paused to look him up and down. "We'll return the mother when you give us the child," he grated. "Until then, keep your scum out of our way."

"Where are you taking her?" Casco asked, but with a grunt, the ashessé pushed past him and started for the nearest portal. The mob parted just enough to let them through.

Gruk bunched his fists and seemed about to attack.

"Stay back," Casco pleaded. "Be letin dem pass. Fracas be makin tings worse."

"Breat-less turna!" Gruk bellowed. "What ud you know?"

"Be knowin enough," Casco yelled back. "Deys itchin a scrap! Itchin a make you dinner! You an all us. Be likin dat, ja?"

Gruk glared at him. Confusion muddied his haze. "I dunna see the way goin," he said at last. "Deys innocent. Tess, Kana, all permies and scrapin true. Dunna see why!"

"I'll be speakin to somat," Casco said firmly. "Get Tess back and meantime keep de wee bless safe, but can do nix natter till sun-up." He sized Gruk up. He was not stupid, just frightened, as they all were. "You're Kana's friend," he said. "Make sure he knows what's happened, and tell him to stay clear until de situation be sorted."

Faces turned, as if he had answers. His first instinct was to shout out to Huldar, but the Ashik had marked him as a troublemaker and it was best to keep his friends in the clear.

Found her! Shan messaged. *What now?*

"Kisha is safe," Casco said.

The message spread like wildfire. Anxiety eased.

"Let's meet back here in the morning," Casco said to them. "I'll do what I can. We'll talk further then. The wee bless is safe, and as for Tess … Gruk, if you could keep in touch with her? She'll want reassurance when she wakes."

Gruk nodded, relieved to have a mission. "We's chatten-hold, yeah? Me an Kana bot."

Some dispersed, others gathered in knots and lit vigil fires outside Tess's house. There was laughter as the fire sparked, and a comment not to let the flames too close to the weatherboards or the whole district might be gone.

"Jus what deys be wantin, sho la!"

Casco was reluctant to leave, but Duvät Gok was alone in his house, and besides, he needed peace to plan his way forward. Sifting psychic chatter from the ether was a constant drain. He would adjust in time, but he had grown used to the quiet of mind only found on a wild planet.

DUVÄT (FORMERLY GOK)

Duvät turned in his sleep and strained to find that happy place of forgetfulness again but it gradually dawned on him that it was lost. He tried to open his eyes but one of them was swollen shut. Despite the soft bed and clean sheets, every move still hurt.

Why me? he moaned. *What have I done to warrant this level of persecution? Had sex with an angel? Killed a few beasts?*

With great effort he sat up and examined his surroundings. It was still dark – the early hours of the morning. Piece by piece he remembered where he was and how it had happened that Casco had brought him into his home.

His stomach rumbled.

A brief scan told him he was alone.

Time to be on my way, he thought.

In the kitchen he found various varieties of nuts and grains. Most looked like they'd been waiting there since before the Uri'madu left for Went, however the fruit bowl seemed fresh. He selected a shiny green globe and bit into it. Juice dribbled down his chin. The sweet green pulp of the guerdi was gone all too soon, and before long, so were two more. He picked out a clump of purple berries and went looking for something to drink.

The wine was Lethian of course, but at least it was from a well-known supplier. He downed the first glass in no time at all then poured himself another and sprawled onto a low lounge to think and plan his next move.

The pain of his bruises faded as the rich yellow vintage took hold, but although his head was full of thoughts, they were fleeting, and no great ideas materialized. He took another swig straight from the bottle and looked around.

Wherever Casco had gone, he would doubtless return; Duvät did not want to be here when he did. Having cleverly escaped his entourage of followers, it was time to slip quietly away to the Imperial Bays, find a cheap navigator and get off Giahn ... except that Casco had taken his coin.

His gaze lit on a cluster of amethyst crystals displayed as a centerpiece on a low table, then travelled to the smaller but infinitely more valuable pair of black-opal netsuke on a shelf nearby. A slow smile creased his cheeks. Not far from the Bays was a dealer who would give him coin and no questions, probably enough to get him to Mecca at least, then maybe, ultimately, to Hesh. There were opportunities for adventurers on Hesh, and so many visitors coming and going that one more Tiamäti would barely be noticed. It was a good plan for sure ... but for the Eyes. How could he leave them behind?

Maybe he could go to Mecca, wait for the fuss to die down, then return, grab the Eyes from their hidey-hole under the bathroom floor and make a run for it? Or perhaps he could hire a Ziquaran to watch the house for him? That way, he needn't risk discovery unless his cache was under threat … But what would he do if someone did find his treasure? He couldn't stop them from stealing it. Mecca was only hours away, but still too far.

And how would running away solve the problem of Huldar?

Huldar could wait, he told himself, but anger swirled in his gut. Why should he wait? Why should he get away with what he had done? He probed the inflammation on his cheek and moved his aching jaw back and forth. His eye would not open at all. He must find a way to get the gems, get Huldar, then get out of Giahn without leaving a trace for Lucaät, Brätan or anyone else to follow.

It was time to be clever again, but alcohol warmed his veins and thinking was difficult. The main thing was to retrieve the Eyes of Bel Nishani before anyone else did. What if he'd inadvertently given Lucaät's inquisitor more clues than he thought he had? Memories of extreme agony ignited his aching head. His jaw clenched. He had tried so hard … but Lucaät hadn't given him up voluntarily, so there was hope. He must still want something from him.

He got to his feet, drawn to the tiny polished carvings: a pair of bento, crouched and ready to spring. The opal shimmered like the coats of the living creatures. He picked them up – smaller than pocket-sized – but when he went to release them into Qalān, they stuck them to his fingers. He flicked them back and forth to no effect. When he tried to prize them away it was as if they had fused to his skin.

With his free hand he reached for the amethyst and gave its smooth face a tentative stroke. Nothing happened. But after he picked it up he found it had also adhered to him.

The purple cluster weighed on his fingers and it hurt to try and shake it off.

He gazed in disbelief at his hands, netsuke stuck in one and a clump of pointy gems in the other. Unless he could work out how to void the charm, his dealer might have to cut them free. Sweat beaded on his brow. Casco had already knocked him down twice – how would he react if he saw this?

Netsuke and all, he ran for the door. It was hard to grab the handle. He tried to pull it open but it wouldn't budge, and then he realised – the doorknob was also charmed. The side of his hand and one free finger were bonded to it as if they had always been one.

With a groan he let his head fall against the door, then quickly lifted it in case it stuck too. Fat tears squeezed like oil from between the swollen lids of his black eye. Where was the Breath now? One minute he had felt it blowing him toward his fortune – then this. Even while the inquisitor had tortured him, somehow he had known he would escape … only to be trapped by a witless half-breed too gullible not to help him!

Hours later, his legs ached from standing in one position and he was sorry he'd drunk so much wine. His bladder ached almost as much as his legs. More tears oozed down his face. When had he ever been so emotional? He couldn't even wipe them away. Anger surged through his haze, so strong it tinged his vision red. He would be contrite when the half-breed came home … he would grovel and plead for forgiveness like the reprobate he was … until his back was turned.

Finally, he heard steps … then a whisper of song. He shuffled back as the door pushed open.

Casco sidled past with a smirk on his face and continued for the kitchen. Water gurgled into a glass … an insult to his tortured bladder.

"You ate my guerdi!" Casco snapped. His boots stomped closer. There was a pause as he reached down and lifted the empty bottle. "Drank my good wine! I don't believe this. And look at you now, you tried to steal from me – disgusting piece of filth!"

Duvät wobbled his head and mouthed, "… Disgusting piece of filth." He pushed the door shut. It was drafty with it open.

"So, you have your uses after all," Casco sniggered.

"If you let me go now," Duvät said, "I won't urinate on it."

"If you urinate on my door," Casco threatened, "I'll cut off your penis and mop the floor with your face!"

Duvät took a deep breath. "Let me go … please."

"How can I trust you?" Casco ranted. "Look what you've done." His voice put on a high-pitched parody. "Save me, please save me! … As if I don't have enough to contend with. You've stolen from me, tried to escape, and drunk all my wine!"

"I wasn't aware I was under arrest!"

"You should be!"

"Yes, I've done the wrong thing," Duvät admitted. "But I was scared … I was." He was surprised to realize that this was the truth.

"Scared of what?"

"Scared you would come home and beat me again." He squeezed his good eye shut and whispered, "Scared I will die a horrible death."

"Scared – like Lind."

Duvät froze.

The netsuke clattered to the floor. The amethyst landed with a clunk on his foot. A small grey pebble landed beside it, but he barely noticed as he turned and raced for the bathroom.

Was that how Lind had felt? His brain seemed unavailable. Was that how Lind had felt … really? He sat on the side of the bath and put his head in his hands. He needed a healer.

Perhaps his fear was different to hers – more intense? But even as the defence formed he recognised how flimsy it was. He had felt her terror, every time, and fed on it.

He hadn't meant for that to happen. He thought it was exciting, and it had been – just not for Lind.

But he hadn't killed her! Her experience trapped in Qalān had broken her mind, not him.

Pots clattered in the kitchen and soon the smell of cooking teased his nostrils – little attar, but inviting nonetheless. He scanned ahead and saw that Casco had set two places. It was far, far more than he deserved.

"Come out before it gets cold." Casco's tone was surly. "I need to use the bathroom myself."

Their hazes crackled as they passed in the doorway. Casco still loathed him, but had cooked him food. Why? What was he supposed to do?

He ladled a generous helping for himself, then noted he'd taken more than half and scooped some back into the pot.

Casco returned and served himself in silence, ate quickly, and cleaned up with practiced economy. The plates clattered back into their place on the shelf. He turned to study Duvät's face, lingering on the black eye and swollen jaw. A slight change in his expression told Duvät that Casco liked what he saw.

"I have to go out again," Casco said, and started for the door. "Please, don't try to leave before I return."

"But you haven't slept!"

Casco might be a half-breed, but his stamina was enviable.

"When will you be back?" he called after him.

"As soon as I can," Casco replied brusquely, then the door snicked shut and he was left alone with his thoughts.

AT THE GOLDEN WHEEL

Casco didn't look back as he left his house. Duvät's presence was a dark blot on his mind. For the first time in his life, he couldn't wait to leave the place. He jogged down the street toward the portal at the far end. From there, the next step was the Golden Wheel. A Hermes was stationed there, and, since the sun was yet to rise, it was unlikely he'd have to wait for an appointment.

He pictured the Guild-Lord's kindly face. When they spoke at Duvät Gok's trial, he had assured him that if ever he needed help … Perhaps he hadn't expected to be asked for this kind of assistance, but Casco felt sure that if anyone *could* help Tess, Shamkarun Pieru of Leth would find a way.

Shera, owner and manager of the Golden Wheel, was already at the counter preparing for another busy day. She beamed as he walked in.

"Casco bless! Bin so long, sho la?"

"Shera gran, days a empty missin you." He gave her a cheeky wink.

"Snuff de gran speak," she grumbled. "Makin un feel sung an gone!"

She looked outside at the Old Town streets, dark and quiet now, then up in the direction of Tess's house where vigil fires still burned. One soft hand patted the counter. "Wa de go?"

Casco nodded. "Need a Hermes, ja?" He peered into the room behind the counter where the Hermes was usually stationed. Because this was Karesk, they often had a younger, un-Marked messenger still looking for experience, but their rates were proportionally cheaper, and Shera was known to have paid on behalf of Kareski in need who couldn't afford the service.

She turned her head toward the back room and, before long, a pale young Hermes in traditional white robes beckoned him in.

"Dere ja go, bless," Shera said kindly. "She be little more dan kinder, sho la, but plenny skilled. I'll be closing de door, ja?"

"Ta, Shera," Casco said with a smile.

He followed the Hermes to a small sitting room. She indicated a narrow table with two chairs facing across it. Casco bowed and positioned himself accordingly.

She returned his bow and responded, "It is my honor to serve." Her voice was surprisingly rich for one so slight. She sat opposite and asked, "How can I help you, Casco of the Uri'madu?"

The title caught him unawares and he couldn't help the flush of pleasure that rippled through his veil. "I need to contact Shamkarun Pieru of Leth."

"You know him, of course." This was a statement rather than a question, and again Casco felt his spirits lift.

"Do you wish direct exchange, or for a message to be sent?" she asked. "There is no charge for a message."

"Direct exchange please."

The Hermes closed her eyes. Her head barely bowed, and he realised that these small contacts must be as easy as breathing for such a one. After a short wait, she opened her eyes again and blinked once.

"Casco? It is still dark outside."

"My apologies, Lord Pieru. I would not have contacted you except that there is a matter of some urgency."

"All right ... of course, but can we please speak less formally? The Hermes won't mind, I'm sure. Now, what's this about?"

"There was a raid last night. Ashessé took Tess, a Nhadu Kareski, hostage. They want me to bring them her child, Kisha, a little one of forty summers. They say the mother is diseased – ill with a sickness of the mind because she married a half-breed – and not fit to have a child. What can I do? If I give them the child, they will take her away, and Tess ... will be bereft."

"They took the child?" Pieru's sense of outrage was mirrored on the Hermes's face.

"No, not yet. We have her," Casco explained. "They have the mother, Tess."

"This is appalling! What of the little one? Is she safe?"

"She's safe, but I don't know what to do. I don't know exactly where they have Tess, but I have asked one of us to stay in contact with her. The family were caught up in that riot the other day, children playing street-ball strayed beyond the enclave ...?"

"Oh yes, I heard about that. And this is retribution?"

"I think so. There was a full squad of ashessé hidden within easy calling distance. All they needed was an excuse and we would've had another riot on our hands, within Karesk this time, inside our borders. The others, the Kareski, they are looking to me to solve this."

"Because you spoke up, didn't you?" Pieru shook his head. "But how could you not?"

"Yes; but I don't have any answers." He shrugged helplessly. "There are none."

"Give me a minute, Casco. I have to think. I suspected there was trouble brewing, but this is far beyond decency, even for the Imperium. Stand by, please."

"Thank you, Lord Pieru."

The Hermes blinked and was herself again. "Tea while we wait?"

"Tea? Err …yes, please," said Casco.

"You are surprised? Why?" she asked with a smile. "Because a Hermes drinks tea, or because I have offered you one?"

"Both, really. I haven't had much experience with your people."

"Is this your first time?"

"No, but –"

"Well, you should not be nervous. We are just like other archangels, really, I expect."

There was a wistfulness in her expression, and he saw how young she was, inside and out. "Do you miss your family?" he asked. "Are they back on Angera?"

She straightened her back. "I miss them, but this is my calling and I am honored to serve."

"Even in Karesk?"

"Especially in Karesk. When I requested this placement, I was not sure I would be accepted. I have much to learn and there were many vying for it. But here I am," she finished brightly.

"Vying for a position in Karesk? Clearly there is much I don't understand about your culture."

She went to the small kitchen where water already simmered gently. "I only have dar-leaf I'm sorry."

"Dar is fine," he said.

Cups clattered softly as she set them on the table.

"I spend most of my time away from home too," Casco said. "I have no family to miss, but my team, the Uri'madu, they are like family for me, and so long as I have a place in Karesk, I have a home to return to when I need it."

"Then we are alike! Is it a good life, the life of a Planet Walker?"

"It is the life I choose."

"You are very wise."

"Me?" Casco snorted. "No, I'm just –"

The Hermes raised her hand. "Lord Pieru returns." She blinked and was gone, her own consciousness set aside so that he, Casco, could communicate directly with another's. He smiled to himself. Hermes were definitely not like other archangels!

"Casco," Pieru said, "I have done some work here. Please, there is no need for you to know how, but Tess will be released and the accusations dropped. She is free to go on the proviso that she and her family leave Giahn."

"Leave Giahn?" Casco blinked at the enormity of this. "Where should they go? Why can't they come home?"

"Let me finish!" Pieru snapped. "They can go to Haaseen. Kana, her husband, identifies as Rukh. Ashemar, the House Leader, has agreed to accept them and their child, and has offered to take as many Kareski as want to come, especially if they have ties to Rukh."

Casco rubbed his forehead and wondered how the Kareski would take the news. Would there be an exodus?

"Matters move swiftly," Pieru continued. "I will be meeting with some of the other House Leaders later today. We will discuss Kareski immigration and re-settlement issues among other things. Be prepared, Casco, and be on your guard. I doubt the Karesk situation will improve. Would you mind if I use you as a contact and representative for your people? Would the Kareski accept this?"

"Maybe," Casco answered. "I've called a meeting for this morning. I'll ask them."

"Good. Shamkarun Huldar has been a fine mentor. If this Hermes is in agreement, we will connect through her. It will be safer for you. The ashessé know your name."

He remembered the Ashik's look and felt a chill in his bones. "How will we get Kisha to the Bays to reunite her with her mother?"

"I will send someone. They will have a token."

"Thank you, Shamkarun Pieru of Leth."

"It is the least I can do, Casco, and you are no less honorable for your lack of title. Breath blow you safe journey. We will talk again soon."

With another blink, Pieru was gone. Casco nodded and closed the session with the ritual remark, "Thank you, Hermes. I trust I need not ask for your respect."

The Hermes bowed and gave the customary reply. "Confidence is maintained, Casco of the Uri'madu. It is the honor of my House to do so."

He sat for a moment, his thoughts awash with the implications of his conversation.

"Would you like more tea?" the Hermes asked. "There is no one else waiting."

Casco gave a rueful smile. "Do you hear what is said?"

"Yes, and no. We are trained to forget. That way we can maintain impartiality. It is the basis of what we do … and where our honor lies."

"Forgetfulness?"

"Impartiality." She smiled. "A Hermes judges no one. We are merely messengers."

Casco returned her smile and put his payment on the table.

"Lord Pieru asks that we maintain contact, for now. Is this agreeable to you? No one can trace our linkages," she assured him. "It is our special gift."

A light shiver went through him, nothing at all like the contact he was used to when exploring with the Uri'madu. A Hermes refinement, he guessed, but he was too shy to ask if he could learn it. Instead, bowed out and started for Tess's house, where a large group of Kareski had already begun to assemble.

FORETELLING

In the heart of the Imperial Bays, Huldar gazed up at the magnificent colored glass in the ceiling and hoped he was doing the right thing.

Inshogi joined him. "Splendid, yes? Ancient. How has such delicacy survived, do you think?"

Huldar shook his head.

"Up to now, the wind of the Breath has been gentle with us, I believe," Inshogi said. "Yet things are changing under our new God-Emperor, and not for the better," he muttered. "I am glad to be leaving this place."

"You have not enjoyed your stay?"

"You will like Frith, Huldar," Inshogi said. "There are no riots. We care for each other. There are no distinctions." He turned to Huldar and looked him in the eye. "As archangels, we have a duty to ensure the wellbeing of our House, the wellbeing of all. It is not for me to say that one's need is more important than another's based on parentage or station, as I'm sure you'd agree."

Huldar nodded. A pall of tension hung over Giahn, as if the planet held its breath and feared the worst.

Over by their designated bay, Andel's emerald green dress – a gift from her mother – flared as she walked between crates and boxes piled high, waiting for the spinners to arrive and embed them in their song. Ninjay, dressed in an imposing royal blue outfit, pointed as she relayed instructions. Fellow travelers gathered in knots awaiting departure and the atmosphere buzzed with anticipation.

Suddenly, Andel turned to look at her mother. Anxiety slammed Huldar's chest.

Father! she called, but as Ninjay fell to the ground, Inshogi was already on the run.

Huldar reached them a moment later. Inshogi crouched beside his wife. Her body was stiff and trembling, her eyes rolled up until only the whites were showing.

What's happening? Huldar asked.

A foretelling, whispered Andel.

Inshogi reached out his hand. *A blanket, if you would?*

Huldar whisked a cover from Qalān and a small pillow to place beneath her head.

"Ninjay? Ninjay my love?" Inshogi spoke softly as he chafed her hand. "Just relax, that's the way. Just let it flow …"

Two ashessé sauntered over. "Everything all right here?" one asked. "Is a healer required?"

"Not necessary, thank you," Inshogi said.

Huldar turned to them. "We have things under control, but …" He nodded toward the gathering crowd of onlookers.

The ashessé bowed. "Move along!" they said to the gawkers. "Give the esteemed Shamkarun some space!"

The ether buzzed with commentary. Huldar imagined ripples of speculation spreading like rings in a pond.

"Give the 'esteemed Shamkarun' space?" he growled. "Your mother's the one on the ground."

Ninjay took a deep and shuddering breath. Inshogi helped her to sit up, but she was breathing hard. She blinked as if emerging from a dark place, then closed her eyes – the light was still too much. Suddenly they snapped open and looked straight into Huldar's. Shards of vision flickered between them, swords flashed and dripped, blood spattered the walls of the Bays.

He blinked in shock and looked away.

"What did you see?" Inshogi asked her gently. "Can you tell us?"

"We must leave here," she said. Her voice was strained as if she'd been forced to run for her life.

"Is there something we should do?" Huldar asked. He glanced at the walls just to check they were clean. "What can we do?"

She looked at him intently and he thought she would speak, but then she shook her head. *Tell no one!*

Inshogi helped her to her feet, wrapped Huldar's blanket around her shoulders and with great gentleness guided her to a nearby seat.

Like vestiges of a dream, the glimpses of violence faded. Huldar turned at a loud burst of banter as the spinner crew arrived. Without ado they began bustling about with the cargo.

Andel stood close beside him. He had the sense she felt almost as awkward as he did.

Ninjay smoothed the blanket's folds with small, repetitive actions. At last, she looked his way. "Trianog has spoken, Huldar, and I need time to fully comprehend."

He hunkered down before her. *What I saw, what you shared …* "Is there anything I can do?"

Her look turned inward. "All the things you should do, you will, and more … and yet … the sacrifice has begun." Her voice closed off.

He was startled to hear the planet's words repeated. "What do you mean?" he said. "What sacrifice?"

She took a heavy breath and turned to Andel. "I'm thirsty."

He searched her face, determined to press for answers, but it was as if that particular light had gone out. Andel's gaze flicked over him. "The refectory is quite close," she said. "We'll be back as quick as we can."

Inshogi put his arm around his wife and drew her in against his shoulder. Her eyes closed, and her head bowed as if she carried a great weight.

Huldar stood up and followed Andel to find a drink for her mother.

A foretelling … I've never seen that before, he said.

Sen'ka – the Wind of the Breath. It hasn't happened for ages … not like that.

Casco told me your mother was gifted in that way.

Yes, it came up when we were on our way to the volcano. He was worried and wondered if I shared her ability also. Lind laughed. She didn't like me much back then.

They pushed through the refectory doors. He wished his friend was with him now.

"Have you heard from Casco?" Andel asked. "I miss him."

"Me too," he admitted. "It's strange without him, but he was determined. I know he's all right, but nothing beyond that." He rubbed his knuckles, remembering a strange sensation from the night before. "I felt some sort of rush yesterday as if he'd been in a fight, and definitely on the winning side! But there are problems; I know there are. And the new half-breed laws, the riots – I worry for him."

"Does he know we're leaving today?"

No.

She frowned. "Shouldn't you tell him?"

They reached the counter and she ordered, "Guerdi, with a touch of kanth, please."

"You're right," he said guiltily. "I don't know why I haven't."

"Why not do it now? I'll take the drink to Mother – you go over to one of those booth-seats there." She indicated a row of alcoves.

He watched her walk away then settled into one of the stalls. People came and went, intent on their meals. He tried to recall what he'd seen in Ninjay's eyes, but could remember no details, only the fear and her words, *Tell no one.*

Without a doubt, he knew he would once have shared this with Casco, but now … Casco was like a brother to him, so why was it so difficult?

He took a deep breath and put his misgivings aside. They were friends. Of course he would welcome the call.

Casco? His mind flowed down the familiar pathway like a stream in its bed. Their contact brought such a sense of relief, he found himself smiling.

Huldar! Casco's voice burst into his head. *I think about you so often, so much has happened … riots, ashessé. I've even been talking to Lord Pieru – he's helping me with Tess and Kana, remember them?*

Is that why my knuckles were hurting?

No, that's another story. A sense of loss welled between them, but Casco remained adamant. *It's best this way, believe me.*

Again Huldar glimpsed the edge of a story – fires, riots, missing children, and strangely, there was even a hint of Duvät Gok, as if their ex-Overlord had something to do with the goings-on in Karesk.

Can I help? Huldar said. *I'm leaving for Frith today – right now actually, but if you need me …*

No! It's not pretty here at the moment, but things are going in the right direction. I'll call if I need you, I promise, but I have to go now. Enjoy Frith – and Andel. She has a way about her, doesn't she? Give her my love.

With that the contact was withdrawn and Huldar was left to wonder if he'd really sensed their former Overlord, or if it was just that Casco still grieved for Lind.

Back in the Imperial Bays, he found Ninjay back on her feet.

"Don't dawdle," she snapped. "The navigator is waiting!"

He rolled his eyes. Things were definitely back to normal with her.

Assessing the group of travellers was a lean archangel with leaf-green eyes and lanky limbs, hallmarks of House Maatu.

Andel's hand wormed its way beneath his arm and tugged gently. Spinners were already manipulating the envelope. It was time to go.

Has your mother told you anything? he asked.

She pulled him closer and murmured, "Only that when I next return to Giahn, it will be for a day of days, whatever that means." She shook her head. "It's confusing for her too. She might tell us more later, perhaps, but I know she's anxious to leave."

"All ready?" the navigator asked. Around them, the chord pulsed with energy.

"Let's go!" one of the passengers cried.

There was a familiar sense of vertigo as the navigator's voice joined with the spinners', then the envelope gelled and they were away.

As the sound settled around him, Huldar felt strangely relieved. Their first break would be at Padmil, then on to Ames, Garden, Lisbo, then a string of moons and planets he had not yet seen – and then finally Rian, the capital city of Frith. But his usual anticipation of new horizons was muted as he speculated about Ninjay's vision and why she wouldn't tell them what she'd seen.

LEAHÄT AND MIRASHAEL

Leahät had been told her walk was a purposeful one, and as she listened to the regular tap of her steps on the cobbles, she supposed it was. Behind her she could sense Rina Gok also heading toward the portal. Rina must have known she'd been noticed, but this time rather than hurrying to catch up, she hung back. Leahät buried her hurt, firmed her veil and continued down the street as if the person she'd once thought of as a friend did not exist.

Before Rina came close enough for the situation to be embarrassing, the portal-keeper gave her a sympathetic look and sang her through. She was ashamed to have no coin to pay him and thanked him instead with a small bag of dharma biscuits.

"I baked them myself," she said quietly and turned before the ripple in her veil became a rift.

She had thought mid-morning might be a quiet time at Mirashael of Cantori's café, as it had been the first time she'd come, but several tables were occupied and a Nhadu family sprawled over two of the elderly divans that crouched against the back wall. She glanced at the corner where the Enna had once sat and polished his knife. It was empty.

"Lady Gok! Lady Gok!"

She turned as Mirashael danced nimbly through the clutter.

"How can I help?" he said. "Please, would you care to sit?"

His veil emanated the merest tinge of polite concern, at odds with the intensity of his gaze.

"Is there somewhere we can talk privately?" she asked.

"But of course, my lady, of course." He shepherded her to the kitchen door and, after a brief nod to the staff, showed her through to his office at the back of the store.

"Now, my lady, what is it you wish to discuss? The bowls you ordered are not available as yet, but I have someone working hard to rectify that situation."

She looked around at the neat shelves and cabinets, not a loose paper or stylus to be seen, then back to Mirashael's colorful, slightly disheveled appearance. He seemed kind-hearted, but ran a stable of killers for hire – seemed casual and carefree, but there was nothing lackadaisical about this room.

"So, have you head the latest from the Palace?" he said blithely. "Another bride refusal from our God-Emperor's only child. Two Enna and a Faythan, presented like goods in a crafter's shop – this will not improve our esteemed ruler's mood, I'm predicting!"

Leahät went to speak, but Mirashael continued with barely a pause. "It's said that Lord Aqumät is waiting for the daughter of Lord Fayenätu Faytha himself, but I have heard her heart is promised to another … and so is his … but really, you are not here to catch up on Imperial gossip, are you?"

She lifted her chin and held her veil steady. "You said … you had work for me?"

Mirashael's head tilted, just a fraction.

"Is this still the case?" she asked.

Through all the blather about Palace politics, Mirashael's thoughts had been expertly veiled, but in the brief pause that followed, he seemed to come to a decision.

"I do need assistance with my accounts, yes," he said.

She looked around the obsessively neat room once more and had the sense that few visitors had been allowed.

"It does not seem so," she said bravely.

"Please, let me show you. One moment – the information is sealed, as you would expect."

He whispered a charm and a set of three polished stone drawers became visible. The stone was bright cerulean blue and glistened as if wet. She almost reached out to touch it.

"Calcite," he explained. "An indulgence, I know, but it takes to secrecy so well. Did you know that?"

"No, I didn't."

He slid the lower drawer open and withdrew a fat ledger.

"You don't keep it in Qalān?" she asked.

"There are techniques …" A swirl of darkness crossed his veil. "Truly, it is safer here."

She looked at him suspiciously.

"I would never harm you, Lady Gok, never! The danger is minimal, I assure you, and you will be handsomely rewarded, yes, yes!"

"Danger?"

"As you already know, some of my business is … of the less visible, less, ah, shall we say –"

"Dishonorable?" she filled in for him. "Illegal?"

"No, not at all! My honor in all dealings is well known! My employees are the best, the very best. All highly trained. But politics is a murky field, even the politics of the heart, as you know – and as for the lawfulness of what I do? That is a murky paddock also. What I meant to say was, clandestine! Yes, clandestine, that's the word. And I will need your utmost undertaking that the information here, in this book, will never be revealed."

He patted the soft suede cover and waited for her to reply.

What did I expect? she asked herself. Of course there would be secrecy involved, but as her clan were traditionally the bureaucrats of the Imperium, all Gok had ability with the keeping of secrets.

"I will understand, of course, if you refuse …"

"I'll do it," she said. What had she to lose? She no longer needed the money since she had Duvät's stash if she really wanted it, but the idea of working for Mirashael was … appealing. There might even be some excitement in it, and it was the last thing her husband would expect – that she, the object of so much of his scorn, would work for an assassin – for the assassin who would kill him!

"Good! Very good! Excellent, in fact."

Mirashael was beaming, and she couldn't help smiling with him.

"And where will you live? Would you care for the rooms above the shop here? They are quite spacious, and no one has lived there for some time."

"What happened to the previous occupant?" she asked doubtfully.

"What happened?" Mirashael's hands flew up. "Oh no! Nothing like that, no. It was me, but I have bought myself a little place down on the Pannias Coast, overlooking the bay. Do you know it?"

"On the east coast?" She had heard of it, a destination for exclusive tourists, and could well imagine why Mirashael would invest in the area.

He nodded agreeably. "Yes, well, it's quite nice. Modest, yes, but the sound of the waves is quite soothing, and now you will be taking some of my workload, I'll have more time to appreciate it." His tone became slightly apologetic. "I may need to sleep over on occasion, so long as that does not inconvenience you? No, I'll be no trouble to you, Lady Gok. Silent as a light-spirit, you'll see."

Leahät took a moment to think this through, but in her current mood, the decision was simple. Even the house … she could leave it empty, make a clean break and start afresh. After a long darkness, a new life beckoned.

Who knows? she thought. *Maybe one day I will have the house I've always dreamed of, with a courtyard and a fountain, and even a guest room for when others – my friends – come to visit.*

With this in mind, she smiled at Mirashael and asked, "May I see the rooms upstairs?

He leaped to his feet. "Of course, of course! Right this way. Three large bedrooms, lovely bright kitchen … I'm sure you will love it!"

At the top of the stairs, the plain iron-wood door opened into a spacious sitting room. Views over the neighboring rooftops were framed by a shaggy vine with hanging clumps of sweet-smelling flowers. Airflow from southerly windows let in the noise of the streets, but kept the space cool.

She turned to him, unable to prevent the smile on her face from forming. "Yes, this will do nicely."

As Leahät Gok made her way from the café, Mirashael's mind followed. Her smile lingered in his thoughts like sunrise after a winter storm. The notion of such loveliness released from the pall Duvät Gok had placed over it warmed his heart indeed. It would be difficult not to let his great attraction for Lady Leahät cloud his judgment, but he knew instinctively he had made the right choice, the right offer to the right person. Her talents were under-realised and, although she would be seen to be working for him, she herself had no history, and no one would suspect her importance to his concerns.

Would she betray him? He smiled. Maybe, but he judged it extremely unlikely. If she could be loyal for so long to an utter worm such as Duvät Gok, then she would be capable of the same for him.

He imagined her smile again as if it were meant for him, and the anticipation of winning such a prize brought a sparkle to his eyes.

CASCO AND DUVÄT

Casco raised his hand and sent a general command for order.

"So far," he continued, "Houses Leth, Rukh, and Nhadu have offered their full and unrestricted support. Naghar, Maatu, and Trianog also offer immediate sanctuary. On Trianog it has always been so. Cantori remain undecided."

"So, is we-un to be believin this, ja? Acause why? Acause you be sayin it?"

"Lord Pieru of Leth has worked tirelessly on our behalf," Casco said. "He has –"

"Lord Shamkarun Pieru of Leth, Lord of the Explorers' Guild?" the heckler jeered. "See? I's be speakin kishlak well as ye, Casco!"

"Pieru be kishlak true," called another. "Why should wes be faidin dat un any more dan oder?"

"I know him, Hamesh –" Casco started.

"Ja, ye be workin for un!" Hamesh said mockingly. "Be some kishlak chippy me so, I'd be tinken dat was de Breat blowin from his arse too, sho la."

There was laughter as an image of an archangel farting golden rainbows was bandied from mind to mind.

"Hamesh," Casco said, "be wantin safety, ja? Bless an kin safe too? Pic an choose, dat be Pieru's game – options, be all. Faid un or no, stay or go, no badun be forcin ye, nor forcin any oder."

"Casco's no kishlak! Be un helpin us true, ye giddy cards!"

He recognized Shera's voice, and was thankful for her support.

Hamesh grunted. Shera's opinion was respected by all. The mood of the meeting began to clear.

"Den why doan de lordy kishlak be comin here and mindin us his lordy self?" Hamesh said loudly.

Casco thought hard. There were many who murmured assent, and he could understand their fears. When had an archangel ever truly helped them? There was always a catch, an ulterior motive … and could it be done? Would someone as important as Shamkarun Pieru visit them here in Karesk?

"If un did, ja … be Shamkarun Pieru of Leth comin here an speakin true – would ye faid un?"

A burst of psychic chatter swirled through the meeting as the Kareski considered this startling idea. It stilled as a consensus was reached.

"Tess an Kisha safe first," Hamesh said. "When bless an moder be safe and sound, den ye be bringin your lord. Den wes be all mind an ears."

Afterward, Casco stayed to answer questions as best he could. He wanted the Kareski to know that not all 'kishlak' were monsters, although, given the state of affairs, this was a hard sell.

Even if the offer was true, as folks said, with permits and overly vigilant ashessé patrolling their every move, how could they travel?

His head swam with calculations of options and means.

As he took the last step toward home, he paused to clear his mind. Would he find Duvät stuck to the door again? Perhaps he'd had found a way to nullify the anti-theft charm, but he doubted it. The toning of the ancient Kareski device was so obscure that few outsiders would even know where to start. He snorted sourly. Charms moved on, but Kareski?

The door pushed open without resistance. His 'guest' sulked in his room.

Eventually, the smell of cooking drew Duvät to the kitchen, where he peered suspiciously at the bubbling pot.

"What is it?" he asked at last.

"Doma," Casco replied. He shoved an empty bowl Duvät's way.

Duvät sneered. "That tells me nothing."

Casco shrugged. After he'd filled his bowl, he handed the dark wooden ladle to Duvät and left him to it while he made himself comfortable at the low table in the next room.

"Well, if this is all there is …" Duvät muttered sourly. There was a clunk as he dipped the ladle into the thick brown broth.

Casco sighed. He'd cooked for the team on assignment. There'd been no complaints then.

Once seated, Duvät lifted his spoon as if death by poison was imminent, but after this first torturous effort, several mouthfuls of doma vanished in rapid succession.

Casco raised his eyebrows.

"Hungry," Duvät said defensively, then slurped back the half-chewed food that had tried to escape his mouth as he spoke. He lifted a full spoon and tipped it. Brown and orange chunks dribbled back into the bowl.

"What is doma anyway?" he asked.

"Made from our own Kareski produce," Casco answered. "Grain and greens we grow for ourselves in secret valleys, fish from the streams, foss bark –" he pointed to a ruffled orange bit "– that's a lichen that grows near the southern ocean – we can't always get it. But the special taste, that sort of salty tang?" He paused for effect. "Fungus from the Imperial sewers."

Duvät's head bobbed absently, then Casco's words sank in and food blasted back into his bowl.

"From the sewers!" Duvät wiped his mouth with savage vigor. "Breath knows what I've just eaten!"

"You seemed to be enjoying it," Casco said. He relished the thought of sharing tales of Duvät's outrage with Huldar and the team, and made a great show of wolfing down the rest of his meal. When he had scraped the last from his own, he reached for Duvät's bowl. "Not as hungry as you thought, then? Do you mind?"

Duvät snatched it back and began eating again, albeit more slowly. "Food from the sewers," he muttered. "I can see in your haze that you're lying. Making fun of me."

"Lying?" replied Casco.

"At least you can speak properly," he said scornfully. "That's something in your favor."

Casco's jaw clenched. "My father, Omar of Leth, made sure it was so," he said tersely. "My parents were good, honorable people."

He pushed back to leave the table and wondered again why he'd offered to help. If he'd hoped adversity might bring out a more pleasant side to the Gok, that certainly hadn't happened. 'Kishlak', the Kareski called outsiders … fruit that was good on the outside but rotten within.

"Honorable?" Doma dripped from Duvät's spoon as he gestured. "Your father married an angel. That's disgusting."

"They loved each other," Casco snapped. "They married and were blessed."

"El despises half-breeds."

"Were you blessed?" Casco retorted.

"Our God-Emperor is El personified," Duvät stated, "and he hates you! Riots? It's an outrage you even exist. And besides, no half-breed ever was Marked."

"Yes, we are! When Kareski are Marked, they are usually adopted into a Great House."

"Rubbish!"

"Whichever one they most identify with," Casco assured him. "Didn't you know? Huldar's grandmother was a half-breed."

Duvät snorted rudely. "That explains a lot."

Casco stalked back to the kitchen and began to clean up. Perhaps he should've poisoned the food.

The heavy silence was only broken when an alarm fizzed against his brain. A tap on the door soon followed. His quick scan revealed a lean and rangy Enna at the door with a guild token held up between his fingers.

Traitor! Duvät screamed. His bowl clattered to the table as he dashed for the back room.

Casco shook his head. No doubt Duvät's experiences at the hands of the Faythan were still raw. When he closed his eyes and looked at the Enna more closely there was something familiar … Maybe he'd seen him at the Guild-Hall. The token seemed genuine.

I've come for the girl, the Enna said. *Lord Shamkarun Pieru sent me.*

What's your name? he asked.

My name is unimportant.

Not to me, Casco replied. *I have to verify who you are.*

The archangel hesitated, then bowed his head slightly. *I am Daric Enna.*

Casco sensed Daric Enna's reluctance, but the name meant nothing to him.

Who sent you? he asked.

I came on orders from Mirashael of Cantori, on behalf of Lord Shamkarun Pieru of Leth.

Casco relaxed. *I'll be right with you*, he said.

In the back room, he found Duvät cowering beneath a pile of bedding. He stank of fear. When Casco stepped closer, he pulled the blankets tighter. "Faithless half-breed … You can't do this to me!" he whispered emphatically. "You promised!"

"Shut up!" Casco snapped.

"You said you'd help me. I won't go without a fight," he hissed. "I won't!"

Casco tried to feel sympathetic, but to see the once arrogant Overlord reduced to such a state by a simple stranger at the door was quite satisfying.

"I have to go out for a while," he said.

"Go? With him?"

"Remember the charm," Casco reminded him. "Keep your hands off my things!" His gaze narrowed. Duvät's fear seemed suspiciously real. Casco was reminded of the hidden watcher outside the Red Weyfal. Had it been Daric Enna who'd lain in wait? Even if that turned out to be the case, Pieru would not have given his token to someone he didn't trust.

His suspicions firmed as Duvät squirmed deeper into the blankets. "Don't let him know I'm here! Please – he doesn't know, does he?"

"Why would he care?" Casco turned away. Clearly, Daric Enna was a good person to count as an ally.

He set the anti-theft charm and, with a nod to the Enna, started down the street.

Daric hesitated. "Do you mind?" Without waiting for a reply, a web of concealment was woven around them, so tight that Casco could feel its pressure on his skin.

"Impressive," he said.

With a slight smile, Daric gestured for him to lead the way.

DARIC AND CASCO

Casco and Daric Enna made their way through a short stretch of lightly wooded forest toward the hidden valley where Shen had made his home. Moonlight painted their footing dappled silver, the crisp and clear air heralded a change of seasons at last, and Casco thought he could quite understand why Shen would come here.

"The 'enclave'," Daric remarked. "Misleading name."

Casco shrugged, but the Enna was right. Karesk was merely the hub of a Qalān system that branched spider-like over the surrounding countryside, and many residents chose, like Shen, to live one or two steps away from the community proper.

As they crested the rise, Casco warned him of their approach. The gentle light from his cottage windows flowed out over a path lined with vegetable gardens and berry bushes, but when he came to the door Shen's warmth faded.

He eyed Daric Enna's outline, lurking in the shadows.

"Who de kishlak?"

"Wid me," Casco explained.

Shen beckoned him closer. "Why sa hidin dere, not showin clear …?"

Daric lowered his screen a little and held up his token.

"Lord Pieru sent un," Casco said. "Here to gadder yon bless, take un to un's moder."

Ye be faid'n?

Casco nodded. *Jus wary is all, an star-bright screener, ja.*

Although he was still a little apprehensive, Shen turned and soon a small girl with pale strawberry hair and serious grey eyes emerged from the passageway behind him.

Casco smiled. "Kisha, bless."

Shen pushed her gently forward. "Go to Casco an dis oder-un ere. Deys taken ye dis time now."

"Cana ye be taken me, una Shen?"

Shen shook his head. "Go now, Kisha bless. Casco be seein ye kind."

Casco squatted to be closer to the little one's height.

She stopped right in front of him and looked him in the eye. "Be ye taken me ta Mama?"

"Aye, sho la." Casco smiled gently, and, with the child's tacit permission, scooped her into his arms. She weighed next to nothing, and through her soft young screens he could feel her thoughts, dark and full of fear.

"Be nt scary now, bless. No worries, ja?"

"Be nt afeared!" she said stoutly. "Jus askin is all."

She looked Daric up and down and whispered into Casco's ear, "He be's a badun."

"Aye," Daric nodded. "But a badun who be doin good for ye, sho la." He smiled at Kisha with surprising tenderness, then turned to Casco. "Time be a passin, ja?"

Casco was more than a little shocked, but there was no time to question how it was that an Enna spoke fluent Kareski. He merely nodded as Daric adjusted his screen to cover the three of them.

"Stay close," he said quietly.

Be tellin Gruk to mind Tess we's comin, Casco said to Shen, then they set off for the Imperial Bays.

They moved from shadow to shadow, unseen in the pale moonlight, careful even in this deserted part of Giahn. Kisha seemed to sense the danger and made no sound. At the first portal, Daric stopped Casco before he could sing them through.

"Let me," he said. "We may be under Guild protection, but best if we have no reason to invoke it, don't you think?"

Casco adjusted the weight of the child in his arms. "Be my guest," he said, and stepped back.

As they travelled from portal to portal via a convoluted route, he soon realized Daric's technique was at a level he had never seen before, perhaps even greater than Huldar's. With combinations of voice and mind he was able to bend the paths they followed so that intersections formed on branches that seemed unrelated. Casco strained to catch on, but without proper preparation the danger of trying such methods for himself would be extreme.

Daric Enna's skill with screens was also extraordinary; he wasn't Marked, but Casco thought he must be very close to it. Near the edge of the enclave's border, they passed a knot of Kareski deep in discussion and, although their elbows nearly brushed, Daric kept them from notice.

"How many be leaving?" Daric asked.

"Leaving?" Casco said. "This is our home. We have nowhere to go." He wondered how much the Enna knew.

Daric nodded. "Big things are happening, Casco – strange times ahead."

"I don't know much about that," Casco replied. He adjusted Kisha's slight weight.

Daric gave him a knowing glance. "Well, whatever the situation," he said, "you have allies. And be sure to use only Maatu navigators, and the older they are the more likely to be trustworthy."

"Why Maatu?"

Daric shrugged. "They remember the righteousness of Ishät Ashik's father. No Maatu at the God-Emperor's side now, is there?"

"What's be Maatu?" Kisha asked. Casco had almost forgotten she would be listening.

"A navigator," he answered. "Deys be tall, wid green eyes."

"Ye be meetin un tonight, bless," Daric added. "Goin far."

"Will Mama be dere?"

"Aye," Daric nodded. "All de way to Haaseen."

The next step took them to a familiar side street just outside the enclave's boundaries. "Hush now, bless," Casco whispered. "Be leavin safe ground and into de wide world, ja?"

Kisha nodded and nestled close. Fearful memories of her broken arm last time she left the enclave were very present. When a party of rowdy drinkers spilled from the Red Weyfal's doors, she buried her head in Casco's shoulder.

Sshh, bless, he soothed. *De badun be keepin us safe*, and sure enough, with minimal adjustment to their screen, they skipped through the gaps undetected. Casco looked up at the sign and knew it had indeed been Daric who'd watched him leave with Duvät Gok in tow. Only a few nights gone, but so much had happened it already seemed an age.

"Can you teach me something of your screening technique?" he asked quietly, "And your way with Qalān? I've never seen the like."

"Aye, sho la. But best be workin on gettin de wee bless to her moder dis time, ja?" Daric looked at him thoughtfully. "Be returnin, be time's good. Maybe trade, ja? Your learnin for mine."

Casco made a non-committal reply and wondered what 'learnin' such a one as Daric might be interested in. If asked to do so, would he betray Duvät? The thought was tempting, but he'd given his word.

"De Rukh, deys be a fine people," Daric said, then his language changed back to the mincing accent of Enna. "If they say they will accept Kareski and welcome them, they will. There are other Kareski there, and while some prejudice still occurs, there are no enclaves. Kisha and her family will be safe there, and, dare I say it, better off."

"Let's hope so," Casco agreed.

"You have travelled widely. Why stay here?"

"As I said, this is my home … but if all goes well I may be tempted."

They moved on, avoiding busy streets. All portals that led to the Imperial Bays were now patrolled, so they made their way on foot. Casco changed Kisha's balance again. She weighed little, but he was getting tired.

"Let me?" Daric offered. "The screen will not be disrupted."

"Just for a minute or two while I give my arms a break," Casco said.

The little one went to Daric without complaint.

"Shame we can't put her in Qalān," he said.

Casco went cold. "Never say that!" he hissed.

"Well, it's impossible anyway … right?"

"You don't know …!" Casco stopped himself from snatching Kisha back.

For a moment, Daric studied him out of the corner of his eye. "De Rukh, now," he said smoothly, "deys be honor made real, ja?"

Casco forced himself to calm. Upwelling emotion could disrupt their screen. Daric meant nothing by his comment. How could he know about what happened to Lind? And it was true that it was impossible to put living beings into your own personal Qalān.

"Yes, the Rukh," he answered, proud of his even tone. "To Honor and Protect … I've met the odd arrogant one, but most … you are right. They would never harm Kisha or her parents, having offered them sanctuary."

"Honor," Daric said. "It binds us in the strangest of ways, in the strangest of places. Merely a concept described by a single simple word, yet our whole great Realm, all that we have wrought, would be meaningless without it – our great civilization would collapse into itself."

"I haven't thought about it that way," Casco remarked.

"Not surprising!" Daric chuckled. "But take your ex-Overlord, for example. He behaved without honor and now he's paying the price. His world is destroyed."

Suspicion crept through Casco's mind, cautioning him with cold little fingers. "Only because he got caught."

Daric nodded slowly.

"There are many who behave dishonorably and don't get caught," Casco went on. "Are their lives being destroyed? No. In fact, they prosper. They don't need permits – a permit to work, to travel, to even exist!"

"No. You are right. But it is my belief that each dishonorable act chips away at the lives of all, whether we know or no. Each incident, small or large, undermines our people's contract with El. Our world is coming to a point of crisis, a tipping-point. I can feel it."

Casco nodded. The truth of Daric's words shivered up his spine.

Daric tilted his head to look at him. "You are a person of honor, Casco. One who holds back the tide. Let's hope we are not both swept away when the flood of El's wrath breaks its banks."

For a time they walked in silence, lost in their thoughts, then, with the high dome of the Bays in sight, Kisha wriggled uncomfortably and Casco took her back.

"What is it you do," he asked, "when you're not ferrying fugitive children through the Imperial City?"

"I work for Mirashael of Cantori, a colorful fellow who appreciates my gifts. He's easily underestimated. Have you tried his omosa?"

"Omosa?"

"The finest in the Realm!" Daric Enna assured him.

They paused when they noticed a short queue before the Imperial Bays. Only one of the huge doors was open. The sentry gestured and the line rippled as people stood aside to let others leave the building, then, at another hand movement, they resumed their forward shuffle.

"Where have all these extra guards come from?" Casco said. "Let's hope the way through the refectory is clear."

"No problem," Daric murmured. "If we go via the trade entry, tonight's supervisor is one of Mirashael's."

They continued on. At the refectory entrance there was no queue, but a pair of ashessé stood on alert.

Around the next corner at an unmarked entrance, a round-faced Nhadu cracked the door open, took a quick glance up and down the alley then turned away. Daric led them through a short corridor where the smell of steaming grains leaked from beneath a shiny metal door. Casco flinched at the sudden clang of a dropped pot. A stream of bad language ensued.

Inside, the dining hall was busy as usual. It was protocol that screens be dropped, but for the moment, theirs drew no attention. Daric motioned toward a pair of black-clad ashessé at the Bays entry, ready to scrutinize all who passed through.

"Be un hungry," Kisha murmured.

Casco looked at the food on display. "Have we time?" he asked.

Daric closed his eyes, presumably to scan or communicate with someone. "A little," he said.

They chose a booth. Casco took a deep breath as the last of their screens dissipated.

"Wait here," he said. From the refectory counter he brought back a plate of fried kosh, small sweet tubers native to Giahn.

Kisha's eyes lit up, but after a short hesitation she offered the plate to Casco. "Ye be takin some?"

"Yea, sho la," he said, and selected a small morsel for himself. "But deys a your'n, ja."

She pushed the bowl toward Daric. "Me's tinkin ye's a nary badun, no true?"

Casco was surprised to catch a pulse of sadness in the Enna's veil.

"Bless … a nary badun true for ye," Daric answered, and Casco felt the hairs on his body rise – not as a response to surveillance, but because he knew that at that point, the mysterious archangel would gladly die to protect their small charge.

Oblivious to the significance of Daric's words, Kisha began happily munching down the feast, but halfway through she stopped and looked up expectantly.

"Be savin some for Mama," she said. "I be knowin she's a bidin – jus dere." She pointed to the Bays.

"Time to pull rank, I think." Daric pulled a paper from Qalān. "The Guild-Lord's promised safe passage."

"Let's go then," Casco said. He gave Kisha a bag for the rest of her kosh.

"Ready?" Daric tipped his chin toward the guards. "Permy wid?"

Casco sighed and pulled his travel permit from Qalān. It had been a while since he'd been obliged to show it and he made a mental note to have the Guild update it.

It was risky to link with another's child, but with Kisha's small hand firm in his own, Casco sidled past her juvenile screens and whispered, *Hush now, bless, don't be speakin …* He kept their contact simple and light and there was no backlash.

The guard looked Casco up and down as if unable to decide, but when Kisha turned her face into Casco's legs a guilty flush stained the angel's haze and she waved them through.

Within the Bays, Kisha soon forgot her unease and looked in wonder as people bustled to and fro. Casco was sure she'd never seen so many annangi in one place before. She pointed with delight as a palate of waving lellit vines floated past, buoyed by a pair of cargo singers. Deltas of containers and crates complicated the flow of traffic. Some sported brightly painted logos, others glowered in dark piles as if embarrassed by their more colorful neighbors.

With a happy cry, Kisha slipped from Casco's grasp and darted off between the islands of luggage. He and Daric gave half-hearted chase, but both knew what they would find. They rounded a last mound of boxes and found her wrapped in the arms of her mother.

They hung back for a moment, then a tall, lean navigator leaned toward mother and child. Tess stood up and beckoned them over.

"See!" Kisha said. "Un be Maatu, una Casco, just like ye's tellin! De eyes, deys green."

"Kisha!" Tess scolded, but the navigator smiled.

"Yes, indeed, young one," she said. "I am of House Maatu. Are you ready now?"

Kisha nodded earnestly, but as her mother took her hand, she stopped and looked at Casco and Daric.

"We be comin back, ja, Mama? Comin home soon?"

"Come, Kisha," Tess said gently. "The navigator can't wait."

"But una Casco an de badun? Deys comin too, ja?"

Casco firmed his veil and hunkered down by her side. "Dis time no, bless, but nary I come visitin, sho la." Huge tears welled in Kisha's serious grey eyes. He brushed imaginary dust from her travel cloak. "Ye be taken kind to your mama," he said. "She speaken, you jumpen, ja?"

Kisha nodded and tried to smile. "I's never done it afore."

"Be dat now's de time, bless. Bye for now, ja?"

"Thank you," Tess said. "Thanks to you both."

"Take good care of them," Daric said to the navigator.

"Of course!" she replied. "The journey will be quick with just the three of us. Don't worry, Lord Pieru of Leth is well used to organizing travel plans." She smiled reassuringly. "All is arranged."

Casco and Daric watched as she moved around their designated bay to find exactly the right spot, then she gathered her passengers close and opened her voice. The purity of the sound caught Casco by surprise. When he'd traveled there'd always been spinners forming the main body of the chord; individual travel was beyond the means of most.

The sound of the navigator closed off with a clear chime. For a time, Casco and Daric stood looking at the space where they had been.

"I need a drink," Casco said.

"Red Weyfal?"

"Let's go."

Although his contact with Kisha had been brief, he felt a dent in his heart where her small presence had been. As they made their way toward the familiar alehouse, he wondered if he would feel it, ever so slightly, when the wee bless's journey through the stars had ended and mother and daughter were safe in Haaseen.

With a jar of Besh before him, Casco's thoughts returned to the mystery of Daric Enna.

"Ye be speakin pure, Daric Enna," he said. "How so? Be nary pures taint deyselves tryin."

"Moder Kareski," Daric answered. "She be Marked wid de Tsemkar, ja, an taken by de Clan. Fine lady gone to de Breat dis long time now."

"May she rest sweet." Casco nodded a bow.

"Aye, may she so."

"Be askin how she met de Breat?"

"No."

Daric nursed his ale, his veil and haze tightly bound. He took a long drink and put his glass back onto the table. "Be sayin she … owe no kind to Clan Ashik," he said at last.

"Is that why you helped us?" Casco asked.

"In part."

Casco twisted his glass, watching the heavy fluid swirl. "The other part?"

"Chippy, acourse!"

Casco gave him a doubtful glance and Daric softly laughed. "That's not all – you're right. Best you know no more, Casco of the Uri'madu." He swilled down the last of his drink and gathered himself to be on his way. "Be sayin dis," he added. "Ye needin help for true, be callin me, sho la."

Casco flinched as Daric reached out to touch his forehead. Daric gave him a look, and he let him complete the contact. In a warm and slightly uncomfortable blast, a convoluted identity was imprinted on his mind.

Daric met his gaze. "Use dat, no oder."

The Enna shimmered before his eyes and was gone. Even the ether seemed clean, although with his uniquely implanted call-sign he could feel his new friend's presence fade as he walked away. With a rueful smile he lifted his glass to the night and thought that of all the people he'd met, this one might be the most complicated.

Had Daric sensed Duvät's presence in his home, he wondered, and did that necessarily matter? The Enna seemed well abreast of developments within Karesk … Did he get his information from Pieru, or elsewhere?

"Best you know no more, Casco of the Uri'madu …" Daric Enna's words came back to him, and Casco was inclined to believe them.

It was time to be getting back. His first call would be to the Golden Wheel and another chat with the Guild-Lord, but when he stepped toward the portal, he was stopped by a mean-faced ashessé.

"Permit, please!"

"Permit?" He raised his shoulders. "Why do I need a permit here?"

"Half-breeds need permits." The ashessé scowled. "Permit. Now."

She examined his paper thoroughly, then showed it to her companion. Casco tried not to let his impatience show. Eventually the two seemed to tire of the game and gave it back.

"Move along," she said firmly.

"May I ask why you are guarding this portal?" he asked, determined to be treated at least with some respect.

The ashessé looked him up and down. "Because the God-Emperor wishes it so." Her haze rippled with antagonism. "Tell your … people – no one is to leave."

"No one? What about these?" He waved his permit.

"Not even with those," she said nastily. "Move along!"

He stepped through to the Golden Wheel, glad that Pieru had acted quickly with Kisha, but what now of the others who wished to leave? Was this the God-Emperor's response? He sighed. There were portals known only to Kareski, but dodging an increased ashessé presence would make the job of getting refugees to safety so much harder.

KARESKI TROUBLES

The next morning, Casco looked from his window onto the unkempt grove of nut trees behind his house and wondered where Huldar was now. It had been a long night, and the warm yellow light of sunrise bathed his face and relaxed already tense muscles, but he had little hope of an easy day. His mood was quickly justified as once again his neck hairs prickled. Whoever had watched him throughout the night was either poorly skilled or wanted him to know. Daric Enna would never have been so clumsy.

Duvät whimpered in his room, convinced the Faythans had finally located him. Casco wondered what the Gok had done to deserve such lasting attention. His treatment of Lind had nothing to do with Faytha, but if the chits Huldar had come by were any indication, fully half of his wage from the Explorers' Guild would have been swallowed by gambling debts. Yet although he had received no wage he'd had a purse full of gold and an expensive brooch.

Lucaät of Faytha had been there to greet them and called Duvät his friend … maybe he'd forgiven him his debt for some reason. But Casco shook his head. The same character had held Duvät and tortured him. They were certainly not friends, and if he wanted him dead, he would be.

Another whimper set his teeth on edge. He recalled the trial on Went – another scene that did not fully make sense. When Huldar had pronounced him guilty, Duvät had not seemed overly concerned. When he'd been ostracized, his tonal expression had been almost triumphant. Even when told by the Guild he would have to pay his entire wage as recompense, Duvät's reaction had seemed somewhat rehearsed ... What else had happened on Went? What had they not seen?

What he did know was he had to get Duvät out of his house as quickly as possible.

It was time for another visit to the Hermes. Although Lord Pieru had offered to come and see the Kareski in person he wanted the visit kept secret, so Casco had revealed portals linked to distant valleys they used to grow crops. It was risky, but he could see no other way. The Kareski were using the underground network to bypass the blockade and obtain necessary supplies, and if even one of the links was discovered by the ashessé, the whole system could be exposed.

Getting groups of emigrating Kareski to the Imperial Bays was another matter. All portals that led directly to Sadir were guarded, as were the doors themselves. He had some ideas, but needed to talk them over with Lord Pieru.

"Ah, Casco. So soon?" the Hermes greeted him. "Nary folk be speakin goss!"

"De learnin be well den," Casco replied. "No time be speakin true."

"I am picking it up, aren't I? Shera's helping me too."

"It's a noble cause, bless, an pleased to be helping, sho la."

"Sho la, yes!" She smiled happily and Casco was captured by the transformation. The closed expression she wore when working was revealed as a mask after all.

"Lord Shamkarun Pieru?"

Casco settled into his place at the table. "Yes please."

"You know you don't have to come here … the link I made?"

He winked. "Be uns beamin visage draws me back, sho la, an de starry tea-makin acourse."

Still grinning, she closed her eyes to make the connection. When they flashed open, her face had changed again.

"Good morning, Casco," Pieru said. "Big day. I have some surprises for you."

"Surprises? Should I be worried?"

"Not at all, well, no more than usual."

"So everything is on track? I'll meet you at Fourth Gate and step you through?"

"As planned," Pieru agreed. "The residents understand what to do?"

"Yes. There will be no rush. Key folk are to gravitate as if by accident. You will cover us."

"We don't want to arouse Imperial suspicion. But seriously, no one is happy with this situation. Businesses have lost their workers, and in some cases, their key patrons as well. House Faytha may even turn out to be an ally, in this matter at least. Stranger things have happened."

"And where coin is involved …"

"Exactly."

"I have some ideas about getting folk to the Bays," Casco said. "It has to do with cargo. Many farmers I deal with for the team ship grain through there. I have spoken to some, and also some crafters, and they may be willing –"

"Save it for our meeting, Casco. We'll talk it through then."

"Two hours from now?"

"Two hours."

The Hermes blinked as the connection ended. After a moment of readjustment, they bowed to each other.

"I trust I need not ask for your discretion?" Casco recited the traditional ritual of closure.

"Confidence is maintained, Casco. It is my honor to serve." The Hermes smiled. "I would offer you the tea you seem to think is so marvelous, but there is another waiting."

"Be rattlin bones den, bless, sho la."

"Noder soon enough," she said.

"Be *neider*," he stressed, "noder is 'another'. Close, but not quite right. Say it?"

"Neider soo enough?"

"Starry shinin, bless, starry shinin," he said.

They grinned at each other, then he turned to leave.

At the counter, Shera directed the next customer through. She tipped her head toward the Hermes's rooms. "Best one yet."

He nodded and passed her the coin, but it was hard to erase the messenger's smile from his mind.

The portal known to Kareski as Fourth Gate had no physical marker, but, like most regional portals, was visible if one knew how to search. It linked the enclave by four wide-ranging steps to the outskirts of the Imperial City, or, with a little vocal tinkering, directly to the city of Clouds, or to a remote island off the coast near the Palace of Gates. Huldar thought it could also be used as a step to a spot within the Imperial Palace compound, a site deep in the forest park, but they hadn't been game to try it.

As he waited, Casco watched the shimmering lines of force, ready to detect the slight ripple that would signal Lord Pieru's imminent arrival. It had been one of the first things Huldar had taught him, way back when he was new to the Guild and they had tackled their first assignments together, before the Uri'madu had even been formed.

He compared the sun's position in the sky to his own internal clock. The Guild-Lord should already be there, but he resisted the urge to message him. Surely Pieru would have said if there were problems.

At last the gate shimmered, but before he could speak, it shimmered again and two more archangels stood at the Guild-Lord's side, one a massive Rukh, the other a slender Leth. Then the Fourth Gate gave another shiver and a tall, distinctly Maatu archangel joined them. The extensive Shamkar on the newcomer's cheek glowed with energy.

Pieru noted Casco's expression and smiled. "Casco, let me introduce Tsemkarun Brechan, First of Rukh, and Tiel, First of Leth." He turned to the Maatu and smiled. "And this distinguished fellow is Shamkarun Mael of Maatu, Lord of the Navigator's Guild."

Casco looked at them, dumbfounded.

"The surprise I mentioned?" Pieru prompted.

Casco remembered his manners and bowed low. "My lords!"

Tiel of Leth smiled. "Casco, isn't it? Casco of the Uri'madu, they're calling you. An honor indeed, I am sure. Shamkarun Pieru has told us much about you, and of the plight of your people. On behalf of my father, Arien Leth, I have come to offer the assistance of House Leth."

"And so have Brechan and I," said Shamkarun Mael of Maatu. He was older than the others, and the lines that graced the corners of his eyes sang of wisdom. "Tsemkarun Brechan has come on behalf of the Rukh of course, and I on behalf of the navigators. I understand from Lord Pieru that there is dissent among the Kareski? That some wish to leave and some do not, but all are suspicious, given the current activities of the ashessé – is that right?"

"Yes, it is," said Casco. "The Kareski have been treated badly – but so it has always been."

"Not always," Mael countered. "During the reign of Zohrät Ashik, Kareski were treated with honor, weren't they?"

"Things were better, to be sure, but there has never been a time when we did not feel uncomfortable mixing with ... others."

Mael's eyes narrowed as he searched Casco's face. "Kishlak, I believe you call us?"

Casco winced. "Some of us, yes."

"Well, let us hope that the term is never warranted by my friends here or by me. May this be the dawn of a new era for those of mixed heritage, Casco," he said. "This is our hope."

"It may not be easy at first," Tsemkarun Brechan said, "but we believe the granting of full, unrestricted citizenship to all Kareski on all the worlds of Rukh is a step in the right direction. Maatu and Leth also uphold this pledge, and others will follow."

"We should follow the Trianog in this," Tiel said. "No one should be judged on their choice of marriage partner."

Brechan tilted his head. "Not in this case at least, but the restriction on marriages between ourselves and the Cantori are not unwarranted."

She smiled kindly. "So you say, but love is love, by Asheru's light, and who are we to gainsay it? Kareski are blessed and marked, the same as all others. They have good and bad, the same as all others."

The Rukh's monumental poise shifted, just slightly, but his veil and haze were held in impeccable neutrality and it was impossible to tell how he felt.

"We of House Leth are proud to support you in this way," Tiel continued. "This sad state of affairs has highlighted the need for an honorable stance rather than a compliant one – a decision which has long been avoided."

Mael nodded slowly. "Well said, but come, we have a meeting to attend. Casco, if you could lead the way?"

"Certainly." Casco bowed again, then led them over the ridge to another portal. Grass crunched lightly behind him, and the pressure of four huge presences made his own haze seem small indeed. He wondered how his people would react when they met the Firsts of two Great Houses and the Lords of the Explorers' and Navigators' Guilds, present in Karesk of their own accord? It was an unprecedented event and he was about to be part of it.

THE AGENT

In a neatly appointed tea-house in Sadir, Lucaät's agent stirred his tea with a disinterested motion and listened to a group of lower-echelon archangels giggle over the latest gossip from the Imperial Palace.

"… and he's so handsome!" The speaker fanned her face. "I'd die if he even looked my way!"

"Well, we'll never see him down here, so you'll not be joining the Breath any time soon," her friend said dryly.

"But how could he refuse them all?"

"And I heard that Aliciiel Enna's gown was positively dripping with tiny fire-opals and her headdress was two full hand-spans high," another said. "All made of the finest purple silver with pearls from Manziat, you know, those blue ones?" She sighed. "So beautiful."

"Symbolizing higher thoughts above …"

"And fire down below!"

There was an eruption of shrill laughter. The Agent drank more tea and wondered why he bothered.

"Aqumät Ashik has a lover," one said salaciously, "female this time, or so I heard."

The Agent sipped again more thoughtfully. This, at least, was news.

"So?" One of the gossipers tapped the table to emphasize her argument. "A lover is one thing – to refuse to marry is another. His father is the God-Emperor. He has a duty."

"Well, it may be that marriage is his duty," their heads bent close as the dour one's voice lowered, "but it is El who blesses, and if his father is anything to go by …?"

There was another bout of laughter, more hushed this time. One glanced over her shoulder and saw the Agent looking at them. She returned to her friends with her fingers over her lips.

The Agent sighed and got up. Furtive eyes watched him leave, but as he stepped through the door he heard them giggle again.

It was almost midday when he reached Crafters, and sweat dribbled down his back. He crossed to the shady side of the street and settled into a rhythmic stride, thinking as he walked. Busy woodworkers filled the air with the smell of exotic timbers. Outside the workshops he saw everything from quaint carvings of Giahn's more exotic flora and fauna to tables and cabinets fit for a lord. They sang as they worked, charms to preserve the use-life of the wood, threads for shaping or binding – the Agent let the sound wash over him while his mind worked furiously on the problems at hand.

He was certain Daric Enna had Duvät Gok hidden somewhere. It was impossible to track Daric, but if he was involved, so was Mirashael of Cantori. Yet for all the time he'd spent watching Mirashael's shop, drinking endless cups of tea and tankards of ale in all the local establishments, he'd seen and heard nothing of use.

Brätan Gok had come to the same dead end. He'd even tried to seize the long-suffering wife and use her marriage bond to locate Duvät, a scandalous move to be sure, and his plan might have yielded results if not foiled by the timely arrival of none other than the enigmatic Mirashael of Cantori. Mirashael again …Then, a few days later, Leahät Gok had come to visit him. His gut feeling was that the two were working together, but neither behaved as if they were hiding anything – well, anything new, at least. Mirashael's collection of secrets was reputedly vast.

Lucaät of Faytha did not seem overly concerned. "Shit floats," he said. "Duvät will bob up soon." But the Agent's Cantori heart couldn't let it rest. And besides, Daric Enna had stolen the Gok from beneath his very nose. There was a score to settle.

A pair of ashessé sauntered by, black leather uniforms shiny and new. They seemed to be everywhere since Duvät had managed to kill one – the thuja nest his boss had promised. But perhaps the 'peace-keepers' would have some useful information for him. He had a friend on duty in the Imperial Bays who might appreciate a free lunch.

Amid the noise and bustle of the refectory, the Agent spotted his contact, a burly Ashik with tightly braided hair.

"Wouldn't you rather the Spring Hatchling?" he suggested. "Nhadu place – much quieter."

"If we stay here there's no chance I'll be late back for my shift," she pointed out, and to be fair, last time he'd eaten with her, time had rather gotten away.

He surveyed the basic range of food on offer. "Are you sure?" he sighed.

"Lucaät of Faytha has spoiled you, sweet-lips," she answered.

"Nothing wrong with a steady income."

He studied his choices again, looking for inspiration, but it was hopeless. The menu hadn't changed for at least a hundred years.

"So, kavesh or omosa?" he said.

"Kosh, I think, and the amberry sauce, that looks nice. And you?"

"It probably looked nice ten years ago," he said. "I'll stick with the omosa."

"They won't be as good as Mirashael's."

"Yes, yes." He rolled his eyes. "The finest in the Realm! Believe me, I know."

"Short on sleep, are we?" his contact said archly.

They wove through the lunchtime crowd to a table at the back, the only one available.

"So," his companion selected a finger-length kosh and bit its end off in a rather decisive way, "what do you want?"

"Information."

Leather creaked as she shrugged. "But who is it, sunshine? You know the cost will vary."

"How about Duvät Gok?"

She didn't even glance at the mental image he showed her.

"Never heard of him," she said flatly.

"Killed an ashessé some weeks back?"

"Oh! Him? Didn't the Gok disown him?" She dipped another kosh into the sauce and ate with enjoyment. "Hated Marvät Gok anyway. Less buck than a maffit."

"How about Leahät Gok?" he tried.

"The wife?" The ashessé paused to wolf down another morsel. "Been seen in Crafters, working for Mirashael."

"What sort of work? Any … connections there?"

"Waiting tables as far as I can tell. Probably needs the income."

The Agent sighed sharply. He already knew as much.

"What do you want me to say, sweet-lips?" the contact said. "That she's some note in Mirashael's shadier dealings? Singing the wrong song there, sunshine. Poor wee thingy looks like a stiff breeze'd blow her over."

He rolled his eyes. His companion's determinedly muscular bulk made most people seem flimsy. It made sense that Leahät Gok would be looking for work, but how did that tie in with Mirashael's "rescue"? Was there a history there that he didn't know about?

"Is that it?" The ashessé said firmly. "Bowl's nearly empty."

"Daric Enna."

At last, she smiled. "Ahh, the elusive Daric Enna. Now you're getting interesting."

"What can you tell me?"

"As it turns out, there has been a sighting right here."

"In the Bays?"

"In the company of a half-breed, Casco. Known Kareski trouble-maker, but the troos on duty didn't detain him. Said he had papers. Child with him – his own maybe?"

The Agent's heart beat faster. "Where did they go?

She put her elbows on the table and beckoned him closer. "No one saw them leave, but later on the half-breed was spotted outside the Red Weyfal, you know it? On the Kareski borders. Mixed clientele, but that's about to change. Can't clean this city up fast enough!"

The Agent put another seafood parcel in his mouth and chewed, but the taste barely registered. His brain whirred. Something was about to make sense: he knew it.

The ashessé leaned back, ready to leave. She put her hand out. "Two golds."

"Two golds!"

"Times are tough, sunshine," she retorted. "Wages have been cut, did you know that? All the coin's in Faytha's coffers, and take more than a good Shamkarun to charm it out again. Steady income like yours is where it's all going."

"The Imperium cut your wages? But there are more ashessé every day."

"Place is a mess."

The Agent was shocked by the venom in her voice. She took the golds and sauntered back to her post. He picked at the last of his meal while his brain spun a web of connections. If Duvät was dead, Leahät would be incapacitated for some time – but she was serving customers with Mirashael of Cantori, so he was still alive. Mirashael owned Daric Enna, and Daric had been seen with Casco, one of the Uri'madu … could it be that Duvät was hidden in Karesk? He hurried to his rendezvous with Lucaät, certain he'd solved the puzzle.

The Agent leaned forward to make his final point. "… however, with the situation in the city of half-breeds, ashessé everywhere and all on high alert, Duvät's re-capture and extraction will be difficult in the extreme."

He waited while Lucaät lifted a glass of fragrant pink wine and took a ruminative sip. His own ale remained untouched.

"But this is excellent," Lucaät congratulated him at last.

"It is?"

"Yes. If Duvät is in Karesk," Lucaät continued, "with the situation as it is, he'll be as trapped there as the rest of the misbegotten scum – for quite some time I've been led to expect. No, my friend, time is coin and I can make better use of you elsewhere. Maybe there is another with information we can use? As I've said, Karesk may be beyond us right now, but Shamkarun Huldar of Leth, where is he?"

"I understand he's on his way to Frith."

Lucaät smiled, and the Agent realised the question about Huldar's movements had been rhetorical.

"Get yourself to the Bays," Lucaät said cheerfully. "There's a navigator on standby. With a short chord, you'll reach Frith in less than a week – soon after they do. I have a plan."

The Agent sighed. Tight travel? Just the navigator and days and days of continuous sound with little room to move and nothing to distract him? "I'll need extra pay to compensate for the stress," he grumbled.

Lucaät laughed sourly. "Perhaps a bonus when you get back. Now, here's what I want you to do. It will be a tricky operation, to undertaken with the utmost sensitivity, you understand? But you are the best I have and more than capable."

ON THE WAY TO FRITH

Huldar flexed his shoulders and tramped his feet up and down to get a feel for the gravity of the planet Lisbo.

A fresco depicting groves of bright yellow flowers spanned the rounded back wall of the Lisbo Bays, but when Huldar looked more closely, he couldn't help but smile. Wart-covered creatures with bristling antennae lurked beneath the blooms, caterpillars munched on stalks and petals, and many of the flowers were past their prime. Supporting the building, one stone pillar was carved to resemble a tree. Flying creatures with long tails and outstretched wings perched among its boughs. Another sported a spiraling relief of the terrifying 'flying teeth' of Bersk.

"Been here before?" Inshogi asked.

"Only once," Huldar replied, "and that was a long time ago." He indicated the fresco. "Can't say I remember this."

"Yes," Inshogi said. "I am a great fan of Bethan of Nhadu's work. There are charms sung into it – have you sensed them yet?"

Huldar stepped closer to the wall. Now he knew the charms were there he could sense a faint psychic hum coming from a group of wide-mouthed amphibians with blue-spotted backs. He recognized them as glubber, native to Cantor.

Inshogi gave an encouraging grin, so he leaned forward and grazed one with his fingertips. His touch triggered the image to jump forward and make a noisy fart.

"Breath!" he swore. "I've never encountered a charm like that!"

Inshogi laughed. "Try another! They're all delightful." They smiled as Andel joined them. "He's found his first charm, my dear. The farting glubber!"

Andel shook her head. "Father," she smiled, "you're such a child."

"He laughed as well!" Inshogi said.

When she took Huldar's arm, a burst of warm affection flowed into him.

"There are other charms set right through it," she said, and led him toward another part of the painting. "I like this one."

She pointed to a group of caterpillars clustered on a bloom they had almost completely destroyed. With a wave of her hand, the caterpillars split open and a grove of singing butterflies took to the skies, their wings the sunny yellow of the flowers they had consumed.

Inshogi called them. "Come away now. There will be time to play with the picture later. Ninjay is exhausted and we must find our lodgings."

"I'm famished," Andel agreed, but as Huldar went to follow, a gentle force whispered through his soul.

Andel said. *You coming?*

I'll be there soon, he assured her, *but I feel something inside.*

Andel turned. He shared his puzzlement.

I think it's … The Breath, he told her. Blood rushed to his cheeks.

The Breath?

The feeling intensified as he acknowledged it, and although he felt embarrassed, he knew he was right.

I have to stay here; I think there's something I have to see – in the picture.

The Breath wants you to look at a fresco?

Andel shrugged, acquiescent but not quite believing, and he had to admit that, 'I feel the Breath in this' was a phrase usually used to assure oneself and/or others a decision had been taken for the right reasons. No one – or at least no one he knew of – felt an actual breeze beneath their ribs. Maybe Lisbo had a soul, just as Went did, and that was what had caused the sensation … but either way, he had to listen.

Catch up as soon as you can, Andel said, and left to find her parents in the food-hall.

Huldar sensed dozens of charms in the imagery on the wall but none had any influence on the strange disturbance he felt. Then he came to a design featuring a beautiful green creature with small, glossy-red wing coverlets that resembled drops of blood, and the wind inside him seemed to pause.

He brushed the charm with his fingertips. The vibration was powerful, but sweet too, like the insect pictured.

Searching for the trigger involved sorting through a complex web of threads and counter-threads, but when he unraveled the knot, the blood bug scuttled for a burrow hidden below the flowers and sealed it behind, leaving no trace. Even the charm faded as if it had never been.

How did it do that? he asked himself. He ran his fingers over the space where the bug had been, but even the tingle of the charm was gone. He waited for the bug to reappear, but the plaster remained empty. He stretched his senses to the limit, but could detect nothing, not even a residue. It seemed impossible.

Bethan of Nhadu? How had she done it? There were skilled charm-singers among the Nhadu of course, but until now, he'd never thought of them as someone he should learn from.

His stomach rumbled. The strange feeling that had led him there had vanished with the creature down the burrow. When a fresh batch of travelers eyed him, he knew it was time to join Andel and her family at their meal. He retraced the charm and committed the steps to memory. It would be good to have a fresh puzzle to occupy his mind while they were in the Chime.

THE MEETING

One by one, in small groups or singly as they came, Casco watched the Kareski dissipate. As they left the cover of Pieru and Mael's screen their walk seemed more purposeful. Each had a task to perform, and most were confident they could achieve it.

"Well done, Casco."

Casco turned and found himself facing Mael of Maatu's neck. He'd forgotten how tall the navigator was.

"I think – no, I am sure our plans can work," Mael continued, "and as many of your people as want to do so will be able to safely relocate." He turned as Shamkarun Pieru approached. "Your thoughts?"

"Yes, I agree," said Pieru. "This is a great thing we have started here. Let's hope the Imperial backlash is not too severe, once he gets wind of what is happening. We must strive to keep our activities hidden for as long as possible.

"With the greatest respect, Casco," Mael said, "your people are of huge importance to the Imperial City as a source of cheap labor. While that can't be condoned, I am surprised by this lock-down. What does Ishät think to accomplish here? It makes no sense. Does he think to force you into slavery?"

"Maybe," said Pieru, "but Kareski make poor slaves."

"How so?"

"Most die. They cannot adapt to those … unspeakable chains!"

"Ah!" Mael searched Casco's face. "Too much the archangel. Stands to reason. Well no Maatu will transport slaves or potential slaves or knowingly support such activities in any conceivable way, I can guarantee you that!"

"Our God-emperor's actions are beyond understanding," Tiel said quietly. "The chains are his own innovation. How can he claim it is El's will to abuse his people so?"

A careful silence followed, but Casco could see that the leaders around him agreed.

"Not all navigators are Maatu," he said to Mael. "What of them? I can believe it of Trianog, but the Enna are Tiamäti."

"Training to be a navigator is intense," Mael replied. "Many centuries of study are needed to achieve full status. In that time, bonds are forged and we become as family. Navigators pride themselves on being their own Realm within the Realm."

"But does this hold true for the Enna among you?"

Mael gave him a wry smile. "As Guild-Lord, I must say yes, but in truth? Have no fear. Only trusted individuals will be tasked with your transport."

Casco wanted to mention an idea he'd had about using other gates, but the matter of transport for Duvät bubbled closer to the surface and he held back.

"I think the God-Emperor wants to divert us from other problems within the Realm," Pieru went on. "Polarize opinions and give people clear alternatives to hold their attention."

"I doubt the Faythans see it that way," Tiel of Leth said softly.

Casco turned as Tiel of Leth and Brechan of Rukh entered the discussion, and wondered again how he had become included in such company. Tiel met his gaze with kindness. The tone of her haze reminded him of Huldar's and a sense of kinship flowed easily between them, but Tsemkarun Brechan of Rukh was even more massive than Cobar, and twice as intimidating. His tawny, archangelic gaze roved the horizon as if he was on constant alert. But when their eyes unexpectedly met, Casco was surprised to sense respect.

"Maybe the Faythans are the very ones he wants to distract," Pieru said to Tiel.

"I have heard conjecture that our God-Emperor is driven mad by gossip," said Mael, "but surely that has nothing to do with this."

"Whatever the reason," Pieru continued, "this is the situation. We are breaking no rules by helping these people escape their circumstances – just bending them a little, and with the majority of Houses in agreement, there should be nothing to fear."

Mael turned to Casco. "I thought you were about to speak, earlier. Was there something?"

He shook his head. "It's nothing. I'm sure you've thought of it already."

"Casco, you are a vital part of this operation. Please, if you have something to add?"

Casco steeled himself, then went ahead, "I was wondering about the other Imperial Palaces."

"Go on."

"Four of them, Winds, Sands, Gates and Snows, each have their own navigational Bays. I know access to them is restricted, but we, the Uri'madu, used Sands once when there was a problem with the Imperial Bays. Is there any way we can utilize them now?" he asked. "For instance, Snows is rarely visited by the Imperial family and usually only inhabited by maintenance staff."

"A good point, Casco," Mael said, "and there are times when the other three are all but vacant also – but the problem is that some navigators, the more talented and experienced among us, can tell if other gates are used. Shamkarun Kandät Enna, for example, is one such."

"But if all navigators are family?"

"We are," Mael said dryly, "but Kandät is also kin to the God-Empress and is the God-Emperor's favored navigator."

"He was our navigator to Went."

"Yes he was." Mael paused as if thinking. "But if we were clever about timing – you may have a good point. One can hear nothing else while in the Chime. Precision coordination would be the key, getting all suspect navigators in transit at the same time. There will be greater risk and a need for rapid mobilization – are your people up to it?"

"Some, certainly."

"Then it is an idea we will take further." He looked at Pieru. "Time to collapse the screen?"

Pieru nodded. "Casco, would you help us? Practice for next time, should you need to use this configuration."

Casco jumped at the chance.

The inner screen, an almost airtight bubble over an area the size of several houses, was conjured with the combined efforts of Brechan's Tsemkar and Mael's song. On its own in Karesk, such massive expertise would have been sure to attract attention, but the inner bubble had been shrouded by an artfully inept outer charm, and the whole had gone unnoticed. He wondered what Daric Enna would make of it. Was he watching them? He couldn't sense him nearby, but that was no good indication.

They paused at Fourth Gate.

"What must be done?" Brechan prompted him.

"Assemble the first group here at the seventh hour after midday tomorrow, ready for passage to Haaseen," Casco recited. "Travel in twos and threes. Permits to be returned for potential reassignment after their owners have reached their new home planets – is there anything else I should be aware of?"

"Best not to know too many details," Brechan said. "Twenty in the first group, no more."

Casco stifled a flash of frustration.

Brechan looked at him sharply.

"There will be more every day, Casco," Tiel soothed. "This is just the first step. Our project has not been so easy to organize, and we are very much feeling our way."

"Despite what Pieru says, the threat of Imperial backlash is real," Brechan said. "I hope your Kareski fully understand."

Casco took a deep breath. "So, with the first party to Haaseen – Lord Brechan of Rukh, will you be here to greet them?" he asked. "I understand you have many more important duties, but it will give confidence to those who wait."

Brechan nodded sharply. "But for subsequent groups, I can only promise that an archangel of Rukh will be in attendance."

"And Lentath, the same," said Tiel of Leth.

"Other Houses will send their representatives," Pieru said. "They will be vouched for, Casco. I will see to it."

"Very well," Casco replied. His heart raced as the reality of action dawned on him.

"Vigilance," the Rukh cautioned, then the visitors were gone.

On his way home, Casco thought hard about his warning. As a House, they did not waste words and were loyal to a fault, but the Kareski had been oppressed for so long and they were frightened. The appearance of such high-status guests had stunned them, and he feared that for many the prospect of resettlement had assumed an air of fantasy. Such exalted beings … even to him it seemed unreal. Despite their best efforts, word would get out, he knew it, and what would happen then?

Nothing good, he said to himself. *Nothing good.*

When he reached his home, Duvät jumped up from the lounge.

"Where have you been?" His gaze darted nervously. "Have you organized a navigator? I must leave here, now. Right now! If they find me, they'll find you, and that won't be good, will it?"

Casco pushed him aside. "I'm working on it," he said. "Glad to see you haven't tried to pilfer anything."

Despite the bruise that lingered on his face, Duvät looked a lot healthier for some rest and a few good meals, but mentally … he was not so good. Casco had to find a way to get him to the Bays, but in this undertaking he was on his own. He thought again of Daric, but something told him it would not be a good idea to involve his new friend. His presence the other night had genuinely unnerved Duvät. Perhaps he should've asked Shamkarun Mael when he had the opportunity, but that didn't seem right either.

"I'll try again this afternoon," he said.

"Should I pack my things?" Duvät sneered.

"There's a blockade around the enclave – no one in or out."

Duvät gave a savage sigh. He turned his face to the wall and bumped his head against it, slowly and rhythmically. "Doomed," he said. "There's no hope, is there? Everyone hates me. Why is it so difficult to get away? If everyone despises me so much, they should make it easy for me to go."

As Casco passed, Duvät reached out and grabbed his arm. A bolt of darkness stabbed through the contact. "They know I'm alive," he whispered emphatically. "They'll come for me."

Casco shook himself free. There was work to do. He had to meet with key organizers, get groups ready, teach others the necessary steps so their movement would be beyond Imperial surveillance – but the deterioration of Duvät's state of mind worried him.

No telling what the vindictive kalla might do, Casco thought to himself. He ate a quick meal and left for the Golden Wheel, determined to get rid of him as soon as may be.

After a short wait, Shera ushered him in ahead of the queue. "Dere ye go, bless," she said. "You de biggun now, sho la, and none be chuckin tanties if deys wise."

The Hermes stood to greet him, but he waved her down. "You look exhausted."

"I am," she replied. "I've sent for help, but there are complications – the same complications that have made me so busy!" When she smiled, a peculiar joy spread through Casco and he smiled in return.

"Lord Pieru again?" she asked.

"No, this time I need to book a navigator."

A very slight frown passed over the Hermes face. "Are you leaving?"

"Not for me. It's for a friend."

He knew she's caught his hesitation over the word 'friend'.

"I shall contact the Navigators' Guild…" she started briskly, but he lifted his hand before she was gone.

"Can you make the actual booking … as if it were for me?"

The Hermes looked at him, her mien politely neutral. "Yes – I can do that."

Casco nodded. "Thank you. A delicate matter. I appreciate your help."

"When and where to?" she asked.

"As soon as possible," he said. "To any remote planet within a seventy-gold radius."

Her eyebrows flickered minutely, then she closed her eyes.

He waited.

"Do you have the coin with you?" she asked.

"Yes, I do."

She nodded, her eyes still closed.

"Erma? Passage for one to the Planet Erma is available."

"Perfect." His lips relaxed in a slight smile. Erma was a rugged outpost in the same galactic region as Manziat. It had few amenities and even fewer visitors.

When the Hermes opened her eyes and looked into his, he noticed a web of pale yellow filaments in the blue.

"Twenty-eight gold," she said. "Tenth hour after midday. Bay twenty-seven – it's near the back?"

"I know where it is," Casco assured her.

"The navigator will meet you there. No need to take coin with you; I've paid on your behalf. Perhaps your 'friend' can take themselves to the Bays and spare you the danger?"

"Perhaps." He smiled and counted coin from the purse Duvät had given him. The sigil on it was Faythan. The Hermes looked at him with questions in her eyes.

He frowned, trying to think what to say, and in that instant, all signs of emotion left her. No shred of curiosity remained. It was as if he was seated opposite a living statue.

"My apologies, Casco of the Uri'madu," she said as if to her hands. "Such disrespect will not happen again."

"Please," he said, "there is nothing to forgive." He floundered. It had been his hesitation. She'd taken it as censure. The open way she'd shown interest, asking personal questions – in the eyes of her people, this Hermes had committed a grave offence, but he enjoyed their easy rapport and even encouraged it. He wished he could take her hand and explain, but this would also be a serious breach of protocol and he doubted it would make things better.

Instead, he continued counting coins. When he was done she swept them into a purse of her own, placed it in Qalān, then looked at him with such complete neutrality that he could think of nothing more to say except the ritual closure, "I trust I need not ask for your discretion?"

His heart twisted as she bowed with immaculate precision and recited the closure, "Confidence is maintained. It is my honor to serve."

MIRASHAEL AND LEAHÄT

Leahät Gok picked up the last ledger and replaced it in Mirashael's strongbox. The breadth and volume of his clientele amazed her, and all from his humble premises in the woodworkers' district. Some of the balance sheets were simple, the day-to-day workings of the shop itself, but the trade in fine carving and wooden utensils was far more complex. There were many high-volume Faythan buyers, as well as individual purchasers, raw materials obtained from Lethian and Rukh growers, bulk supplies from Cantori, goods delivered and received and meticulous records of commissions paid to Nhadu crafters. She could feel her horizons widening. There was a whole Realm out there she'd forgotten even existed.

As for her employer's less reputable dealings, it was highly unlikely a Cantori would keep no records, but at this stage she had seen nothing of them. With luck he would continue to keep such matters entirely to himself.

There was a light scritch-scratch on the door and Mirashael entered bearing two fragrant juices and a bowl of steaming omosa.

"Ah! My lady Gok is finished already?" He placed the food and drink on the table. "Truly, you are a miracle, and a more fitting reward shall be found."

He dashed from the room and returned in short order with a bunch of gloriously scented hereny flowers.

She put her nose to the blooms and breathed deep. Was this scoundrel courting her?

"Hopefully my books will continue to smell as sweet!" he quipped.

"Mirashael of Cantori!" Although she tried to sound scandalized, her heart fluttered like a girl's and sadness crept up from beneath.

"Eat," he said, and pushed the omosa toward her. "You are too thin, dear lady. I worry about you."

She frowned. "Why did you come to my house?" she asked. "You knew Brätan Gok's ashessé were there."

There was a moment of buzzing silence, and her new friend looked at her; she had never seen him uncertain of himself before. "I admit to an interest in you," he blustered. "Ever since you came here, so lost, so desperate, yet strong enough to strike a hard bargain, I … was watching out for you."

"But I felt no one's presence," she said – was it comforting that he had been watching her, or a little off-putting?

"No. There are ways, my lady, not so ingenuous as this side of my business I'm afraid. But you need not worry about such things! No, no, no. You are a ray of light come to ease my day, and I would not burden you with such darkness."

"But I am already burdened, Mirashael. My husband is still alive, if you recall."

"We can rescind the contract, if this is your desire," he said cautiously.

"No!" She struggled as difficult emotions welled up beneath her careful veil. "I want nothing more than to be free of his bond, and he deserves death, believe me." She pulled a handkerchief from Qalān and dabbed at her face. "I'm sorry. It's just that … you are very kind, yet I imagined you such a rogue. And I am so tired."

"Tired?"

"The things he did still prey on my dreams." She glanced upward, toward her new rooms. "I hoped that with the change of residence … but I fear I will never be able to sleep well again."

"Sometimes it helps to talk," Mirashael said. "In my line of work, there is little I have not seen, and I will be as a Naghari in this. Your trust will not be betrayed."

His kindly gaze held her, but how could she tell him, or anyone, of the horrors she had been made to live through?

"What haunts you, Leahät?" he pressed. "What has he done to hurt you so badly?"

She drew a ragged breath. "Night after night," she began, "I relive the events. Our marriage bond – I was forced to share his experiences, almost as if I was doing those things myself." Horrid images flooded her mind even though she battled to keep them hidden. "Lind, that poor angel, how could he use her so brutally? And those creatures, poor defenseless things, he took such joy in …" Her voice choked on the words.

"In what, my lady?" Mirashael prompted cautiously.

"… In ripping out their eyes!"

"In what?" His face twisted in abhorrence.

"He ripped out their eyes!" she sobbed. "They were singing and he ripped them out – with his fingers! And he laughed!" Tears flowed as she remembered the horror of it. "Then Lind found them. That was what he used to trap her. Soon after, I went to Shamkarun Kraviel Enna and he helped me shut down the bond as far as we possibly could, and it hurt, Mirashael, it hurt a lot! But that pain was good and clean compared to the pain my husband caused. How could he do that?"

She hugged herself with crossed arms and tried smother the vile scenes beneath veils of politeness, but as if it had life of its own, the truth refused to be buried again so soon.

Mirashael's tentative touch made her flinch. "I would not hurt you, Lady Gok. Leahät ..." he said quietly. "I would never hurt you – I promise."

He touched her shoulder again, and she let him draw her into his arms. Fresh pain bubbled to the surface, almost too much to bear, and he let it wash through them both without resistance.

The pain is real, he said to her tears, *and justified. There is no shame in the release of such malignancy. Let it come, let us face it together and in its own time, it will pass. I know this,* he whispered. *It will flow with the Breath, drawn in by El and breathed again out by Lady Asheru, whole and clean again ...*

I didn't want him to suffer ...

And neither should you, but I can understand why you seek his death. I have tried to fulfill your contract, however there are others who wish him dead also ... but not before they discover what he is hiding. Tentatively he turned to her. "My lady, I think this is it. This is the secret ... this terrible thing."

"But the trial had been conducted."

"No, the suffering of poor Lind is horrible, but no mystery – yes, but the creatures, their eyes. What else can you share with me about them?"

Her soul convulsed and Mirashael said quickly, "Not the hideous things, no, no, no! Not that, not for now – but what else do you remember? What were the events leading up to it?"

"I'll try," said Leahät. She recalled the creatures again. Duvät's great bloodlust was still there, but now she had shared with Mirashael, it was no longer her standing on the lonely beach. Now she could see it was her husband who committed the atrocity, and he who had forced her to bear witness. She started to think – there had been many trips to that long, sandy shore, but before that – and before that again … what had changed?

She lifted her gaze to Mirashael's. "My husband's grandfather died and Duvät inherited his desk. At first, he hated it," she said, "but before I could arrange for it to be removed, he changed his tune – seemed to fall in love with it … so much so he even took it to Went with him."

"A desk? Where is it now?" Mirashael asked.

"At the Explorers' Guild with the rest of his belongings, I expect," she replied.

When he smiled, the old shrewdness had returned, and Leahät decided she liked it.

He gestured toward the door. "Then, my lady, we should accept this challenge! We should go to the Guild and see what secrets this artifact holds."

———

Leahät's heart skipped nervously as she and Mirashael approached the glowing pillars of the Explorers' Guild. "What if they won't let me see it?"

Mirashael paused. "Has anyone indicated that such might be the case?"

"No."

"As it happens, I have a few connections within the Guild. Did you receive a letter?"

She nodded. "It said that since the Guild paid for their transport and Duvät had been evicted from his membership, ownership of his possessions had reverted to me and I could claim or dispose of them as I wish."

Sympathy shone in his gaze. "I will be with you," he said. "But if it is too much, we will leave and return when you are stronger."

"Leave?" The offer surprised her. "But you would be disappointed."

"Dear lady, it is true that there is an element of selfishness among my motivations. The potential for financial gain, and the answer to a riddle – these are games I play, but I would never amuse myself at your expense. If it is too much, we will go."

Leahät looked back the way they'd come. Afternoon parasols bobbed to and fro in the golden heat. Parties of tourists chatted excitedly and craned their necks to study the architecture of the Guild precinct. Soaring above the rest of the city, the famous glass dome of the Imperial Bays caught the light in multicolored rays. Once, the Navigators' Guild had resided there. Now they made their home in a new hall in Hesh, but there were still offices and Guild representatives at work in the ancient building, organizing the comings to and goings from the heart of the Realm. She had heard it said that without them, the whole of Giahn would draw to a halt.

"If we left for now, would I still be able to work for you?" she asked Mirashael.

He smiled, his shrewd self again. "I would be devastated if it were not so."

With that, her mind was made up.

"Let's see what we can find, then." She turned for the Explorers' Guild's magnificent double doors. "We're here now, and I have the letter."

After a brief consultation at the front desk, an usher came to guide them to where Duvät's effects were held. Leahät started to follow, but paused as Mirashael lingered by the counter. She sensed a rapid psychic exchange between himself and the receptionist.

"The concierge is an old friend of mine," he explained as he joined her. His smile never slipped. "I merely asked that he safeguard our privacy."

She tried to gauge the level of shrewdness beneath his innocuous veil and decided that there was probably more to it than he'd said.

As they made their way through the maze of halls and passageways, she was glad of the guide. Finally they arrived at an enormous open room crammed with boxes and miscellany. Despondent white tags hung from each pile.

"Over there, to the left." The usher passed a quick image of the location.

Leahät thanked her, but she could already sense her husband's belongings as if they gave off their own particular stench. Beyond a long row of tall shelves, in between a stack of dark wooden crates and a shapeless heap of carpets, they cowered beneath the plush floor rug that had seen so many planets.

She froze, unprepared for the emotional bolt they provoked.

Mirashael continued on. With a flick of his wrist, the rug slipped aside, and there was that bed, that divan, those cushions – Leahät could barely breathe as images of Lind's distress flooded back. The desk crouched among the objects like a waiting beast. Images of mutilated sea creatures haunted her.

"I can cover it again?" Mirashael offered.

She shook her head. This must be faced.

Mirashael stood beside her and quietly took her hand. Compassion came through with unexpected strength. Her eyes blurred with tears.

It was not your fault, he said.

The words moved slowly through her psyche.

You could not have stopped him.

But the things he did! I knew he was bad, but … not evil. Should I have known? I married him. How could I have been so … naïve? She hung her head. *At some level I must have known.*

Mirashael gave her fingers a gentle squeeze. "It is past, Lady Gok, and you are here. It has taken courage and strength for you to come to this place. Are you ready to look?"

She nodded and wiped her eyes. The song was sung, as the saying went. An coda of tears added nothing.

The dented timbers loomed large in her mind. "That's it."

Mirashael pushed the divan aside to examine the desk and its contents. At first she hung back, but when another drawer was opened the smell of anise came to her and she stepped forward. Suddenly it was as if she could see Duvät standing there, and she remembered something, a furtive movement, a guilty look ... "Try the little ones at the top."

Mirashael turned his attention to a nest of four small, square draws almost at eye-level. His fingers danced above the simple latches. "There's a charm at work there," he said, "but I think ... yes! There it is."

The first held a collection of notes. He said, "Gambling chits, I believe," and with a sympathetic glance, passed them to Leahät.

She started reading. A large figure swam into focus, then another even larger. Sheet by sheet, the sums added quickly. "We would have nothing left!" she exclaimed. Yet Duvät had come to her with coin from Lucaät of Faytha, his principal creditor. How could that be?

"You knew?" her companion asked.

"I did know that he gambled," she admitted hopelessly. "I was constantly bailing him out – my jewelry, furniture, there was nothing much left. I thought I had paid all that was owed … but he had hidden this!"

"No wonder Lucaät of Faytha was after him!" Mirashael said. "Met him in the Bays, I believe. Had no intention of letting him out of his sight."

"Lucaät of Faytha?

"Yes, I assure you, my lady, it was as if they were the greatest of friends."

"Duvät came to me … it was the day before you came – before Brätan Gok. He had coin, lots of it, in a purse with the rune of Faytha worked into the leather. I still have most of it."

"You still have it?"

She nodded.

Mirashael seemed at a loss for words, something she'd never thought to see.

"Then you don't need my employment?" he said slowly. His veil rippled. Puzzlement drew his brows together.

"That coin, I couldn't stand to touch it," she explained. "I hid it away, never want to see it again. When ashessé came to my door, I thought that was the reason."

Still Mirashael seemed mystified. "Why did you come?"

She thought for a moment then answered, "Because I was afraid and I wanted to die. I wanted my life to mean something."

He returned to the drawers and opened another.

"Empty," he said. "And so is this one … but what have we here?" As the last slid open he reached inside. There was a rustle of paper unfolding, then, "Come! Look!" he said excitedly.

Leahät gazed at the wonderful gem in Mirashael's hand. A gentle glow emanated from its heart, touching his face with color.

"It's like a prism," she said, "but round, and the light is inside." Although it was fascinating, before long she felt compelled to look away. "There's something sad about it. Whimsical. A fragile thing that's lost and alone … far from its home."

"My lady is more sensitive than I," said Mirashael. "Where would this fabulous stone have come from? Did he bring it back with him? But no, if he had found it there, it would have gone to the Guild – to the Imperium."

Leahät picked up the wrapping. "There are marks here." She turned the crumpled paper around. "Writing – and some pictures … oh! It's a map! Look here, I think these are meant to represent the creatures I saw. The ones that –" She looked at the globe again and slowly backed away in horror.

With one hand, Mirashael cradled the crystal against his stomach, with the other, he reached for the map.

"These are navigator's marks," he said.

"His grandfather, the one who left him the desk, he was a navigator."

"… And images sung into the page … a planet of ice with a central sea that looks like an eye. Could this be the planet your husband went to? And what does this say?" He held the map to the light and read slowly, "*The Eyes of Bel Nishani* … I think we have our answer."

"We should tell the guild."

"Perhaps," he said slowly. "This mesmerizing gem is yours now, Lady Gok, to do with as you wish, and if relinquishing it to our esteemed God-Emperor is what you desire, then that is what we will do."

Leahät hesitated. "Why would it go to the God-Emperor?"

"Because the planet Went has been claimed for Tiamät. But not only that. There are whispers, rumors one hears, that the normal protocols will be overlooked. Riches so great, so rare, that our glorious ruler cannot wait for Leth to grant approval."

He plumped himself down on the divan. "Already it seems this planet will start a storm, a political tempest which such as I can either ride – or be drowned by." He studied the gem, deep in thought. "But does he know of these?"

"Who?" Leahät asked.

Mirashael turned to her. "Lucaät. This is the answer, I'm sure of it. I've never seen anything like it. How much does he know? Is that where Duvät's coin came from? My lady, please think. Are there more of these? Do not throw aside our chance for great wealth so blithely."

She nodded slowly. "There are – many more. But as to where they might be?" She shrugged. "He only came home the once. They could be anywhere."

"Why did he come home? Did he say?"

"I was out. He called me when he arrived. When I got in he gave me the coin. Yelled at me. Said he'd worked hard and I'd thank him one day … But he has a hiding place, a loose stone in the bathroom. If he's hidden them in the house, that's where they'll be."

"Let's go then, yes, yes, yes!" He whisked the globe and the map into Qalān. "A treasure hunt? How exciting."

Despite her reservations, Mirashael's enthusiasm brought a smile to Leahät's mind and she followed, almost as eager as he to find the hidden stash. Memories of sea creatures receded, lost in a rush of fresh attraction for her wily Cantori benefactor.

However, as he passed the concierge, Mirashael stopped again and this time his exchange was longer.

Leahät waited, puzzled by his rudeness.

With a final nod to his contact, Mirashael hastened to her side, his enthusiasm somewhat dimmed.

"My apologies, dear lady," he said. "Sad as it seems, we must hurry home now and leave our quest for another day. Perhaps by tomorrow the troubles will be over, yes?"

"Troubles?" she looked out onto the sunny street. "I see no troubles."

"They are elsewhere, yet they must take my attention for now." He winked at her. "Indeed, I have troubles of another kind that need to be orchestrated."

"Orchestrated?" Her mood plummeted. "What do you mean?"

Have no fear!" He placed his hands on her shoulders. "You are in no danger, and together we will continue our quest – but not today."

For a time she allowed herself to be shepherded toward Mirashael's café in Crafters, but as her head cleared, she stopped. "What are you involved in?"

He blinked innocuously. "Involved in? My lady, I assure you –"

"I am in no danger? Yes, I understand and I believe you, but I've endured centuries of being brushed off and I will no longer tolerate it. If you trust me, as you say, then tell me. What's going on, and what are these troubles."

Instead of the anger she'd braced herself for, there was a level of admiration in Mirashael's steady gaze.

He took her hand again. *When we are safely home I will answer your questions,* he said. *But in part this concerns our bowls, and I wonder how much you truly want to know.*

The realization that Duvät's death might be near sent her already bruised heart into hiding. She hurried on with Mirashael, anxious to be away from the crowds but dreading what the ensuing days might bring. The ending of a marriage bond caused great psychic trauma, no matter the circumstances.

She gave Mirashael's hand a little squeeze. *At least your books are up to date … if I …*

He pulled her gently closer. *My lady, the books are the least of my worries when compared with my concern for your welfare. Have no fear that you will be cast aside to deal with this alone. I will be with you, you will see. You need never feel unvalued again, this I promise.*

DOOR KNOCK

In Karesk, a sudden shower cleared the winding Old Town streets. Water sluiced down the cobbles and the smell of wet stone and leather competed with the sweaty aroma of humid people crushed together under what awnings there were.

Casco knew he should be thinking about organizing his first batch of émigrés, or making plans to get Duvät to the Imperial Bays and return safely, but the closed face of the Hermes wouldn't leave him. He didn't even know her name – but then, no one knew a Hermes' name.

A familiar hail came from behind and he half turned as Shen pushed through to his side.

Starry times! Shen bumped his shoulder. *Smokin, ja?*

Shen knew his level of admiration was embarrassing, but he continued regardless, counting off on his fingers, "First o' Rukh, First o' Leth – *an she be a starry lass, sho la!* – an two Guild-Lords, one, two, be un right here, and all ta to you." He gave Casco's ribs a playful jab. "Movin in de soarin sky dese days, sho la. Be nary too flash to speak wid us Kareski folk. Ja, maybe I should be an explorer too!"

Casco shook his head. *Yon folks all set?*

Shen's tone became more serious. *Ja, be flighty but keepin low. Canna give cred, not really, but seemin for true.*

Be true, Casco assured him. *All sorted. Meet at Four Gate, den be faidin de Rukh.*

They walked in silence for a moment, then Shen pictured the First of Rukh and combined the image with a hint of the snowy peaks of the Southern Alps. *Biggun for true, sho la.*

Casco's bark of laughter turned some nearby heads. He took Shen's description and made the mountain snows crack into an avalanche as it flexed its muscles. *Ja, biggun for true!*

By the time he reached home, the rain had stopped and a gentle summer mist crept through the valleys. He paused for a last look, then pushed open his door.

"You're leaving tonight," he announced to Duvät.

"Tonight?" Duvät appeared from his room.

"Erma," Casco informed him.

"Erma? That hole? Is that the best my coin could buy?"

Casco continued to the kitchen and poured himself a drink. He still had no idea how he would get Duvät to the Bays. It had been hard enough to get there with Kisha, even with Daric's help and a pass from the Guild. Before the incident with Tess, no one on the outside had looked at him too closely, but now it seemed that every ashessé on Giahn knew his face – and as for Duvät, the Gok was a prime target in his own right.

Duvät leaned against the bench. "When Lucaät's agent saved me from Brätan Gok," he drawled, "we pretended to be lovers and nobody looked."

Casco turned to him, aghast.

"Ask yourself why you saved me," Duvät smirked. "You might enjoy it."

"Go away," Casco snapped. "I need to think!"

He sprawled on his favorite divan. The fluid in his glass ebbed slowly. A sense of deep unease filled him, and ideas darted like fish in a pond. Maybe it was best to simply set out for the Bays and deal with problems as they arose. The appointment was made and Duvät had to go.

With a long groan, he got up to pour another drink, but en route to the kitchen he was stopped in his tracks by Shen's sending of black-clad ashessé moving military style from house to house, banging on doors, demanding permits, brutalizing any who resisted.

Permy raiders! Shen shouted. *Deys be takin dem, takin dem all. We's be fightin dis time, ja!* Images jolted as armed with his garden hoe he ran to join the battle, high on anger and adrenaline. *Deys sayin about a new Agency! Our lives no more dan bits of paper!*

Dat old scam? It'll never happen, Casco assured him.

He sharpened his farsight and saw Kareski lining up for portals. They were gathering in Old Town, anxious to make a stand.

On another street, an ashessé hammered on a bright blue door. "All permits are revoked!" he cried. "Half-breeds must apply for new permits with the Agency."

The door cracked open.

"Agency?" the Kareski inside retorted. "Empty threats and lies …!"

A muscular glove thrust through the gap and grabbed the Kareski's throat.

"Get me the permit," the ashessé grated.

He threw the Kareski aside and watched him scuttle to obey.

You comin? Shen sent imagery of a black-clad back in motion as a group of excited Kareski gave chase. *We got un here!*

But when Casco sent his farsight ahead he saw a troop of ashessé lying in wait, weapons at the ready.

Stop! he cried. *Deys sly, set trap!*

Shen slowed. *Set trap?*

Round de next bend! I's vizzin mebbe tirty, all weapons drawn.

The group stopped abruptly.

Sneak tru de dwellins, ja? Casco said. He sent Shen an overview of the streets and houses around them. *Get behind all quiet and yous get de jump.* He paused, wondering why he didn't tell his friend to go home and stay safe, but where was that safety when troops of ashessé stood with swords drawn, ready to kill people forbidden to hold arms?

Star-bright screens, he advised. *Surprize de baduns, ja? Look ahead. Tink wid de brains!*

Ja, Shen said ruefully. *De brains, no de brawn. You vizzin more?*

Don't wait for me, Casco said. *Haden, she be starry vizzer. Get her on de job. An Shera? She should be sortin de ruckus. I's back later.*

Shen's hurt came to him loud and clear, but with all eyes on Karesk, this was the chance he needed to get Duvät to the Bays.

A plume of flame shot skyward as Old Town caught alight. Shen's enthusiasts quickly regrouped. He watched until their screens were in place, then tore his vision away. It seemed wrong to leave, but a plan had formed at last and if he missed this chance, he might never be rid of Duvät. If they were quick, he could still help when he got back.

"Duvät! Get dressed," he called out. "Look important. We have to go as soon as possible."

"Won't I stand out?"

"We'll go together. I'll pass myself off as an archangel."

"You?" Duvät sneered. "The eyes are a bit of a giveaway, don't you think?"

"Fourth level braid, keep my head down. The city will be distracted. No one will know the difference."

"Distracted?"

"Riots. Get moving."

"If they catch you with a status braid, they'll shave your head."

"That's the least of my worries right now," he replied.

He'd seen Huldar do a Lethian version of the fourth-level style many times. The songs he used weren't complicated, but because high braiding was forbidden for half-breeds, Casco had never tried to learn. He placed the image of what he wanted to achieve firmly in mind and set out to recreate the style by hand. Fortunately there were many interpretations. So long as the key elements were there, the rest merely had to be neat.

Duvät paced up and down outside his room. "Aren't you done yet?" he snapped. "We have to go!"

Casco didn't answer. Any comment would take his attention from the next twist and the whole arrangement could cascade into disaster. He didn't want to have to start again.

A few more turns and the hair was passable. He thonged the ends in brown leather and picked up a small Lethian insignia Huldar had given him – 'Just in case you're ever Marked,' his friend had said. But the penalties for fraudulent House affiliation would doubtless be more severe than head-shaving so he tucked it into Qalān for luck.

"Let's go," he said. As he pushed past he tried not to see the sneer on Duvät's face.

Outside, a red glow had begun to spread across the horizon.

"Who cares?" Duvät snapped. "Let's go before someone sees me."

They cut north through surrounding orchards to the secret portal chain that led to Fourth Gate. To take a non-Kareski that way was to risk their security, but he saw no option. From there, four short steps emptied them into Crafters.

Duvät blanched. "Everyone knows me here!" he whispered.

"Smile," Casco suggested. "No one will recognize you."

When Duvät's scowl deepened, Casco shook his head and pointed to his own up-turned corners. Duvät's mouth moved through a series of ugly twists as it slowly followed suit.

Two ashessé strolled their way.

Casco turned to a woodworker's display, picked up a bowl and rotated it from side to side. "Lovely, don't you think?"

Duvät's hard won smile slipped a little.

The ashessé sauntered past without a second glance.

"My wife has bowls like this," Duvät said. "Two of them."

Casco turned before the stallholder could see his face.

"Lovely," he said, and presented the bowl to Duvät. "Let's get her two more."

Duvät made no move to accept. Casco shrugged and replaced the item.

They continued toward a narrow laneway, aware that anything out of place could attract attention.

"Just up here," he said, "a step through to Sadir."

Duvät slowed. "It will be guarded. They'll see us!"

"If we seem confident, there'll be no reason to look," Casco assured him. Like many Kareski, he'd learned basic shoplifting skills in his early years as a matter of survival.

"This is stupid," Duvät hissed. "All you've got to lose is your hair!"

As they stepped onto a busy Sadir street, Casco pointed to a shop across the road and strode toward it. Crowds clustered outside shops and eateries, heads abuzz with news of fresh riots in the enclave. Black uniforms dotted the mix like dung in a well-grazed paddock. Eight staunch Ashik patrolled the main entrance to the Imperial Bays. Casco put his head down and hurried Duvät toward the refectory entrance.

Two ashessé hovered either side of the back door, but scrutinized the out-going more than those who went in. While a large party of holiday travelers tried to exit, Casco and Duvät slipped between them and made it through unhindered.

Hearts thumping, they entered the packed dining hall. Casco pointed as if he'd spotted someone he knew, then waved as if they'd seen him.

"Important business!" Duvät said in his most officious tone.

The ether was noisy with a wary edge. As he and Duvät wound their way through the patrons, Casco kept his eyes half closed and tried to look as if he belonged.

He almost collided with an angel juggling several bowls of steaming talemgal and had to stop himself from apologizing. She bowed as best she could and said, "Excuse me, my lord." Narrowing his eyes to mere slits, he nodded cold acceptance.

A pair of uniforms glanced their way. One spoke to the other and started toward them.

"They've seen me!" Duvät whispered through clenched teeth.

"Keep walking," Casco said. "Look normal."

The guard picked up pace. Those at the inner doors looked up also, and Casco's heart fell.

"What do we do?" Duvät muttered.

"I don't know," he said. He kept his head turned and feigned interest in someone's meal.

His heart froze as a voice behind them barked, "Hey! You there!"

"Thief!" it continued. "He stole my purse!"

The ashessé turned toward the trouble.

Keep walking! Casco said.

From the back alcoves, someone cried, "Breath! He's been stabbed!"

A plate crashed to the ground.

"Healer! Get the Healer now!"

Someone screamed. Black uniforms muscled through panicky crowds. More food went flying as a lithe figure bolted for the refectory door. Another group cried out for help as an elderly angel fainted.

"What about my purse?" the theft victim cried. "Over there! He's getting away!"

"Watch it!" another growled. "Get out of my space!" A scuffle broke out.

"Half-breeds!" someone yelled. "It's a riot!"

Terrified people streamed for the doors.

Casco put his head down and allowed himself to be swept toward the Bays. Duvät struggled to stay at his side. Sentries were shoved aside in the crush.

"Bay twenty-seven," Casco said as they squeezed through. "It's down the back."

"I know where it is!" Duvät snapped.

"Don't run," Casco reminded him. "You'll draw attention."

"You've already drawn attention," Duvät said. "If we get caught and I die, it's your fault! You and your stupid plan."

Half running, half walking, he dodged between piles of cargo as Duvät fled toward the designated bay.

"We're too early," Casco called. "Slow down." Automatically, he began checking for places to hide. He rubbed his forehead where the call-sign had been imprinted ... screens were forbidden in the Bays, but Daric could probably hide anywhere, even there.

Just before bay twenty-seven, he spun toward the tread of boots and saw a neatly built Enna coming toward them. For a split second he thought it was Daric, then he realised the newcomer was female.

"Passage for one to Erma? You're early." She turned to Casco. "Saphela of Hermes asked me to look out for you. I am Shamkarun Darine Enna, your Navigator."

Saphela? The realization was a light-burst in his soul. He pictured her solemn face, and the moment when it broke into her beautiful, shy smile and everything about her seemed to change. Saphela of Hermes ... With a start, Casco remembered to avert his gaze.

The navigator glanced quickly at his braid but gave no sign she'd noticed anything amiss.

"Yes, Erma," Duvät said. He looked back the way they'd come. "Quick as you can!"

When the navigator returned to Casco, her brows flickered. He tensed, certain now that she knew who he was, but a tiny wave of reassurance brushed his mind and Daric's sigil warmed as if his friend was nearby.

"You'd best leave now," the navigator said, "while things are in disarray. There's a door ..." She indicated the shadowy area at the bay's edge. "Take the passage, office at the end. Go that way, *Casco of Leth*, and you will draw no attention. Breath blow you good fortune."

Casco bowed respectfully and started for the exit she'd shown him.

"What are we waiting for?" Duvät barked, already pacing impatiently.

No thanks – not even a backward glance! Casco thought to himself.

As the navigator's hidden door closed, the clamor of the Bays shut off. He continued down the narrow passage toward a soft light that glowed from beneath a door at the end. This opened into a roomy office as promised, but instead of the usual desk and chair, he found a scattering of cushions and a low table strewn with official-looking papers. The tired remains of a half-eaten meal sat on top of them along with several used mugs and glasses.

It made him smile to think that in some ways navigators might be as ordinary as the travelers they ferried from star to star. *And where do all the papers go?* he wondered. *Even here! Does anyone ever read these never-ending reports?* Again he thought of the Imperium's threat to make a registry of all half-breeds and sniggered at the mountains of paperwork that would generate for some unlucky Gok.

Through the office he went on to a wide, vaulted corridor. From the residual vibrations that clung to the stone, he was in one of the most ancient sections of the building. Carved stone filigree draped the ceiling. Designs based on Giahn's fauna and flora so skillfully rendered it was as if living figures had been turned to rock between one breath and the next. Casco drank them in as best he could, knowing it was unlikely he'd have the chance to revisit, then he smiled. He was the only non-navigator he knew who had been allowed beyond the actual Bays – Huldar would be seriously jealous if he ever found out.

Ahead, the hallway turned at a right angle with an exit he thought might lead to the street. At first approach the charm that sealed it seemed quite complex, but on closer examination he saw its similarity to a Kareski style. From there, it was simply a matter of unpicking the notes and singing the key, but instead of the street it led to a quadrangle enclosed by featureless walls.

As he stepped through, he looked back to see the opening disappear into the stonework.

In the center of the courtyard, a covered portal hummed with latent power. The rune of Tiamät stood tall at its peak and ten intricately carved tentacles drooped from the canopy to form supports. The tiles beneath were patterned into three wedges for the three clans of Tiamät, arranged around a central disc of white gold.

Casco fought the urge to flee. Surely there was another way out?

In the eastern corner he was relieved to sense another, more modest portal and he sidled rapidly toward it, wary that at any moment a hidden door might manifest and he would be discovered.

At first, the portal presented him with a bewildering array of possible exits, but when he placed the resonance of Four Gates foremost in his mind, it simply opened there. It was as if Qalān itself was intuitive, but perhaps in the home of the navigators such things were to be expected.

His braid was also eager to escape and as he jogged toward the next step, he loosed its ties and let it work its way free. The wind combed it with fine fingers and he spared a moment to laugh at his own audacity, thankful he'd made it home with his tawny mane intact.

Saphela of Hermes – he mouthed the name, the first Hermes name he'd known … but as he stepped to the outskirts of Karesk and saw the red glow on the horizon, his rosy daydreams fled.

Dogged with guilt for abandoning his friends, he called out to Shen and hurried toward the fray.

DUVÄT

"What are we waiting for?" Duvät cried.

The navigator studied him as if she didn't like what she saw, but what did he care? There was terrible trouble all around him. Surely she could feel it too?

"What is wrong with you?" he barked. "Singing a chord can't be that hard!"

Her steely veil gave a momentary glow, but still there was no move to sing. Instead, she smiled over Duvät's shoulder and he turned to see another Enna stepping along with all the arrogance inherent to the clan.

As he opened his mouth to vent his frustration, alarm was triggered. He looked again. He knew that face. Fear welled in his heart. Surely Casco, that simple fool, had not betrayed him!

"I'll take it from here," said Daric Enna.

The navigator gave a decisive nod. "Very well, brother. I wish you joy in your undertaking."

Duvät let out a strangled cry, but it was already too late to run. "You'll never get me out of here," he said. "I'll fight you every step of the way!"

"No need."

A brief glimpse of the round fungi in Daric's hand was all the warning he had before a puff of brown spores carried him into darkness.

At a certain point during his return to consciousness, Duvät realized what was happening. He tried go back to the comfort of oblivion, but the picrcing pain in his head denied him that luxury. He found himself bound upright in a chair. A weak yellow globe threw more shadow than light. Small sounds of Daric Enna's presence exploded into yet more pain.

"How did you find me?" he croaked.

"I traced you to Karesk with a little beacon stone I slipped into your pocket." The Enna's tone was self-congratulatory. "I know a charm that will make it stick to fabric," he went on. "I'll bet you never even knew it was there."

So the half-breed hadn't turned him in. Duvät remembered the stone falling from his pocket when Casco had released the anti-theft charm on his house. Why hadn't he looked at it more closely?

"Might have known," he whispered. His mouth felt like the inside of a sand-miner's latrine. He tested his restraints, but they were more than firm.

"So, who do you work for?" he asked. "You're not Brätan's, or the Faythan's."

"Actually, I'm working for your wife," Daric answered cheerfully.

"Leahät?" Duvät closed his eyes and slowly reopened first one, then the other. This was not a dream. Surely he'd misheard.

"There is something you have that could benefit her," Daric was saying, "and I can't stand not knowing. I must solve every puzzle, get to the guts of every mystery – and you are the answer to my current conundrum."

Duvät barely heard. He struggled with the concept that his wife, the whining yet submissive creature he'd been shackled to all these years, had actually organized for him to be killed.

His captor prattled on, but Duvät's attention was swallowed by the outlandish notion that his wife could do such a thing.

"Leahät Gok?" he interrupted. "My wife?"

"A bit of a surprise for you, I see."

"She wants to kill me?"

"No, of course she doesn't. That's my job," Daric said. "But still, perhaps if you give me the information I want, no fuss, no trouble – I'll tell her you've escaped and you'll never return to bother her again." He put his hand on the back of the chair. "Never return to make me a liar."

He leaned so close that Duvät could smell the seafood on his breath. His haze jangled and rasped against the contact, and he realized his captor was quite unhinged. The ordeal he faced would be nothing like the organized extraction the inquisitor had tried to perform.

"And that will be the truth, won't it?" Daric whispered.

The menace he projected was infinitely dark. Terror bloomed in the pit of Duvät's stomach. He gagged and tried not to vomit. He wasn't ready to face this, not again …

Daric's fist thumped the table. "Say it!"

Every muscle spasmed. "Yes," he wheezed brokenly. "That will be the truth."

"Good, good," Daric smiled again. "But in case there's any doubt," he fished in his pocket and pulled out a fine, silvery chain, "I respect your wife enough to make certain it is so."

The chain slipped between his fingers, running from hand to hand.

"In fact," he continued, "and this is such a shame – but honesty has never been your strongest suit, would you say?"

Duvät flinched as Daric leaned close again and murmured into his ear, "Perhaps you should have stayed with me the first time."

He watched in horror as elegant fingers pulled the ends of the chain apart.

"You know – or perhaps you don't," Daric said quietly, "that once this is on, you won't be able to remove it yourself. The charm is sealed with a very special kind of song that combines the powers of mind and voice, Tsemkar and Shamkar together. Brilliant, really."

He dangled the slave chain in a loop before Duvät's face. Wan light flickered on the links.

"Once it's closed, your higher self will cease to function," his captor continued. "The only way your wife will know you haven't died is that you won't have sent a death-cry … Of course, the chain will kill you in the end. Archangels never survive it for long."

Daric moved behind him and lowered the chain. Duvät flinched as cold metal touched his cheek. Silver shivered against his skin like the teeth of a weyfal about to strike. He remembered the terror in Lucaät's slave girl – the sadness. Tears burned his eyes. He did not want to be that. The links dribbled over his lips. He tried to spit them away.

"Stop!" he gasped. "Please, don't do this!"

"Why not?" Daric asked. His tone was as innocent as a child's.

Duvät squirmed against the ropes in a vain attempt at escape. "No!" he cried. "I'll tell you. Please let me tell you!"

The ends of the chain closed around his neck, almost touching. He felt nauseated. His skin crawled.

"Please!" he whimpered. "They're in the bathroom, under a stone, that's where they are. Lucaät took the others but the best ones, the true ones – they're under a stone in the bathroom. They are! Take it off. I'll take you to them. Just take it off me! Please!"

"I already know that," Daric said.

"No! You can't!" Duvät cried, but there was no compromise in Daric's gaze. "How could you know that?" He started to cry. What else could this person want? There must be something. Words burbled from his lips. "There's more in the strongbox, just a few, not very many …"

"Go on," Daric said.

"They came from the inner sea, the inner sea of Went. I got them myself. They're mine! I have a map! My grandfather was a navigator; he gave me the map and I found them, just as he wanted. But I did better, better than him. I ripped out their eyes – I ripped out their eyes and they became my fortune …" His litany slowed. "I'll never see it now, will I?"

"No, you won't," Daric said.

The links closed.

Duvät convulsed.

Words forced their way into his darkness. "Your wife can't feel this, not like the sick torments you visited on her." He paused, his attention raw against Duvät's exposed senses, then came a ray of hope …

"But enough's enough, right?" Daric said.

He tried to nod but his mind streamed from his grasp, crumbled like old cake and vanished as if carried away by a million tiny insects. "Take it off," he managed to whimper.

Daric stepped back, his head cocked as if considering. "I can't leave you like that," he said. "Not really."

His sympathy seemed honest. Duvät dared not look up. Tears of relief welled in his eyes. Daric's hand came to his forehead as if to bestow a blessing, and with a simple touch, reached into his exposed mind to sever the life from his body.

Pain ceased.

A sense of lightness filled him.

He looked into Daric's face, but Daric didn't see him, only the corpse he had become.

The brooch he'd bought Leahät, how terribly inadequate a gift it had been. He remembered her smile when they were first married, when she had still believed in him.

Time began to thin, drawing like toffee while it waited for his cry to be made. What could he say? Nothing he could tell Leahät would matter, yet he must make his death-cry or become a light-spirit, trapped between worlds until those Last Words could be uttered.

He turned to Casco and found him in the thick of an unfair battle. Black clad, sword-wielding arms chopped at determined Kareski equipped with only with what weaponry they could find. Then a group of better-armed defenders threw themselves at the ashessé from behind and the tide turned. Duvät found himself hoping the Kareski would win.

Long brown hair flying, Casco shoved a short-sword through someone's chest, but as his enemy fell, the half-breed seemed sad, not triumphant. He looked up, as if sensing he was watched. His spirit shone in Duvät's eyes, on fire with anger, accepting of his deep loneliness, resourceful in the face of opposition and filled with potential still to be realized. Casco had sheltered him even though because of him, Lind had faced this very moment, the moment of the Cry.

Thank you … he whispered, and then he was gone.

Seconds later, Leahät crumpled into Mirashael's arms, her soul rent by the breaking of the bond.

Mirashael gently kissed her forehead. "He will return to El's embrace and be breathed out again, cleansed and beloved." He looked down at her and stroked her face. "Let us hope he makes better choices in the life to come."

———

In Karesk, at some unheard signal, the ashessé withdrew.

"Let them go!" Casco ordered. "Tend their wounded too, if necessary."

Gruk kicked at a downed ashessé, but Shen stopped him.

"No, Casco be seein sharp," he said. "Not us the baduns. We's be wantin quiet livin, is all."

Casco nodded his thanks. Every muscle ached. He massaged his sword arm and wondered what would happen now.

Shen, set guards on each entry, he said. *Be wary mind? Sunup soon, den we's seein clear wha de go.*

While his friend organized sentries, Casco found a quiet place and messaged Pieru.

Casco! You're all right? Pieru seemed flatteringly relieved. *That Breath should blow such times.*

What's going to happen now, do you know? Casco asked him. *Will they be back? Can you tell?*

There was a pause, then Pieru replied, *Brechan seems to think not. There is a meeting with Faytha in progress. He thinks the embargo will be lifted. Too much disruption to the workforce.*

So we go ahead as planned?

There was another pause, then, *Yes, proceed as planned. Get some rest. Brechan will let us know of any further developments, although he warns of a deep schism. Clan Ashik have the God-Emperor's ear.*

That can't be good.

He visualized a haughty, sword-wielding Ashik running around with a golden ear in his hand.

Casco! Pieru laughed.

I must be over-tired, Casco apologized. *Didn't realize I'd shared.*

But still with a sense of humor. The more I learn about you, Casco, the more I appreciate your value.

While Shen set sentries, Casco asked for anyone who had tents to help put them up as temporary accommodation.

A message came to him from a lookout at the City-side street entry, *Kishlak. Four-un. Recon deys Naghari.*

Be Marked? Casco asked.

… Ja.

Sen dem to Shera at de Wheel. I's be meetin un dere.

He arrived at the Wheel just in time to follow the Naghari in. Emanations of distress had turned the ether inside the guest-house into a dissonant soup. Casco turned to a sturdy archangel with care-worn eyes.

"You and your people are a welcome sight."

"What's the situation?" she asked.

"Twenty-three with serious wounds, breaks and lacerations," Casco informed her. "We have no Marked healer among us, but Doba and Chere," he pointed out two Kareski, "are doing a great job with first aid. Any herbs or substrates you need, talk to Shera at the counter." He'd already put out the word that whatever bandages and medicines could be found should be sent here, and Shera had her head down sorting and dispensing those supplies.

"You've done well in a short time," the healer said. "Field training?"

"Explorers' Guild."

"Ahh." She nodded. "Excellent. We'll get started."

"I can't thank you enough."

He looked up as Saphela of Hermes emerged from her rooms. She bent close to Shera as they examined a sheaf of dried leaves, and he realised she must be helping with the dispensary. She gave him a swift glance, then turned back to her work.

"If you need me," he continued, "either of those two can find me."

The Naghari glanced toward the makeshift pharmacy then hurried off as one of her team called for help.

Casco looked toward Saphela again and their eyes met. He saw the hint of an answering smile and started toward her, but Shera tipped her head toward the door, a definite suggestion that he should leave them to it. It was true they could never marry – he would not condemn her free spirit to the life of an outcast – but friendship, surely that was accessible? Reluctantly he made his way back to the growing tent city.

Early morning light filtered through smoky residue, painting the easterly tent-leathers orange, and it was then that he remembered Duvät Gok's death-cry and wondered why it had come to him. Surely such a moment belonged to one's most beloved? He remembered the Gok's offer of sex and shuddered. To be intimate with such a one would surely leave a scar.

Had an accident in Qalān taken his life? If so, he was sorry for the navigator, she'd seemed a decent sort, but as far as the Gok was concerned, perhaps such a lonely death was fitting.

MIRASHAEL AND DARIC

From beyond a bank of brush-covered dunes, the hush and sigh of summer wavelets drifted through the muted windows of Mirashael's seaside mansion. Flower heads nodded in their vases as a breeze swirled lightly through the room, ruffling the curtains around the huge four-poster bed where Leahät Gok slept soundly at last, thanks to the ministrations of the Naghari healer commissioned to tend her.

With a last look at Leahät's Gokish face, typically plain but beautiful to him, Mirashael followed the Naghari out onto the wide veranda and stood a moment, sharing the sweeping ocean view. It was certainly far removed from his dingy shop in Crafters.

"Would Shamkarun Obrel of Naghar care for a drink?" he asked the healer pleasantly. "Guerdi, perhaps, or tea? I'm sure such deep and delicate healing is thirsty work."

"You have no servants?" Obrel asked.

"No, but there are several on their way. I seldom stay here and only call in help if needed. A drink?" he repeated.

"My thanks," the healer said, "but I will return to the Crafters Chapter-House. Your friend will sleep for now. Don't expect her to wake until tomorrow, and then be sure she is not left alone for even a moment. Expect her psyche to be fragile for some weeks yet, but because the bond was already abridged, her recovery time will be much reduced. I will come again tomorrow, possibly midday, unless you have need of me beforehand."

"A thousand thank yous, Shamkarun Obrel." Mirashael bowed. "Without your assistance …"

"Such wounds are hard to bear and slow to heal," Obrel agreed. "Be sure to call me if our patient wakes in the night, or seems overly distressed. Otherwise …" He inclined his head. "Until tomorrow."

With that, the Naghari set out among the dunes, following a faint track toward the portal further up the beach. Mirashael watched for a moment, then returned indoors.

Now that Leahät had been seen to he realized he hadn't eaten since the night before. He took a smoked fish from his pantry and, with an exquisitely patterned pair of hanta, pulled the flesh slowly from the bones.

The Eyes of Bel Nishani were the key to the puzzle, he was certain of it! But how to fit the key to the lock – and what would be inside that figurative box once opened? A shit-storm, he expected.

He pictured his friend, Daric Enna. The assassin had performed well, as always, but although he had found and confirmed what knowledge they had, he had not been shy in communicating his misgivings.

They are not evil in themselves, he had said of the eyes. *It's what they represent. They should be returned to the planet whence they came and never disturbed again.*

Mirashael agreed. Some things should not be bought and sold. But already too many players had sighted the prize and the option to return them to Went was no longer available. There was a wealth of factors in play and none of them simple. Whatever action he took would have to be set in motion quite quickly, and with no room for error. If he played this incorrectly, his story could end, and then what would become of Leahät? And although the eyes were nominally hers, the only legacy of value from what had been a horrible marriage, ultimately they belonged to the God-Emperor.

He maneuvered a sliver of fish from one side of the plate to the other. Perhaps he should offer them to both Brätan and Lucaät at the same time and deliver them to the highest bidder.

If he envisaged Brätan Gok as an ashut piece, he would be the Ranger – powerful moves, but constrained by honor.

Lucaät, as acquisitive as only a Faythan could be – was the Fish. Slippery, able to swim between levels at will, the Fish had far more glamor but without the power of the Ranger. However, the fish could work as a shoal and strike in many places at once.

Tsemkarun Ishät Ashik, the God-Emperor, was represented by the Mother in this game. Singular and unpredictable, the Mother would have the final say, but this piece was the slave of fate and could only react to what it could see.

And if the eyes represented the Palace – the ultimate prize … then Daric was the Huntress, and he, Mirashael, must then play the Moon; a subtle influence with the power to deceive.

And where was the lady Leahät in this not-quite-imaginary game? Certainly not a simple fled to be sacrificed at will; no, she was far too precious for that. Perhaps a second huntress won from the enemy and played in tandem? It could be done.

With a delicate touch he prized another piece of flesh from his meal and finally the flavor came through – it really was delicious. By the time the bones were picked clean, he'd had word from Daric Enna that he'd recovered the trove and was on his way to Pannias Cove.

Mirashael waited on the veranda as the lean assassin tramped up the same path by which the Naghari had left.

"No trouble?" he asked.

"Easy," Daric assured him. "Attention still on the enclave. Leahät's house is watched by Lucaät's people, but without real conviction, and the Agent is deployed elsewhere – either that, or he's had a serious skills upgrade. My guess is that the Faythan already feels he knows enough for whatever he has planned … and we know there'll be something."

"Sure as rope and rada," Mirashael agreed. He pushed a broad cushion toward his assassin and waved toward the dimple in its center. "Show me."

Daric spilled the contents of a leather bag onto the soft fabric, and they both stared in shock.

Mirashael played his fingers through the series of rainbows the gems projected. "It's as if they have seen deity itself … and here we see some small imprint of its glory," he murmured. "No wonder Lucaät of Faytha is desperate to have them. Oh, yes, he would definitely want such splendor for the honor of his House."

He moved the cushion and watched the display splinter into dots of color then reform into distinct bands once more.

"Put them away," he said abruptly.

With a deft touch of mind, Daric shepherded the orbs back into their bag. "What will you do?" he asked.

"They belong to my lady, Leahät."

"That may well be," said Daric, "but what will you do? Once word of Duvät's demise gets about, it won't take Lucaät long to work out where they are. He'll come for them."

"He will," Mirashael agreed.

Daric stared glumly at the cushion where the eyes had been. "You're smarter, but he has far greater resources."

"Could we hide them in Karesk?" Mirashael suggested. "Your friend Casco?"

No!

"Or smuggle them off-world with a group of Kareski refugees?"

"Is that the best you can come up with?" Daric said scathingly.

"Just a thought." Mirashael slowly rubbed his chin. "If I were Lucaät," he mused, "I'd go to Brätan Gok and tell him that they are with me, Mirashael. Then I'd join forces with Gok, get the Ashik involved – we wouldn't stand a chance.

But after a moment his gloom began to lift.

"How well did you hide the body?" he asked. "Have you destroyed it?"

"It's where I left it," Daric replied. "In the room below the warehouse in Crafters. Thought you wanted a Shamkarun to sing its belongings from Qalān?"

Mirashael nodded happily. "Good, good! Is it preserved?"

"Of course, ready to be sung."

"Good, good, good! Excellent. Yes. Well, we have a little time yet to get that job done, but in the meantime, no one but my lady Leahät knows he's gone, and the healer of course, but that's no problem. Lucaät won't act quickly. As far as he knows, Duvät is still in hiding."

"What are you thinking?" Daric's eyes bored into him. *I could find out for myself …*

You respect me too much for that. Mirashael smiled. "It occurred to me that our friend Lucaät, thanks to his coin-hungry Faythan soul, will not join forces with anyone because he has no intention of sharing, and I doubt very strongly that he'd even relinquish the Eyes of Bel Nishani to the God-Emperor, if he did have them, except under extreme duress. But our friend Brätan, he's the opposite. He wants them returned to the Imperium, and from what I hear –"

Which is quite a bit –

So much noise! "Anyway, I hear that he actually made an appointment with Ishät Ashik himself regarding the gems, had to cancel when Lucaät took Duvät Gok, and now he's angry with Lucaät and desperate to save face."

Daric raised his shoulders, *You heard that from me.*

Quite so! Mirashael smiled. "Just wait. You won't be disappointed! Your sister, make sure she tells no one – has told no one. Then we must wait for my lady to wake. The gems are hers. She must have the final say."

The pause that followed was measured by the hush and sigh of the small, curling waves that lapped the sandy shore of Pannias Cove. Sea birds called above azure waters and the scent of pink hereny floated delicately on the vagrant breeze. A group of three angels meandered up the beach, heading for Mirashael's manor. They waved as they sent greeting, and Mirashael waved back.

He returned to Daric Enna. "You will stay? It may be a few days, and you've certainly earned the break."

Daric looked around at the luxurious surroundings, then back to the gentle waves. "Could do far worse."

"Far worse indeed!" Mirashael chuckled, and together they went inside, ready to help the servants get settled.

FRITH

Every planet had its own feel, an underlying ambience Huldar could sense as soon as he set foot on it. The planet Giahn was warm and welcoming despite the current political climate – Haas, the principle world of Rukh, had a somber note, while Hesh, sub-world of Nhadu, had an inescapable air of euphoria. Frith, however, kept him guessing. The mystery of it tantalized him, but made him a little jittery as well.

The last-but-one step toward Aventhe brought them to a ridge above a verdant glen. Bright morning sunlight warmed his back. Fluffy white clouds scudded overhead like a playful group of summer-sprites consigned to the clear blue sky.

In the distance, he made out a nest of spires and turrets poking needle-sharp above a forested rise. In the valley below, swathes of impossibly green moss coursed between groves of ancient trees, many of which were entirely cloaked in pink or yellow blooms. Brightly colored birds chirped and chattered as they fluttered among the branches, and family groups of small, four-legged beasties bounced happily across the clearings.

All that's missing are the rainbows, he thought, then chided himself for the cynicism.

He noticed a shrill sound pulsing faintly from the valley floor and turned to Andel.

"Vesa!" she said, and passed on an image of creatures with palm-sized iridescent red-and-blue wings. "It's their mating time. They gather all around our house – the spires, look, you can see them from here."

Inshogi glanced at the sky. "Best move along," he said, "or we'll be caught in the rain."

Huldar followed his gaze and saw the formerly innocent clouds had already grown and darkened into a cohesive front. A gossamer curtain of rain drooped from the leading edge.

"Fairly typical for the time of year," Inshogi assured him.

He leaned toward Andel. "Remind you of somewhere?"

"Went!" She turned to her father. "It was unbelievable. Made our weather seem quite tame."

From their vantage on the ridge, Huldar watched the storm unfold like a story in the telling. In no time at all, the veil deepened from gauzy silver to a leaden blanket. Small creatures ducked for cover and birds retreated among the trees. Soon, a moist gust announced the storm's imminence, the rustle of the approaching shower grew to a roar, and the love-song of the vesa was lost to its passion.

Andel took his arm and drew him south to a portal marked by a ring of worn paving stones.

They stepped through into a covered colonnade. Water sluiced from the transparent roof and the sweet white rayno blooms that draped its archways clashed and tinkled in the downpour. Clumps of vesa clung to the ancient stonework of Aventhe's walls like multicolored tiles, the vibration of their wings reduced to a mere hum while they waited for the sun to return.

"Wait until they fly again." Andel fluttered her fingers in the air. "You'll love it!"

After hearing them from a distance, Huldar wasn't so sure.

Inshogi paused at the entrance to their house and swept a bow. "Welcome to Aventhe! Until Breath blows us different paths, Shamkarun Huldar of Leth, our home is as yours."

Ninjay nodded stiffly. "Welcome."

Huldar bowed in return, then followed as Andel burst through the door into a wide, wood-lined foyer. Twin staircases stood at its end, either side of a pair of shell-like translucent doors. A huge, brightly patterned rug covered the floor. Vivid artworks contrasted with the dark timber walls, but what they depicted, if anything, Huldar couldn't tell.

"Home!" Andel cried. "Home at last." She breathed deeply as if savoring its scent.

Even Ninjay managed a smile. "It is good you have returned unharmed," she said. "Let's make the most of it."

"Yes, indeed," said Inshogi. "There is work to do, work aplenty, but for now let's relax. Drinks in the sitting room, eh? And a few more tales of the wild weather of Went."

They turned as a buxom angel rushed to greet them. "Lady Andel!"

"Jeiah!" Andel beamed, "And Kalel?"

"He'll be back any minute. Just fetching extra supplies. Oh, my lady – let me look at you! More lovely than ever – even your Mark has grown ..." She lowered her eyes demurely and leaned her head closer to Andel's. "And who's this handsome lord?"

Huldar smiled and bowed again as Andel introduced him, "Shamkarun Huldar of Leth, meet Jeiah, our housekeeper. She and Kalel have lived with us since I was a baby."

Ninjay pushed past them. "Have you prepare the eastern turret for our guest, as I asked?" she said. "I will have tea in my room."

Jeiah blinked and dusted off her apron. "Of course, my lady. Right away!"

"No need to rush," Ninjay snapped. "I've only just arrived. Where's Alma?"

"On her way. She'll be so pleased to see you."

Ninjay paused. "And I her. I'm sorry, Jeiah, I am pleased to be home and everything looks lovely, but I am quite exhausted by the trip and in need of tea and a rest."

"Should I send for a healer?"

"No, just tea."

"Yes, my lady," Jeiah said, and bowed as Ninjay continued toward the staircase.

Huldar peered after her.

Andel tilted her head. "Are you all right, Jeiah?"

"Yes, Lady Andel, of course. She's often a bit short after time in the chime. But if I may ask, has something else happened?"

"She is tired," said Inshogi. "The journey was most taxing for her."

"I see," said Jeiah. She smiled at Huldar. "The turret is all ready for you. It's lovely up there, young sir, and I'm sure you'll be most comfortable."

"Thank you. I'm sure I will." Huldar gave a small bow and Jeiah turned to Andel with a nod of approval.

"Just give me a minute to make sure the room is perfect," she said before heading up the stairs.

Huldar leaned closer to Andel and murmured, "Are we expected to sleep separately?"

"We'll share the turret," Andel assured him. "It's quite large enough, and private."

"Quite so," Inshogi said. "Yes, indeed. Well, Andel will show you the way, and then I'm sure she'll give you a tour of our home, just so you know your way around. Don't get lost, eh?"

"Drinks in the sitting room?" Andel prompted.

Inshogi peered in the direction his wife had gone. "I'll let you know when dinner is served?"

"Thank you, Father," said Andel, but before they could leave, the portal at the end of the colonnade shimmered to life and Huldar realised there was something else unique about Aventhe.

"You have no screens?" he asked.

Inshogi shrugged. "No need, dear boy, no need."

"We have never had house screens," Andel explained. "It is our duty to care for our people. They trust us, we trust them, and we have no need for concealment."

Her face lit up as two more angels came through the door, one older and another who looked to be his son.

"Kalel!" she cried. "And Amber! It's so good to see you!"

Huldar smiled and nodded as fresh introductions were made, but his mind was lost to the novel lifestyle of the Trianogi. Andel's disarming naïveté must have its roots here – and Inshogi had that same ingenuous nature.

"Is this openness," he waved his hand toward the ceiling, "this lack of screening, a part of Trianogi culture?"

"Yes, it is," Inshogi assured him. "Only at Trianog House itself will you find any such shielding at all, and even there it is minimal, in accordance with our customs."

"Businesses?"

"All open."

"Personal privacy?"

Inshogi winked. "We choose not to look."

"Our inner defenses are the same as anyone else's," Andel assured him, "but our actions? We have nothing to hide. And if we don't know what others are doing, how they are faring, how can we know when or where help is needed?"

Inshogi smiled at his daughter. "As I said, Huldar lad, there are no riots here, no segregation of peoples, no need for 'ashessé'. The Imperium could learn from us, I reckon!"

"Perhaps it could," Huldar agreed.

"People come to us with what excess produce they can spare, you see – this is the way we do things. We archangels store those goods for redistribution when they are needed. That way, no one in our community, our protectorate goes without. All have food, shelter, clothing, even coin if that is what is necessary. And our retainers stay here because that is what they wish. They are treated as family. All Trianogi are family."

"And halfbreeds?"

"There is no enclave here. If not for the expense of travel – and other difficulties imposed by our imperium, I am sure more mixed couples would choose to settle on Frith."

"A very different system to any I have encountered," Huldar said. "I look forward to a deeper understanding of its intricacies."

Inshogi bowed. "Until dinner, then."

From a landing on the next level, Huldar followed Andel up a spiral staircase to a faceted room beneath a high ceiling. Skylights surrounded a central tall hollow that disappeared into the dark interior of a needle-like spire, a large bed with short curvy legs jutted from between two windows and, on another wall, cushions and a low divan surrounded a squat round table with a bowl of fruit still wet from the rain outside.

The bed creaked as Huldar threw himself onto it. He patted the space beside him and Andel stretched out there, looking up at the raindrops as they drained from the clear panels in the roof.

It's sort of like a tent, she said. *I never noticed that before.*

A very large and comfy tent! Huldar chuckled.

This was Aanjay's room. I used to come up here when I was young. He had some crystals with images sung into them, and one with a navigator's song.

What were the images of?

One had pictures of a Terric colony, another showed the flying wings of Germane. My Uncle Roshan gave them to him. He's dead too now.

As Andel's fingers entwined with his own, memories of her brother's face came through. They were hazy with time, but Huldar saw his brilliant smile and deep blue eyes. Then he saw Roshan, the navigator, and how he had changed after the accident, always seeming sad and tired.

He died some time later, Andel said. *It was as if he blamed himself, but he had nothing to do with it really. He just dropped us off there on Germane and we made our own way to the cliffs. We saw the wings there,* she remembered, *gliding so gracefully, but when they land, it's more of a splat against the rocks, then they hang there in clusters, like the vesa on the walls – only much, much bigger.*

Do you still have the crystal? I'd like to see them.

Mother threw it away.

You are still angry with her.

She's hiding something, I know it. Something about the foretelling.

He leaned across and kissed her. *I'm sure she'll tell us in good time.*

But what if it's something important? Something we should know?

He kissed her again. *If it was important … even your mother could not be so bloody-minded.*

Bloody-minded?

You must admit, she's hardly been welcoming.

She is doing the best she can, Andel said. *She didn't want me to be an explorer, and now I've arrived back with an extra one in tow! Of course she finds it difficult!*

Anger stung his fingers. He released her hand.

In tow? Like baggage? He thought of all they had done together – all he had done to save her and Lind from Qalān …

No, that's not what I meant! Andel said.

Then what did you mean? he snapped. *Because if I'm just weighing you down, I have more important things I could be doing.*

Their minds closed to each other.

He went to the far window and stood with his back to the bed. As if on cue, the sun came out. Yellow evening light shone through wisps of steam that lifted from the garden below. Glades of emerald moss gleamed like the coat of a living creature – then the vesa took to the skies. Their strident buzz rattled his eardrums, but as he watched the couples pair off in a complex dance, flashing wings filled the air with color and the discomfort of their song was forgotten.

Hesitantly, Andel came to join him. Their hands brushed, then intertwined again. Regret for harsh words broke the banks between them, combined with a certain amount of fear that each might lose the other. He drew her close and kissed the top of her head.

A pair of vesa danced past the window in an intricate series of spirals.

Andel hugged his waist. *I told you …* she said quietly.

Yes, he agreed. *They are beautiful …*

He closed his eyes, lost in the affirmation of love. It was true her mother had been rude at times, they agreed, but it was also clear her foretelling had affected her deeply. His criticism had been overly harsh, and they were both tired and on edge.

I can think of a better way to vent pent-up feelings, he said.

With a grin, he swept her into his arms and deposited her onto the window ledge. Their lips met hungrily. Her underwear shimmied gracelessly down her legs, caught between two minds at once. While lust-filled vesa screeched jangling love songs, Andel's legs wrapped hard around him and his fingers opened a rapid path for their own song of desire.

He gasped as he entered her, and bowed his head, lost in their shared sensation. With his hands cupped around her buttocks he thrust again as deeply as he could, and again. Their hazes merged, finesse lost to urgency.

Beyond the window, storms of fluttering creatures filled the air with noise, and Huldar let it wrap around them, drawing on its unsubtle message.

Her breath blew warm and rhythmic against his chest. He felt her need for him and was hungry to feed it.

Just as he hoped the intense pleasure could last forever, they both knew it could not, and when climax rushed upon them their auras reached consonance in a single deep note that played between their bodies like a pounding bell. Huldar threw his head back in a tortured groan while Andel's hands pushed hard against the window frame; her mound crushed against him and small cries amplified his joy still more.

When the last shivers of orgasm had passed, he carried her to the bed and lay down with her slim body still wrapped in his arms.

Her hand came to his cheek. *I'll never be able to hear the vesa in quite the same way again,* she said softly.

Relaxation spread like a balm through his muscles and he wondered how long it had been since he'd felt so good. Then he remembered the house was not screened.

Do you think anyone was watching? he asked.

Hard to say, she replied. *But if they were, I hope they learned something.*

His fingers slid downward and found their way between her legs, slowly enacting the third rule of touch.

Her eyes widened. *Again?*

She arched upward and he turned to share her small gasp with his lips.

I think we have a thing or two to show them yet, he whispered.

INSHOGI'S STORY

Huldar woke to Andel's light shake.

"Get dressed," she said. "Dinner's ready." *I'll meet you down there.* The door closed and she started down the stairs. *Oh, and wear something nice?* she added.

Something nice?

Her smile found him through the ether. He rolled out of bed and thought about what clothes he'd brought with him. Unlike Casco, he had no permanent residence in Giahn, so most of his belongings remained in storage at the Guild. He wished she'd stayed to help him, and entertained the secret suspicion that she liked to see him struggle with social niceties.

In the end, he chose the blue shirt she said matched his eyes, and a pair of soft, bone-colored leather trousers.

Good choice, she said as he entered the dining room.

Although the weather was not overly cold, a welcoming fire crackled with flame. Multi-tiered light crystals spread gentle warmth over a long table decorated with rayno blooms. The tasseled white cloth was embroidered with the rune of Trianog at each corner. Steaming tureens and bowls of mysterious baked vegetables already lay in wait and household staff stood ready to serve.

Andel's mother smiled valiantly.

Inshogi stood and bowed.

"Be welcome at our table," the serving staff intoned.

"Thank you," Huldar said, and bowed to Inshogi in return. Everyone looked at him, and he hoped there wasn't some secret Trianogi protocol he'd missed, but then Andel tipped her head toward the empty seat beside her.

As he sat, the staff stepped forward, and he heard the gentle voice of Jeiah at his shoulder asking if he'd care for some lamoway.

The purple tubers, Andel informed him. *Local delicacy.*

Jeiah noted their subliminal speech and grinned a little.

"Perhaps you would like to try them with the goranda casserole?" she said kindly, and pointed out a creamy dish in a sturdy ceramic bowl.

"Yes, thank you," he said, and wondered what goranda was.

"The omi-peel garnish has a nice, tangy bite." She whisked some curly green strings from a nearby plate. "Should complement it nicely." She smiled as she positioned his meal in front of him and seemed about to say something more, but Ninjay's glance stopped her.

"Is something wrong?" Andel asked her mother.

Ninjay turned to the wafer-thin angel who waited behind her. "Cadewi, Alma, and some lamoway."

Inshogi looked at the table with relish. "Ah," he said. "Eat and enjoy!" He scissored a purple chunk between his hanta and held it up. "Our bodies are a love-song constructed by our souls from the bounty of El," he proclaimed. "Without a body to utilize it, the soul must be satisfied with love alone."

Huldar smiled. "Andel has shared your wisdom with us on a number of occasions," he said. "'To live so close to the Breath makes a friend of every breath' ... This is one of my favorites."

"Ah yes, one of my brother's." Inshogi nodded. "He was a navigator, has Andel told you?"

"She has told me, yes. May he rest sweetly in the Breath."

"Were you often in such danger?" Inshogi asked.

"Such danger as navigators face – no, but at the time Andel quoted him, we were on an island in the deep south ..." He turned to Andel.

She smiled. "You're the master storyteller! ... but yes." She turned to her father. "On a beach, slushy with ice. There were huge worms with beautiful markings – blue and white stripes ..."

"Were they dangerous?" Alma asked.

"No, not at all," Andel replied, "but packs of bright red lizards hunted them ..."

"Six legs ..." Huldar added, "and the front ones held up high, like this!" He demonstrated the leg position as best he could.

"Do many creatures have six legs?" Inshogi asked. "As you may know, our family has traveled a bit, but I've not seen any six-legged animals."

"Six legs and multiple eyes," Andel said. "It's a feature of that planet." She flashed an image of a scaly red face with three scarlet eyes, two on either side and one on its forehead. "They weren't very big, but they swarmed over the dunes right in front of us and overcame a giant worm that had already been injured by something else. Ate it alive."

The staff looked at each other, trading sub-audible messages.

"Huldar wanted to stay and watch what happened," Andel continued. "That poor creature! But the drama of it was amazing … then one of the lizards turned around and looked right at me, and my heart just stopped!"

Ninjay frowned. "That my daughter should be exposed to such terrors!"

"We were in no true danger," Huldar was quick to assure her. "The portal was right at our backs."

"Well, that is fascinating," Inshogi said. "I must say, I envy you two." He smiled encouragingly at his wife. "Such adventures, eh, my love?"

"It is a wonder they survived," Ninjay snapped. "Perhaps they will not be so lucky in the future. I have already lost one child. Is this all I have to look forward to?"

"Come now, love, life is to be treasured. And we have had some exploits of our own, eh? I remember camping on Haas, determined to see a wild Rukh. The bird of course," he explained. "The annangi Rukh are not so hard to find! Anyway, there we were, far from civilization, and we came face to face with a bento!"

"A bento?" Huldar raised his eyebrows appreciatively. "Remarkable creatures, and very dangerous!"

"Yes indeed!" Inshogi said. "At first I could see it quite clearly. We froze, not sure what we should do. When it saw us, it looked so surprised, didn't it, my love? Almost comical. But then … you know about their cryptic abilities?"

Huldar nodded. "You were lucky to see it at all."

"Well! It faded away, the whole creature – all the colors melting, disappearing, until all we could see were its huge, hungry eyes – which were at a level with our waists, I might add! And its big red tongue as it licked its invisible lips!"

Ninjay scowled. "Hardly suitable discussion for the dinner table."

"How did you get away, Father?" Andel asked. "You never told me this before."

Inshogi raised his hands theatrically. "Well, we stayed motionless, almost too frightened to breathe. If we'd even blinked, I think it would have eaten us, but eventually it padded on. It was quite some time before we were game to move again, wasn't it Ninjay, love? I mean, even their psychic signature fades, so how could we tell if it was still there?"

"Fascinating," Huldar said. "Face to face with the most elusive of predators? Now it's my turn to envy you."

"All this was before we were blessed." Ninjay said. Her lips tightened. "Young and irresponsible! Little did I understand the consequences if anything had happened. What death really meant."

Her wave of sorrow washed through the room. Huldar studied his now-empty plate.

"A storyteller are you, Huldar, eh?" Inshogi said brightly.

"Yes, Father," Andel said. "He has stories from all over the Known."

Huldar nodded, relieved to be back on safe ground. "I am most interested in the ancient oral histories, although who we are and where we came from – I haven't worked that one out yet."

"No one has," said Inshogi. "Perhaps our origins are El's secret, never to be disclosed." He paused, eyes twinkling beneath his brows. "A collector of stories?"

"Yes, I am," Huldar assured him.

"Well, I have a story you might like," he said. "Have you heard How the Trianogi Found Their Home?"

"Will you tell us?" Andel asked him. "We could sit by the fire, just as if we were camping. You could wear the shawl."

Huldar smiled. "I've brought some Lethian Besh with me, if you like?"

"It's quite strong stuff …" Inshogi said teasingly.

"Just to add atmosphere," Huldar laughed.

Inshogi turned to Ninjay and she sighed heavily. "If we must."

She got to her feet as if weighed down by an over-stocked personal Qalān and joined them as they settled on plump cushions by the fire. Huldar passed the white shawl to Inshogi and the three of them clinked the necks of bottles of Besh. Ninjay raised her glass of wine, but her smile looked forced.

"We dedicate this story of our beginnings to the bounty of El." Inshogi raised his bottle high. "Hear my words! After the birth of the archangels," he began, "all annangi lived in peace and harmony together on Giahn. At first, their daily lives continued much as they had in the past, but in time the differences between each House became more clearly defined and they bickered as children do while they are finding their way in the world."

He glanced at Huldar and Andel, and Huldar recalled that, without house screens, his hosts may have heard their earlier argument – among other things.

"Hermes was the first House to leave the greater tribe," Inshogi continued. "They claimed it was impossible for them to perform their duties with true impartiality when they were living among, and involved in, the everyday tussles that had begun to mar the annangi's lives – so when the navigators found a new habitable planet, they left. Angera they called it – still the Hermes' home-world to this day."

"Next to leave was Nhadu – their creativity compromised in the same way as the Hermes' impartiality had been. They settled on Grath, a lush world the annangi had visited before coming to Giahn, and it quickly became the creative hub of the Realm.

"On Giahn, the remaining Houses grew more restless and antagonistic. The actions of Hermes and Nhadu were questioned. No one had ever left the tribe before, and their loss made the annangi uncertain of who they were.

"So, Kahlishel Tiamät, the fourth God-Emperor, decided on a project to divert his people from their struggles and unite them in achievement, and all the Houses were invited to participate in the design and construction of a Palace to reflect their veneration of El. It would be the greatest architectural feat ever attempted, and, although the magnificent building we saw there in the Imperial City has grown on those bones, it is said that its design remains true to this day.

"Everyone waited while Trianog archangels meditated with the idea in mind, and when their vision was clear, the concept was shared with the Nhadu, who drew it as pictures. Maatu took those images and, with clever engineering, turned them into designs that could be built. During the construction stage, Cantori labored tirelessly, with total commitment to the plan. Faytha provided the necessary wealth for adornment, inside and out, while Leth grew food and made beautiful gardens to enhance the exterior, Naghari healed hurts, and Rukh kept an eye out for danger. Hermes relayed messages between all houses with complete impartiality and Tiamät was well pleased because it seemed the plan had worked.

"Finally the day came when the project was complete. The Imperial Palace was open to all and a huge celebration was held. The Imperial family moved into their rooms and for a while all were content. But without a common cause to unite them, the annangi soon reverted to their argumentative ways.

"After a spate of particularly aggressive brawling, many lives were lost and the Houses were shocked into an uneasy truce. The Leaders gathered and marched into the Palace. When Kahlishel would not speak to them, they banged on his door, demanding another solution.

"But instead of an answer, El's Chosen ordered the Rukh to move into the Palace to better protect him – there were no ashik in these early times – and the doors were locked against their noise.

"With the God-Emperor inaccessible, the remaining annangi turned to the Maatu to find them new homes among the stars, but the navigators were inexperienced in their craft, and finding new, habitable planets was slow.

"Soon, many dwellings were locked. Great Houses kept to themselves and every fresh outrage sparked another battle. Old scores were slow to settle, and weapon-smiths were in high demand.

"Then an angel of the Trianogi had a vision in which he was shown a solution to their problems.

"Full of joy, he rushed to tell the God-Emperor.

"'Please,' he said to the Rukh at the palace gates. 'El has sent me a prophecy. Our new homes are waiting for us, just as the Breath has blown.'

"The Rukh sneered that a lowly angel should imagine El had spoken to him. 'Only the God-Emperor Kahlishel speaks for El,' they said, and would not let him in.

"He knocked at the gates again. 'Please, let me speak to the God-Emperor and show him what El has shown me!'

"Finally the Rukh grew tired of the clamor and let him in, but to no avail.

"'I, El's Chosen, have meditated day and night!' the God-Emperor said to him. 'My head is sore from the strain, and still no words have come to me on the wind of the Breath. If El will not speak to His Chosen, why would he speak to you, a mere angel?'

"The angel wandered away, miserable and confused.

"On his way home, he passed the House of Maatu and one of the navigators saw him.

"'You look so sad,' she said. 'Is everything all right?'

"'No, it is not all right,' the Trianogi replied. 'I have had a vision and no one will listen to me. Our houses are locked, and so are our hearts. In order for annangi to grow, our hearts must be open, and so to each of us, El has allocated a planet where we can find our true natures and grow in peace. El has shown me this, and shown me how to find them, but the God-Emperor Kahlishel won't listen and the Rukh have sent me away.'

"'El speaks to whom he will,' said the Maatu, 'and I am listening. Planets are everywhere, but those capable of supporting annangi life are few. If your vision can help us find them, surely we must try?'

"Filled with new hope, they went together beneath the great dome of House Maatu to sit where the gate to the outer galaxy vibrated at its strongest.

"The Trianogi stilled his mind and waited, just as El had shown him. They stayed that way for some time, but nothing had happened and he was filled with shame.

"'I must have been mistaken after all,' he said dejectedly. 'You have been most kind, Lady Maatu, but I will go home now.'

"'Wait,' the Maatu said. 'Didn't you say something about opening our hearts? Maybe you and I should open our hearts to each other? Perhaps that is the full meaning of the vision?'

"The Trianogi agreed to try again, and joined hands with his Maatu friend. Almost immediately, their souls were taken as if by a mighty gust and swept into the vast unknown.

"'What can you see?' asked the Maatu.

"'I can see a sun, yellow like Giahn's, and ten planets spinning around it!' the Trianogi said.

"'Are any of them blue?' the Maatu asked.

"'Yes! There is a blue planet with green lands, and two blue moons like smaller sisters.'

"The Maatu followed him and saw a point where a portal through galactic Qalān could be made.

"'I need to get closer,' she said, 'to hear the vibration more clearly.'

"Together, they honed in on the location and saw a huge black bird soaring high above it.

"'Rukh!' the Trianogi cried. 'This is the home of the Rukh!'

"The very next day, they found the Unicorn of Cantori, then the serpent of Naghar and the Sword of Maatu were discovered in quick succession. Each time, the harmonies were committed to memory and passed on to the archangels of Maatu so that a chord of translation could be made.

"The labyrinth of Faytha was next to be revealed, then the scythes of Leth – but still there was no new home for Trianog.

"'Perhaps we are destined to be homeless,' the angel said.

"'I think not,' replied the Maatu. 'You must open your heart to the song of the galaxy in the same way as you have opened your heart to me.'

"With that, they tried again, and this time the Trianogi felt himself filled with the most magnificent sound his mind could comprehend.

"'That is the song of the stars,' the Maatu told him.

"He surrendered to the great vibration and let it draw him from Giahn to a green and blue world more beautiful than any other, and there, at last, the three feathers of Trianog hung in perfect balance.

"When he returned, his face burned in agony, and he found himself Marked with the first ever Shamkar. He took the name Oriien, and eventually married the God-Emperor's daughter … but that is another story!

"This is why we Trianogi pride ourselves on our open hearts and minds. As archangels, it is our duty to ensure the welfare of our people, but we are always aware that El speaks to whom He will; our sixth God-Emperor was a half-breed, and angels too can be Marked.

"Hear my words," Inshogi said, then he bowed and handed the shawl back to Huldar.

"Wonderful!" Huldar congratulated him.

Andel took his arm. "I think you have a rival, Huldar my love!"

Inshogi smiled at them both. "Love is the soft veil that shields the soul," he said gently. "And I am overjoyed to hear the connection between you spoken aloud." He lifted his bottle again and toasted, "To love!"

"If you don't mind me asking," Huldar said, "Inshogi is an unusual name. Where does it originate?"

"That is another interesting story," Inshogi winked. "There is a Hermes in our ancestry, but stranger still, Inisha of Hermes was the daughter of a navigator, Shamkarun Oman of Maatu, brother to the then leader of House Maatu. She was a wild and headstrong character by all accounts, but when her husband, my great-grandfather, died, her heart was broken. Inisha left her life here on Frith and returned to Angera. That's where the wanderlust comes from in our family, eh, Andel my dear? And my name is a derivative of hers – a proud heritage!"

"Proud heritage?" Ninjay shook her head. "How can you say that? Our 'proud heritage' killed our son, my Aanjay!" She rounded on Andel. "And you! Traipsing around the furthest reaches of the Realm with nothing but a degenerate Gok, a handful of angels – one of them a half-breed – and this stubborn romantic between you and disaster?" Her eyes half-closed with pain. "You don't know …"

"What don't I know?" Andel retorted. "Why won't you tell us? Here's Father telling a story about why our people are so open and honest and yet you are keeping secrets!"

Ninjay got to her feet. "Now is not the time!"

"It's your foretelling, isn't it?" Andel cried. "What did you see? Why can't you tell us?"

Huldar had never seen Andel so furious. He reached for her mind but anger closed him out. "Andel," he said soothingly, "your mother will tell us when she is ready."

"Stay out of this!" she barked. "I have been a good, submissive daughter. I have paid for Aanjay's 'crime' for long enough!"

"Andel! Please!" her father cried.

With a sob, Ninjay raced from the room and slammed the door. There was another bang as she left the house.

Andel shrugged her shoulders helplessly. "But it's true, Father. For years I have blamed myself, accepted my mother's unending punishment for my brother's death as justified, but it's not. I was a child. I didn't kill him. It was an accident!"

"Of course you didn't kill him!" Inshogi said. "Whoever said you did? But your mother was inconsolable, and she knows she couldn't face it again. All the time you were away, she suffered." He paused, watching the fireplace. "She loves you so much. If anything happened to you it would break her."

A gust of wind moaned around the house and disturbed the flames, so Huldar went to the window to adjust the charm. The thought of Ninjay outside in the weather, distraught with grief, was a hard one. After years living rough, he well knew the effects of exposure.

"Where would she go?" he asked. "I should find her."

"No, I'll go," Andel said heavily. "It's my fault."

"We'll go together," Huldar offered.

"I can find my own mother, thank you," she said firmly. *Don't come after us*, she added more gently. *Maybe we'll be better able to talk when we're alone.*

The outside door slammed again. Inshogi and Huldar looked at each other.

"Children," Inshogi said. "So beloved it's hard to remember they are not ourselves and have their own threads in El's great tapestry … Drink?" He placed two small glasses on the table. "I have a fine liqueur, local stuff, excellent. Perhaps now while we wait would be a good time to try it?"

Uncorked, the bottle released a sweet scent reminiscent of easanberries. Thick red-brown fluid tumbled into the glass and swirled lazily. Huldar lifted it to his mouth. The aroma alone was intoxicating – but before he could drink, Inshogi looked up, his eyes fixed on the middle distance.

"What is it?" Huldar asked.

"I'm not sure. Ninjay called out, and now – nothing."

"'Nothing' as if she doesn't want to talk, or 'nothing' as if she's unconscious?"

Inshogi's face crumpled. "Something is wrong."

Have you found your mother? Huldar called to Andel. *Your father senses something.*

An image of moonlit trees came back to him as Andel followed her mother's faint tracks in the moss. She came across an area that seemed scuffled. Her vision darted sideways to a shadowy figure. Huldar received a burst of alarm then her presence went dark.

"Come on!" he cried.

He and Inshogi raced for the door. With their minds lightly linked, they quickly found the place where Andel and Ninjay had been. Huldar sharpened his eyesight until his surroundings seemed bright as day.

See here! He pointed out an area of bruised moss. A nearby section seemed stained with a fine brown powder. He rolled a pinch between thumb and forefinger and noted its smooth, dry texture.

These may be spores of some kind … He brought them to his nose to test the odor …

Huldar, no! Inshogi cried, but the warning was too late and Huldar fell to the ground, rendered unconscious by the action of the puff-ball fungus, seshura.

THE AGENT'S FATE

You fool! Lucaät of Faytha yelled through his Hermes's connection. *Why did you take her too?*

I've been watching them, as per your orders, the Agent replied. *He hates her. Won't get anything from him on her behalf.*

Of course you would. Andel loves her mother and he loves Andel! That's enough!

Yes, Tsemkarun Andel, the Agent stressed the title, *but she's a diviner, not some Ashik warrior. Like all Trianogi, she's as weak as a Hermes' smile in that department and the spores will make her weaker still. If you want information about mineral deposits, she's far more useful than the Lethian. And besides, the only safe hideout we have here is a cave, and she's a diviner – think about it. And also besides, she was about to find me with her mother. You said no deaths.*

I thought you were smarter than this. How do you plan to hold her?

Same way I'll hold the mother.

Ninjay might be an archangel, but the Agent knew she was not strong, and in her weakened state he could easily find the chord that tethered her soul to her body and hold her life to ransom. The Agent passed this plan along to Lucaät. It wasn't hugely imaginative, but brutal enough to work. Perhaps he should have discussed it with his boss first, but what was the purpose of reconnaissance if not to refine plans?

She'll tell us all we need to know, he said. *No need to risk any involvement with Huldar, and the secrecy of our information can be preserved. Secrecy is vital. You said that. No one else knows what we know about the eyes, and no one else knows about the nacrite. If this works, by the time the Guild releases the relevant reports, we'll be way ahead. I'll get the intel quickly, knock them out again, pop them back to Rian and get Tsemkarun Jaldan to fuddle their memories.* He showed Lucaät the face of the seemingly affable Trianogi, someone they'd used similarly in the past.

Lucaät paused, and the Agent knew he was getting his point across.

This is not some seedy Gok, here, no valueless slave for you to practice on! Lucaät cautioned. *This is a powerful Tsemkarun and her even more powerful lover. If you kill any one of them – or if they somehow find out I'm involved – you're dead.*

You don't mean that, the Agent said glibly, but without doubt he knew his boss meant every word. In his head, he reviewed his plan yet again. Maybe he had made a mistake … but he didn't think so.

The mother will be waking any minute. Do you want me to let them go? he offered.

It's too late now, Lucaät said caustically. *We'll never get another chance. Don't forget to use that mask thing. Cost me a fortune. If they see your face, Tsemkarun Jaldan's work will be compromised.*

After Lucaät withdrew, the Agent returned to the cave and considered his options. Neither captive had woken, but that time was not far off. His thoughts drifted to the Explorers' Guild. They'd been very tight indeed with reports from the new Imperial planet, and he wondered why. But that was Lucaät's business, and if more information was required, it was up to him to get it. He didn't have to know the reason.

From Qalān he withdrew a mask made of sheer fabric, charmed to hide his face and shape. For a long time, its existence had been little more than a rumor, but once Lucaät had heard about it, he'd persisted until he'd tracked it down. And as for his plan to hold Andel's mother, the inquisitor had taught him one did not require great strength to find the force that tethered a soul to its body, just skill and tenacity. The risk was that it was an either-or ploy. The victim could certainly be tortured or killed, but because of the skill needed to hold the cord, there would be little energy left to finesse the extraction of information. In this case, that would not matter. Andel would hand him what he needed on a platter. He just had to be careful not to accidentally kill her mother before he had what he wanted.

Ninjay of Trianog stirred. He donned his mask. Soon there would be a small window of opportunity, a gap between the natural defenses of sleep and the contrived protections of consciousness. It was then the assault could be made.

The seshura spores would lengthen the period of weakness, but there was no time to hesitate. As soon as there were signs of emerging consciousness, he gripped the bare skin of her arm and forced himself past barriers in flux.

Like disturbed fish in a murky pond, the memories he bumped flashed their insights, but if she came to full wakefulness her natural defenses would burn his mind. Instead, he used the inquisitor's technique to grasp the silvery cord that bound her to this existence.

As her awareness surfaced, he cautioned her not to move and congratulated himself on work well done.

Soon after, Tsemkarun Andel's eyes opened to gummy slits. She wriggled a bit and tried to move her hands and feet, then seemed to understand they were bound. The Agent waited. There was no more to do until she was fully awake, not long now …

"What have you done to my mother?"

He was shocked to see her bonds fly apart and smack into the walls of the cave.

She struggled to her feet and steadied herself against the chair, but her Tsemkar glowed white, anger ran like flames through her haze, and it dawned on him that that he may have underestimated her aggressive potential.

"Release her immediately!"

He buried his uncertainty and stroked her mother's head. "Of course I will, Lady Andel," he soothed. "Just as soon as I have what I want."

Andel made a brave show of standing tall, although sweat beaded her brow and he knew from experience the cracking headache she must have.

"Who are you?" She blinked at his mask as if trying to force her senses beyond it. "Let us go! Huldar and my father will find us, and there won't be much left of you when they do!"

"An ecologist and an elderly landlord?" He sniggered. "I can't say I'm overly worried."

"You should be."

She tottered a step closer, but stopped when he held up his hand.

"All in good time," he said. "If you look you will see that I hold your mother's life." Ninjay gasped as he squeezed the cord with his mind, then lay still again, too afraid to do anything but listen. "Tell me what I want to know and I'll set you both free."

"And if I don't have it?"

"It will be a long time before anyone finds your remains."

Andel glared at him coldly, and he smiled to himself. As the inquisitor had said, time and time again, it was simply a matter of leverage. Despite her power, his plan was unfolding as it should.

"There is nacrite on the Imperial planet Went," he said. "I want to know where it is and how it can be extracted."

"Nacrite?" She seemed nonplussed. "All this for nacrite? Why not simply read the reports?"

He shrugged. "The Guild won't release them. I'm sure they have their reasons."

"Probably so people like you won't be involved," she sneered.

He moved his hand toward her mother's neck and squeezed the cord again. Ninjay's eyes rolled back in her head.

"Don't you hurt her!"

"Then tell me!"

"How? I have no map. I can't draw it for you!"

Here came the risky part of his plan … He held out his hand. "Show me."

Andel barely hesitated, doubtless aware of the discrepancy in their strengths and abilities. "I have your mother's life," he reminded her. "The slightest trouble from you and I'll end it. It's a reflex, a compulsion so ingrained you won't have time to stop it.

She nodded and completed the connection, but if a mere look could murder, he knew he'd be dead.

He shuddered as she rushed into him, full of strength and rage, but Ninjay gasped as his mind reacted and she backed off.

Please, daughter, tell him what he wants! … It was odd to have someone speak through him. He could feel her reluctant acknowledgement.

How are we going to do this? she asked him.

Just transfer the knowledge.

It takes time to prepare.

He replied with a thought-cluster that made it clear he would not wait.

Decisions snapped through her brain with blinding speed. He could not hope to keep up, but he could feel potential amassing.

No tricks, he warned.

She ignored him and continued to gather information and render it into a form that could be transferred.

The process slowed, then stopped. *Are you ready?* she asked.

He opened his mind just a sliver and offered a tendril of connection. Every ounce of energy that was not holding her mother was directed toward guarding against a trap, but the transfer began seamlessly. He blinked as images of locations, statistics, strata and volume flickered through his visual cortex. There was no time to analyze the information and he stifled his mind's tendency toward rebellion. Faster and faster it streamed, the link pushed to capacity. Lucaät would be pleased. There was more than enough there to prepare a full mining operation.

Darker images began to flow and he had the sense of being underwater. His mind reeled. How much data did he really need?

Then whiteness bloomed in the dark … cottony whiteness, and fear that grew like a beast inside him. How could this seemingly fragile diviner have known such terror? He tried to cut the link, but found it jammed it open.

Don't you care about your mother? he shrieked. There were ways to turn her attack back on itself, but they slipped beyond him and fear of the never-ending whiteness consumed him.

Make it stop, he whimpered.

I lived through this, she said. *And if you think I survived it just to be bullied by a sniveling glubber like you, you're wrong!*

When the Agent awoke, it was dark. At first, he remembered he was in a cave, then a bud of whiteness grew and bloomed until it was all there was. Fear filled him. He huddled in on himself and tried to stop shaking. Every sense contracted, lest he draw attention to himself.

Voices came. Something moved in the white like the reverse of a shadow.

He tried to back away, but there was nothing to touch, nowhere to go. The shape came closer. He screamed in frustration. White moved on white. He couldn't let it touch him.

Help me! he cried, but there was no one to hear.

The thing reached out.

I'm Tsemkarun Jaldan, it said. *I've come to help you.*

The sounds were meaningless. It was almost on him. Liquid terror oozed over his skin. He fought back as hard as he could and screamed again, a hopeless wail … *Don't touch me!* DON'T TOUCH ME!

ANDEL AND HER MOTHER

Andel looked down at her mother's pale face and wiped the loose hair from her forehead. She was so deeply unconscious that it was hard to find signs of life, but they were there. As she'd searched for them, she'd also seen the damage. Her attachment to this body was so fine now that only by her own will could she return.

"Please, Mother, stay with me …"

Tears landed on her mother's eyelids and dribbled downward as if they belonged.

"I'm sorry we fought," she whispered. "I know you will tell me what you saw when the time is right. I was wrong. I won't argue … please. Just speak …"

It seemed ironic that she had used her experience of being imprisoned in Qalān to trap and destroy their captor, and now her mother lay in her lap as Lind had done – sleeping, but broken beyond repair.

She put a blanket over her mother's still body, and folded another to place beneath her head.

When their captor had fallen, she had not known what to do. Her mother was too heavy for her to carry, but they had to get away. The force she used to move stones could not be used to lift living things … but the chair! She could lift the chair and her mother in it quite easily.

Quickly, she found the ropes and retied them around Ninjay's torso. Her fingers stiffened, juggling the weight as she picked up speed, running with the levitated chair before her.

Soon, there had been no light at all and even her archangel eyes could see nothing, but her mind could sense ahead, it was used to doing so, and her flight continued through twisting caverns and narrow spaces until she could carry the weight no further. It was only after she'd stopped that she'd remembered the globe she kept in Qalān, the legacy of an explorer's regime.

Huldar! she cried. *Huldar, we're here!* But the rock around them was too dense, and her voice would not carry. If only they had become dabaku as he'd wanted to, their bond would have led him to her.

She closed her eyes to divine further through the cave system and found they'd stopped not far from a sinkhole that plunged deep into an underground lake.

She redirected her senses upward … a strange sensation, as if the world had turned upside down, and quickly guessed they were buried far beneath a mountain chain.

Perhaps they could go back the way they'd come? How long would their captor stay unconscious? She had no idea, but perhaps someone knew where he was and would come to find him and then, when the cave was empty, she would either know the way out because she'd seen it, or she would be able to find it herself … because there must be one.

Satisfied with her plan, she raised the globe with her mind and suspended it a little way ahead. It was hard to return her mother's dead weight to the chair, but when she had her in place she retied the ropes and started back, following the trail of her footprints in the pristine dust.

After the rest her psychic strength had somewhat returned, but the effects of the seshura lingered. Ninjay's limp body tipped at the slightest imbalance and without the adrenaline boost, it was much more difficult to keep her upright. When she stumbled on a boulder and nearly sent them both tumbling, Andel knew she needed another break.

She propped the chair up against the cave wall and checked for signs of life.

There were none.

Her heart raced. It could not be! How could her mother have left her? She tried again … and there it was, the tiniest flicker of warmth. She was not gone yet. She was still fighting.

She ducked as a scream echoed through the chamber, and she knew her captor had woken. Then another cry bounced through the caverns and another, each more horrific than the last, and she began to cry. Had she done this? She looked at her mother's slack features. Had she killed her mother and inflicted this terrible pain, all from anger?

The terrible sounds gurgled to silence. She heard faint murmurs and quickly screened them both with the tightest cover she knew – flinched as the quiver of another's awareness passed them by.

Minutes passed. She estimated the time she'd run through the caverns, subtracted the short distance she'd retraced and decided to risk using farsight.

Her vision zoomed through the cave complex, but in the utter darkness it was impossible to see the traces of her flight. Still, her unerring sense of direction took her through the maze, and by trial and error led her to the faint glimmer of an abandoned globe.

The room was empty but the trail of her footsteps was obvious. Whoever had come for their captor might return.

She looked at her mother's face, gently illuminated by the light of her own globe. There were features she had not noticed before – faint lines of worry on her brow and of pain beside her mouth. Her hair was the same color as her own, and her eyebrows formed perfect shallow arcs above slightly tilted eyes. How she wished those eyes would open. However angry her mother might be for what she had done, it would be worth it.

With a sigh, she hoisted her again and stumbled on, but the effort was telling. How she wished she had Casco or Cobar to watch over her now.

Whatever her mother thought, she'd loved every minute of the Uri'madu … except for the time between gates in Qalān … poor Lind rocking from side to side, counting her toes over and over.

She paused to catch her breath. Darkness pressed down as if the light of her globe was a sin. She tried not to think of what had happened to their attacker.

"Huldar …" The whispered name caught in her throat. He must be frantic with worry; her father too … And then came another memory of Went. The beacon stone – the small orange marker she had carried with her into Qalān. He had replaced it with the opalised seashell she'd given him, and said that if ever she needed him all she had to do was whisper his name into its fiery heart. The sound would reach him no matter where he was, and he would come to her.

She fished frantically for the tone that would summon it from Qalān. At last her fingers closed around its delicate ridges.

She brought its small hollow to her lips and whispered, "Huldar …"

The silence was complete. Tears fell on her hands.

"Huldar!"

Had he heard?

"Andel, listen to me," her mother croaked.

"Mother? You're alive!"

"I don't have much time. You must listen."

"What do you mean, not much time? Oh, Mother I'm so sorry!" she cried. "I should've just given him what he wanted. I thought we could escape, but look, look what he's done to you."

"There is no time for this," Ninjay rasped. "You must marry Huldar. Promise me!" Her wandering gaze fixed on Andel's face, demanding obedience.

"I will, I promise!"

"Good. You must return to Went. The planet calls you. Strange things – a long road … long, dark, and very far."

Her voice trailed off. Andel wept harder as tears flooded her mother's eyes. A vision came to her, one bright moment mind to mind, of a beautiful young archangel dressed in impossible finery, and a tall, handsome husband beside her.

"You'll be there! You'll see it too," she sobbed. "You said we'd return to Giahn for a 'day of days'. You said so!"

Ninjay smiled through her tears. "My granddaughter," she whispered proudly. "Who would have thought it?"

Andel's head bowed. The regal vision was not of her and Huldar …

Her mother's head shook weakly from side to side. Her fingers moved. Andel took her hand. More vision of her foretelling streamed through the contact. Streets full of people running in terror, wild-eyed warriors dropping from the sky, then those same streets with crumbling façades, doors ajar, overgrown and empty. She saw herself leaving Went, her face wet with tears, a baby in her arms, the whisper of a name, Innana, carried on the Breath like a song. Strange creatures paraded before her, a wild world of hardship and beauty, and then …

Wild little thing, Ninjay whispered. *You must keep her safe. No cost is too great. Her gift is worth more to the Realm than even your own beloved's* … Her staring eyes dulled. Her mind darkened … *Remember the story of Apen's bride* …

For a time, they sat together, motionless in the deep silence of the cavern. Gradually, Ninjay's labored breaths drifted further apart, until each one seemed it would be the last.

Andel held her hands tightly and kissed them. *Please stay with me!* she cried. *I love you! Please, hold on!* But finally there was no more breath to breathe. As Ninjay's soul left her body, a slight breeze moved Andel's hair with a joyful tousle like her loving fingers once had, so long ago.

Sweet daughter, her death-cry came, *their deaths are not your fault, and neither is mine. Take care of your father … a better parent than I …*

Ages later, she opened bleary eyes to see a light bobbing cautiously toward her. Huldar's relief rushed into her heart, filling empty spaces with love, but the space that had been her mother's remained cold, never to be filled again.

Where's Father? she whispered.

He could not come, Huldar wept, *but Jeiah and Kalel are here to help bring her home.*

MIRASHAEL'S PLAN

Mirashael hovered around the huge soft bed, a shadowy shape in slippered feet.

Leahät yawned and stretched a little, more comfortable than she thought she'd ever been, and he parted the curtain to look inside.

"Ah, dearest lady, you are awake?"

His expression was so anxious, she tried not to smile.

"Feeling better, yes? Your color is certainly much, much better! Shall I bring you something? Some food perhaps, luscious fruit from the Faraway Isles, or a lovely cold guerdi to quench your thirst?"

She groaned weakly, just for effect, and passed him an image of a steaming pot of tea. "Only if it's not too much trouble?" she murmured.

As Mirashael dashed off to comply she added two cups to the image, and a small pot of honey – she did like some honey in her tea.

He soon returned with a steaming pot and two dainty cups. "How are you feeling?" he asked as he set the tea on the bed beside her.

"You have servants who could do this," she said.

"But would they do it as well as I? With the same consideration?" He whisked a flower from behind his back and laid it on the tray.

"Probably not," she conceded. She brought the bright red bloom to her nose and inhaled its fine aroma. Her haze glowed with happiness and she didn't mind him seeing her so, but as Mirashael prepared the tea, she noticed a certain precision to his movements, as if ritual was necessary for the containment of his energy.

"Is there something on your mind?" she enquired.

"Only if my lady is feeling up to it."

"I am," she assured him. "There is still a little residual pain, but in myself? I've never felt better." A sudden rush of affection brought moisture to her eyes. "Thank you, Mirashael," she smiled. "Thank you so much."

"As promised!" He bowed with a flourish. "You will never feel unwanted again."

He sat beside her on the bed and served her tea with a dab of sweetness, just how she liked it.

"If it's the books," she said, "I am quite ready to resume, although I fear that serving in the café might be beyond me for a little while yet."

"No, no! Dear lady, no! It is not with such mundane matters that I disturb you. No, it is another thing, entirely un-mundane, if there is such a word. I know the concept quite well, at least."

"What is it?" she asked, genuinely curious now.

"My lady, it is to do with your husband." After a short pause he continued, "I cannot find it in me to ask that he rest sweetly in the Breath. But if we are clever about it, he has left you a legacy of great value."

"The Eyes?"

"Indeed yes. They are yours, but if truth be told, they should be the property of the Imperium, and if the Tiamät gets hold of them, you will get nothing in return. But worse, much worse: I am afraid that if the situation is handled the wrong way we may lose our lives."

"Our lives?"

"Once Lucaät of Faytha figures out who has your husband's treasure, and it won't take much – his influence in court is far greater than mine, as you can imagine – he may try to convince the God-Emperor that we have attempted to steal what was rightfully his."

"And he would do this?"

"Most certainly. Sadly, Lucaät has been known to be vindictive where it will do him the greatest good, and this stroke of genius would both eliminate me, paltry rival that I am, and set him in Ishät Ashik's great good favor."

The answer seemed simple. "Then just give them to him!" she said. "Or give them to the God-Emperor and that's an end to it."

"Yes, we could do that," Mirashael nodded, "but how? We have no means of getting them to the God-Emperor in person. I have my contacts, to be sure, but none so highly placed. And even if we pursued this most honorable of pathways, the gems being what they are, we may be still accused of trying to keep them for ourselves."

Leahät thought for a moment. "And we can't sell them, can we, because they are too unique."

"Exactly!" Mirashael nodded as if she'd passed some sort of test. "They would be traced to us and again, we could be accused of trying to keep them from their rightful owner."

"And the Faythans know about them?"

"Yes, and I'm afraid that Lord Brätan Gok knows of them also, but here's the thing. Neither luminary has traced them to us – as yet."

"And that shrewdness in your eyes …" She smiled. "You have a plan?"

"Indeed, yes, I do, but the prize is yours, my lady, and I will do nothing except with your permission."

"Then, I give you permission, Mirashael." She hitched herself up higher against the headboard. "What is this plan? I am anxious to hear it!"

He smiled and nestled closer. "I'm afraid your one-time husband must be 'found'. Lucaät will come to see the body … Faythans are acquisitive. He thinks it belongs to him. When he turns up, I sell him the Eyes. Soon after, I will tell Brätan Gok that Lucaät of Faytha has them. Brätan has power enough to get them from Lucaät and then *he* returns them to the God-Emperor," he concluded triumphantly.

Leahät though about this for a moment. It seemed terribly clever, but what could go wrong? Her mother had often talked politics, but it had been very long ago. "So, Faytha will respect you and Brätan will owe us a favor?"

Mirashael's eyes sparkled as he took another sip from his dainty little teacup.

"And you will have recompense for your inheritance," he said.

She drank more tea and thought about this. Perhaps she should have felt remorse for the idea of using her husband's body so, but she didn't. "Are you sure he will come to see? It seems very macabre. What if he already knows he is dead?"

"He won't be able to help himself," Mirashael said. "His spies are still watching your house, just as they are watching Karesk, the Imperial Bays and all the Bays on all nearby planets. He does not know."

"Then we should act soon, before he does realize," she said. "Duvät's death-cry must have gone to someone."

"I am sorry, my lady. It must pain you to be ignored at the last after all you have suffered."

"I think my pride is hurt," she admitted, "but very little else. To be honest, I didn't want it, and this way he is gone and there is no residue to hold me back. So, when do we start?"

"You are the bravest and best of all the ladies I know – and that is a fair portion." He gave her a cheeky grin.

"And the body?" she prompted.

He winked at her. "Very nice indeed!"

"Mirashael!" Leahät felt the blood rush to her cheeks.

Mirashael's grin broadened. "Ah then, if it's Duvät's body we're talking about, I'll have a Shamkarun sing it clean and I estimate that Lucaät of Faytha will be there to see it by some time tonight. All we need do is wait."

A chilling thought dampened her optimism. "Will he kill you rather than pay you?"

"It is unlikely," Mirashael assured her. "Faythans respect coin. They understand the need for an exchange."

"Unlikely?" Her heart clanged with sudden fear. "That's not good enough! Please, don't put yourself in danger. I couldn't bear it if anything happened to you."

He studied her face for a moment, as if every line and angle was significant, and his haze flushed with pleasure. "Dearest lady, your care … is so precious to me – more wonderful than any jewel or gem. But would you think less of me if I sent someone in my place?"

She looked into his tawny eyes. If he was killed, she would be devastated, but this was the other side of the coin, the side he begged her to accept. And if, because of her, someone was killed in his stead … he would feel it deeply and the dishonor would forever stain their relationship.

"Then take someone with you, a bodyguard, please!" she insisted. "Someone you can trust. I know you have suitable employees."

He saluted her with his teacup. "I know just the one."

"Good!" She relaxed and drained the last of her tea.

"Another?" he suggested. "And I must tell you, I heard the most tantalizing gossip from the shop last night …"

She listened with half an ear as he related an improbable story about the Commissioner of Mines and an exotic beast. The tea slipped warmly down her throat, and she felt comfortable and treasured for the first time in her life, yet a new anxiety muted her happiness. Whatever Mirashael truly was, the only thing she could not forgive him for at this point would be his death.

LUCAÄT AND MIRASHAEL

Lucaät of Faytha stepped from a broad street in the jewelers' district of Crafters into a narrow alley adjacent to the enclave. A barrel-chested Cantori named Sender, the Agent's potential replacement, came through with him.

The portal guard stared at Lucaät's high-status braid, as if unsure what to say.

Lucaät gestured toward Sender. "He's with me."

"Yes, my lord!" The ashessé bowed and waved them on.

"Tiresome," he murmured to Sender, but he doubted his new operative understood why.

A heavy screen slapped into place, and Lucaät frowned. His former aide would never have been so clumsy. What exactly had been done to the Agent even Tsemkarun Jaldan of Trianog, a specialist in matters of the mind, did not know – but it was obscene. The information he'd been sent to get was all there, but completely irretrievable, and while Lucaät wasted no energy on plans for revenge, he knew in his Faythan soul that one day he would make Tsemkarun Andel of Trianog pay.

With a flick of his fingers Sender signaled him toward an uninviting street on the edge of the enclave.

Again, Lucaät stifled his irritation. He knew where they were going. He was the one who'd given Sender the location in the first place.

Heads turned as they pushed through a battered door into a seedy bar. His nose wrinkled at the smell of old ale and the half-breeds he imagined would have been there if the embargo was not still in place. The barkeep looked him up and down, then spoke to Sender.

"What does he want?"

Sender slouched casually against the counter. The barkeep leaned closer.

"Body been found hereabouts?" Sender asked quietly.

The barkeep tossed his head. "Back room. Nasty business."

"No one claimed it?"

"Not yet, but clean as clean, apart from his clothes, that is, and a few other stains. You taking it?"

"We'll see," Sender told him.

"Well someone's got to get rid of it," the barkeeper grumbled. He wiped the counter with a discolored damp rag. "Who's your high and mighty there?" His chin jutted toward Lucaät.

"None of your business." Sender's tone was matter-of-fact, but his stony veil spoke volumes.

The barkeep backed off. Lucaät was impressed. Maybe Sender would work out after all. Just a slightly different skill-set.

The back room was a sorry affair, with bare floorboards and peeling walls. As they pushed aside the door curtain, he saw Duvät's body sprawled on the bed. Pale insects scuttled from the light. As their friend at the bar had noted, a Shamkarun had already attended and there was no sign of his personal Qalān.

Sender prodded the remains. "This what you wanted to see?"

What had he expected to find? Lucaät asked himself. How could a Breathless body lead him to the missing Eyes? Then his neck prickled. Someone stepped from the shadows and Sender crouched, ready for action.

The interloper held a steaming vessel in his hands. With a small flourish he removed the lid and a delicious smell filled the room.

"Finest in the Realm!" he said, and lifted the bowl a little. "Do try one."

"Mirashael of Cantori." Lucaät winced a little at the shirt. It looked like it had been involved in a dyers' riot. "It's been a while."

Mirashael looked him up and down. "And you, Lucaät of Faytha, so very stylish! But then, I would expect nothing less. And your new best friend?" He tipped his head toward Sender.

"What are you doing here?" Lucaät asked.

"I came to talk terms." Mirashael placed the bowl of omosa on Duvät's chest and pulled another covered dish from Qalān. He opened the lid, just a crack, and released a flare of rainbow light that could only have come from an Eye of Bel Nishani. Moments later it closed.

Lucaät's mind whirled.

Stand down! he ordered Sender. *Wait outside!*

He missed the Agent with an almost physical pang. How many games of ashut had they played together … most of them lost? How had Mirashael of Cantori found the eyes when they'd tried everything and failed?

Mirashael dusted something from the front of his hideous shirt. His face was politely inquiring, his veil a shield of perfection and haze annoyingly unreadable. How could one play such an enigmatic foe?

"I'm listening," he said at last.

Mirashael cocked his head. "My client has instructed me to offer the entire cache of these singular … omosa … for sale."

"How much?"

"If you would allow me?"

Lucaät nodded. The air firmed as a stout screen cut the room from outside interference, and he received Mirashael's sending, an extraordinary sum written on virtual paper.

"My, my!" He blinked. "Your client certainly appreciates their food."

"As do you," Mirashael replied. "Your only chance," he said firmly. "Here and now."

"Limited shelf-life?"

"As always with seafood."

Mirashael returned the covered dish to Qalān. The smell of the real omosa pervaded the shabby sleeping quarters, trapped by the density of their screen. The asking price was enormous, almost all the projected revenue from his gambling operations for the entire standard year to come, and then some. He looked at Duvät's empty face, no more beautiful in death than it had been in life. What would the Agent have advised?

"And if I don't agree?"

Mirashael gave a florid wink. "I've heard that Brätan Gok might have a taste for omosa, or maybe even the God-Emperor himself."

"They won't pay nearly so much."

"No," Mirashael agreed. "But then Tiamät will own the prize, not you."

"I need a moment to think."

"Of course! Do try one." The Cantori selected an omosa for himself. "They are not poisoned. I would not compromise the taste!"

Lucaät reached over Duvät's body and picked a seafood parcel from the bowl. The first bite filled his mouth with wonderful flavor.

"Congratulations," he said to Mirashael. "These are a sensation."

"Worth every coin, as I'm sure you'd agree."

"I have some big mining leases coming my way," Lucaät said eventually. "Remote planets … it can be hard to find labor, even harder to find good caterers. Perhaps, for a small reduction in your client's terms, I could ensure these prospects come your way?"

"Show me."

Lucaät sent the virtual paper back to Mirashael with the figure somewhat reduced, but below it was a long-term option for him to supply the mining operations on the Imperial Planet Went with skilled and unskilled labor, and another, separate Imperial contract to feed the entire mission. Their combined value far outstripped the immediate cash pruned from the original figure.

As Mirashael's eyebrows gave an involuntary twitch, Lucaät could almost see the Agent smiling.

"Do you have these opportunities to offer?" the Cantori asked.

"I do," he assured him, and in a few weeks' time it would be true.

"Even the Imperial one?"

"I have secured exclusive rights." That at least was verifiable.

He watched as Mirashael took another omosa from the bowl and slowly ate. In this type of negotiation, it was unwritten law that no external communication could take place. If Sender had remained within the perimeter of the screen, Mirashael would no doubt have used the assistance of his assassin, Daric Enna, to come to a decision. Perhaps it was good that Agent was no longer available.

Mirashael swished the last piece of fish around his mouth and swallowed. "How about this," he said, and returned the virtual paper as Lucaät had sent it, but with exactly half of what had been cut from the figure restored.

"These terms are enticing," he added, "but exploration on the planet you mention has only recently begun. I have no guarantee as to when, if ever, these operations will take place."

Lucaät took a deep breath. "Agreed, these contacts represent a longer-term profit projection," he argued, "but overall you will have secured an opportunity to continue as my principal supplier of labor and provender. Surely you see? This extends the potential return on your own investment immeasurably."

"Why would you offer me this?" Mirashael asked. "Coin is here and now – clean, no further attachment, no questions, no ongoing drama …"

"And this from someone whose shirt fairly screams its presence to the Realm?"

The corners of Mirashael's eyes creased. Lucaät noted a slight softening of his haze and almost smiled in return. The game was his.

"And you have not wiped my offer completely from the sheet?" he continued. "I think you will accept this proposal, my friend – perhaps in your heart you already have. I think you are too clever not to."

"I must think of my client's fortunes," Mirashael countered. "Not my own."

"Your client?" Lucaät paused. Was there truly someone else involved? Did someone else know? He looked at the body again. The death-cry. "The wife."

"Yes, indeed. You are most perceptive," said Mirashael. "About to be a very wealthy lady indeed."

"I'm sure she'll be most grateful," Lucaät said sarcastically. "Alone with all those assets? She'll need expert guidance, of course."

Mirashael's head tilted and Lucaät was surprised to see a steely hint of anger. "It's clear you don't know her. The Lady Leahät is a very special lady, yes, and most honorable. It is with her you will be dealing, so you'd best remember her name for next time, and become accustomed to speaking of her with respect."

"My apologies," Lucaät said. He made a mental note to be careful. Cantori, once bought, made it their honor to see a project through, as he knew only too well from his association with the Agent. Despite his apparent insouciance and limited resources, Mirashael was never to be underestimated, and with this boost to his range and potential, and his apparent affection for the widow, it would certainly be in Lucaät's best interests to keep him close.

"Are we done then?" he asked. "Will you accept my terms?"

"Do you have the coin?" Mirashael responded.

"Yes, although you must understand that such a vast sum cannot be carried in person."

"Sad," Mirashael said. "I was looking forward to seeing you and the Lady Leahät working together."

The Cantori got up to leave. Lucaät's heart raced. For the glory of Faytha, he had to have those Eyes! "I can give you a note! To be filled by the Faythan himself in person!"

"I am not interested in a note." Mirashael shrugged.

Lucaät saw his mouth move, about to release their shield. If that happened, their negotiation was done.

"I'll give you all the coin," he blurted. "All the coin you asked for originally, and the contracts as promised. Went will be mined within its next rotation, I have it on very high authority."

Mirashael paused.

"There will not be long to wait, not long at all!" Lucaät assured him.

"And the coin?"

"Come to my house, you will have it tomorrow."

"No. You come to my café," said Mirashael. "Be there alone with the full amount within the hour or the deal is off."

"I accept," Lucaät said.

With that, the shield was released. For the briefest of moments, he considered having Sender kill the Cantori for his insolence, but if he did, the Eyes would never be his, and he would have lost. Now the challenge would be to raise that amount of capital within the next half-hour.

He snapped his fingers as he hurried from the room. *Sender! With me!*

Sender complied without hesitation.

It was only after the enormous sum was finally gathered and promissory notes of contract drawn that Lucaät of Faytha had a fleeting moment of anxiety – was he really was the winner? But then he remembered the brilliant show of light that burst from beneath the cover of the dish and he hurried on his way to Crafters.

Neither he nor Sender had seen the emergence of Daric Enna from the shadows at the back of Duvät's impromptu mausoleum, nor the triumphant smile that bloomed on Mirashael of Cantori's face as the two sat together over the body to enjoy the rest of the food.

"Harka! Come join us," Mirashael called. *And call the others.* Seconds later the barkeep came through the curtain, a wide grin on his face, soon to be followed by four more who had posed as drinkers.

"Plenty for all, yes?" Mirashael congratulated them. "Keep your strength up for the next round."

"Giddy trap, mates!" Harka picked up an omosa and held it high. "I's be winnin dis one square, sho la? Bidin dere, ja, while you slyuns be schemin wid de coin-lord, an I's tinkin of his lordy face an hurtin not to laugh!"

THE EXCHANGE

Daric Enna and Mirashael of Cantori sat together in Daric's favorite corner of the café. All was in readiness for the exchange to take place, every situation discussed and planned for – including escape routes should there be an attack by Lucaät's Ashik.

I am sorry, you'd better go now, my friend, Mirashael said. *My lady is on her way, and some things it is best for her not to know.*

Daric smiled slightly. *It's more comfortable this way. I killed her husband, after all … but there is something we need to talk about afterward, something you can do for me.*

I am in your debt. Mirashael bowed slightly, then made a shooing gesture with his hands. *She comes! We'll talk later, as you wish.*

Daric slipped through into Mirashael's sanctum just as Harka led Leahät Gok to the café door.

"Ah, my lady!"

The assassin smiled to hear genuine joy in his boss's voice.

"Just the sight of you back here in my humble café lifts my heart," Mirashael said. "The trip has not overtaxed you?"

"I am a little tired," Leahät replied. "But, oh, Mirashael! A mining contract? Whoever thought I would be doing such things! But … he'll see right through me, won't he?"

"See right through to what?" Mirashael said kindly. "Your strength? Your intelligence? Let us hope he does." There was a short pause, then, "Are you ready?"

Daric Enna left off eavesdropping and with his acute, short-range farsight, began to scan for any suspicious activity.

When Harka had taken his place by the nearest portal, he sent him a tiny psychic prod and received an irritated poke in return. The Kareski was always edgy when Mirashael's safety was at stake. It was odd that if a half-breed threw more to the angel, they could live anonymously in the outer world with barely a worry, but for those of Casco's ilk, the safest place had always been Karesk – until now.

Deys comin, Harka whispered.

Moments later, Lucaät stepped through the portal with Sender. There was another with them – a fighter, clearly Ashik. He redoubled his vigilance, but there was no sign that the remainder of the force were nearby. Lucaät stationed his lackeys outside the café and entered alone, as agreed. His haze seemed misshapen, a sure sign that his Qalān was overburdened.

After an appropriate round of greetings, Leahät was introduced and the party moved into an alcove at the back of the dining area. Mirashael signaled with a seemingly innocuous twitch of mind and for the second time that night, Daric sang a tight screen around them. Since the screen was his, he could monitor what went on inside it and Mirashael was free to be immersed in the negotiation at hand.

Scattered in strategic positions, Harka and his team waited on full alert, keyed in and ready to act on his say-so.

Another benefit of using Kareski. Although they might appear to be simple angels, they were often quite powerful in one particular field. The operatives he was working with tonight had been chosen for their potential for violence but also for their strength with screens and songs of combat, talents which Daric had personally honed.

Sooner than he'd anticipated, Lucaät reached into Qalān and began to divest himself of purse after purse of coin. Slowly his haze resumed a more normal shape.

Leahät sat with admirable poise while Mirashael checked random bags and counted the contents. Her former nerves seemed forgotten.

When the giant mound lay neatly stacked on a groaning table beside them, the Faythan produced two rolled papers. Leahät took them as if she had been born to status, and handed one to Mirashael while she read the other.

Between them, several points were found to need alteration or clarification, but at last both contracts had been signed and it was time for the exchange.

With typical Gokish practicality, Leahät simply popped the Eyes of Bel Nishani onto the table.

Lucaät reached for them as if every moment of his life had led to that action. He caressed their bulges with reverent intensity, but when he tried to open one, his fingers fumbled with the drawstring.

"Charm, please!" he said urgently.

"Let me," Leahät said, and she sang the release aloud so Lucaät could hear it.

The rainbow blazed to life as the top of the bag opened. Tears glinted like jewels on the Faythan's cheek. In an instant, Mirashael's shabby premises had become a place of splendor. Even Leahät seemed completely awestruck and Daric realised she had only seen the gems second-hand via her husband.

Lucaät had to close his eyes before he could bring himself to reseal the bag.

With little further ceremony, the meeting was over. Daric collapsed the screen and Lucaät of Faytha led his henchmen back the way they'd come.

He signaled Harka to stand down but remain vigilant.

Tell them to stay nearby, Mirashael instructed.

"Who has been guarding us?" Leahät asked.

"My lady, you know you have my complete trust, but this – it's best you don't know," Mirashael replied.

Leahät nodded, but Daric wondered how long it would be until she was no longer content with such answers.

She turned to gaze at the heaping bags of Imperials. "I've never seen so much coin! What shall we do with it?"

Mirashael grinned broadly. "It is yours, my lady, to do with as you will. I have a strong-room hidden beneath the beach-house at Pannias. Perhaps you would care to store it there until we can make other arrangements? And don't forget, this gold will finance preparations for your new venture, or ventures I should say."

"Our ventures, Mirashael," Leahät said firmly. "I am counting on your involvement … let's say half and half?"

Mirashael beamed, comfortably open with his happiness, and Daric smiled, bemused by the convolutions of the Breath.

"And now, my lady," Mirashael said, "I will make us some nice refreshing tea, and if you will give me a few moments before we go out to celebrate?"

"Out?" Leahät's gaze followed him as he headed for the kitchen, dancing between the chairs with typical flair. "I am exhausted," she called after him, "and more than happy to simply return to the beach house – as soon as you finish whatever business you have."

While Leahät nursed a cup of her favorite brew, Mirashael joined Daric Enna in his office.

"That went well," Daric greeted him.

"Yes, my Lady Leahät continues to impress! But can you lower your screens, just a bit?" Mirashael replied. "It's only that I know you're there …"

Daric eased his cover and Mirashael's gaze settled on his face.

"Ah! That's better."

Daric smiled. "Harka and his team are standing by to escort you back to Pannias."

"Good, good," said Mirashael. "Well done, Daric my friend, well done. The Faythan was so enamored of his prize; it seems a shame to take them off him. Perhaps we should wait a day or two before telling Brätan Gok?"

The Enna thought for a moment then suggested, "Let's play it both ways, tell Brätan and then at the same time, tell Lucaät that Brätan knows he has them."

"Yes, yes! Excellent!" Mirashael agreed. "What would I do without you?"

Daric paused, then said, "That brings me to my request."

Mirashael's face fell. "You are not leaving me?" He put his cup down, suddenly very serious. "Daric, you can't. I won't allow it!"

"Don't be silly," Daric replied. "You couldn't stop me anyway. But I fear I will be absent for a time. I want you to help me join the Uri'madu."

Mirashael frowned.

"Think about it," Daric said. "The planet Went is beyond contact and there's no way that slimy Faythan intends to honor any agreement he can get out of – and I wouldn't like the chances of any random administrator or overseer you'd care to send, whether it's written into the contract or not."

"A good point," Mirashael conceded. "And so, your plans and mine coincide?"

"He would never let me join the host as an observer, but he can't stop me if I'm part of the Explorers' contingent." Daric explained. "It's an Imperial requirement for every mining venture on a newly assessed planet now – the original Guild exploratory team must be present to supervise as operations commence, not just a Lethian representative."

"Yes … " Mirashael said slowly.

"And we have another seven years, almost, before I have to go. Time enough to train someone to take my place."

"No one can take your place, Daric," Mirashael said. "Have you considered the extreme demands made of exploratory teams? Horrible accommodation, danger lurking around every corner –"

"Just as it is now."

"And another point – what if these conditions, the new learning and adaptations that must take place – what if they lead you to be Marked? You'll be useless to your current profession the instant that happens."

Daric nodded. This complication had occurred to him, but it was a risk he took with every refinement of his skill-set. To be Marked would certainly change his life – and what would he be Marked with? Tsemkar? Shamkar? He had to admit to a certain curiosity. He used voice and mind with equal dexterity. It was what gave him the special edge in his field.

"I hope I'll still be able to find work if that happens," he said. "If I am successful with the Uri'madu, maybe that's where my future lies."

"There are Rukh on the team. You know how they feel about assassins."

"I'll sing that song when I come to it. Honor is the key to any Rukh's regard."

Mirashael sighed in resignation. He looked toward the café. "My lady has all but fallen asleep. She's worked so hard – one would never realize how fragile her spirit still is. Yet I believe this victory has buoyed her … the first of many to come."

Daric held out his hand.

With a sigh, Mirashael took it, and reluctant agreement flowed through their touch.

You will always have a place with me, Mirashael said. *You are as a blessing to me, Marked or not.*

Daric bowed over his hand and kissed it. The Cantori had taken him in when no one else would and given him room to grow, but this decision would take him on the right path. He knew it in his heart.

For a short time, their attachment to each other kept their hands from separating, then Mirashael laughed. *It's not as if you're leaving yet!* "And just as well," he continued as their grip parted. "Lots of work yet to move your Kareski refugees from place to place – right under the Imperium's vaunted nose. I like it!"

"I'm off to find Casco now," Daric told him. "I'll tell him the good news."

"And I must take my dear lady home before she collapses with exhaustion." Mirashael's gaze twinkled. "I'm becoming quite fond of her, you know."

"I'd never have guessed!" Daric chuckled. With that, he alerted Harka and his gang that they were required to escort their employer, and when he was sure all was quiet, he headed for Karesk.

DARIC ENNA AND CASCO

The Golden Wheel was dark but for a few muted globes. Daric Enna looked up at the moons before he went in. It was about the fourth hour since midnight, and a good time to find a quiet space.

Shera looked his way as the doors opened. Did she ever sleep?

"Need some quiet," he said by way of explanation.

She waved him into a deserted sitting room and he settled on a comfy couch. Moments later his clever mind had breached Casco's house-screens.

Casco! … Casco! he called, and shook his head when he realised he'd whispered the name aloud, an old habit from childhood.

Casco tossed and turned in the grips of a troubled sleep, then suddenly sat up. His hand went to his forehead.

Daric Enna?

Can you meet me at the Wheel? Daric asked.

Now? The Kareski passed his hands down his face and scowled. *How did you get in?*

Daric sent a sardonic smile. *Giddy, ja?*

Without another word, Casco snatched clothing from the floor and fumbled into it with the clumsiness of sleep disturbed. Daric watched until he was on his way to the first step, then asked Shera to make them tea.

"When you givin up dis badun life, Daric Enna?" she scolded. "Be joinin de Breat soon enough, sho la. Tinkin un's moder be cryin out, nary she be here."

"Shera Gran, I's here and doin starry best." He winked. "But maybe goss comin soon, sho la."

"You'll no be draggin Casco onto your darksome track," she said crossly.

"No, Gran. I's goodun here. Helpin you, Casco, everyone. Ye'll be knowin soon enough."

"Believin be vizzin, ja?" Shera snorted, but then she looked him up and down and her expression softened. "I's vizzin ye true, Daric Enna, known ye since wee youngun and faid ye be goodun at heart. Moder wouldna had it be any oder, an doan ye be forgettin." She set a warm brown pot before him and two cups. "Dar-leaf. Casco likes dar-leaf."

"No panic – I's good on dar-leaf too," Daric assured her.

"Dat be luck, den," she said sarcastically, and left him to it.

A few minutes later, Casco hurried in.

Daric stood and bowed. "My apologies, my friend. I know how busy you are, but I have news that can't wait."

"I'm sorry Daric … News? Is it important? I've barely slept for weeks now."

"Please," he indicated the dar-leaf, "join me?"

As Casco watched the heavy brown fluid pour from the spout of the teapot, Daric noticed the tiredness in his posture and the tightness of worry in his haze. It was as if shreds of nightmare still clung to him.

"How are the relocations going?" he asked.

"Relocations?" Casco said sharply.

"Come now, my friend. When the heirs to two Great Houses and the leaders of two Guilds all visit the enclave at the same time it won't be kept secret for long. I have connections, remember?"

Casco gave a non-committal grunt and sipped his tea. "It's a lot of work," he said at last.

"I have heard that the ban will be lifted … just as soon as all known Kareski have registered with the new registry office."

"An empty threat." Casco snarled. "There is no registry office!"

"There will be tomorrow," Daric said. "They are coming in and setting up in what remains of Old Town."

"Breathless bastards!" Casco's teacup clunked to the table. "Have they no respect? Apologizing for our lives to some meat-brained, no-chin Gok? It's an outrage!"

Daric's eyebrows twitched as Casco's normal decorum disintegrated. "We're worth nothing in their eyes," he stormed on. "Label us abominations, yet our parents married for love. Touched by the Breath of Asheru it's said, and blessed, yes, blessed just the same as any 'pure' couple might be." He flung an accusatory gesture toward the Imperial Palace. "And who's he to talk! Where's his blessings? One single son and heir? El's Chosen? Far from it!"

Shera poked her head around the corner. "All's well out here, Casco bless?"

Casco blinked as if only just becoming aware of the tenor of his outburst.

"Sorry, Shera gran." He bowed to her and with some effort, stifled his emotions to a more acceptable state. "Permies be settin up de registry for true. Best be gossin de word, ja?"

Shera nodded. "An ye's bein starry-fine?" She looked suspiciously at the two of them.

They both nodded. Casco smiled convincingly and she left them alone.

"I've also heard that Arien Leth is buying swords," Daric said. "Word of a secret militia."

"That won't help us with this latest cock-up," Casco said. "Stupid," he snarled. "I'm so stupid! I thought our efforts at resistance had gained us a little respect."

Daric nodded in commiseration. "Actually it's the Faythans who are behind it. They can't afford to lose too many of you, it seems."

"As if we're kreth. Well they're going to be mighty disappointed when the bulk of the herd have found new homes on more welcoming planets."

"That's something to look forward to," said Daric, "but my most important news may have more personal repercussions. It concerns the planet Went."

Casco's eyes narrowed.

"Mining operations are to begin on the next cycle." Daric told him. "It's the nacrite ... the God-Emperor wants it for weaponry. Amazingly, it seems he senses unrest."

"The Guild will never stand for it!" Casco exploded again. "They can't. You must be mistaken." He worked his knuckles as if he wanted to hit someone, but wasn't sure who. "How do you know all this?" he demanded.

"And there's more," said Daric. "Duvät Gok, your one-time Overlord, had a secret. A very nasty secret …"

As he told Casco the story of the eyes, the explorer sat in stony silence, but every so often a fresh slice of anger flashed through his haze.

By the time he finished, Casco had slumped forward, head in his hands. Feelings of guilt stained his veil. "I saw the signs," he groaned. "How could I have missed this? Even when we put him on trial I knew there was something not right," he went on, "but we all hated him so much for what he did to Lind, even to think about him sullied the mind. I guess he knew it, the slimy kalla, and played on it."

He paused. "Yet his death-cry came to me," he said, and shared his deep puzzlement.

Daric tilted his head. A death-cry was a final discharge of love, as he understood it, but in Duvät's last, painful moments there had been no evidence of true regard for anyone except himself.

"He stayed with me at my home … Breath knows why I offered," Casco said. "He was pretty beat up when I found him, and I must admit I put in a few good ones too. He gave me all his coin, even the brooch he'd bought for his wife, to find him passage off-world. It was risky, but I did it." He shook his head. "And then the death-cry. I was caught up in the fighting here. He didn't make it far – and part of me rejoiced."

Daric took a deep breath, *Casco, there's something more I have to tell you, but I'm afraid you'll hate me.*

Casco shrugged tiredly. *If there's something you need to get off your chest, just say it.*

This is hard for me … His heart quailed. He considered making something up – something to tell him that was important but forgivable … but Casco deserved the truth. He gritted his teeth and plunged on.

"I killed him."

You? Casco's gaze rolled skyward as if wondering where the next rock would fall from.

It's what I was paid to do, Daric admitted carefully.

Just as he'd feared, the pain of betrayal ripped through Casco's veil. The Kareski thrust to his feet and strode toward the exit, anxious to put space between them. Daric stared after him, stunned by the hurt he'd caused. Right before the doorway, Casco turned. His hand came up to his forehead as if to grasp the sigil he'd implanted and rip it out.

An assassin? he cried. *I trusted you!* A wave of fury punched into Daric's chest.

Daric remembered the moment he'd implanted the sign – so spontaneous, as if his heart knew what his mind had not yet grasped. There were so few people worthy of attachment.

You can still trust me! he cried. He tried not to sound as if he was pleading. *I would never harm you,* he continued in more level tones. *Please, give me a chance to prove myself.*

Casco raised his hand. *Just stop.*

I told you about Duvät's duplicity as soon as I could, Daric rushed on. *I came in friendship, and because I believed it was the right thing to do. You needed to know.* He tried to order his thoughts. Casco was shocked, and rightly so, but there'd been no reason to tell him before now. He recalled the sight of his friend with his hair braided, posing as an Archangel. The bravery of it brought tears to his eyes. Would Casco ever know that he'd seen him? That he and Mirashael together had organized the distraction in the Refectory and saved him from arrest?

The Guild must be warned, he said. *Please, if you can't think of me as a friend right now, can you just do that? Warn the Guild.*

The force of Casco's antipathy wavered. Daric could almost feel his mind working. He wanted to trust, he was sure of it, but assassins were a taboo even stronger than Kareski. He tried again … *If the protocols are broken, what does this say about the future of the Realm? About the God-Emperor himself and the archangels who support him? Who would sanction such a thing?*

Slowly, Casco's tension eased – small signs at first, but then his shoulders slumped and Daric's heart began to race as if catching up on the beats it had missed.

Slyun! Casco said fiercely. *Here's I tinkin you's a goodun, Kareski heart, speakin pure, sad history – but wee Kisha viz un true.* Slowly he nodded. *Ye be two-sided coin, Daric Enna, an I'll be so minded.*

Daric stood up. "Ye'll no be saddened," he said. "Be swearin on moder's heart."

Casco took a step toward him, then another, still reluctant. "All hale an starry," he said gruffly. "Must be giddy, ja? Losin de pram."

"Mebee so," Daric agreed, "an I's a losin it too, sho la. Be askin to join de Uri'madu next."

The advance stopped. "You? Loose in de wild?" Casco looked at him askance.

Daric nodded. "Savin shiniest for last."

Casco returned to the couch and stared over the rim of his teacup for some time before taking a drink.

Daric waited quietly.

At last, Casco's haze cleared, and he turned to look at him. "Thank you for your honor in this at least. It wasn't easy for you to tell me the truth of who you are, and now you are trusting that I will tell no one else. Assuming your bid to join the Uri'madu is successful, you must tell them too. If you can promise me this, I will welcome you to our team."

He bowed deeply. "I promise," he said. "And I have a feeling you may need my skills and insider knowledge, given the circumstances unfolding. Lucaät of Faytha is ruthless in his pursuit of wealth."

"And the boss you mention, Mirashael of Cantori? What of him? Who owns his loyalty?"

"In this? Leahät Gok."

Casco's brow creased at this fresh revelation. "Duvät's wife?"

"It was she who paid for his passage back to the Breath."

Casco shook his head. "What next?" he said. "Ishät Ashik himself handing out gold coins on the street? Annangi growing wings and flying?" He got to his feet. "I've had enough. I need a drink. I'll warn Huldar what's going on, then I'm going home … join me if you like."

Daric didn't try to stop the smile he felt seeping through him. The feeling of honest acceptance was a revelation. "I'd love to," he said, and he meant it whole-heartedly. He couldn't remember the last time anyone but Mirashael had invited his company. "I'll take the tea things back to Shera gran while I wait."

Casco paused, *Shera gran?*

Known her all my life, Daric responded.

Casco shook his head again and continued toward the Hermes rooms.

KISHA

On the planet Haas, in a tidy terrace-house on the outskirts of the city of Haaseen, the dawn's first rays filtered between the tall buildings of the city's heart. Kisha looked out of the front window as sunlight kissed frost, and the steady drip, drip, drip of melt-water began to sound in the down-pipes.

She turned as her ma pulled a jumper and leggings from the welcome-pack they'd been given and held them up as if comparing her for size. Kisha made a face. They looked nothing like what she'd wear back in Old Town, but her ma had that determined look and she knew she'd have to put them on anyway.

Their new place was made of stone, much nicer than the ancient timbers of their last house. There was no chance this one would burn down. At first, her ma had cried a lot, but since Da started his new job at the brewery – a place where they made beer, she'd been told – her parents smiled more often.

In the corner where the sunlight first came, Da sat with his new sword across his knee. He held a leather cloth and worked it up the blade in rhythmic motion.

Keeps the edge fine as fine, he said. From his mind she saw the need to use a stone first, with long even strokes to polish out any nicks or dents, then the leather for fine honing, *Just like the commander showed me.* "You're a Rukh now too," he said. "All Rukh are warriors."

An me-un? she asked.

Even you, my bless.

Whenever her Da called her that, she felt warm inside, but there was no room to snuggle on his lap with the sword in the way.

He glanced up at her from under his brows. "Swords are important here." With narrowed eyes, he aimed the blade straight at her and gazed directly down its glinting edge. "Every Rukh has a sword, sharp and battle-ready. The commander's put me down for training with battle techniques. I's be playin keepers den."

"What's 'techniques', Da?"

He put the sword away and fixed her with a stare so intense she had to giggle. "Wrappin badun's minds. Stop un first afore deys be stopin me!" he said ferociously, then she shrieked with laughter as he pounced with his arms outstretched.

Held close and surrounded by his love, she felt happiness grow inside like a rosy bubble chasing all the bad times away.

If all goes well I might be asked to enlist as a full-time soldier. Knock some Ashik heads – what do you think about that?

Deys Ashik best mind out den!

Deres my bless!

He kissed her head and hugged her tight. Warm sunshine fell on her face and she looked outside.

Bein sunup in Karesk, Da, or moder moon an weeuns? She patterned her fingers across the sky, imagining the big mother moon and her five little ones trailing along behind. Here on Haas there were three giant moons and one smaller one.

"'What time is it in Karesk?'" her ma corrected. "Say it properly."

"What-time-is-it-in-Karesk?" she repeated obediently. "Why deys be speakin all giddy here?"

"Not giddy, bless." Her da winked. "Strange, or confusing."

Kisha giggled with her father.

"Kana! Don't encourage her," Ma scolded. "We're the ones wid de giddy speak … oh!" Laughing, her mother swept her from her father's arms and swirled her about. "Look what you made me do!"

Her da stood up and kissed them both. "Better be going. Early start."

"This new job, Kana," said Ma. "I'm so proud of you!"

"Only by a we be livin hereabouts dese days, ja?" Kana grinned as his wife swatted at him. He picked up his lunchbox with a deft twist of mind and stowed it in Qalān.

"Practice, see?" he said to Kisha.

"I's be practicin too, ja?" she replied. In her imagination she saw herself as a mighty Tsemkarun, Marked and all, and her ma and da starry-proud …

Ma shook her head. *Maybe one day …*

"Using it at work," Da said. "Actually employed to use tsemkar, I keep looking over my shoulder."

"I know." Her ma smiled. "Who would have thought that Breath could blow this?"

"And better pay as well!" he added as he opened the door.

"Mind you don't drink all the profits!" her mother called after him.

"Mandatory military." He winked at Kisha. "Ma knows I won't. Commander forbids it."

The door closed with a solid clunk.

"I like seein Da every day," Kisha said.

She looked up as her mother's arms closed around her. "Come on, let's get you dressed. We've got to go to the markets this morning, and after lunch, I thought you might like to play with Brekka? Her mother is Nhadu like me."

"Brekka has a brother," Kisha said. "Will I ever have a brother?" She pictured their neighbor's tiny new baby. "Where do blessings come from, Ma? We getin un too, now we's be Rukh?"

"Perhaps," Ma smiled. "That's up to El. But in the meantime, look what I have for you."

She went to the kitchen and opened the lid of a bubbling pan. The delicious smell of fried kosh filled the room.

"My favorite!" Kisha squealed. But before she started to eat, she put two aside, just like she had last time, just in case.

"Dats for una Casco and de badun," she said sternly, and when she looked up she was surprised to see tears in her ma's gentle eyes.

THE EMPRESS ISHIQUEL

The God-Emperor's Chosen, Empress Ishiquel Enna Tiamät, felt her languor dissipate in a flash of glorious, multi-hued light. Her surroundings, already the most opulent in the Realm, were instantly transformed, as if she had seamlessly and soundlessly stepped onto a brand new world. Even the rather ordinary face of the Faythan who had brought this wonder to her had been made more interesting by the play of light.

"From … Went, you say? A curious thing to name a planet?"

"Yes, most exalted of ladies," he said. His voice was slightly nasal, but he spoke with a pleasing reverence. "They are the product of a creature that grows there, a worm-like thing that squirms from the sea to the shore in order to nest."

"An ugly, wriggling thing produced this? Incredible!" She held it toward her slaves. "Even they seem more engaging," she muttered.

With a flick of her mind she summoned a mirror. The slave was careful to hold it so no gripping fingers obscured her view. If she held the orb just so, her tawny yellow eyes seemed to blaze like molten gold. Color rippled over her yellow-blond hair as if she were at the bottom of a pool of liquid light. She examined her face in detail, high cheek-bones and tilted Tiamäti eyes – the set of her lips, her delicate nose, how novel they looked when bathed in this glow. It was difficult to look away, so she had the mirror turned to reflect her benefactor as well.

"A marvelous gift, Lord Lycrät."

"Ah – that's Lucaät, Royal Lady," he corrected with delicacy. "Lucaät of Faytha …?"

She held the gem to her hair and imagined a headdress, totally unique. More beautiful than any other. Her husband would find her completely irresistible and … maybe that would encourage El to bless them as he should.

"Are there more?"

"Yes, glorious Empress, as it happens, there are several more."

"I want them."

"Certainly, highest of ladies," the Faythan said stoutly. "It would be my honor to present them to you."

Ishiquel smiled to herself. The Faythan, whatever his name was, had nearly choked at the idea of giving up such treasures for free. If she'd been alone, her eyes would have rolled.

"How excellent," she said. "You were wise to come to me before any other. Such loyalty has not gone unnoticed."

"Your majesty is too kind."

Even as the words were spoken, Ishiquel felt her husband's attention shift and knew he was on his way to see the novel jewel for himself.

As he neared her chamber, a wave of terror crossed the slave's minds. They backed hurriedly toward the walls and stood still as statues. The Faythan showed only a moment of puzzlement, then he too turned toward the door and bowed as low as it was possible for a portly archangel to bow without snapping in two.

The doors parted and her husband swept in, tall and muscular beneath his regal robes, yellow eyes alight with curiosity. The tsemkar on his forehead shone with the after-light of use, and briefly, she wondered what he'd been doing. Probably fine-tuning the surveillance network he'd devised. The observances of very slave in the Palace were open to him – it was just a matter of coordination now, and filtering out any trivia. She smiled and lifted the orb in the capable grip of her mind, turning it for him to see.

He took it between his fingers and held it to the window. *It's not a trick of the light ... fascinating.* He indicated her visitor's bent back. *And this Faythan, Lucaät, brought it to us?*

However do you remember their names?

I've seen him in the Palace recently – a visit to the Commissioner of Mines. Sadly, we need Faytha's support. I sense a conflict coming, as I've said, and –

Yes, you have said, husband dear. But this? She retrieved the stone from him. *I have never seen anything more beautiful.*

He smoothed his elaborate coiffure and turned to the bowing spine. "Rise, Lucaät of Faytha, and tell me more about this singular jewel. How is it that you have it? I have the full report from the Planet Went. Why was this not included?"

Lucaät paused as if unable to speak. Ishiquel's lips curled. Even this smooth-talker was awestruck to be addressed by her husband. They all were.

"Great and Holy Emperor, Chosen of El," he began. "The villainous Duvät Gok, former Overlord to the exploratory team responsible, managed to conceal his find from all, even his own team members."

"Until now."

"Yes, Holy Emperor. He called them 'The Eyes of Bel Nishani'. My dealings with him after their return led me to believe something was amiss, and I –"

"The Explorers' Guild?"

"I came directly to you."

"To the Empress."

"Yes. I have a connection …"

"Of course."

Ishiquel waited as her husband paused in thought and wondered how the news of this great oversight would affect the Explorers' Guild, if at all, and the substantial discredit to the Gok – would Brätan suffer for it? He had an appointment for the eleventh hour this morning, and Ishät's moods these days had become quite unpredictable.

"The Overlord, you say?" Ishät continued. "Has he been made accountable for his thievery?"

Lucaät bowed. "Greatest of Lords, he has rejoined the Breath."

Her husband nodded. Through their bond, she felt his mind continue to whir through possibilities then come to a conclusion.

"But you know where these originated?" he said. "How to obtain them?" He turned to her and smiled fondly. "My wife, you see, has a deep desire to increase her collection."

Ishiquel's heart beat a little faster. Was that a flash of desire in his mind? Her loins tingled to think so.

"Certainly, Great Lord," Lucaät simpered, "but their procurement is not without great risk and depends upon highly specialized and expensive methods."

"I am not suggesting that you give them to us without recompense," the God-Emperor replied. He rolled his gaze to the ceiling. "Faytha would writhe with agony were I even to think such a thing!"

Ishät sent her an image of the Faythan House-Leader's daughter and their own son, Aqumät, beside each other … *What do you think, Ishiquel? Will this tempt him to marriage at last?*

She nodded approvingly. *You will have to be strong with him, but this is the perfect excuse. And as for Faytha, if you couch this as a reward? They cannot refuse, and they will be able to refuse us nothing else once the two are wed.*

"Yes, " her husband continued seamlessly, " I am reminded that my son is as yet unmarried, and Faytha's daughter likewise. It is unusual for the direct offspring of Great House Leaders to marry, but in this case, perhaps the protocols may be set aside? What are protocols anyway? Mere guidelines. I am directly attuned to the Breath itself, and it is for me to say what guiding principles should be upheld, and which are merely holding us up."

"Holy Emperor," Lucaät spluttered. "Surely such great matters are not for me to say! Such a concession to my house … immeasurable worth, an inconceivable honor! But, if I may say –"

Ishät severed the babble. "You, yourself require payment." He measured the Faythan in his gaze. "It is ever more clear that the singular wealth of this new planet has been blown to me by El's Great Design," he proclaimed. "Mining cannot wait. Therefore, as a reward for your honesty and loyalty I grant Lucaät of Faytha the full and exclusive right to mine the Imperial Planet Went. In return, I will have all nacrite for the Imperium, but Lucaät shall own one half of the yield of Eyes – a bonus for his loyalty."

Ishät's gaze followed Lucaät as he bowed low.

"My Imperial Lord," the Faythan began, "such honors will go a long way to ameliorating the extreme expense of mining operations on such a distant and inhospitable planet, I am sure. But if I am not funded securely from the outset, yields will be adversely affected. The amount of nacrite I am able to secure for you may be reduced, and the harvest of the Eyes of Bel Nishani may not be as productive as one would hope."

Is he actually trying to bargain with me? Ishät said to her indignantly. *Faythans!*

Ishiquel rotated the gem so that its light caught her husband's eye. *Give him what he wants! We've already turned the situation to greater advantage.* She held the gem near her face, then lowered it suggestively down her neck toward her ample bosom. *El may yet bless …*

Ishät's mind smiled a secret smile, just for her.

"Very well," he said sternly. "I have no time to pander to a Faythan's delight in bargaining. I grant you one third of the nacrite, and ten thousand gold imperials for each Eye of Bel Nishani delivered to my Empress, excepting for this one which I am to understand was presented as a gift. Does that please you, Faythan?"

"Greatest and Holiest of Emperors, I am ecstatic. I have over fifty Eyes in my possession, enough to make a headdress fit for our Imperial jewel."

Ishiquel smiled as the Faythan bowed again. Her mind immediately turned to who she should hire to fashion this wonderful new adornment. It was so exciting! The entire Realm would crave such beauty!

Lucaät prattled on. "You can be guaranteed that the greatest possible yields of all minable goods will be achieved, and the continuing favor of my House assured."

Ishiquel started as the tentacles of Tiamät on her husband's back rustled to life – a small movement, but an extreme caution nonetheless. The Imperial Mark manifested more readily these days – whenever he was annoyed.

"Has the 'favor' of House Faytha been somehow in question?" he asked quietly.

Lucaät paled and hurriedly bowed again. "Greatest and most respected of lords, Faytha has always been the most stalwart supporter of the Imperium. In this time of flux and unrest, I merely wished to reiterate our commitment."

The tentacles calmed, but Ishiquel could still feel their presence, as if they had will of their own and were watching …

"Very well," Ishät said at last. "Deliver my wife's new baubles to Enasha of Nhadu by this evening."

Without waiting for the usual pleasantries, the God-Emperor turned and started for the door.

"And the payment?" Lucaät ventured.

Ishiquel's heart chilled as the ghostly tentacles of the sea-creature, Tiamät, manifested more substantially on her husband's back.

"Fool!" She raised her hand to silence the Faythan, lest he exacerbate the situation. There had been enough deaths of late for their staff to tidy up.

For a long moment, Lucaät of Faytha stared in horror as the reality of his situation sank in, then he bowed more deeply than she would have thought possible. *And well he might*, she thought. These days, few saw the creature and lived to tell of it. Her husband continued through the doors on his way to a meeting with Brätan Gok. No wonder his mood was uncertain! The Faythan did not rise until he heard the doors close. For one second, they shared a glance. Almost, she felt like crying, then her veil firmed with slow anger.

"I thank you for bringing the Eyes of Bel Nishani to me," she said coldly, "and congratulate you on the retention of your life. Payment will be arranged through the exchequer. You knew this, yet you dared to anger El's Chosen. If it weren't for the loyalty you have shown us just now, I would have you killed myself! Have a care, Faythan, and tell your House as much. Breathe no word of our intentions toward Faytha's marriage until you are instructed to do so."

She stood, cold and proud as he backed toward the doors, bowing at every step. Her heart still thundered against her ribs.

She watched the corridors where her husband walked. Rage boiled in the set of his shoulders and the predatory grace of his stride, and whatever Brätan Gok wished to speak about, she was glad she was not in his shoes.

For the time being, Ishät's mind was closed to her, but she took heart that the promise made across her fabulous new trinket would soon be fulfilled, and for those few moments his tension would ease.

Why had El not blessed them with a second child, she asked herself for the thousandth time, or even a third? Most previous God-Emperors had boasted at least three children, some as many as six! It was a source of constant distress to her, and fuel for the minds of malicious court gossips.

As if her longing for another child had somehow affected the orb in her hand, rainbow light streamed between her fingers, and she opened them to examine the gem more closely. With gentle strokes of her fingertips, she transferred wisps of energy into it, then listened with all her senses. It responded quickly with a resonance almost as if it lived. There was more to it than simple stone.

She held it to the light, much as her husband had done. Was a life somehow trapped inside it? The question curled her lips in a smile. The mysterious Eyes of Bel Nishani would make excellent ornaments indeed.

MIRASHAEL AND LEAHÄT

As rain beat down on the convoluted streets of Crafters, a steady stream of lunchtime patrons streamed into the warmth of Mirashael's café to seat themselves on tastefully upgraded furniture. The look was still rustic, but much cleaner, and the decrepit divans that had once lurked in the shadows at the back had been replaced with a series of cozy and quite private nooks.

From behind the counter, Leahät paused halfway through receiving payment from one of their regulars and directed new serving staff to a table that had been missed.

Mirashael hurried past in a burst of tropical color with several bowls of steaming omosa held high on a tray. Although they had other employees now, she could not convince him to stop personally serving his guests whenever he could – and the lurid shirts … well … she had to admit she loved them too, if only for the varied reactions of their guests.

She returned to her customer. "My apologies, Tethrät Enna."

"Accepted," he replied. "New help needs training … some more than others." As he paused, his eyes followed the erring waitress. "I have noticed an unusual accent with one or two of your employees?" he remarked.

"There is no need to hedge," Leahät said coolly. "They are Kareski."

"I thought they'd all gone? There's a Faythan consortium moved in on the enclave, or where it used to be before it burned down. A whole new military precinct going up there."

"As you can see, that song has yet to be concluded," said Leahät. "Many strive to remain on Giahn, the only world they have known, in homes they have occupied for generations."

"But half-breeds …" He glanced quickly around the café as if assessing the patrons, then leaned closer. "I hope you have your valuables firmly tied down."

Leahät worked hard to keep her expression within the range of acceptable politeness. "They are as trustworthy as any other, Tethrät Enna – perhaps more so since many feel they have something to prove."

"And this has not affected your trade?"

Leahät gave a gentle snort. "Look around, sir. We are full to capacity and sending orders via runner to many other local establishments as well. Our trade has more than doubled."

"Well, the quality of your omosa certainly hasn't declined, and for that I am most thankful!"

"Still the finest in the Realm?"

"Most certainly!" Tethrät assured her.

Leahät's answering smile was somewhat triumphant. "Then I will be sure to give Shen, our trainee chef, your kind feedback."

With a slight bow, she turned to the next in line. "Table for four? I'm afraid you'll have to wait."

That night as the doors finally closed, Mirashael and Leahät slumped into one of the nooks while others cleaned and prepared for the next day's onslaught.

"It's these new tables and chairs," Mirashael complained. "Dear lady, they are altogether too inviting."

"I overheard some gossip from the Palace," she said. "This time next year, we'll be getting organized for our new venture."

Mirashael groaned. "More work."

"And, the Clan Chief of Gok asked for a reservation for tomorrow night, table for eight."

"What did you tell him?"

She paused. Mirashael seemed a little short, and that was unlike him. "I reminded him of our 'no reserve' policy," she replied, "and said he'd have to take his chances like everyone else." She rolled her eyes as she shared the Clan Chief's response, but although he would normally have laughed with her, Mirashael barely reacted. She wondered what had happened to upset him.

"You're right," she went on brightly. "We can't start being all exclusive here … but what of my idea for a second place, perhaps in Sadir?"

Mirashael raised his eyebrows and tried to seem interested.

Leahät plowed on. "We have Shen now, and he's going so well. Customers are complimenting without ever knowing it wasn't you who made their omosa, let alone a Kareski. You're such a good trainer. Perhaps if we –"

They turned to a rap, rap, rap on the window.

"Please! Just tell them we're closed!" Mirashael called out.

"No, wait," Leahät said. "It's a Hermes."

A willowy archangel with pale skin and pale blond hair was allowed in.

She gave Leahät a small bow. "I have a message for Leahät Gok? And a small parcel – a gift. I was asked to wait until your shop was less busy."

"Oh?" Leahät said. "A gift?"

The Hermes held out her hand. "The message is personal."

Mirashael made a wry face. "Competition?"

Leahät smiled fondly. "There could be none, and you know it, you rogue." Perhaps it was time they took a few days off.

She held hands with the Hermes and received a message with no distinct words or vision attached, although she detected hints of Kareski. There was just the knowledge that the gift had been purchased for her by her husband shortly before his death, an apology for its late return, and the sender's wish that her future be bright and full of promise.

She released the hand quite hurriedly. Why now after so many years?

"What is it?" Mirashael asked.

The Hermes placed a small box on the table and waited.

"Oh," Leahät stammered. "Um … I trust I need not ask for your discretion …"

"Confidence is maintained, Lady Gok," the Hermes replied promptly, and with that, she left.

"What is it?" Mirashael asked again. He peered into her with eyes full of love and concern, his former worry forgotten. "Come, come, dear lady, what has distressed you so?"

Leahät shook her head, unwilling to speak. A tear scrolled down her cheek, unnoticed until Mirashael wiped it away.

Hesitantly, she slid the box toward her and fumbled with the catch. It gave a small snick, and the lid popped open. Inside, nestled in a cushion of deep velvet blue she found a spray of jewels fashioned into a sprig of pink hereny, her favorite flower.

For a time she could do little but stare.

Mirashael reached for her hand, and she passed him the message as the Hermes had delivered it.

With her permission, he pulled the piece from its nest.

"A brooch," he said, and examined the clasp.

Almost, she reached out to take it from him, but at the last minute she changed her mind.

"Put it back."

No sooner had he closed the lid than Shen placed their meal before them, presented in their favorite bowls.

"Thank you, Shen," Mirashael said, his tone a touch over-bright. "There were more compliments on your work today. Excellent progress!"

"Ta, boss," the Kareski said. "I's be every-day grateful dat ye's takin faid wid me, ja?"

"And I do have great faith in you," Mirashael assured him. "Thank you again! Now go and get some sleep."

Shen left them for the upstairs apartment and quiet finally descended over the nameless café.

Leahät looked at the wooden bowls with their ochre rims and green enamel finish in the 'accidental' style, and couldn't help a glance toward the corner where the mysterious Enna had once sat sharpening his knife.

Mirashael pushed the box from between them and placed his hands over hers.

"My life has changed too," he said. A warm and soothing love flowed from his soul into hers. He took her hands to his lips and kissed them. "You are the special sauce, the unexpected burst of flavor that makes the meal of life worthwhile."

He paused and took a deep breath. "Lady Leahät, dearest lady," he began. He tried to hide his question from her, but she could see it was a big one. This must be the worry that had afflicted him. Her heart started to flutter.

"Loveliest and most intelligent," he stammered. "Capable, strong and gracious, yes? … no … Oh dear, this is not coming out right …"

His light brown eyes looked deeply into her own; love swirled through her soul into places she had never thought would be reawakened and her long abandoned inner child rejoiced.

"My lady, it comes to this," he said firmly. "And I am not expecting an immediate answer, you understand? No, no! … But in you, I have found the love of my heart. Such a thing has never happened to this poor Cantori before." As he gazed around his restaurant as if in search of inspiration, she was touched to see his eyes bright with moisture.

"And, if it might be agreeable to you," he kissed her hand lightly, "I ask," he kissed her hand again, "that you become my wife."

"Leahät of Cantori?" She smiled through sudden tears.

"Exactly," he answered.

"Married?" She moved her finger back and forth to simulate the bond that would bind them.

He nodded, but the excitement in his haze began to dim as despite his eternal optimism, part of him, the hidden Mirashael, entertained the specter of rejection.

"It is too soon, my lady, isn't it?" he said dejectedly. "Alas, for my impatience …"

"No, no!" she stopped him. "Mirashael, you are so dear to me! My life has been blighted till now, and I have made poor choices and such truths are hard to face. I came to you first seeking change, and then again because I knew there was more to living than the mere performance of life. Now that former darkness has passed away … and I am left behind."

She ran her fingers around the rim of her bowl, amazed by what it represented.

"I love being with you," she said. "I have wonderful new roles, serving customers in your café, helping our Kareski, your secret book-keeper ... I love it Mirashael, and I love you – and maybe, with your help, I'll even find I have an entrepreneurial flair." she grinned. "Who knows? But if I do, I want to find it with you by my side."

"So it's yes?"

In answer, she took his hands and opened her heart to him and their hazes glowed rosy gold.

"Then let us enjoy this meal in its accidental bowls to its very fullest," he said gladly, "and promise that we shall never stint on life again."

She could feel the last shadowed shreds of her time with Duvät melting away, all that pain, the dreadful acts he had made her party to ... and she studied Mirashael again.

A Cantori, she mused.

There were shadows there too, and things he did not yet wish to share, but whatever they represented she felt utterly certain that Mirashael of Cantori loved her, and it amazed her that she, a plain and lowly Gok, could own such depth of feeling in another. It was an experience she'd never anticipated.

My transformation will be complete, she said softly.

Transformation? He shook his head and gave her a loving smile. *No, my lady! You and I, we are in the process of being revealed ... all the things that we are, dark and light ... and I would not change any part of it, only see more.*